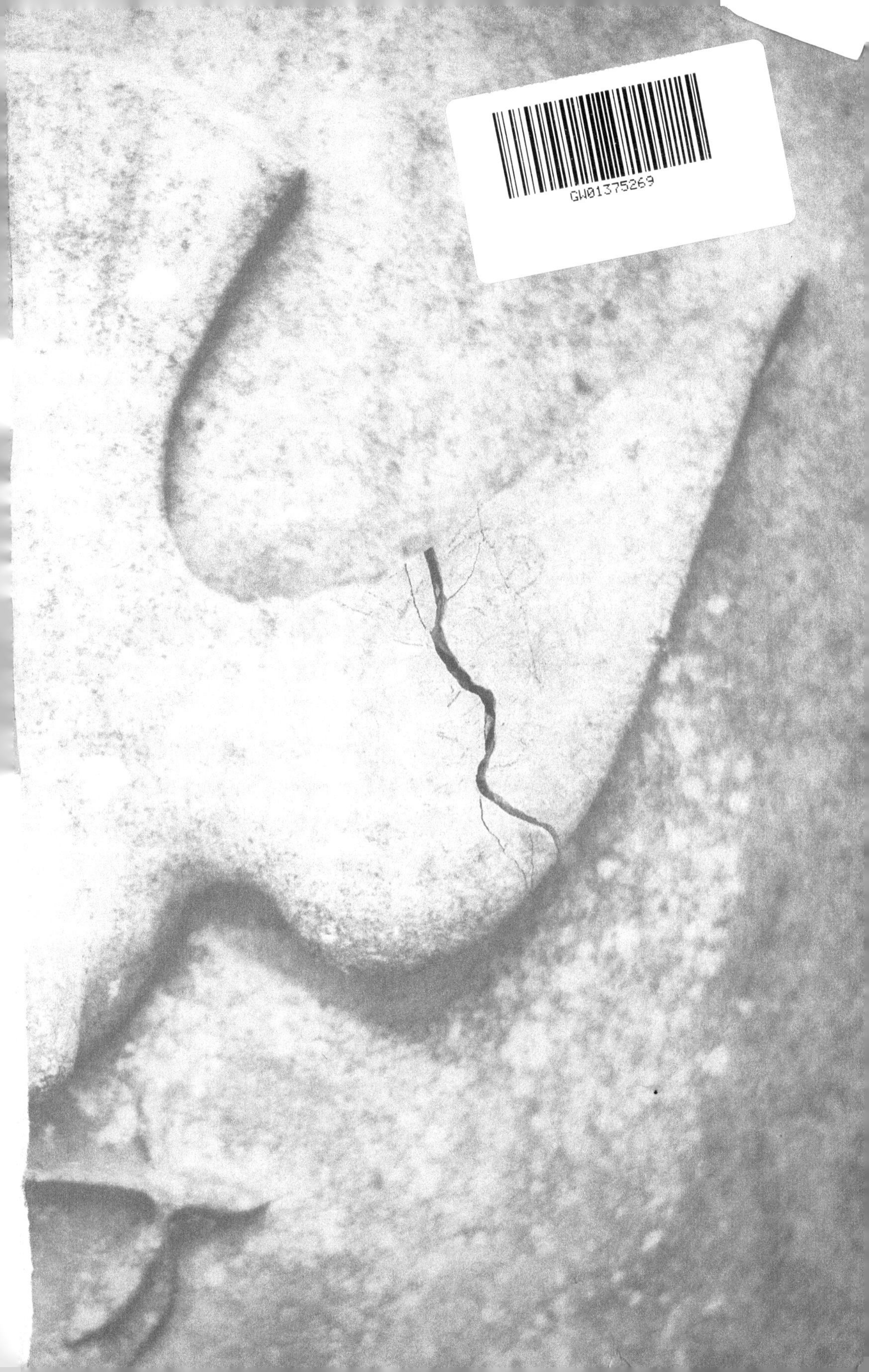

ABOUT THE AUTHOR

Pamela Allinson was born in Yorkshire in 1935, with an early passion to write. However, she trained to be a nurse, and on marrying moved to Birmingham where, with her Police Officer husband, she brought up her son and daughter. While managing to write on and off she continued her career, working as a District Nurse, School Nurse, and Health Visitor Fieldwork Teacher. Pamela lived for 20 years in Cornwall where she taught for a few years at a local Further Education College. As well as writing she was involved with various community activities: local drama group, voluntary hospital work, museum steward; loves reading, walking, WI and spending time with her husband, family and friends. Pamela spent her last years in Henley in Arden in Warwickshire where in 2015 she lost her battle with cancer.

THE BROKEN WING

BY
PAMELA ALLINSON

Copyright © 2016 Pamela Allinson

The moral right of the author has been asserted.

Apart from any fair dealing for the purposes of research or private study, or criticism or review, as permitted under the Copyright, Designs and Patents Act 1988, this publication may only be reproduced, stored or transmitted, in any form or by any means, with the prior permission in writing of the publishers, or in the case of reprographic reproduction in accordance with the terms of licences issued by the Copyright Licensing Agency. Enquiries concerning reproduction outside those terms should be sent to the publishers.

This is a work of fiction. Names, characters, businesses, places, events and incidents are either the products of the author's imagination or used in a fictitious manner. Any resemblance to actual persons, living or dead, or actual events is purely coincidental.

Matador
9 Priory Business Park,
Wistow Road, Kibworth Beauchamp,
Leicestershire. LE8 0RX
Tel: 0116 279 2299
Email: books@troubador.co.uk
Web: www.troubador.co.uk/matador
Twitter: @matadorbooks

ISBN 978 1785892 844

British Library Cataloguing in Publication Data.
A catalogue record for this book is available from the British Library.

Typeset in 11pt Garamond by Troubador Publishing Ltd, Leicester, UK

Matador is an imprint of Troubador Publishing Ltd

Dedicated to my beloved wife Pam and with thanks to our daughter Jan for her help in making it happen.

1

Rosamund

Treblissick, Cornwall, 1954.

Rosamund looked with sadness at the dilapidated front of the granite Victorian house with its many gables and bay windows. For many years now it had housed only Rosamund, her invalid father and a host of spiders in its high-ceilinged rooms.

'I simply have to go back into the house one last time. How long have I got before the auction starts?'

Francis looked at his watch. 'About twenty minutes.' He brushed her cheek, concerned. 'Are you sure, Rosamund?'

'Yes, I'm okay. Let me know when it's time.'

She took a deep breath and stepped into the porch, avoiding the broken terracotta and blue tile which rocked when you stepped on it, and wrinkled her nose for the last time at the smell of mildew, mice and the dust she had never managed to conquer. Why had Pa hung on so long here, until he died? But she knew why. She loved the place as he had done: loved the lofty rooms and damp-marked wallpaper, the stubborn kitchen range, the cantankerous noisy water system. Especially she loved the stained glass peacock window on the stairs, and the view from her bedroom over the garden and Cornish fields sweeping up to the moor. It was – well, had been – home for all her eighteen years. Trailing through the rooms she sought to escape the lot numbers staring at her from every surface. She needed to find a way to say goodbye.

The brass knob with a dent that fitted the heel of her hand turned, and she slipped through the door into the drawing room. It was quiet in here. The faded green of the brocade curtains and soft colours in the worn turkey carpet; the pictures and ornaments; the hollows of the chintz covered sofa where she had nestled with Francis among frayed silk cushions, and the fat leather armchair in which Pa presided over the Sunday hearth would be imprinted forever on her mind. The light was muted, shaded by branches of the lilac tree outside the window, and the lot numbers were scarcely visible. This still felt like home, and Rosamund sat in her father's chair and became absorbed into the peace of the room.

In the far corner the Chinese cabinet gleamed in the shadow, and she got up to stroke its delicate carving for the last time. This above all things in the house she would have liked to keep. It was a lovely thing, brought from the Far East to the family home by a long ago uncle. The wood was rich and dark, and there were many cupboards and dim shelved recesses. Set in the carved scrolls and curling leaves were tiny birds, beasts, butterflies and fish made of mother of pearl and ivory. She stroked the outline of a favourite mother of pearl dragon, and knelt to wonder for the last time at the intricate tracery on an ivory bird. It was broken. A bare patch of wood showed where the wing had been.

'Oh no,' Rosamund cried. 'Where is it?' She felt carefully around the floor until her fingers closed on the tiny fragment. Leaning forward to fit it into place, her eye was caught by a fold of paper just visible under a low drawer. She eased it out and smoothed the thin paper until she could make out the spidery writing.

'*My Darling Edgar*,' it said in large spiky letters.

'Ro-osamund. They're coming in now,' Edith called.

She wrapped the piece of broken ivory in the paper and thrust it into her pocket.

'Coming,' she called, and left the room to its secrets.

As Rosamund emerged from the house, Edith was walking towards her.

'They're beginning to arrive.' She glanced back over her shoulder. 'Let's go inside.'

Rosamund marvelled. Her cool, collected sister was nervous. She felt a sudden alarm herself.

'Where's Francis?' Edith asked.

Rosamund pushed away her panicky feeling, and looked across the yard to the stables where no horses had been stabled in her lifetime.

'Over there with Alan Phipps. Remember him? He was in the same year as Francis at school – went into estate agency and auctioneering with his father.'

Francis had his back to her, chestnut head bent to look at the papers Alan held. She called out. 'We're going back inside till things get going.'

Even from where she stood, she could see the clear green of his eyes disappear into crinkles as he sent her his special grin.

'See you later,' he called.

Alan waved, and the two men turned back to the papers.

As the sisters passed through the hall, Edith picked up a catalogue and glanced at the heading.

> Gelling Gelling and Phipps Auctioneers
> Catalogue price 6d
> The Old Rectory, Treblissick
> Friday 3rd November 1954 at 11am
> Viewing on the day prior (Thurs 2-5pm)
> Clearance Sale following the death of the late Mr Arthur Hambly

She put it down hurriedly, and looked around. 'Where shall we go?'

Rosamund stopped. Where indeed? There was nowhere to hide. The house was truly no longer her home, and the first prospective bidders were entering the hall. 'In the morning room. If we stand by the garden door we can see what's going on outside too.'

Her panic had passed, and she was feeling vaguely excited.

People were moving about the house now, pink catalogues well in evidence. There had been quite a crowd to view yesterday, and these early arrivals were looking over lots today before bidding began. Many glanced curiously at the two women in the morning room. Rosamund knew they didn't look like sisters. She, ten years younger, was slender and fair, with high cheekbones, a longish nose and what Pa had called a determined chin. Edith was dark and slightly swarthy like Pa. Dressed in a cream crepe blouse and a black suit which emphasised her complexion, she betrayed her nervousness by drumming her fingers on the wall against which she leaned.

'This is awful, Rosie. It hasn't been my home for years, but I feel as if these people are turning my life over. It makes me feel naked. Aren't you hating it too?'

'I thought I'd be awfully upset. Instead I feel numb, as if none of this is happening to me. It's as if there's a glass bowl over me. I can see and hear what's going on, but nothing can touch me.' Rosamund leaned calmly against the windowsill. She felt odd, a stranger in a familiar room. None of the emotions – love, sadness, pleasure, boredom, which had punctuated her life so far, had left the faintest mark on this room. But her memories she would take with her. Even now she could feel Edith's arms round her after her first day at school because another girl had taunted her with having no mother. 'I have got a mother, haven't I, Edith – somewhere?' she'd implored her sister. Edith had buried her face in her hair, and told her that Mother had died when Rosie was a baby; that she and Pa and Edith were all each other needed, and come on now, it was time to feed the hens.

Rosamund smiled. All each other needed. It was only four years later that Edith came home with a diamond on her finger, and within a year was married and living in South Africa. It was lovely to see her again, even though she'd had to leave Leslie and the twin nephews Rosamund had never seen, behind. But Edith wouldn't be here now if Pa hadn't died.

She turned to the window. Below on the lawn rugs in piles, plant pots, deck chairs, the mower and a wheelbarrow stood forlornly in the November murk. Even from here she could see the white patches where a number marked each lot. That was all it took to turn old friends into a heap of junk.

'Whoever would want to buy a ginger deckchair with a broken canopy?' murmured Edith, following Rosamund's gaze.

'Pa never did get round to mending it.' She blinked away a tear. 'I can't get used to him not being here. He used to potter about the house and garden on that gammy leg of his. And all those lovely things he made in the old wash house…'

'Toys and gadgets, our bookcases, all the dolls' house furniture…'

'When he was well enough.'

They smiled at each other, remembering with affection. A fat woman stopped to peer at the threadbare chair beside them, then moved on.

'His tools should fetch a good price,' Edith observed. 'It's a pity there's no one left in the family who would want them. Still, we need to make as much as possible in this sale.'

'I didn't know till after he died that we were in debt. He never told me.'

Edith glanced sharply at Rosamund, then turned away.

'I wonder how much longer Francis will be,' she said.

The moment passed.

Rosamund stroked the seed pearl and garnet ring on her left hand against her cheek.

'I don't know what I'd have done without Francis, specially these last few weeks, helping with Pa, and then the funeral.' She choked, then lifted her chin. 'It wasn't always like that, though. Remember how he used to tease me when we were children? But I often got my own back. Didn't we squabble – fists and feet, and no holds barred!'

'You once bit me when I tried to separate you,' Edith grinned.

Rosamund smiled, then sobered. 'He wouldn't let anyone else touch me, though. I couldn't believe it when he came home after National Service and fell in love with me.'

'As if we didn't notice. Everyone took it for granted that you and Francis would marry. You've always loved each other.'

'Yes, I think we have. Now Pa's gone Francis doesn't want us to wait to get married.' She turned back to the room, tugging down the jacket of the grey suit with a pencil skirt suit she'd worn for the funeral. Edith was in black because it was done, but Rosamund wouldn't wear black for Pa. She chose grey because it was subdued, but her blouse was the bluebell colour he'd liked to see her wear. 'Matches your eyes, poppet,' he'd said.

'I do miss him, Edith.'

Her earlier excitement had subsided. The glass bowl feeling disappeared and sadness came flooding back. Glad when Francis's steady features appeared among the thinning crowd, she met his eyes with relief, and saw them soften with compassion. His glance took in Edith too as he reached their side.

'The auction's about to start. It's going to be a long drawn out business. Shall we go over to the farm? Mother said she'll have coffee ready.'

He tucked an arm of each into his as they made their way out. Rosamund nuzzled her cheek against the roughness of his coat, and he gave her arm a comforting squeeze.

She could hear the auctioneer's voice from the stableyard and caught a glimpse of him raised above the clustered crowd.

'What am I bid for lot fifteen, assorted woodworking tools?'

Rosamund swallowed and quickened her pace.

'No coffee for me, thanks,' called Edith five minutes later as she disappeared upstairs.

'I'll just have a quick one, then I'd better see where Dan's to.' Francis propped himself against the dresser.

Rosamund flopped into a chair. 'I don't ever want to go through that again, Aunt Maud.' She took a steaming mug from Francis's mother. 'Thanks. You should have seen people turning the stuff over. Things I've been using for years without taking much notice. They seemed so shabby and ordinary today. I'll be glad when it's all over.'

'I said you'd be better keeping away, Rosamund. My, you're in some hurry,' as Francis drained his mug. 'Dan's taken the tractor up Top field with some hay for the sheep.'

'Right. Thanks. I shouldn't be long, Rosamund.' He headed for the door.

Aunt Maud raised her eyebrows. She lifted a plump arm and floury hand to push back a wave of red-gold hair streaked with grey, before returning to the dough she had been kneading at one end of the vast kitchen table.

Rosamund smiled at her across her mug. Dear Aunt Maud, she thought. No relation yet, but she'll make a wonderful mother-in-law. She's always been there, ready to listen to my tales of woe, or to kiss a bruised knee better. She watched as she deftly turned and kneaded, turned and kneaded, rocking in ancient rhythm. Even when Uncle Edgar died in that terrible tractor accident six years ago she was the same – always there for others. From babyhood she and Uncle Edgar had taken the place of a real aunt and uncle, rambling Pennygarra Farm as familiar to her as the Old Rectory.

She'd always loved this kitchen which enclosed Aunt Maud like a jewel in its setting – its low beams festooned with dried herbs and strings of onions; the creamy walls smoke-darkened from the fireplace with its cloam oven where the bread would be baked, and the slate floor where soft greys, golds and purples echoed the misty distances of the moor that lay above the farm. She settled lower into the high backed Windsor chair, soothed by thuds of dough and the slow tick of the grandfather clock. Across the hearth Tilly was washing the latest batch of kittens, not yet with their eyes open. Her eyelids drooped, and she slept.

She woke to Francis's footfall, and stirred.

'There you are,' she said, her eyes soft.

'Come for a walk, my bird. Dan'll manage on his own this afternoon.'

'Just give me time to change out of these clothes.'

She left the kitchen and climbed to the room under the eaves she'd shared with Edith for the last few weeks.

'I didn't realise I'd brought so much with me.' Edith had spread clothes over both beds and was busy packing a large brown suitcase ready to start her return journey to Johannesburg the next day.

'Like some help?'

'No thanks, I'm better sorting it out on my own.'

'I know what you mean,' Rosamund grinned, relieved. She stepped out of the grey skirt and threw it with the jacket across a chair, then pulled on tan trousers, a high-necked turquoise jumper and an old tweed jacket. 'I'll put these away later.' She hunted under the bed for a pair of stout shoes. 'Francis and I are going for a walk. Don't forget to leave a dress out for tonight.'

'Where's he taking us?'

'The Royal Oak. It's not too far as we don't want to be late back, and the food's good. It's where we went for Francis's twenty third birthday last March. Pa was with us, it was the last outing he had.' She lowered her head to tie her shoelaces, then straightened up. 'See you later,' and dashed out of the room.

Francis waited in the yard as Floss, his black and white sheep dog, ran to the gate and back in anticipation, tail waving like a flag. With Rosamund's hand in his warm grip, together they swung out of the farmyard. By tacit agreement they avoided the direction of The Old Rectory, and took the field path that led towards the moor. A granite stile led them into a field of cows who greeted them with soft moos, and lifted curious heads to watch their progress. In the next field sheep scurried out of their path, bleating like a bunch of well upholstered matrons disturbed at afternoon tea.

Francis stopped, narrowing his eyes to appraise the flock, while Rosamund shaded her eyes to watch a pair of buzzards as they lazily circled in a thermal over an old quarry.

'I almost envied Edith when she was talking about South Africa last night,' she said. 'But look at all this. I never want to be anywhere else but here.'

He put his arm over her shoulders as they carried on down the sloping field. 'You won't have to, my lover, if I've anything to do with it.

We could travel later on, in a few years' time if you want to. Visit Edith and Leslie perhaps.'

Rosamund laughed. 'We'll not be able to for years and years if we have the string of children you plan on.'

'We'll take them all with us, you'll see.'

'Pipe dreams, that's what they are.'

Floss scrambled onto the last stile beside a glossy holly tree, and they followed her, dipping down into a wooded valley where a clear stream burbled its way to the river below. There were few birds about, and the raucous call of rooks which followed them from the edge of the wood soon faded. When they reached the wooden bridge over the stream there was only the sound of running water.

Here Francis stopped and swung Rosamund towards him, held her close. His heart was bounding beneath her cheek, and she saw the throb of a pulse close to the small indented scar on his neck which she loved to kiss. She lifted her face to his and they kissed long and deep.

'Oh, Rosamund.' His breath was warm on her hair. 'I love you so much. We must get married soon. I want to be close, to be part of you – never let you go. I can't wait much longer.'

'Oh, yes,' she promised. 'How soon is soon?'

'How about tomorrow?' She laughed and nuzzled his ear. 'No? Next spring then? Mother wants to stay on in the farmhouse some time longer, so we could have one of the farm cottages at the end of the lane. I'm serious, Rosamund. The one next to Dan's has been empty since Michaelmas. It'll only take a couple of months to get ready.'

'And it will take two or three months to arrange the church and everything.' Rosamund sobered, but her eyes shone.

Francis held her away from him, and looked down into her eyes. 'It's going to be very difficult.'

'What is?'

'Living in the same house as you, sleeping in a bedroom near you.' She felt his arms tremble as he gripped her tighter.

'I'm not going to the altar in the family way, Francis Durrant, and that's that.' She pulled away from him reluctantly. 'And we're not taking any chances either,' as he drew her to him again. 'Although I'm not saying I wouldn't like to.'

'Rosamund Hambly, you have the makings of a Scarlet Woman.'

'At the right time, and in the right place, boy. And that's not here.'

She put her head on one side. 'Shall we get up to the moor today, d'you think?'

'I can see I'm going to be henpecked. You win – this time. Race you to the kissing gate.'

Where, of course it began all over again.

Rosamund never forgot that walk. When they emerged from the wood onto the edge of the moor the clouds were clearing, and a soft blue sky such as early winter in Cornwall sometimes brings circled the hills, and sheep cries came thinly down the turf-scented wind. They climbed to the summit of a tor, the world at their feet. Francis had loaded his pockets with cheese, apples and chocolate while Rosamund was changing, and they shared the food with some moorland ponies who were old hands at gatecrashing picnics. When they had eaten, Francis took out the tin whistle his father had brought home from a long ago fair and taught him to play. He played now – jaunty tunes that had Rosamund tapping her feet, then haunting strains that drifted over the slopes below. She sat beside him among a tumble of boulders, and leaned against a granite outcrop, eyes closed, lost in the melody and the moment, hands resting on cool turf.

The music died away.

'Time to go, my bird. It'll be dark before we're home.'

Smiling into his eyes, she reached up and he lifted her to her feet. They kissed with loving tenderness under the luminous sky, then turned to go. On the way back they skirted an ancient stone circle where the curlews cried, and beside a still moorland pool the remnants of cotton grass breathed memories of harebells and high summer. The ponies followed them to the edge of the moor, then whisked their tails and tossed their heads and scampered with flying hooves back to the heights.

Dusk was falling as the lovers tramped along the road towards the farm, arms around each other's waists. Cottage lights winked on, vying with the rising moon, and the evening was magical with the scent of woodsmoke. They came to the shuttered cottage that was to be their home, mysterious in the deepening dusk.

'I'll get the key tomorrow, and we'll have a look round,' promised Francis with glowing eyes.

2

'Are you sure you want to stay here on your own, Rosamund?' Aunt Maud got up from the breakfast table and started to gather crockery.

'Yes, I'll be fine. Leave those and go put your hat on. If you don't hurry, Mrs Hicks'll have bagged the best end of the stall and left you the part where the canopy leaks. Francis'll be back by lunchtime. He's only got to put Edith on the train and do a few errands in Bodmin. Go on, Aunt Maud, I said leave them.' She took the dishes from her and gave her a gentle push towards the door.

Aunt Maud armed herself into her second best coat and pulled on a grey beret. 'You're a good girl,' she told Rosamund, and bustled out into the yard to the ancient Land Rover. She pushed her umbrella and money pouch in among the stacked eggs, butter and other produce that Francis had stowed in the back before setting off with Edith. 'Don't do too much, mind. Take some time for yourself.'

Rosamund stood in the doorway until the Land Rover had clattered out of the yard.

'Morning, Dan,' she called to the shadowy figure in the dairy.

'Marnin', Rosamund. I'll be down Bottom Field when I'm finished 'ere.'

She nodded, closed the door and leaned on it for a moment. A few hours alone, what luxury. She felt quiet today after the emotion of yesterday, with the house sale, plans for their wedding and a cottage home. Then the meal out in the evening had been bright on the surface, but after such a short time together there was sadness at Edith's leaving.

It'll be a few days before we know the proceeds of the sale, she reflected as she washed and dried the breakfast pots. Edith is all right for money, and Francis'll look after me when we're married. I've enough to manage on with my Post Office wages until then. It doesn't matter how much the sale raised, so long as this wretched debt can be paid off. Poor Pa, to have that hanging over him all these years. I suppose I'll never know what it was for. She sat down suddenly at the table, put her head on her arms, and wept.

When her sobs had subsided, she stayed where she was for a few minutes, resting. No one had told her grief would be so tiring.

After a while she sat up. There was a small patch of sunlight on the floor, and it reminded her that she'd intended to do some washing. If the sun stayed out, the clothes might even dry outside. Her spirits revived and she went upstairs, her thoughts on the cottage home she would soon be caring for.

Edith had stripped her bed, and Rosamund added her own discarded garments to the heap of sheets. She made her own bed, then picked up the grey suit still lying on the chair where she had left it yesterday. As she put it on a hanger, feeling in a pocket for a handkerchief that need to be washed, a piece of flimsy paper fell out.

'What's…? Of course, it's the letter I found in the Chinese cabinet yesterday.'

Rosamund sat on the bed and unfolded the paper. Yellowed and brittle, it smelled slightly musty – of old wood and forgotten sunlight. With the fragment of ivory wing in her hand, she read the slanting words.

My Darling Edgar,

I brought the baby home yesterday. She is the image of you, with fair hair, and I have called her Rosamund. Arthur has no idea, and is already besotted with her, (although I believe he would have preferred a boy this time). I know you wanted a girl, so you're in luck.

I MUST see you soon. I have the wildest dreams about us, you can't imagine. The baby screams in the night, and I hate her for interrupting my dreams.

I saw you from the window this morning and cannot bear to be parted from you. All I want is to…'

Rosamund's face grew hot, and she threw the letter away from her as if it were a lighted match. Her mother had written that? Her MOTHER. But Edgar? She picked up the paper and scanned the jerky writing again.

'My Darling Edgar…

She is the image of you, and I have called her Rosamund…'

She knew only one Edgar. Francis's father. So Uncle Edgar was…? Her heart shrank into a lump of iron. 'Francis, oh Francis,' she whispered, white to the lips, as the deadful realisation crystallized. Then her head went back, and a cry rang out, anguished and desolate as the wastes of the moon. 'Fraan – ci-is.'

She sat on, mute and still. Hens squarked comfortably in the yard below, and a train whistled in the valley.

Emotions swirled in her brain like muddy water after a storm. Mother, whose memory she had worshipped, for whose death she had felt herself to be guilty. Mother, whom no one would talk to her about. Was it because of this monstrous thing she had discovered? No, it couldn't be. If it was, Aunt Maud wouldn't have cared for her like she did. She and Uncle Edgar wouldn't have been friends with Pa. And they'd never have let her and Francis fall in love. No, Pa loved her like a true father. He could not have known.

She picked up the letter with her fingertips. Perhaps she had misread it. But there was no doubt – she and Francis could never marry.

A feeling deep inside flickered, then grew until it filled every fibre of her body. An unfamiliar feeling of overwhelming sorrow – and anger, tinged with horror and fear. Mother and Uncle Edgar, whom she had loved and trusted had hoodwinked poor unsuspecting Pa and Aunt Maud. And robbed herself and Francis of their love and their future.

She didn't cry, yet shudder after shudder washed through her in great waves, and left her gasping for breath. Shocked at the violence of her emotion she rode it out, fought to regain control. At last the tide receded. Weak and drenched in cold sweat, coherent thought became once more possible.

Then she panicked. How can I tell Francis? What shall I say? How will he feel about me once he knows the truth? I wish I could just run away and not have to do this. She twisted the ring on her finger. This shouldn't be here she thought, yet kept it on.

Don't be stupid, she told herself. Of course you can't run away. You owe Francis more than that, whatever it costs, even though telling him about this dreadful thing'll shatter all our dreams. A sob nearly choked her. We'll never marry in the village church, never set up home in the cottage. She threw herself down on the bed burying her head in the pillow in a vain effort to shut out reality. Gone the promise of days and nights of delight in each other, gone the promise of children to fill the farm with love and laughter as they themselves had done. No grandchildren to keep them young, no gentle slide into old age…

I must tell him, she resolved, and with a determined effort sat up and tried the words aloud. 'Francis, I am your half sister.' No, I simply can't do it like that, but I'll find a way somehow. It'll be the hardest thing I'll ever have to do – and the worst – so it needs to be done as soon as possible, or I won't have the courage.

***

When Francis returned from Bodmin there was a note for him propped against the kitchen clock.

'Meet me at the Jubilee Stone as soon as poss. R.'

It wasn't like Rosamund to be so brusque. Something was wrong. He had a list of farmwork as long as your arm, but nothing that wouldn't keep for a while longer. He tore up the steep lane above the farmhouse lined with mossy boulders under dripping trees, vaulted the ancient gate which hadn't been opened within his memory, and burst out onto the lower reaches of the moor.

The Jubilee Rock was their place, his and Rosamund's. They'd known the huge granite rock since they were children; traced their fingers in the eighteenth century carvings commemorating the Jubilee of King George the third, which adorned the sides. The top was approached from above. It lay below the skyline tucked into the grassy slope, dotted by wind-stunted hawthorns and gorse bushes, from where you could step straight onto the top of the rock. It was here they'd come for picnics, sometimes with other village children, and played on and around the rock until they knew every nook and cranny. When he was thirteen or fourteen and almost too old for childish games, Francis caught Rosamund in a game of tag, and laid a first tentative kiss on her cheek. She, five years younger, had pushed him away with a 'Don't be soppy, Francis,' but when he returned from National Service two years ago and found she had become a beautiful young woman of sixteen, they had both been more than ready fo fall in love.

He could see her now as he swarmed up from below through wet grass wreathed with spiderwebs. A lonely figure, she crouched on top of the rock, arms round bent knees, gazing out across the moor. She looked lost and somehow diminished. A finger of dread stirred in Francis' chest, and he quickened his pace. When he scrambled up beside her, panting, she didn't move.

'Rosamund?'

Hunkering down, he raised a hand to stroke her hair. 'What is it, my bird?'

'Don't touch me.' Her voice low, tight as a sprung trap.

Francis's dread deepened, his heart thudding against his ribs, but he kept still and waited.

Without turning her head, she held out a folded piece of paper. 'I found this in the Chinese cabinet yesterday. I only read it this morning.'

Carefully he unfolded the paper and began to read.

Rosamund couldn't bear to look at him. This was the moment when their lives would change for ever. Until now she could have screwed up the letter, burned it in the kitchen range, never to acknowledge who she truly was. She wouldn't have to tear their future to pieces, to cast their love to the moorland wind as though it had never been. Wouldn't have to bring betrayal and pain to Aunt Maud who, unknowing, had loved and cared for her husband's child. But all her life Rosamund would have known that Francis was her half brother. Young as she was she knew that that kernel of guilty knowledge would sour their love – grow like a cancer, to push its deadly fingers into every crevice of their lives until it destroyed the very thing she sought to save. Besides, she had never hidden anything from Francis, and wouldn't do even now.

She didn't need to read it again, the words were blazed onto her brain. 'My darling Edgar … she is the image of you, and I have called her Rosamund.' At his quick intake of breath his whole body tensed, and she recognised the moment when he realised what the letter meant. In the long silence that followed, she gazed unseeing over the moor, towards the distant gleam of the estuary where it launched itself into the sea, her vision blurred by tears.

Suddenly Francis dropped the letter. Grabbed her shoulders in an angry vice and twisted her round to face him. 'No-oo!' he raged in disbelief.

'Stop it, Francis! Don't do this, it won't help!'

He stared into her hopeless eyes until his own brimmed, then let go abruptly so that, off balance, she almost fell backwards off the rock. Instinctively he reached for her and clutched her to him.

'I'm sorry, my darling, I'm sorry. Tell me it's not true. It can't be true,' he whispered fiercely into her hair.

Instinctively, she'd relaxed against him as she always did, but at his words she stiffened and pushed him away.

'Read it again.' She gestured to where the folded missive had dropped into a crevice.

'I don't see how it can not be true,' said Rosamund at last, as she took the letter from him before refolding it and thrusting it into her pocket. 'It was hidden under a bottom drawer of the cabinet in our drawing room. It's obvious that your father and my mother… had a baby together… me. That makes us…'

'Half brother and sister!' He shook his head. 'But I love you, Rosamund. We were meant to be together… every one says so. To marry, to have children…'

She buried her head in her hands, tears streaming between her fingers. 'I want your children… so much… but it's impossible now.'

'I know, my love.' He rocked her, unresisting in his arms, 'Couldn't we just forget this letter ever existed, tear it up and let it blow away over the moor?'

'Don't you think I thought of that, exactly that?' with a sad smile at his same train of thought. 'No, eventually it would destroy us.'

'There must be something we can do.

Blindly they reached for each other.

In their grief they touched a depth of closeness they had never before experienced. Conscious already of guilt, they forged a bond which would endure a lifetime of separation. Wrapped in his warmth and tenderness, Rosamund drank in Francis's own special smell mingled with hay and cattle, feeling the strength and solidity of his body as it enfolded hers, committing the sense of him to her memory. Passion sparked, and grew. Grew until it threatened to overwhelm them both…

Francis wrenched himself from her.

'Oh God, how can I be without you' he said, broken voiced. 'I need you so.' He rose and backed away from her one painful step at a time, both hands raised in a gesture of despair.

Abandoned on the hard rock, Rosamund felt each step that took him from her like a blow. Knowing what it cost him made no difference. That Francis, although he might not have realised, had made the first move in their necessary separation, felt like betrayal. It took all her strength to struggle to her feet.

'It's over,' she said, and walked away onto the moor.

She hadn't gone far when she heard him call.

'Rosamund. Wait.'

She hesitated, without turning. Stopped.

'It might not be hopeless,' he said when he caught up. 'Look, on the face of it the letter seems genuine, but it might not be. We could ask for advice. See what some one else thinks about it.' He clapped his hand to his head. 'God, how am I going to tell Mother? I can't imagine how she'll feel. She'll be terribly upset! Dad – how could he!' He took a deep breath and swallowed. 'But she might be able to shed some light on things. Don't lose heart yet, sweetheart.'

***

Maud was upset, most dreadfully. She had not been able to have any more children after Francis, now this letter showed that Edgar had not only been unfaithful, but had fathered another child.

After a good weep she wiped her eyes, blew her nose hard and made a pot of tea.

'I never noticed anything at the time, but then I wouldn't, would I? We didn't really know your parents that well, Rosamund – at least I didn't – until your mother went into hospital and Arthur came round and asked if I'd look after you and Edith.'

'I didn't know that, Mother. I thought we'd known them for ever.'

'Pa wouldn't have brought us to you if he'd known what was going on, would he?' Rosamund blinked back tears.

'I should think not! Anyway, to begin with I had you all the time, with your pa coming to see you when he could. Then after his wife was moved to another hospital and he couldn't visit her so often, I just had you in the daytime while he was teaching. He and Edith used to come after school to fetch you. They stayed to tea, then he took you both home. And that's how it went on. But that doesn't help you now m'dears, does it?'

'You've been all the mother I ever knew, and I'd give the world not to have brought this on you now.' They were both in tears.

Francis became impatient and demanded 'Have you any ideas how we can get out of this mess?'

'Well, I never saw your ma's handwriting, Rosamund, but who did write it was well upset. Did you ever see such jerky writing!' she said. 'But why don't you show it the vicar, see what he thinks.'

***

Francis closed the gate behind them as they left the vicarage, and they were silent as they crossed the green with more space between them than there had ever been.

The Reverend Trevail had welcomed them heartily, a twinkle in his pale blue eyes, thinking that they had come to arrange for the banns to be called. He'd listened to their story, eyes clouding with sympathy, and when he'd read the letter took it to the telephone where he'd called a solicitor friend. When he returned, he'd told them that Mr Julian considered that on the strength of the letter, there was too much doubt that a marriage, civil or otherwise would be lawful. The solicitor had only confirmed his own conclusions, and with deep regret the vicar told them that he could not marry them.

In the stunned silence that followed, a strange feeling had stirred in Rosamund, something abhorrent that she did not want to face. Her throat seized up, and leaving Francis to mumble faint thanks she'd made for the door, head high and left with her dignity intact and her heart in tatters.

Beyond the green they set off up the road, and it wasn't until they turned into the farm lane that Francis spoke.

'What's to become of us, Rosamund?' he said despairingly. 'I couldn't bear it if we had to stay in the same house. I can't leave the farm – it's Mother's livelihood as well as mine. It doesn't seem fair, but I'll try to find you somewhere to live.'

'Of course you can't leave the farm. I wouldn't expect you to. But it would be hopeless if I lived anywhere near you. You know what we're like. We'd be back together in no time, and who knows what would happen then.' She took a deep breath and said the unthinkable. 'I shall go away, Francis. Right away.'

'No!'

'I'll make a new life for myself, and you won't know where I am.'

'But you've always lived in Treblissick, you don't know anywhere else.'.

'It's the only way.'

They lingered in the dip in the lane where the stream tumbled down from the moor running silver beneath an arch of ferns, like time that was running away from them so unbearably swiftly. Both had now faced the reality of parting, and a barrier of pain had already begun to fill the space between them.

'When will you go?' he asked at last.

'Soon,' she replied, and turned away up the steep lane.

3

Leadersfield, Yorkshire.

Rosamund remembered little of the journey to the North of England, and it was dark when the train began to slow through the grimy suburbs of Leadersfield and drew into the city station.

Outside the station she hesitated. Streetlights and neon signs leered through the murk, and wet pavements gleamed, greasy and sullen. Tall buildings peered across the station forecourt, and the sooty air was full of clanks and rushes of steam from the station behind. Cars and lorries ground in low gear into the caverns of the streets with a whoosh of tyres on wet tarmac. A tram swayed and clattered up the hill and come to a halt in front of Rosamund. It was the only friendly thing in sight and she decided to board it.

'Taxi Miss?'

She hadn't noticed the line of taxis drawn up to the left of the station entrance. That would be better.

'Yes, please. Can you take me somewhere I can get a room? Somewhere respectable – and cheap?'

'Hop in, luv. I know just the place. I'll tekk yer to Mrs Wilson's.'

Mrs Wilson's was in Sebastapol Road, an endless row of Victorian villas about a mile from the city centre. As the taxi drew up before twin pillars guarding three storeys of net curtained windows, Rosamund saw the curtain to the left of the door twitch. A few moments later, as she finished paying the taxi driver, a figure appeared at the top of the steps silhouetted against the light.

'What've you brought me tonight, Alf?' The figure heaved her bulk down the flight of steps and peered into Rosamund's face. 'Oh you poor thing. Come on in and let's get you settled. It'll be a room you're wanting? Not too expensive? I've a nice one on the top floor. We'll soon have you cosy.'

Rosamund followed Mrs Wilson's flowered behind up three flights of stairs to a tiny attic room, furnished with the bare necessities of bed, table, cupboard and a sagging armchair propped on a house brick, all standing on shiny yellow lino and presided over by a vase of red plastic roses and bilious-looking seascape above the gas fire. The main feature of the room was two greedy looking meters prominently stationed alongside the table. Mrs Wilson bent to turn on the gas fire, which hissed and popped into life, immediately bringing cheer into the room.

'There's a bit of gas left, luv, but you'll need to put some shillings in soon.'

'I'll see if I've got some.' Rosamund fumbled in her purse. 'Just one.'

'Come back down with me and I'll find you some more.'

Downstairs Mrs Wilson clucked over her, insisted on giving her cheese on toast and a cup of cocoa.

'Just this once, mind, and only because it's as plain as the nose on your face that you've had neither bite not sup since I don't know when.'

Placing five shilling pieces in return for Rosamund's two half crowns on the table, she added bread, butter, milk, tea and sugar ('I'll add it to the rent, luv,'), and a large iron key.

Rosamund climbed the stairs again, the key clutched in her hand. She felt its coldness and hardness as she turned it in the lock, and caught back a half-formed thought ready to escape and wing its way to the South West. Determined not to think of the past, she undressed quickly and lay on the cold bed. All night long the traffic rumbled in the street below. At dawn she slept.

Several hours later the rumble was the first thing Rosamund was aware of as she opened her eyes to a dim green light, and the curtained window was in the wrong place. Memory flooded back in the first defenceless moments, and filled her with such pain that it blotted out all other thought or feeling. She had held herself together to do what was necessary to sever herself from her old life, and now the enormity of what had happened overwhelmed her. For the rest of her life she must deny her love for Francis, and would never be whole again. What have I done to him? He'll be wild with grief, not knowing why I've gone without a word. Better that than the shame of the truth, for him as well as for me. I'd still have had to leave – it wouldn't have been possible for us both to live in the same village.

A great sob erupted, and she turned over in the strange bed and cried her heart out.

When the worst of the weeping was over she slept, to be wakened some time later by a knock on the door.

'Who is it?'

'Mrs Wilson, luv. Are you all right?'

'Yes. Just a minute.'

Rosamund stumbled across the cold lino, fumbled for the key and unlocked the door. Mrs Wilson saw Rosamund's tearstained face and summed up the situation. She crossed the room and pulled back the curtains.

'It's nearly three o'clock, and not a sign of you, so I thought I'd come up and see. Have you been comfortable then?'

Rosamund nodded. Mrs Wilson looked at the untouched food on the table.

'You'll be wanting to go out and get some food afore the shops shut, won't you? Have you enough money?'

'Yes, but I'll need to get a job soon.'

'Well, it's a bit late to go job-hunting today, but you never know. Why don't you mekk yourself a pot of tea, and have a bite afore you get ready to go out? There's a row of shops just down the road, you'll get all you need for the moment there.'

'I forgot about buying food. I'm not really used to anything yet.' She shivered in her thin nightdress.

'You'll catch your death, stood there like that. I mustn't keep you gossiping. You know where I am if you want me.' She wheezed her way to the stairs.

'Thank you,' Rosamund called after her, grateful that someone in this strange world cared enough to be interested in her.

She didn't look for work straight away. Each morning she left Mrs Wilson's and trudged about the city, getting to know this different world. She missed the friendly faces from the village where every one knew her, and couldn't get used to seeing only strangers in the streets.

In the Market Hall, prices were low and the stall keepers friendly, calling to each other from stall to stall in the northern accent that until now she had only heard on the wireless. Here pungent smells assaulted her nose, of flowers and fish, hot pies, and firelighters and paraffin. The stalls were a tapestry of colour and texture. Oranges and apples, nobbly potatoes, cabbages and peas, heaped in profusion next to a stall swathed with exotic silks and satins, sensible flannelette and good Yorkshire woollen cloth. Under the clock tower in the centre of the market, Rosamund found a stall where jars of jelly babies and humbugs and twists of liquorice sat next to tubes of Smarties and bars of chocolate. Here she treated herself to a triangular paper bag of peardrops from the sweet stall under the central clock tower, and crunched them as she wandered the stalls. Over it all arched the wrought iron and glass dome, beneath which ancient gas jets sizzled and glowed, warming the booted and scarved people below.

There was a park only a few streets from Sebastapol Terrace. It was a far cry from her beloved woods and moors, but here Rosamund could see the sky and walk in open green spaces where mothers parked their prams and children played. Paths wound between neat beds of newly planted wallflowers, to a small lake where a row of bare trees loitered along its banks. Ducks clamoured for food, and she brought crusts for them, saving some for the dusty city sparrows that chattered and squabbled for her favours.

She found a library, and bore books home to fill the long lonely evenings, silent except for the sounds of other people moving about the house, and the ever-present traffic. But after a few pages her thoughts would wander, the book fell from her lap, and she'd sit gazing guiltily into the past. The future she dared not contemplate, and the present, despite her resolution and new experiences, was a desert to be crossed with slow painful steps. She couldn't stop herself from searching for Francis. The glimpse of a copper head, the set of a pair of shoulders, the sound of a light warm voice would set her heart pounding, palms wet and mouth dry, only to find with sorrow yet another stranger, and the familiar sinking feeling of despair would return.

She seldom saw the other lodgers, occasionally nodding a quiet 'good morning' as she passed someone in the hall or on the stairs. Rosamund was grateful that for the most part Mrs Wilson left her alone, although she was aware of her watchful care.

As she looked idly in a dress shop window one day, she realised that she needed new clothes. She hadn't brought much away with her.

Besides, everything she possessed reminded her of Francis and the old life. When she saw the prices, she decided it really was time to find work. How? A newspaper. There would be a situations vacant column in the local paper. She bought one on the way back to the bus station and, with time to spare before her bus was due, took it to the Jester Coffee Bar nearby to read.

Rosamund had been in here several times already. She liked the red formica-topped tables and the mosaic glass mirror behind the counter that jumbled up the colours and outlines of everything it reflected. On the end wall a gaudy Jester capered above a jukebox with its diet of modern songs, an overlay to the buzz of conversation and clink of spoons on crockery. The shiny coffee machine spluttered and fizzed, and turned out frothy coffee in wide glass cups, filling the air with the friendly smell.

She sipped a cup now, feeling the warmth of the hot liquid spread to a glow inside her, and unfolded the paper. She ran her eye down the column. There were plenty of jobs, but what could she do? She hadn't a lot of experience, only the village Post Office shop until Pa was too ill to leave him… She refused to allow her mind to travel further in that direction, and looked again at the newspaper. Secretary? That was no good. Greengrocer's assistant? On the other side of the city, and she didn't want to move from Mrs Wilson's. Counter assistant, city centre coffee bar. She looked up. Could it be here? There was a card tucked into the mirror behind the bar. 'Counter Assistant Required.' It *was* here.

Rosamund sat and watched for a while. There was only one assistant behind the bar, and there were pots of tea, hot chocolate, milk shakes and squash to serve, the spluttering coffee machine working overtime. There were sandwiches, cakes and pies, and baked beans on toast. The assistant had a pleasant word for everyone she served, and it was clear many were regular customers.

The girl came out from behind the counter to collect dirty crockery and wipe the tables with a bright green sponge. When she reached the next table Rosamund plucked up courage.

'Has anyone filled the post?' she ventured, nodding in the direction of the notice.

The girl stopped scooping up crumbs.

'I wish we had, luv. I'm rushed off me feet. Why? You interested?'

'Yes. Who do I see. You?'

'Oh no,' she laughed. 'My boss, Mr Holroyd. He's got the tobacconist's next door as well as this place. He'll be round soon, if you want to see him.'

'Yes I do. I'll wait till he comes.'

'Righto. I can't stop now, there's a queue at the counter already. I'll tell him when he comes in.'

'Thanks.' Rosamund watched the girl busy with the customers, and felt a small tingle of excitement. I'll enjoy working here – if I get the job. I'll meet lots of people, and the girl seems nice. With a rosy face and dark eyes with a wicked sparkle, she was obviously popular with the customers.

Soon a long thin man with big bushy eyebrows came in and lifted the end of the counter to go through to the back. Rosamund saw the assistant speak to him, and they both looked over in her direction. The girl smiled encouragingly as the man made his way across to Rosamund's table. She got to her feet, not knowing what to say.

'You want to apply for t'job here I gather, lass?'

'Yes, I can see you need someone.'

'Come through to t'back then.' He gestured with his head, and held up the counter for Rosamund to go through, leading her to a room that combined kitchen and storeroom. They sat either side of a small table littered with paraphernalia for making sandwiches, flanked by piles of dirty cups and saucers stacked beside the sink. The room was untidy but basically clean.

'Now then lass. What was your last job?' The eyes were shrewd, the tone businesslike.

'I worked in a village Post Office and store.'

'Why did you leave?'

'After my father died I was going to get married.' Rosamund flushed. 'Then I – I moved away from the district instead.'

'Any references?'

'No, there wasn't time to ask for any…' Her voice trailed off.

Mr Holroyd leaned back. 'What mekks you think I might employ you? No references, stranger to these parts – I could be tekkin' on a load of trouble. Eh?'

Rosamund took a deep breath, and looked directly at him. 'My parents are both dead, my father only recently. My only sister lives abroad and I've no other relatives. I left the district where I was born because of a broken engagement. I liked my work in the village shop, and I think I was reasonably competent. I've watched what your assistant has to do here, and there's obviously more than enough work for one.' She glanced at the littered table and piled up crockery, 'And I'm sure I could do it well. I like the atmosphere in here, and the clients, and – I do *need* a job, Mr Holroyd.'

This was the first time since ariving here that she had spoken of her circumstances, and she wondered at the strange feeling of relief which it gave her to have spoken even so briefly of her past.

'Can you work evenings?' he asked suddenly from under his eyebrows, making no reference to what she had just said.

Rosamund was astonished. 'Yes.'

'Right. One thirty till ten, with half an hour for tea, Monday till Saturday with a sliding day off. Seven pounds a week, and your food and overall free. You'll work a week in hand. One week's notice either side. When can you start?'

'Tomorrow?'

'Good. You'll work with Susan. She'll show you what to do. Pauline does mornings, and two evenings, relieving you and Susan at the busy times on your day off. Any questions? '

'No, I think you've covered everything, Mr Holroyd, thank you. I'm looking forward to starting.' Surprisingly, she was.

'Mekk sure you've some comfortable shoes on your feet, lass. It's hard work. I think you'll get on all right with Susan, She's been with us from t'start. Come and have a chat with her.'

***

So it was that Rosamund started work at the Jester Coffee Bar. Mr Holroyd's advice about wearing comfortable shoes was well founded. It was hard work and long hours. Rosamund caught the last bus home each night with aching legs and feet, and the latest tune from the jukebox ringing in her ears. She fell into bed and slept dreamlessly well into the mornings. Some colour and animation gradually returned to the face in her mirror, but there was still a haunted look about her, and sometimes her gaze would lengthen and her eyes darken with memory and pain.

She soon learned the ropes from Susan, and they became quite friendly. Susan was outgoing, and the customers liked to talk to her. She was also a flirt. She would flutter her eyelashes and clear the tables with a wiggle and a cheerful toss of her dark head, and there was no shortage of young men eager to see her home after the coffee bar closed at night. She would come in the following day full of what had happened – or not, as the case might be.

'You'd never believe it. That Brian – the quiet one 'at sits in the corner. Well, he's hands like an octopus. Most offended when I wouldn't let him kiss me goodnight. What does he take me for?' Or; 'George took me home last night, Rosamund. You know, that suave Romeo type with the big feet. Never been so disappointed in me life. He never even tried to hold my hand, and hadn't a word to say for himself.'

Rosamund was amused by these confidences, but resisted all invitations to talk about herself. She took an interest in the customers. Many of them were on their way to or from the bus station across the road, just in for a quick drink or a packet of cigarettes. There were the women who struggled in laden with shopping, who eased their tight shoes surreptitiously under the table while they sipped tea, their chattering children sticky with buns and ice cream. There was a tramp who came in occasionally on a rainy day. He smelled, and no one wanted to sit near him. Rosamund spread butter extra thick on his currant teacake and gave him a special smile, but she took care to give the chair he had used a good wipe when he had gone. A bevy of nurses came in, with navy blue storm caps and gabardine coats over their hospital uniforms, and she strained her ears to hear snippets of their mysterious conversations. Then there were the lovers. She tried hard not to notice them, but inevitably she saw the way they looked at each other. The only time she felt annoyed with Susan was when she joked about the lovers. Lovers were no joke, and they didn't know how lucky they were.

Mostly she enjoyed her work, and offered to do overtime when needed. That way she had very little time to spare for grief.

The Jester was a meeting place for a group of young people. They drifted in during the evening, boys in drape suits and thick rubber-soled shoes, and girls in full swinging skirts and low heels. They played the jukebox non-stop, smoked, drank coffee and enjoyed themselves with dedication.

Rosamund felt she was watching a stage from the other side of the counter, relieved that she was for the most part a spectator, becoming only briefly involved on her forays among the tables. But straight away the young men in the group were interested in her. Susan was well known to them, in fact she had been out with most of them at some time or other. The first evening they came in Rosamund was greeted with cries of 'What a smasher'! and 'Where have you been all my life, darlin'?' Rosamund was discomfited, and Susan, taking pity on her, intervened.

'What about me then? Don't I count any more when there's a new face around?' The young man leaned on the counter and smirked in Susan's face.

'Course you do, luv. But we know you, don't we?'

'Some better than others,' one of the girls sniggered.

'Pipe down you.' He turned with a half-mocking raised fist. 'We know you an' all, don't we lads?'

There was a general guffaw, and the girl who had interrupted hastily took out a handbag mirror and made a minor adjustment to her kiss curl.

'That's Ace,' Susan beckoned Rosamund into the back room and whispered. 'His real name's Cyril. Ace is a'seudname', he told me. I don't blame him reely for having one of those. Not with a name like Cyril I don't.'

'No, you're kidding.' Rosamund didn't know whether to believe her. 'It doesn't suit him at all.'

'It's true as I stand here. Coming luv,' she called to a waiting customer.

Back behind the counter, Rosamund observed Ace with curiosity. He was darkly handsome, with an olive complexion and unbelievably red lips. His Teddy Boy jacket of the deepest drape sported a maroon velvet collar, his blue suede 'brothel creeper' shoes had the thickest crepe soles, while his hair had the biggest quiff and the smartest DA cut at the back. The others hung on his every word, and he had only to flick cigarette-stained fingers and someone sprang to his bidding. He was clearly the leader of the group, and of course was first to make advances to Rosamund.

One evening he took a comb from his breast pocket, swept it through his already immaculate hair, then sauntered to the counter hands in pockets. The girls nudged each other and giggled, the boys egged him on. 'Go it lad'.

'Hiya honey, how's about me walking you home tonight?' in a pseudo-American drawl.

'Sorry, but no thanks. I catch the bus.' Rosamund looked around for help, but there was no way out. Susan was in the back washing up, and Rosamund couldn't leave the counter.

'Okay kid, we'll go on the bus then,' with a broad wink.

'I said no. I don't want anyone to take me home.'

'Aw, c'm on. Be a bit friendly.'

But Rosamund had turned away to serve another customer, and Ace swaggered back to the corner by the jukebox. The others were laughing, and someone put Norman Wisdom singing 'Don't Laugh at Me 'cos I'm a Fool' on the jukebox.

'She turned you down then, Ace?'

'Just playing hard to get. She won't resist me for long, wait and see.'

'She didn't fancy you, you mean,' his last girlfriend, June, said spitefully, 'and I'm not surprised.'

'What do you mean?' He stood over her threateningly.

'Aw, let it go, Ace,' said Dave. 'Put another record on. Let's have 'Happy Wanderer' for a change. Who's got sixpence?'

An argument started about which record to play, but Ace didn't join in. He sat moodily watching Rosamund under his eyebrows. She, aware of his attention, was glad when Susan came back.

'Ace asked if he could take me home,' she whispered.

'Are you going to?' Susan's eyes gleamed with interest.

'No. You know I don't want a boyfriend, Susan.'

'You want to watch Ace. He's not used to being turned down. He could get nasty. You might be as well going out with him once or twice, then he'd lose interest.'

'I told you, I don't want a boyfriend, and I'm not going out with anybody unless I want to. He'll soon find someone else.'

Susan looked doubtful, but said no more.

***

The next evening soon after Rosamund arrived for work, Ace came in. He bought an Espresso and sat down at his usual table, knees and arms spread, facing the counter. He watched her as she juggled plates and cups and saucers, cleared up, cashed money, wiped tables. Others of the group arrived one by one, the cigarette smoke thickened and the jukebox blared. Rosamund went home with the memory of his dark eyes on her every move, and the strains of Max Bygraves' 'Heart of my Heart' ringing in her ears. Francis used to play that to her, and it broke her heart to hear it now. It was the same every evening. The coffees, the cigarettes, the music. Ace tried asking her to the pictures, for a walk in the park, even a meal out, but her answer was always no. He now took little part in the group's conversation, and gradually fewer of them came.

'I'd put him out of his misery if I was you,' Susan counselled. 'He's got it real bad. I've never seen him like this before. You might regret it, else.'

But Rosamund didn't let Ace's attentions worry her. She was struggling to still her love for Francis, and that was taking all the emotional strength she had. In spite of this, she was enjoying her work and meeting new people, but still her heart was searching. Every man she saw in the street, every man who entered the coffee bar had something about him to remind her of Francis.

Then one day just before Christmas, it *was* Francis.

4

He was standing in the light of a gas lamp just outside the coffee bar, hands thrust deep into the pockets of his trench coat, eyes seeking hers, just as he had stood a thousand times, waiting for her.

Rosamund felt the blood drain from her face, her legs like cotton wool, her heart fit to burst out of her chest. How on earth had he found her! But she'd known he would – somehow. She took a deep breath, and picked up the tray of empty cups to carry it, shaking like an aspen, towards the counter.

'Here, give me that, before you drop it. You're mekking the cups rattle.' It was Ace at her elbow.

'What? Oh, thanks.' Gratefully she surrendered the tray and took refuge behind the counter.

'You all right? You look like you've seen a ghost?'

I might as well have seen a ghost, she thought. That's what Fancis must be to me. 'I do feel a bit peculiar.' She focussed her eyes with difficulty. 'I'll be all right in a minute.'

'You look fair peaky, Rosamund,' Ace said. 'Want to take me up on that offer to see you home?' He looked genuinely concerned and there was no trace of a swagger.

She hesitated, and he pressed on.

'You don't look fit to go alone. I'll look after you,' Ace said. 'Don't worry.'

That's it, she thought with relief. If Francis speaks to me I'm lost. If I'm with Ace he won't interfere.

'All right. Wait for me by the door. I'll only be a few more minutes.'

The coffee bar was empty, the last few cups washed up.

Ace put a proprietorial hand under her arm and crossed with care over to the bus station. Rosamund daren't look about her, and she felt sure Francis was still somewhere near. Her mouth was dry and her legs felt rubbery. Ace murmured into her ear, but she heard nothing, and allowed him to help her onto the bus and up the stairs.

When they got off near Mrs Wilson's, Rosamund was relieved to see that Ace took no notice of the young man who left the bus from the lower deck at the same stop. He put his arm round her waist, and feeling Francis's gaze from behind, she didn't resist.

'This is the house,' she whispered as they approached Mrs Wilson's gateway.

'Don't go in yet. Let's talk a minute.' Ace backed her expertly against the gatepost, and imprisoned her between his outstretched arms. Rosamund stiffened, then caught sight of Francis in the shadows. Afraid that he would intervene, she determined to act it out. He would take some convincing, she knew. As she relaxed, Ace's head blotted out her view of Francis, and his mouth came down on hers, loose and wet, tasting of stale cigarettes. It took all her strength not to cry out and push him away. Forgive me, Francis, she cried wordlessly as she put her arms round Ace. He became more excited, and pushed his knee between hers.

'Let's go to your room,' he grunted.

'No. Mrs Wilson doesn't allow visitors.' She turned her head towards the lighted window, as Ace groped at her breast.

'You want it really, I can tell. I've waited a long time for this, Rosamund.' His mouth came down greedily into her neck. Rosamund searched the darkness beyond his head – and Francis had gone.

As Ace came up for air, she twisted furiously out of his grasp and darted up the steps.

'Thanks for bringing me home,' she flung over her shoulder, before she fled to the safety of her room.

The curtain at the window beside the door twitched as she passed, leaving Ace throbbing with rage and frustration in the deserted street.

***

Next day was Rosamund's day off, and she was thankful to be able to stay at home. She slept badly and got up late. Unable to face food, after a cup of tea she began an onslaught on her room. She wasn't fond of housework and was normally comfortable with a degree of untidiness, but today she scrubbed and polished until the room shone, in an effort to ease the grief and pain that had come flooding back with the shock of seeing Francis. She was also unbearably homesick for the village and Cornwall, for all the dear people she knew, and for Pa. She sat in her spotless room in a bleakness of spirit that was worse than anything she had felt up to now.

When she heard carol singers in the distance she realised it was long after dark. Smells of cooking drifted up from the window below, reminding her that she hadn't eaten all day. She heated a tin of baked beans on the gas ring, and toasted bread. Spread thickly with butter, she piled it high with steaming beans, and ate ravenously before the toast went soggy. Afterwards, with a mug of tea between her hands she sat beside the gas fire. Slightly comforted, she still felt lonely, and wished she had a radio. She would save up for one, perhaps even be able to buy it as a Christmas present for herself. It was a certain fact no one else would. It was rent day, and having cleared away the debris of her meal she counted out the rent money and went downstairs to knock on Mrs Wilson's door.

'Oh it's you, love. Come in a minute and sit yourself down.'

'I've only brought the rent. I won't stop.'

'That's all right. I'm going out myself soon. Our Dolly wants me to babysit while she and her husband go to the pictures. It's 'Doctor in the House'. Have you seen it? I don't often get the chance of having the grandchildren to myself.' She chuckled in anticipation.

Rosamund perched on a chair near the door. 'How many grandchildren have you?'

'Just the two. There's our Tessa, she's four. And Steven, he's the baby, only eighteen months. Proper caution he is.' Mrs Wilson was packing her bag with knitting, purse and several packets of sweets.

'Here's the rent Mrs Wilson. I really mustn't stay.'

Mrs Wilson took the book and money, and cast a shrewd look at Rosamund.

'Got yourself a boyfriend I see?'

'No, not really. He just walked me home.'

'Just walked you home, did he? You'd better watch your step, young lady, or you'll be getting a name for yourself going on like that if he's just walked you home.' Mrs Wilson pursed her lips, and pulled a round felt hat over her iron grey bun, then jammed in a hat pin.

'I shan't be going out with him again. I don't really like him.'

'That's not what it looked like last night. Still, if you say so. This is a respectable house, and always has been. There's plenty of nice boys around, and it pays to be choosy.'

'I'm not interested in boys. I've enough with my job at the moment. Oh good – I hoped there'd be shillings. I must go – the gas has nearly run out.' And Rosamund escaped to the sanctuary of her room.

A few minutes later she heard the outside door close. Most of the other occupants seemed to be out and the house was quiet. It was Christmas next week, and Rosamund supposed there would be parties and dances to go to. None for her, even supposing she felt like celebrating. She decided to have a bath.

In the bathroom on the next floor down she ran the water. The small room filled with steam, and she undressed ready to step into the hot water.

'Bother, I've forgotten the towel.'

She slipped into her dressing gown and climbed the stairs back to her room. The girl from the room opposite hers passed with a hurried 'Hello', and continued at a run down the stairs to the hall. Rosamund heard a murmur of voices, one male and one female, then the front door slammed.

She had just picked up a towel when a slight sound startled her. She turned, and there in the open doorway was Ace with smouldering eyes. He slid into the room, closed the door and turned the key. Rosamund stood with the towel clutched to her, petrified.

'Get out,' she said through stiff lips.

Ace leaned against the door.

'No one leaves me high and dry like you did last night, yer cheating bitch.' His voice was smooth, menacing. Rosamund backed away.

'I'll soon stop yer fancy airs and graces. D'you think I'm not good enough for yer? Well, try this for size.' He undid the front of his trousers and thrust his hips towards her, thumbs hooked into his leather belt with its huge metal buckle.

Rosamund shrank away too shocked to scream, and in one stride he grabbed her. She closed her eyes as he thrust aside her dressing gown, and her bare flesh crawled under his searching fingers. Desperate to escape his hold, she turned and twisted in his grasp, went momentarily limp, then tried again to wrench herself away. He was ready for that, and swung her round by shoulder and hip to sprawl across the bed. Then he was on her, lips wet and loose, but the rest of his body hard and cruel, and the metal buckle dug into the soft skin of her abdomen. He panted faster, shoved her legs apart, and raised himself to enter her.

But he couldn't wait, and collapsed jerking convulsively on top of her, until at last he lay limp and spent, and Rosamund felt warm stickiness seep across her belly. She lay inert, head turned away, eyes closed.

After a while Ace rolled away and stood beside the bed. Rosamund didn't move or open her eyes. Already her body felt bruised, and she was sore where were his buckle had dug into her flesh. She sensed him fumble with his trouser buttons, then his belt clunked against the bed edge. With clumsy dabs of the towel he wiped her belly. Still she didn't move, and at last she felt him draw the discarded dressing gown across her, heard him stumble from the room.

For a long time Rosamund lay as he had left her, feeling nothing. Nothing at all. At length she rose and pulled on the gown, picked up the towel and returned to the bathroom as though nothing had happened. Her gaze was focussed into the distance, all her movements mechanical as she stepped into the lukewarm water and soaped and scrubbed her whole body.

Returning to her room she straightened the bed. Then she dressed in outdoor clothes, and packed the bag she had brought with her to the city.

As she reached the front door it opened, and there was Mrs Wilson back from her babysitting.

'Hello, Rosamund. Where're you off to this time of night?' she asked in surprise.

Rosamund neither saw nor heard, but passed through the door without looking left or right, down the steps, across the pavement and out into the road. There was a bus approaching, and for a brief moment she returned to reality to see the radiator grill above her as she fell before the screeching wheels.

***

'How does that feel, Mrs Grant?' Nurse Tait tucked the sheet round the woman's thin shoulders.

'Lovely, nurse – except, – could you just push the pillow further into my back? That's right. Thank you.'

'Here's a drink before you go back to sleep.'

She held the spouted cup expertly so that Mrs Grant could drink without spilling. 'Sleep tight,' and she moved quietly down the dim ward, glancing carefully at each sleeping form as she passed. The only light was from an orange bulb high in the ceiling, but it was sufficient to see that all was well, and her torch remained unused in her hand. It was quiet, except for light snores from Mrs Mount who had had her bunions done that morning. The other operation cases were all sleeping peacefully.

She came to where today's only casualty was lying behind screens in the bed nearest the ward door. She was still unconscious. Time to do her blood pressure again. As she pumped the air into the cuff, the girl's eyelids fluttered slightly. By the time Nurse Tait had recorded a normal blood pressure, a pair of very blue eyes were staring curiously at her.

'Hello,' the nurse spoke softly, and waited as the eyes flickered, then closed again. 'Miss Hambly.' She stroked the girl's wrist. 'Miss Hambly – Rosamund.'

The eyes opened again, and stayed open, wide.

'You're a nurse.'

'Yes. You're in hospital. You were in a road accident.'

She groaned. 'That's why I hurt. What happened?'

'You have a broken leg, and lots of bruises. Concussion too.'

Rosamund did not answer, she had drifted off into unconsciousness again. Nurse Tait left her and went to the telephone in the office.

'Night Sister, please.'

That would set the ball rolling. Night Sister would phone the Houseman before coming to the ward herself, and he would come to examine Miss Hambly, and eventually the police officer who had been patiently consuming cups of tea ever since he started his night duty would be allowed to take a statement. She had seen it all before. She yawned, and went to meet Night Sister as she came through the ward door.

***

Rosamund swam frantically towards the surface. There was something huge and evil following her. She felt its hugeness in the swirling waters and knew it would soon be upon her. Francis was leaning over the water holding out his arms, but she was swept past him into a yawning whirlpool. A metal ring lay at the bottom, with a sharp spike pointing upwards. She fell nearer and nearer the spike until she felt it penetrate her right leg. The pain grew until there was nothing left except her and the pain.

***

A cool hand took her wrist. 'Hello,' said a woman's voice. 'You're safe in hospital. You were in an accident with a bus, and you've a broken leg and concussion.'

Back in the whirlpool, she was dragging her right leg. She could see it hanging at an angle below. Someone was calling her name, and she knew it was her brother. But she didn't have a brother – did she?

'Can you hear me?' a voice said.

'Where are you?'

'Right here with you. Open your eyes, Rosamund.'

With an effort she opened them. A face swam into focus, a blur of white below.

'That's better. How do you feel?'

The face belonged to a doctor in a white coat, and she dimly remembered someone had told her she was in hospital, had had an accident. Pain. Her leg. She tried to lift her head and couldn't. *The whirlpool again.*

'We'll give you something for the pain. There.' A sharp sensation in her arm. 'Soon it will go.' And to someone she couldn't see, 'Sponge her hands and face, we'll see if that will rouse her a little.'

The warm water felt good and the whirlpool faded. The pain receded too. The doctor was here again.

'Feeling a bit better now?'

She managed a nod.

'Good. There's a policeman here to see you. He needs to know what you can remember about the accident. Try and talk to him, but if you're not feeling up to it he can come back another time.'

'All right, I'll try.' She smiled weakly at the young man who sat by the bed, balancing his helmet and open notebook on his lap, pen poised.

But try as she would she could not remember anything before waking up here. Anything. She was frightened. Who was she? Where had she come from? What was her life? She knew her name because she had responded to it, but how did these people know it? She was too confused to work it out.

'Know anyone called Wilson?' the policeman tried.

At that first that meant nothing, then hazily she remembered. 'She's my landlady?'

'Can you remember when you last saw her?'

Rosamund wrinkled her brow. 'When I paid my rent' she managed.

'Good,' he encouraged, 'and then?'

'I don't know – oh, I think I had a bath. Yes I did – I had a bath.'

'What happened after that?'

'Nothing.'

'What do you mean?'

'Nothing. Then I woke up here.'

It was no use. She could remember nothing more, and the young man put his notebook away and went.

Rosamund slept on and off for several days. At the end of it she was no wiser about herself.

***

'Give it time,' they all said to her, but she didn't mind. She was happy in an odd sort of way. If she was in pain she had only to say, and an injection took care of it. The Houseman came to see her every day, and he told her that her mind was numbing the memory of what had happened in the same way that the injection numbed the pain in her leg and head, and the spectacular bruises she had.

One day Mrs Wilson came to see her, and she recognised her at once, hair drawn back in a tight bun, bright inquisitive eyes above the straining bosom of her best coat. She even remembered the way she wheezed and waddled when she walked. As she creaked into a chair beside her Rosamund smiled broadly, so pleased to see a remembered face.

'How are you luv? My but you do look poorly. Here, I've brought your bag for you. Picked it up out of the road that night. Took it straight into the house in case anyone should run off with it. I'll put it in here till you're ready for it.' She bent with difficulty into the depths of the locker, then came up gasping for air and with reddened cheeks. 'Gave me a real fright, you did, that night. Just walked past me as if you was dreamwalking, down the steps, and straight under that bus. The poor driver never stood a chance. Oh, he's all right now I b'lieve. But whatever made you go and do a thing like that, Rosamund?'

'I wish I knew. I've been trying to remember. But I'm very glad to see you, Mrs Wilson. Please tell me what you know about me.'

Mrs Wilson needed no second asking, although it was little enough when she had done, but Rosamund heard the story as if it were about a stranger. When she had gone, promising to come again next week after Christmas, Rosamund lay quietly in bed, thinking. After a while she asked a nurse to pass her handbag, which had been stowed with the other things Mrs Wilson had brought. She looked at the assortment of things that made up her identity. So few articles to tell so much. She remembered now who she was and where she had come from, but the jigsaw was still incomplete until she found the letter with the spidery writing which enclosed a small piece of broken ivory, and she knew why she was here in this northern city. The numbness in her mind wore off, and all the pain of her broken dreams flooded back. But the reason for the accident did not emerge, and she remembered nothing of the events surrounding the bath she took that night.

***

As Rosamund watched Nurse Tait wheel the night drinks trolley down the ward, she swung her broken leg in its splint suspended on pulleys from a beam above the bed. Now her memory had returned, her body was responding to treatment, to rest and kindness, but she knew her mind and emotions would take much longer to mend. Mrs Wilson had been again and brought fruit and magazines, and news of the Jester where she had called to tell Mr Holroyd what had happened to Rosamund. He had sent her a note saying not to worry, he would have to fill her place for now seeing it was Christmas, but there would be a job for her when she was well again. Christmas. Earlier today the nurses had hung brightly coloured streamers and balloons in the ward, and there was a large Christmas tree twinkling in the corner.

'Tea, coffee or Horlicks, Rosamund?' Nurse Tait interrupted Rosamund's reverie.

'Horlicks please, nurse.'

She stirred vigorously and brought over the frothing cup. 'Please note – no lumps. Must do it right for the expert,' she grinned.

'I know. You saw me at the Jester.' They all teased her about that. 'Thanks. Don't you wish you were off duty tonight – it's Christmas Eve?'

'Not a bit. Christmas in hospital is special. I shall stay on the ward in the morning too.'

'You'll never stay awake. What's so special about it, anyway?'

'You'll see.'

The ward was settled for the night, and Nurse Tait called softly, 'Good Night' before she switched out the lights. Most of the patients had gone home, either discharged or for the Christmas holiday. The few that were left were grouped together at one end of the ward. There was a rustling and a murmuring as each made herself comfortable for the night, and gradually it became quiet except for the occasional chink as a piece of coke dropped into the tray beneath one of the iron stoves in the middle of the ward. It was dim and mysterious in the orange glow from the nightlights and the glimmering lights on the tree.

Rosamund could smell the tree from where she lay, and it smelled like all the Christmases she had ever known. She was a little girl again, climbing with Edith onto Pa's high bed to empty the fat stockings they were clutching, and a few years later she and Francis were Joseph and Mary in the Nativity play. Then the farm kitchen was full of exciting Christmas cooking smells, and there was Aunt Maud, red-gold hair falling into her eyes as she basted the turkey. Uncle Edgar teasing her as he handed her a parcel from under the Christmas tree. Carol singing. She and Francis arm in arm singing 'Angels from the Realms of Glory' at old Mrs Simmons' cottage, before the whole group of them finished up at church for the midnight service. Francis's face, serious and loving, as he slipped the ring on her finger last Christmas Eve at midnight. She closed her eyes and desolation swamped her.

Then in the distance came the strains of 'It Came Upon the Midnight Clear.' Was it real or part of her forbidden longings? It *was* real. She held her thoughts and listened. It stopped, then there were moving lights outside the windows. Nurse Tait opened the double doors and the singing began again, as a group of scarlet-cloaked figures, white caps gleaming in the light from the lanterns they carried, floated into the ward to the strains of 'O Little Town of Bethlehem'. Time stood still as the clear voices filled the night with the magic of the eternal story. There was a fluttering of white handkerchiefs in the dimness, and sounds of quiet weeping. The last notes lingered as the door closed on the scarlet cloaks, and a sigh gusted from the throats of each patient lying there. As 'Good King Wenceslas' began on the next ward, women began to murmur to each other. Nurse Tait talked quietly to Mrs Grant, who everyone knew would not see another Christmas. Rosamund was cocooned in comfort, though she had wept with the others at the sheer beauty of the experience. The effort to keep away thoughts of the past had gone, and she could no longer believe that it was wrong to treasure her memories. Nurse Tait moved from bed to bed, smoothing a sheet here, straightening a pillow there, with a gentle 'Goodnight, Happy Christmas,' for each one, and came at last to Rosamund's bed.

'Are you all right, Rosamund?'

'Yes, I believe I am. You said it would be special, and it is. And I've been remembering past Christmases.'

'You look more peaceful than I've seen you before. Do you think you'll sleep now?'

'Yes, I'm sure I will.'

'Then goodnight and a Happy Christmas.'

5

There was quite a bit of activity in the hospital corridor. The man from the dispensary had parked his trolley near the ward door, and waited until Rosamund had carefully negotiated the corner. He whisked into the ward, large wicker basket rattling with lotions and medicine bottles, as Rosamund leaned on her crutches to get her bearings. She could see a porter pushing a theatre trolley with a green-sheeted figure on it, a nurse walking alongside holding a drip bottle high. They turned into a ward further up the corridor, and a group of nurses came chattering by, white caps bobbing as they filtered off into their respective wards. The library trolley was not far away. Rosamund hesitated. No, she'd change her books next time they came. Today was too good a chance to miss. After several weeks of wind and rain while she had been learning to walk with crutches today had dawned clear and unusually mild, and Sister had said she could go out on her own into the hospital gardens.

A porter winked at her. 'Going my way, luv?'

She smiled at him, shook her head, and concentrated on the arch of daylight at the end of the corridor. A consultant and his retinue marched purposefully from one ward to another, and Rosamund could hear a woman singing in the sluice in ward B, as she emerged safely into the sunlight.

She rested on her crutches, easing the pressure under her arms as she filled her lungs with freshness after the pervading antiseptic smells of the ward. Eagerly she looked about to get her bearings. There was the tree-lined avenue which Sister had told her led to the gardens. Buds were swelling, and trees beckoned with pink-tipped fingers to the end of the avenue. She skirted the Victorian administrative building, into a wide drive with a view above distant trees to the chimney of the laundry building and the roofs of the mental hospital. The drive was flanked by trim borders, where crocuses bloomed and spears of daffodils showed. There were tennis courts off to the left where no one was playing on this March day, and beyond them what looked to be an orchard.

Her leg ached. 'It's time I sat down,' she murmured, nearing a summerhouse.

'Who are you talking to?' Nurse Tait's bright face peeped out at her from the summerhouse.

'I didn't know there was anyone here. Mind if I sit down a minute?' Then seeing books spread on the seat, 'Sorry, I can see you're studying. I'll find another seat.'

'No, don't do that. It's okay, I'm ready for a break. Here, let me move these, there's plenty of room.'

'That's better.' Rosamund eased herself onto the seat and propped her crutches beside her.

'You're a long way from home.'

'Yes, that's the furthest I've walked. I didn't know there were gardens out here – tennis courts too. Who uses them?'

'Trained staff, sisters and staff nurses, and doctors and their friends, mostly.' She glanced with concern at Rosamund, who was rubbing her aching muscles. 'I hope you haven't overdone it.'

'I don't think so. Sister said it would be good practice, and the physio approved.' She pulled a face. 'I was ready for a rest though. What are you studying?' She picked up a text book.

'Fractures,' Nurse Tait said with a wry grin.

'Don't I know about that! From the wrong side, of course. I'll bet it's interesting.' She fanned the pages. 'Is mine in here?'

'That's what I was reading. See. "Fractures of the Shaft of Femur".'

'This picture? My leg looked like that.' Then reading, 'Balanced weight traction on a Thomas's bed splint with Pearson knee flexion attachment'. Sounds impressive – and complicated.'

'Mm. I was revising how to put one up.'

'I don't remember mine being put on. It was there when I woke up.'

'You wouldn't. The fracture was reduced in theatre and the splint put on there.'

'I remember what it felt like with the weights going up and down every time I moved my leg. It throws you off balance having one leg in the air all the time, but you soon get used to it.'

'It's easy to forget the patient when you're concentrating on the nuts and bolts. Would you test me on it, I have to know it for the exam?'

'Course I will. Let's see…' She picked up the book and selected a passage. 'Right.' She smoothed the page. 'What do you need to set up a Thomas's bed splint?'

They settled to the task.

***

Rosamund was late for lunch, but she didn't get into trouble. Even if had, she wouldn't have minded. She felt more lively and energetic than she had done for months, even though her leg did ache.

The two girls became friends. Helen Tait, with her dark eyes and shiny black hair, was lively and popular. At first her interest in Rosamund and the problems she suspected lay in her background was professional, but as their acquaintance grew into friendship she found she had much in common with the soft spoken Cornish girl. To Rosamund, her friendship with Helen eased the loneliness and despair in which she had been living, and the knowledge that she was liked for herself gave her confidence to face the future.

She was ready for discharge at last, and the Hospital Almoner visited Mrs Wilson to see whether she had a ground floor room to spare instead of the top floor room with its long climb up steep stairs, which Rosamund had occupied before.

'Bless me, I'll find her one, the poor luv.' Mrs Wilson was in her element. 'Course me ground floor ones costs more than me others, but till she's back at work she can 'ave it at the rent she paid afore.'

With help from the 'Dole' arranged by the Almoner, and the little she had managed to save, Rosamund had enough to manage on until she could return to the Jester.

So it was that for the second time Rosamund arrived at the portals of number 310 Sebastopol Road in a taxi, and this time it was daylight. Carefully she manoeuvred herself up the steps to the doorway where Mrs Wilson waited to welcome her with a hug, which nearly knocked Rosamund off her crutches.

'Ah'm right glad to see you, Rosamund love. My, you do do well with those crutches. Still, you'd never have managed all those stairs. I can see why the Lady Almoner wanted you to have a ground floor room. T'student that was in there moved in with a friend nearer the college, so it all fell right. I've made it nice for you. Come and see.' She ushered her into her ground floor room.

'It's lovely, Mrs Wilson.' Rosamund gazed appreciatively round the gleaming room, smelling of Mansion Polish and Vim. She crossed the room and bent to sniff the scent of jonquils in a vase on the table. The gas fire hissed merrily, and she saw that this room had a square of red and green carpet and a surround of brown lino. There was a bowl of plastic roses on the sideboard, a brightly coloured cushion on the worn green armchair and a view of Land's End over the mantelpiece.

'Its me best room, and me meters is 'id.' With a flourish Mrs Wilson flung back a flowery curtain, which hung from the edge of a low shelf to reveal the twin grey monsters. 'There.' She stepped back with satisfaction, hands resting upon the swell of her purple and yellow pinafore.

'Thank you, Mrs Wilson. You really have gone to a lot of trouble. I shall be fine here.' She hopped across and planted a kiss on the soft folds of Mrs Wilson's cheek.

'Go on with you. There's a few things in the cupboard to get you going. Just let me know if there's anything else you need or can't manage. Right, then. I'll leave you to get settled in.' She withdrew, dabbing surreptitiously at her eyes.

When she had gone Rosamund sat in the green chair, properly alone for the first time in three months. The quiet surged round her in the room, with muted rumbles of traffic in the background, and she rested her head against the antimacassar on the chair back. How strange and different from her former life this one was. Instead of fields, woods and bare moorland, she was surrounded by buildings and noise and people with unfamiliar accents. But they were kind, the Yorkshire folk, with down to earth bustling liveliness instead of the slow speech and easy pace she had grown up with. I mustn't think of those times, she thought resolutely, or goodness knows where it'll lead. I've a lot to be thankful for, and a future to make. Her bag stood just inside the door where Mrs Wilson had left it. Yes, best to settle in now, make it home. She unpacked the hold-all, and rediscovered her other possessions where Mrs Wilson had stowed them about the room.

Other tenants dropped in to say hello – she was surprised to find they remembered her – and with Mrs Wilson only across the hall Rosamund had plenty of company. She missed the ward, and was apprehensive at first about being back in real life with all its problems. Hospital had seemed so safe.

As soon as she could do without her crutches, she went into town on the bus. She went to the Jester where Susan was pleased to see her, and sent the new girl, Margaret, to fetch Mr Holroyd. He shook her hand and said, 'Let me know when you're ready to start back, lass. Business's booming and Ah could do with you as soon as maybe.'

When he'd gone, Rosamund perched on a high stool at the counter, the familiar hissing Gaggia coffee machine at her elbow, and smiled at the mirrored view of customers eating, drinking and gossiping at the formica topped tables. Susan made a cup of tea for them both and settled down for a chat across the counter, breaking off now and again to serve someone.

'Well, what's been going on since I've been away?'

'All sorts of things. You hadn't been here long, Rosamund,' said Susan, heaping sugar into her tea and stirring vigorously, 'but some of the regulars was asking after you.'

'Were they? I don't remember any of them.'

Susan looked surprised. 'You don't?'

'No – I'm a bit hazy about working here. I lost my memory for a while, after the accident.' She sipped the hot liquid. 'It hasn't come back completely yet.'

'Go on… I've never met anyone who reelly lost their mem'ry – only in stories. You mean to say you don't remember old Mrs Crowther that always takes her shoes off and can't find them under the table. And the tramp? And Ace and his lot…?'

'Ace?' Rosamund had the queerest feeling in the pit of her stomach.

'You surely haven't forgotten Ace? He nearly drove you mad to go with him. Funny thing, none of 'em comes in here now. Not since just after your accident. They go down Westgate to t'Rising Sun where there's a skiffle group, I believe. There's a few lads and lasses come in here on their way home from school. They haven't got much money for cups of coffee, it's the jukebox they like. Then there's… .' Susan went on and on, and didn't notice how pale Rosamund had gone.

There were strange bubblings in her chest. They churned and grew until she could bear it no more, and broke into Susan's ramblings.

'Sorry Susan, I have to go – my bus is due. Lovely to see you. Keep in touch. Goodbye.'

As fast as her limp would let her she dashed out of the coffee bar, oblivious to Susan's and the customers' stares.

She crossed the road in a wild dot-and-carry-one, threading her way between green and cream double-decker buses going in and out of the bus station, their gutteral engines in low gear. Unaware of petrol fumes and gusts of passenger warmth as the buses passed within inches of her dodging figure, she reached the bus station waiting room before her knees let her down. Just. She landed on a hard bench, among a scatter of used tickets and an old newspaper. Her whole body shook, and doubled over with her face clutched in her hands, the past caught up with her.

She saw again Francis's dear figure, the chestnut sheen of his hair in the misty street light, hands thrust deep into his coat pockets, head slightly tilted back just like he used to wait for her, eyes glinting under half closed lids, mouth curved in a grin. She wanted to dash outside and throw herself into the familiar circle of his arms, to smell the fresh scent of his skin. But she only felt again the grip of Ace's fingers on her arm as he helped her onto the bus; relived the sickening feeling of her betrayal as his wet loose lips fastened on hers, and saw the desolation of the empty street behind his head. Francis gone. Gone from the spot where he had stood and watched Ace kiss her outside Mrs Wilson's door. She saw like a slow motion film the ugly twist of anger and lust on his features, and the obsidian glare of his eyes as he closed her room door and leaned on it, the big buckle gleaming… She relived the horror as she twisted hopelessly in his grasp; the despair as she felt his hardness and the weight of his body on hers; and the terrible feeling of loneliness and degradation as he left her, the air cold on her damp skin. She remembered the feeling of utter futility as she scrubbed her soiled body in lukewarm water, with the water heater popping madly in the cold bathroom; then the overwhelming urge to take flight, and the bus driver's horrified face as she fell in front of him.

Shuddering she moaned, 'Francis, what have I done to you? As if leaving you wasn't enough.' Again she shuddered at what Ace so nearly did to her.

'Rosamund. I was on my way to see you. You all right?' Helen was gripping her shoulders. 'Hey, what's wrong?' Rosamund lifted anguished eyes. 'Come on, the bus is in.' Helen pulled her to her feet, and she allowed herself to be led home to Mrs Wilson's.

'You've had a shock haven't you?' Helen put the kettle on. 'Come on love, tell Auntie Helen all about it.'

Rosamund broke down. Helen held her and let her cry, stroked her hair and rocked her until the sobs ceased, and she lifted a blotched and swollen face.

'I remembered, Helen. I remembered why I walked into the bus.'

'What is it, then?' She set a cup and saucer before Rosamund, and pushed the sugar basin towards her. 'Tell me while you drink your tea.'

Rosamund ignored the tea, and forced the painful words out. 'Before I came here – to Leadersfield, I was engaged to be married. His mother helped to bring me up, so we grew up together on the farm. I love him so much.' Tears welled up, but she lifted her chin and continued. 'I was closer to him than anyone in the world – the other half of my self.'

Screwing her sodden handkerchief into a ball, she got up to search through a dresser drawer for a clean one. She blew her nose and looked across the table at Helen.

'There are some biscuits in that cupboard if you want one.'

Helen shook her head. 'Go on, Roz,' she urged.

Rosamund sat down opposite her friend, and with head lowered started to trace patterns with her forefinger on the table top, backwards and forwards. 'It was after Pa died – just after the funeral, and the day my sister Edith went back to South Africa.' The finger stopped and curled into her palm. 'I discovered something terrible about myself. No, don't ask me what it was. It meant I could never marry – my boyfriend. I couldn't stay and mess up his and other people's lives. So I got on a train and found myself here.'

Helen's gaze was fixed on Rosamund's face, chin cupped in her hand.

'I was just beginning to make a new life for myself – though I hadn't got over what had happened, and I was missing Fr… .' She daren't say his name. ' …my fiancé, dreadfully. I was doing fine at the Jester. Ace pestered me – he's one of the gang that came to the coffee bar most nights. Susan said he wouldn't like being turned down – but I thought I was handling it all right. Then one night my fiancé turned up outside. Goodness knows how he found me. It would have been fatal to talk to him, and I panicked. I used Ace to make my boyfriend go away. I let him kiss me and he got a bit passionate. When I wouldn't follow through, Ace tricked himself into my room and tried to rape me. He didn't quite make it, but after everything else I couldn't cope, ran out of the house, got knocked down by a bus and landed here, with a broken leg and no memory.'

Helen gave a low whistle, but said nothing.

'Most of my memory came back as you know, except for the last bit with Ace. But when I went to the Jester today to see Susan she was talking about him, and it brought it all back. I remembered it all. And – oh Helen, I can't bear it.' She laid her head on her arms and sobbed.

Helen waited, and when Rosamund was quiet again observed sympathetically, 'What a rotten thing to happen, especially after splitting up with your boyfriend.' She sipped her tea and looked at Rosamund, with narrowed eyes. 'But you did rather ask for it, you know.'

'I did what?'

'You did rather ask for it.'

'Well, of all the...' Rosamund leapt up and banged both fists on the table. 'I thought you were my friend, Helen. How could you? Just because I...' Helen looked at her steadily.

Rosamund paused, and swallowed. 'I – I suppose I did – in a way. But I never dreamed...'

'Of course you didn't. Yet Susan warned you, you said.'

'Yes, she tried to, but I didn't take too much notice of Ace. I was only really aware of – of the other man, and how to make him go away. I should have realised what was happening, and I never dreamed that Ace would lose control like that. Ugh.' She shuddered again at the memory. 'After, he – he covered me up.'

'I expect he was as surprised as you were at what happened. It doesn't sound as if he was used to being crossed. Well there's no harm done, and you've had a good cry now. It's better out than in, if you'll pardon the pun.'

Rosamund gasped, then spluttered. 'Helen, you're outrageous.' She laughed out loud, then sobered. 'You're right though. There is no harm done, and I should try to forget it. Let's change the subject. Tell me what's happening in the ward. How's Mrs Grant?'

'Much weaker I'm afraid. Her husband's there most of the time now. Sometimes he brings the boys, but they get bored and embarrassed, and she can't talk to them much. It's very sad. Poor Miss Wilkins got a bladder infection and we've nearly been run off our feet with bedpans for her. Oh, and I'm going on Theatre next week. No bedpans there, thank goodness. Sometimes I wonder why I ever went in for this job.'

'Why did you, Helen?' Rosamund looked thoughtful.

'I don't quite know. It just seemed right. I don't really regret it, that's just talk. There's nothing else I'd rather do. After the Orthopaedic finals this summer, if I pass, I'll go straight on to General Training.'

'What qualifications do you need?'

'What, for nursing? They like you to have some 'O' levels, but it's the interview that really counts. Rosamund, you aren't thinking…? You are.'

'Do you think I'd get in? I believe I would like nursing. I never minded looking after Pa. Liked it in fact, except that it was Pa and he wasn't going to get better. And I learned a lot from just watching in the ward these last three months. I can't stay at the Jester for ever, and like you, it feels right. Do you think they'll have me? How would I go about it?'

Helen stared in astonishment. 'You are serious. You really mean it, don't you?' Rosamund nodded with assurance. 'You ought to think about it first. It's harder than you may think. There's being on your feet for hours, working shifts – you don't get much chance of a social life; then there's lifting, bedpans, lots of boring jobs like sluicing soiled laundry. Then there's the emotional side, like when relatives are upset when a patient's very ill, and when someone's dying or dies.'

Rosamund was certain. 'I did all that for Pa, with very little time off, and mostly on my own,' she said quietly. 'I know it's more than all that, but I don't need to think about it. I know it's what I want. Probably have done for ages without realising.'

'If you're sure, write to Matron and ask for an interview. Do it soon, and if you're successful you'll be in the next PTS… .'

'What's that ?' interrupted Rosamund.

'Preliminary Training School. Then we'd start on the wards at the same time. That'd be absolutely super, we'd do the whole three years together.'

***

Rosamund wrote to Matron, and was duly granted an interview. Her medical reports were satisfactory, especially as her memory had returned completely. Mr Holroyd agreed to give her a reference, and so did the Sister of the ward where she had been a patient for three months. She had seen how Rosamund helped other patients and recognised her potential for nursing. There was a sticky moment in the interview when Matron asked about permission of next of kin as she was still under twenty-one. Rosamund was reluctant to bring Edith into it in case Francis got to know, but admitted to having a sister and promised to write to South Africa for her permission.

It was May before Rosamund picked up a flimsy blue envelope with a South African stamp from the table outside Mrs Wilson's kitchen. She carried it across to her room, ignoring Mrs Wilson's inquiring cough through her open door. With her own door firmly closed and a coffee in front of her, she sat beside the open sash window in a patch of sunlight. A mild spring breeze stirred the net curtain, and a bundle of sparrows in full voice did their best to drown the noise of the passing traffic. She looked at her name in her sister's clear upright handwriting on the envelope. What would Edith say? Would she keep her confidence about where Rosamund was? She was longing for contact with the only family she had, and opened the letter with eager fingers.

As she unfolded the flimsy pages a piece of bright yellow paper fell out, and she looked at this first. In vivid wax crayon colours was a child's drawing of a bed with a figure with spiky purple hair sitting at one end. Another figure stood beside the bed with a white apron, round blobs for shoes and wearing a peculiar white edifice with wings on its head. In large wobbly letters it was signed 'love Greg and Tris', with a border of large multicoloured kisses.

Rosamund touched the waxy imprint with wondering fingers. They sent her love, these two little nephews who had never seen her. With a lump in her throat she opened their mother's letter.

> *Dear Rosamund,* wrote Edith.
>
> *What a surprise to hear from you after so long. We have been so worried about you since Aunt Maud's distressed letter to say how you had left without explanation. I'm sure you must have had good reason, but you can't imagine how upset they are, especially Francis.* 'Oh, I can,' Rosamund murmured. 'I can.' *But Aunt Maud said Francis found you, and you appeared to be tied up with someone else!!! Still, I won't mention where you are or what you are doing if you really don't want them to know. I have to say I think it's all very peculiar. I'm so glad to hear from you and know you are all right, especially after such a nasty accident, that I'll say no more about that side of things.*
>
> *Of course I'll give permission for you to train as a nurse. I've already written*

to Matron. It does seem a bit ridiculous having to give it, but if that's what it takes… I think you'll make a marvellous nurse, especially after all you did for Pa. I always felt guilty (still do) that I couldn't help with all that, but it was no good coming back to Cornwall when there were no jobs. It was good to be together when I was there for Pa's funeral, and I often wonder if I had stayed longer I could have helped with whatever crisis came up for you. Still, it wasn't to be, but please, please keep in touch now.

There are two boys here who want to know all I can tell them about Auntie Rosamund. They had their tonsils out recently so they know all about nurses – as you see from their letter. They are five now, and full of mischief. They played their usual trick of pretending to be each other until I gave the game away to Sister by telling her about the mole on Tristan's right ear.

We're all fine here. Leslie is happy (sends his love), and earning good money at the mine. (Who knows, we might even be able to afford to go back to Cornwall one day!) But this really is a wonderful place to bring up children – and the climate's not bad either!

Please write back soon and give us all your news, and good luck with your new career.

Lots of love from us all at Jo'burg,

Edith xxxxxxxx.

Rosamund wept over her letter, but was glad to feel part of a family again. She ached for news of Francis. His name didn't stir memories for her, because he was always with her however she tried to banish him. Everything that happened to her she longed to share with him.

She went back to the Jester for the summer, with only a slight limp. Mr Holroyd said he would be sorry to lose her again, but she ought to be in a better job than that anyway. When the nurses came in there were some she knew, and they included her in their chatter if she had time.

The summer months passed, and Rosamund's leg grew strong again. She bought low heeled black lace-up shoes, and embroidered her name on all her underclothes. She pirouetted in front of Helen in her outdoor uniform of navy gabardine coat and storm cap, her cap at a rakish angle.

'Do I look like a nurse?'

Helen laughed. 'Not yet. You'll be sick of uniform before your three years are up. Wait until your neck is rubbed raw with all those starched collars.'

Sore neck or not, Rosamund eagerly looked forward to the great day in September.

***

It came at last. She said her goodbyes at the Jester, handed the key of her room to Mrs Wilson, who wiped her eyes and implored her to come and see her often. Soon she was at the bus station, bag in hand, a new suitcase in the other, to board the bus for the hospital and the nurses' home.

6

FRANCIS

Treblissick, Cornwall. 1955.

'You look some handsome, Mother.'

Maud rearranged the full skirts of her pre-war black taffeta dress. 'Thank you, Francis. I wish I could say the same for you.' She eyed his worn brown corduroys, collarless flannel shirt and unbuttoned waistcoat that had once belonged to his father's best suit. Slumped in front of the fire, his feet in thick home-knitted socks rested against the slate hearth. He was clearly going nowhere tonight. He's thinner, she realised, taking in the new hard line of his chin and hollow cheeks, and green eyes dulled like muddy pools, purple shadowed below. Looking older than he should, too, and more and more like his father, except that she had never seen Edgar look so unhappy. Her voice softened. 'Won't you change your mind and come with me to the Easter Dance? No matter if we are late, I'm sure Alan and all the others'd be glad to see you.'

'No.'

'He asked if you were going. Said the gang'll all be there as usual. You know, there's …'

'I'm not going. And you know well why.'

'Yes I do, Francis, but I wish you would come. They're having the St Brevan band, so the dancing should go well…'

'Who the devil would I be dancing with? Tell me that.'

'Well… Anyway, the hall looks lovely all trimmed up with fairy lights and balloons, and Colin Raddy's fixed up one of those revolving balls that reflect the lights. And Dan's helped bring the beer barrels over for the bar.'

She crossed to the mirror on the back wall and rubbing at an imaginary speck on her cheek, watched in the mirror for a reaction to her words. There was none, so she moved back to the hearth and sat down facing him across the hearthrug.

'Come with me, my dear,' she coaxed.

'Tchaa.'

Francis turned away and slumped even further into the chair. The chair where he'd come in after the house auction and found Rosamund asleep, honey-gold head resting against its wooden back, hands relaxed along the arms. She'd looked exhausted, defenceless, poor kid, gold tipped lashes fanned over pale cheeks. He'd wanted to gather her into his arms and keep her safe for ever.

'Francis.' His mother's exasperated voice brought him back with a start. 'Did you hear me?

No response.

'Oh, for Heaven's sake pull yourself together. You sit there like a great clod every evening with a face as long as a wet week, feeling sorry for yourself. I've put up with that surly face every morning, watched you stamp through your jobs with never a word for anybody. You keep your friends at a distance and…'

'Leave me be.'

'No I won't. You can't go on like this, and neither can I. It's like living with a stranger.' She paused. 'Even Floss looks puzzled after you.'

'I said leave me be.'

'I can't. It hurts to see you destroying yourself – and me.' She put out a tentative hand to touch his shoulder. He shook it off, and she stepped away. 'How do you think I feel? I've lost the nearest I've ever had to a daughter, and now you're not here either – or as good as. I don't know this grumpy oaf who's lost all pride in himself, doesn't shave, doesn't bother to do up his buttons…'

Francis dragged himself out of his chair and, making quacking movements with his hand, stomped into the scullery. He emerged with a mug of cider and a wet dribble down his chin.

'…and doesn't eat enough to keep a sparrow alive, and…' eyeing the mug upended over his face, '…pours far more of that stuff down his neck than's good for him.'

The empty mug crashed down on the table. Maud leapt to her feet.

'That's enough,' he snarled into his mother's frightened face. 'It's nag, nag, nag. Do this Francis, do that Francis; it'll do you good Francis. Eyes on me all the time, watching, criticising, finding fault.' He threw himself into the chair and glared at the fire. 'My God, I'd leave the place myself if it wasn't for the farm.'

'That's another thing. The farm was your passion before. Everything up to scratch, nothing too much trouble. Now you just about manage the basics – if that. There's slates loose on the linhay, fences to mend, feed to order, books to get up to date – Lord knows what else.'

He took an angry breath and set his jaw.

'You haven't neglected the beasts, I'll give you that. But where's my Francis – my boy, my sunny contented boy?'

Francis stood up with a roar, fists clenched tight at his side.

'Shut up, shut up, shut up,' he shouted, anguished, ugly. 'How else can I be? I don't know how else to be. I've blamed myself, but what for? I've done nothing wrong that I can see. There's nothing left now – no more meaning to anything without Rosamund. My whole life's wasted. And you stand there telling me to pull myself together. You can't possibly know how I'm feeling, smug there in your finery. How could you know?'

'Of course I know.' Maud, calm now, her eyes full of unshed tears. 'I lost your father.'

Silence stretched between them.

'Yes,' he said at last. 'I'm sorry.' Then after a long pause, he squared his shoulders. 'If you're ready, let's go. I'll drive you down, but I'm not getting out of the van, so you can forget any little schemes you might have.'

***

Floss came running out of the barn as he drove back into the stable yard. 'Good girl, Floss.' He fondled her head and she followed him into the house, something she would not normally dare to do. He threw himself into the Windsor chair again before the hearth, and gazed morosely into the red heart of the fire. After a while the logs settled audibly, sending soft white flakes of wood ash onto the hearth. Francis heaved himself up and pulled the half-burnt logs together with the hooked poker, and threw on a couple more pieces of wood. Then he wandered into the scullery where he downed a glass of water from the single tap above the stone sink. Restlessly he prowled round the farmhouse, where everything reminded him of Rosamund and precious times lost. He came at last to the room under the eaves which she had shared with Edith after moving out of the Old Rectory. His mother had packed away the things she left, thinking to spare him pain, and the room looked bare. He stretched out on the bed Rosamund had slept in, his head fitting into the hollow of the pillow where her head had lain. He closed his eyes. Immediately the scene replayed itself against the screen of his eyelids, as it had replayed over and over in the empty weeks. Rosamund being helped into her best grey coat by that – Teddy Boy, in the brightly lit coffee bar. Rosamund, slightly unsteady, stepping onto the bus platform with an incongruous hand under her elbow. Rosamund's face, pale against the stone gatepost, her hands spread around the back of the stranger, and his dark head blotting out her face as he bent to kiss her. He opened his eyes wide, trying to banish the image. In vain. Then, rolling over with a sob, he curled into a ball.

Some time later he heard Floss whining at the foot of the stairs, rose and stumbled down to the kitchen. He let her out into the yard, pulled on boots and a coat, grabbed a torch, and followed her. It was bright moonlight and the air was crisp with cold, a March frost riming the roofs of the farm buildings. He shone the torch into the linhay, registered the liquid eyes and warm breath of the cattle shadowy in their stalls, and the pungent smell of trodden straw and dung. In the pigsty the sow snuffled contentedly in her pen, and he crossed the cobbles to unlatch the stable door where, since Captain and Daisy the carthorses were gone, bales of straw were stacked in the stalls, and bags of feed and fertiliser. He swung the torch round the floor and walls, lighting the pale circle of an barn owl's face as it shifted from foot to foot on a rafter above. It swivelled its head to stare at him disdainfully. He moved the beam on. Nothing out of place. He closed the stable door and leaned on it, listening to sleepy squarking from the henhouse. There was a 'cree-ee –ick' from the trees in the lane where the barn owl's mate hunted, then quiet flowed back through the frosty night.

Floss looked up at him, her plumed tail a question mark. 'What is it my handsome? Fancy a tramp on the moor then?' An enthusiastic wag, and she bounded to the gate. 'No, we'll take the van, go up the lane.'

Beside him in the passenger seat her tongue was rough and warm on his cheek. He drove up and up, twisting between steep hedges, and skirted the wood where he and Rosamund had walked on that last happy day. Then he turned off into a rutted lane that ended where the headlights revealed a barred gate, and beyond the moor. A stony track wound away to where a rocky tor lay clear in the moonlight, and bleached wastes patched by dark shapes of gorse and dead bracken stretched on either hand to meet the spangled sky. Floss, through the gate before Francis had slammed the van door, turned to wait for him, tongue hanging. He passed through the gate and latched it behind him, and the two figures moved out onto the moor, Floss flickering black and white against the the moonlit landscape. Francis's step was jerky, tight with anger and grief, and his boots pounded the stony ground unmercifully, (whether in punishment of himself or some nameless other he didn't know.) Usually to stride out like this would soothe him. But not tonight. Eventually his anger subsided, but in its place a black despair gripped him. So tightly did it grip that he lost all sense of time and space, didn't see the dark shapes of ponies in the distance, the grey humps of granite dotted about, was unaware of the vast silence. His feet of their own accord found safe places to tread, and he passed without knowing through the ancient stone circle. Floss trotted by his side instead of bounding off in glorious exploration as she normally did, and cast puzzled looks at him from the sides of her eyes. Francis was oblivious.

He came to himself suddenly when Floss pressed herself across the front of his legs and halted his progress. There was spongy turf beneath his feet, and the toes of his boots dipped to the brim of a reed-fringed pool. He stood there a long time without moving, enclosed in a darkness of spirit deeper than ever before. The pool lay before him, a path of moonlight across its cold surface, and dry reeds crackled and whispered in the frosty air. Slowly he lifted one foot then the other, and moved forward into the freezing water with scarcely a ripple, drawn by the silvery light. There was nothing left in the world except to become one with the pure moonlight. Then Floss gave a single bark, and there came a cry, breaking the spell. The cry of a sheep in distress, not far away. Francis stopped and listened. There it was again, and he discovered to his terror that he was up to his thighs in icy water, cold as death. He turned, and in a flurry of foaming silver floundered back to the shore. Floss dashed backwards and forwards, ears pricked towards a tumble of granite on the brink of an old quarry about a hundred yards away.

'Find it Floss,' She leapt away.

When he caught up with her, Francis found her standing over a two-tooth, a ewe in lamb for the first time. It was lying in a hollow and panting with pain.

'You shouldn't be up here, my girl. Let's have a look at you.' He propped the torch against a rock, and bent over her hind quarters to find a tiny pair of hooves protruding. The ewe turned her head to look with puzzled eyes over her heaving flank.

He watched for a while. Each time the ewe strained, the hooves advanced then retreated, and seeing the labour could not progress, he took the feet gently and firmly in his hand, and with the next contraction made a sustained pull down. He forgot his wet legs, and kneeling on the springy turf with Floss lying quietly nearby he worked steadily, pulling and resting with the ewe until he felt movement, and the legs slid further outside the ewe's body. Next time he eased the lamb's legs towards its mother's tail, until the whole body slithered suddenly free and he laid it gently beside her. When the after birth was delivered and the cord severed he swung the lamb, head down, until it gasped and gave a protesting bleat.

'You'll do all right now, I reckon,' he murmured as he placed the lamb, still wet and skinny-looking, in front of its mother. Tentatively at first she nosed it, then began to lick. Francis gave a sigh of satisfaction as he wiped his brow and sat back on his heels to watch the pair. The ewe heaved herself to standing, and nudged the lamb into taking its first wobbly steps. He watched as the lamb rooted under its mother's fleece and started to suck. There was nothing more he could do here. They'd be all right. It was thanks to Floss and good luck that they were safe.

'Mister!'

Floss pricked up her ears in the moonlight, and ran to the edge of the quarry hidden by a brake of furze.

'Mister!'

There's someone down there, Francis realised, and went over to peer into the shadowed depths. A pale blur emerged as an upturned face.

'Here,' he called. 'What's wrong?'

'Fell down. Hurt me ankle. Can't climb up nor down.'

'Are you safe where you are?'

'Mebbe. If I'm still.'

'Can you wait till I come back with a rope? I've a vehicle at the edge of the moor.'

'Aye. Best be quick.'

As Francis reached the van, he heard the bells from St Hyldroc's in the village far below, as they chimed midnight on the clear air. Another day without Rosamund. But Mother is right, he thought. I must try to move on even though I know I'll never forget, never mend. He grabbed a hank of binder twine from the back of the van and closed the doors. I hope that poor devil down the quarry's managed to hang on.

He had, and before long Francis had hauled the man, scrabbling and cursing over the broken edge of the quarry onto the safety of the thick rimed turf.

'Ta, mister.'

Francis knelt to examine the man's injury, but was shoved out of the way by a sharp elbow.

'I sees to meself.' He leaned forward to wrap his hands round the ankle, already swollen above his boot, then looked up at Francis, white teeth chattering. 'That's not to say I'm not grateful. Been down there a long time. A goner if you hadn't come by.'

Under black curls beneath a flat cap Francis looked into the black slanting eyes of a man about his own age. Slight and swarthy, he wore an army greatcoat much too big for him and tied round his waist with twine, a red scarf round his neck. A Gypsy.

'I'll take you back to the farm, and get Mother to look at your foot.'

'Said sees to meself, didn't I?'

'Let me at least give you a hot meal, and a bed for the night. You needn't come in the house if you don't want, there's hay in the barn to make you comfortable.'

'No need. Bender's down yonder under the hedge.' Then seeing Francis's puzzled look explained. 'Tent, see. And I'll not starve.' He pulled a catapult from one pocket of his coat, and from the depths of another the long ears of a dead hare. He grinned. 'Broke my fall, he did. Still taste good, see.'

Francis chuckled. There was something in the man's crusty independence and defiant grin that struck a chord.

He stuck out his hand. 'Francis Durrant, from the farm down yonder. D'you want work? Lambing's starting.'

'Eli.' His grip was rough and hard as tree roots in Francis's broad farmer's hand. 'Naw, not this time. Promised down west – join me family daffodil picking, see.'

'Well, when you're this way again, perhaps.'

'Aye. Likely.'

He struggled to standing and tested his weight on the injured foot. Sweat stood out on his forehead, cheekbones sharp as blades above a mouth blue with cold and exhaustion. Peastick thin wrists stuck out from the end of his coat sleeves, but he held his head high as he staggered to keep his balance.

'Steady, boy.' Francis's strong arm held him. 'I'll take you back to your bender at least, and no arguing.'

Francis bumped the van over the moorland track at Eli's direction, to the canvas shelter under the Top Field hedge, bent to the ground with soft branches and supported by stronger ones.

'Have you water?'

'Aye. And fire.' Eli lifted a turf in front of the bender where the remains of a former fire lay. 'Soon be snug and fed. Never fear.'

'Right.'

Francis left the odd little man with reluctance. It's not because I think he won't manage, he thought, I can see he will. I like him, and I'd like to get to know him. What a night it's been. To think I'd sunk so low as to almost drown myself. If it hadn't been for Floss I would have done, too. He shuddered. But I'm still here, and glad to be, for all my troubles – thankful for a second chance.

'I owe you one, Floss,' he told her later, as he placed a big bone in front of her kennel, and rubbed her under her soft chin.

Next morning at daybreak Francis returned to the bender at the edge of the moor with bread and milk and cold meat pie, and salve for a painful ankle. The canvas had gone, the turf replaced. It was as though Eli had never been there.

7

ROSAMUND

Leadersfield, Yorkshire.

She was here. It was really happening.

Rosamund, surrounded by eager figures clutching assorted items of luggage and led by a brown-coated hospital porter, walked along a winding drive with trees on one side and open fields on the other. It was dusk, and tall lamps already illuminated their progress. Her heart thumped, and she was breathless with excitement. Or was it fear? She didn't know. But what she did know was that this was IT.

'That's never the nurses' home – it's much too posh?' A small thin girl with freckles visible even in this light put down her enormous suitcase, pushed back a straggle of brown hair and stared accusingly at the hospital porter.

'That's reight,' he affirmed with a grin. 'That's Danby 'All.'

'Well I never.' The thin girl picked up her suitcase and dropped a brown paper carrier bag. 'Drat.'

'Here let me.' Laughing, Rosamund picked up the bag and slung the string handle over her own wrist. 'I'll bring this one.'

'Please hurry up miss.' The porter was looking at his watch. "Ome Sister's expecting us, and she doan't like to be kept waiting.'

'Ta,' with a wink at Rosamund. They set off to catch up the rest of the group, but the thin girl paused again. 'Shan't we be toffs then? I fancy living in a big house like that.'

It was impressive. They had left the familiar hospital gates and crossed the road. At the end of a long drive bordered by trees, Rosamund could see a large Georgian house, windows brightly lit. She felt a moment of panic. This was not what she had expected. What had she got herself into? Who was she, a fugitive from a forbidden relationship, to undertake such a high calling as nursing? Nevertheless she held her head high and strode with the others towards a fanlighted doorway spilling light onto the gravel approach.

An elegant silhouette peered out into the dusk at the group of new recruits. 'Thank you, Dawson.' Frosty eyes under a lace cap perched on iron-grey hair dismissed the porter. Home Sister stepped back to allow the girls to enter. 'Welcome to Leadersfield Hospital.'

Her doubts forgotten, Rosamund looked about her. The wide hall was floored in pale wood polished to a satin gleam, the only furniture a round pedestal table with a bowl of bronze crysanthemums, and beside the table dangled the handpiece of a wall-mounted telephone.

'Caaarter. Telepho-one,' a voice screeched in the distance, and a girl in a dressing gown, hair wrapped in a striped towel, scuttled from a side corridor. Nestling against the wall, she whispered into the telephone with nervous glances towards Home Sister. Ignoring the girl she, ramrod-backed, preceded her new charges up the staircase. Upstairs the girls were shown into a large room divided into curtained cubicles each furnished with a bed, wardrobe-cum-dressing table and a bedside cabinet.

Home Sister turned to face them.

'I am Miss Garbutt, Home Sister of this hospital, and you will be in my care while you are living here. These will be your quarters while you are in Training School, after that you will be allocated other rooms. You will be awakened each morning by one of the maids at a quarter to seven to report for duty in the schoolroom at eight a.m. Lights out is at ten o'clock. My room is next to this one, and noise after ten o'clock will not be tolerated. Unpack now, and in thirty minutes you will be shown round the Nurses' Home, then taken to the dining room for supper. Time is your own then until lights out.' Miss Garbutt cast a smile of infinite sweetness on her charges, revealing a mouthful of the most discoloured teeth Rosamund had ever seen, drew up her neat grey figure, pursed her lips and left the dormitory.

'Wow.' The thin girl flopped onto her bed. 'Talk about Lady of t'Manor. What does that mekk us?'

'The lowest of the low, so don't get ideas above your station,' a voice from the end row called. 'My sister's in her third year here, so I know all about it.'

'You don't say,' the thin one whistled. 'Hey, this bed's nice and soft. I wonder how many blankets they've given us.'

There began rustles and thuds, clicks of wardrobe doors and shuttings of drawers, until at last curtains were drawn back and faces looked out to examine their new companions. Tentatively at first they started to talk to each other. The thin girl, Amy Weston, was on Rosamund's right, a tall dark girl called Muriel across the aisle. The one who 'knew all about it' was Sandra Clegg. She lost no time in telling the others that her father was on the Town Council.

'Tell Councillor Clegg it's time he sent t'roadmenders down our way. Shutt End's full o' potholes. My father's allus black afore he gets to t'pit, it's that muddy.' Amy was irrepressible.

'Are you all ready for the conducted tour?' A nurse wearing a blue belt over her white apron broke in as she came down the steps into the aisle. 'Yes? Then follow me.'

There was a bewildering succession of bedrooms, and bathrooms with deep blue enamelled baths with mahogany surrounds and enormous copper taps. The bath at the Old Rectory had had curly feet and brass taps, but Rosamund had never seen anything like these.

'Bye, I could lose mysen' in one of them. Better 'n a zinc bath in front of t'fire,' commented Amy.

In the sitting room, several girls clustered round the television set beside a coal fire, watching Dixon of Dock Green. Some were in uniform, others in ordinary clothes, and they each glanced up to smile a welcome to the newcomers.

After a peep into the empty study, the dining room was cheerful, with formica-topped tables where groups of nurses were eating. The room was noisy and warm, redolent with the smell of rabbit stew. For a moment Rosamund was back in Aunt Maud's kitchen, supper on the scrubbed table, and Francis glowing and hungry just in from the fields. She shook her head resolutely and sat down with the others to their first meal as student nurses.

***

'How did your first day go then, Nurse Hambly?' A familiar face peered round the curtains of her cubicle.

'Oh it's you, Helen.' Rosamund looked up from the pile of white overalls on the bed. 'Quite well thanks, but confusing.'

'Yes it is rather a whirl on the first day, but isn't Mr Archer a poppet? I'm glad you've got him for your tutor – Mr Smart doesn't have a sense of humour. Aren't you going to ask me in?'

'Of course. Sorry.' She made room on the bed. 'Careful!' as Helen flopped down causing a dozen or so loose buttons lying on the counterpane to bounce around.

'I'd forgotten what a bind it is changing those every time you change overalls. But never mind, you'll soon be in proper uniform.'

'We were measured for it today. Helen, however do you turn this oblong into one of those pretty caps?'

'A butterfly you mean. You need safety pins. Got any?'

Rosamund shook her head.

'I've got some spare ones.' She dug in her pocket. 'Here we are. First pin the cap to the bedspread like this.'

Her fingers folded and pleated, and Rosamund watched intently as she deftly produced a crisp cap with butterfly wings and a long pointed tail.

'There we are. Got any white hair grips?'

'Yes. I noticed yours. Is this how it goes?' She perched the cap on her head, secured it to her waves and looked in the mirror. 'Oh, I really do look like a nurse now. How strange.'

'That's looks fine, Roz.' Helen called out, 'Anyone else want a hand folding their cap?'

There were a few replies of 'Yes', but Sandra had already gathered most of them around herself. 'Our Wendy showed me how,' she purred.

When everyone had made a butterfly, somewhat crumpled for the most part, (especially Muriel's, who had managed to get hers grubby too) ready for the next day, Helen turned to Rosamund. 'Come on, I'll show you where I sleep.'

She followed her to a four-bedded corner room with windows looking out over stubble fields and the pithead gear of a colliery in the distance. Turning back to look into the room she exclaimed, 'This is super.' A scarlet-lined cloak lay across the foot of one chintz covered divan bed, and each dressing table held photographs and ornaments as well as the paraphernalia of toiletry, so that the room glowed with its occupants' personalities.

'This place is not at all what I expected – it's more like a stately home than part of a hospital,' said Rosamund.

'It used to be – a stately home, I mean – the home of the Danby family. It is unusual for a Nurses' Home. A bit different from Mrs Wilson's though, isn't it?'

'Yes it is. And so is the training school. You didn't tell me where it was.'

'Didn't I?' Helen looked innocent.

'No you didn't. It's scary being let in by that enormous nurse jangling with keys, and knowing we're locked in all day, except for dinner. Then being escorted through locked doors to go to the lavatory. And the weird noises from next door!'

'You'll get used to it. It's just that the school shares one of the Mental Hospital wards.' Rosamund shook her head. 'Most of the poor souls in there have been in for years – many'll be there for the rest of their lives.'

'Mr Archer explained.' Rosamund shuddered. 'The nurses look so brawny, all with big bunches of keys – and the smell of carbolic…'

'You'll see all sorts now you're here, Rosamund – and have to deal with it. Are you getting cold feet?'

'No, of course not. You know how much I want to do this.' She paused and her face broke into a grin. 'Mr Archer introduced us to Annie today. We'll be seeing a lot of her, he said.'

'You will too. You'll be giving her bedbaths and sticking needles in her before you know where you are. You'll throw her around as you'll never be able to throw a real patient around.'

Rosamund chuckled, then became serious. 'There's such a lot to learn before we go on the wards. D'you think I'll make it?'

'Of course you will. The time will fly like magic, then there'll be times you wish you were back in the safety of PTS.'

'Never,' declared Rosamund.

***

The time did fly – if not quite like magic.

Each morning, wrapped in cloaks over their white overalls, they trooped through the hospital to the redbrick building standing on its own near a copse of gloomy trees. Here a burly female with a large bunch of keys admitted them to climb a stone staircase up to the schoolroom. Their tutor, Mr Archer, looked like a cleanshaven Father Christmas with round belly and rosy face set with twinkling blue eyes. The school soon became familiar, with its two classrooms, one for practical work, with trolleys, screens, a bed and cabinets full of curious implements; and a room for written work. Everything they did was new and exciting – except for note-taking.

'I thought I'd finished with this sort of thing,' Muriel remarked crossly when Mr Archer left them to finish a long session of note-taking on Ward Hygiene from the blackboard. 'I never did like school – never was any good at it.' She frowned, dark brows meeting in a line under a shock of black hair which always managed to escape her cap. She threw her pen down. 'I can't keep up.'

Rosamund, next to her, was still scribbling madly to take down the last few words. 'You can copy mine later if you like – if you can read it,' she mumbled. 'There, that's it.' She screwed the cap onto her fountain pen and leaned back. 'Whose turn is it to make tea?'

'Amy's. She's gone to put the kettle on. Should be ready by now.' Sandra packed up her notebook. 'I shan't bother with notes, I can always look at our Wendy's.'

'You'll get bored,' warned Rosamund.

'There's plenty to look at.' She wiggled smugly out of the room.

There was. A grey-white skeleton stood in the corner, with whose scratchy hands they'd already become acquainted; a skull and a collection of bones lay on top of a cabinet. Anatomical charts, with their lines of red and blue blood vessels, hung on the walls, shiny and yellowing with age. Rosamund had known little about the mysteries of the human body, and explored its structure and functions with fascination. Her eyes were drawn to a cross section of a full term foetus lying head-down in its mother's uterus, waiting to be born. The baby was curled up, eyes closed, thumb in its mouth, looking so cosy and contented that it stirred her to wonder mixed with sadness and a hunger she could not explain.

Weeks passed in a blur of 'Trays and Trolleys', giving bedpans, injecting Annie, shaving balloons with a cut throat razor, and becoming acquainted with rubber catheters, funnels and lengths of rusty coloured rubber tubing. There were notes to take on everything from how to give medicines to administering an ice pack or an enema. And Last Offices. No one looked forward to laying out a body, but it was a necessary part of their job.

Rosamund never got used to being locked in on the mental ward side of the training school. One day as they were being let through to the lavatories at break time, she heard bloodcurdling howls and screams coming from a bathroom. To her horror, she saw one of the nurses wrestling with a scrawny woman in a bath. She was struggling to get out, arms and legs flailing in great swirls of water and writhing wet hair. The floor was awash and the nurse nearly as wet as her charge. Rosamund could see why the mental nurses had to be brawny. She recoiled from the sight, thankful that general nursing would not be like that – she hoped.

'Oh my Gawd.' Amy looked set to join in and help the nurse, but Helen grabbed her arm and hauled her away. The students looked at each other with discomfort, and as soon as possible bundled back through the door to their own side, where the sound of wails and screeches continued for some time. Mr Archer serenely continued to teach, and eventually his students settled down.

They were learning how to move patients in bed, working in threes. Rosamund and Muriel worked together, while Sandra was the patient lying flat in the bed. She lost no time in giving orders to the others. 'You're supposed to hold each others' wrists across my lower back and underneath my thighs.'

'Do shut up Sandra. We know what we're supposed to do.' Rosamund fumbled for Muriel's hand beneath the bedclothes. 'I can't see what I'm doing. Where's your hand?'

Muriel let go and turned the sheets back. 'Is that better?'

'Much. Keep still Sandra, do.'

'Mind my stockings, they've already got one hole in them.'

'Never mind your stockings. You wouldn't be wearing any if you were a real patient,' Rosamund panted. 'Right Muriel? One two three…'

Mr Archer watched. 'Keep the patient covered at all times, Miss Hambly, Miss Wright. Just the sheet will do. That's right. Now ask your patient to tuck in her chin and bend her knees. Good. Now – LIFT.'

At the first lift nothing happened. At the second, Sandra shot up the bed and banged her head on the bed rail. The other two collapsed into laughter, but Sandra was none too pleased. She had thought she had chosen the easy option. After a few more tries they got it right, and Sandra was lying comfortably propped against a pile of beautifully arranged pillows.

'Now ladies, we'll try changing the draw sheet. After that, putting the patient on a bed pan.'

'Oh no you don't. It's someone else's turn to be the patient.' Sandra scrambled out of the bed.

'Giving of the bedpan will be done using Annie, but you will each practice every procedure until you are proficient, ladies.' Mr Archer turned away to hide his smile behind a cough.

Sandra gave in, and they carried on until Mr Archer was satisfied. It wasn't easy lifting, especially when the nurses were different heights and weights. 'You'll have to work with whoever is on duty with you, and learn to do it properly, so that your back is protected and the patient does not suffer discomfort,' Mr Archer told them. 'More nurses go sick, or have to leave the profession with a back injury than for any other reason. So learn to lift well.'

Muriel was tall and gangly with long arms, Sandra short and rounded, and Rosamund, although slight was strong, but they got the hang of it and learned to work together.

8

Gradually the new students' knowledge and confidence increased. They began to know each other better, friendships and alliances were formed. Helen and Rosamund were already friends, and Amy became an easy third. Surprisingly Sandra attached herself to them. There seemed to be an unwilling attraction between her and Amy, who had no time for Sandra's airs and graces. There was often friction between them, much to the amusement of Rosamund and Helen.

As Amy said, 'There's nowt so queer as folk, and none queerer than Sandra here.'

'I'd have you know Amy Weston, Daddy says I look like Marilyn Monroe.' She struck an attitude, fluttering her lashes over baby blue eyes and tossing blond curls.

'An' Ah'm Doris Day – I don't think.' But they got on well enough on the whole.

***

It was the middle of the afternoon, and Rosamund was last to return to the schoolroom from the lavatories. Unusually the door into the ward was open, and curious, Rosamund peered in. A smell of stale urine and fear, overlaid with carbolic and a draught of cold air from wide-open windows filled the large room, where row upon row of beds were placed so close together that there was no room even for a locker between them. Shocked, she wondered how many patients had a bed they could call their own. A young woman sat alone in the sea of beds, rocking. Lank head down, shoulders in institutional stripes hunched. Mindless, rocking. Profoundly moved, Rosamund wondered what had brought the woman to this terrible place? What demons of the mind did she suffer in the midst of this bleakness? Where was her family? Did they know what was happening to her? Did they care? There was anguish and hopelessness in every line of the solitary figure. After a long moment Rosamund withdrew, returned to the normal world on the other side of the dividing door. The image of the young woman stayed with her.

***

One evening towards the end of October a green and cream bus chuntered along Sebastopol Road and deposited Rosamund and Helen outside Mrs Wilson's house. It had been raining most of the day, and wet leaves lay in dank drifts in the gutters and in the corners by the gateposts. Raindrops sparkled in the light of the gas lamp as the two girls ran up the steps between the pillars, to where in her flowery wrap-round pinafore Mrs Wilson waited.

'Come on in before you catch your deaths of cold.' She ushered them into her kitchen where they laughed as they shed wet coats and shook raindrops from their hair. 'And take them shoes off an' all. I can't do wi' you dripping on me clean lino,' Mrs Wilson scolded.

They sat beside the gleaming blackleaded range, and the orange and black glow of a good coal fire warmed their feet where they wiggled stockinged toes on the rag rug.

'How've you been, Mrs Wilson? It seems ages since I was here.' Rosamund looked round the familiar room.

'Middling, middling, thank you Rosamund. But I want to hear more about what you're doing in that PTS of yours. When are you going to be proper nurses?'

'Not for ages yet. We'll still be student nurses for another three years after we finish in PTS. And there are exams to take before then.' Helen warmed her hands round the mug of hot tea which had found its way into her hands. 'We were allowed onto the wards this week, on Thursday afternoon.'

'Go on then. What was it like?'

'We-e-ll.' Rosamund hesitated, looked at Helen who encouraged her with a grin. 'Well it was all right for Helen. She'd done it before – when she did her orthopaedics.'

'Get on with it Roz, or I'll answer myself.'

Rosamund took a gulp of tea. 'I was on Women's Medical. I'd felt quite confident before I got there, but I looked round the ward and it was vast. All those women, ill. And I was supposed to do something about it. But I needn't have worried. Sister put me at ease straight away, and asked Nurse Smith, who was just starting a temperature round, to take me under her wing. I just pushed the trolley at first, then she asked me to put the thermometers into patients' mouths and she'd follow on, read and record them. That went fine for a while until I found a thermometer that hadn't been shaken down. I remembered it had to register zero to start with, so I gave it what I thought was a professional shake. Unfortunately I shook it to one side, and the thermometer smashed on the handle of a wheel chair. I was mortified, but no one shouted at me.

'What a shame. What did you do then?' Mrs Wilson was agog.

'I helped Smith give an old lady a bed bath. Well she left me to it mostly, so it took ages. The lady wanted to talk, and I didn't like to stop her. By the time I'd finished and cleared up it was time to go off duty. I suspect I was given a bed bath to do to keep me occupied for the rest of the afternoon. Out of harm's way at least.' She grinned. 'I'll improve, I know I will.'

Helen gazed into the glowing cave of the fire. Mrs Wilson turned to her. 'You're quiet. What did…?'

'I was on Women's Surgical. I went to theatre with a woman for a breast removal.' Her eyes were sombre.

'Oh.'

No one spoke for several moments, then Rosamund turned to Mrs Wilson. 'It's good to see you again. To be here. I don't know what I'd have done without you when I had my accident.'

'Get away with you. I did nowt. I hope you'll come again, and bring more of your friends. T'lodgers come and go – no chance to get to know them properly. My daughter's moved ovver t'other side of town, her husband's got a better job. I don't see so much of them now, and it's too far to go to babysit. I miss that. I miss my grandchildren.'

'Of course I'll come again. And I'll take you out to tea. We could meet in town, have our tea at the Jester?'

'That'd be grand, love.' Mrs Wilson's corsets creaked as she reached across the table for a plate piled with crumpets, and a dish of butter. 'Here, tekk hold of that toasting fork, Helen, and do us some crumpets, there's a good girl.'

She replenished the flowery mugs with tea, and the girls fell on the crumpets as they came off the toasting fork.

There were footsteps down the stairs and across the hall, then the outside door banged. Mrs Wilson sighed. 'Why do they allus bang that door?'

'Who's in my old room now?' asked Rosamund with butter running down her chin.

Mrs Wilson launched into tales of her present lodgers, and the time sped until Rosamund suddenly looked at her watch. 'Goodness look at the time. We'll get locked out.'

Helen stretched. 'It's okay. We'll be all right if we get the next bus.'

Rosamund was quiet on the way back. Good as hospital life was, her time at Sebastopol Road was precious, and she basked in Mrs Wilson's homely kindness. It was the nearest to a home and family she had now. Most of the other girls went home at weekends, but there were always other off duty nurses in the nurses home, so she needn't be lonely. I must write to Edith, she remembered. She'll be wondering how I'm getting on. Besides I'd like another picture from Tristan and Greg to pin up beside the one in Edith's last letter.

The porter was shaking his keys as they passed the lodge at two minutes to eleven and dashed up the drive to the nurse' home.

***

Rosamund woke one morning in early November in the depths of despair. She knew what it was. It had been creeping up on her for some time. Today was just one year since that truly dreadful day when she had found the letter from her mother to Uncle Edgar at the house sale, and her life was brutally changed. She dragged herself out of bed and down to breakfast, but she scarcely knew how she did it.

'What's up, Roz? You look as though you've lost a shilling and found a farthing.' Even first thing in the morning you could depend on Amy for a quip.

'Nothing, just feeling a bit off.'

Helen looked at her carefully. 'It's more than that. Are you ill?'

'No. Memories. An anniversary.'

'Ah. Can you cope?'

'I'll be okay.'

Helen tucked her arm through Rosamund's, and said no more.

But she kept her eye on her just the same. She didn't know what the memories were, but she did know there was more to Rosamund than she had revealed, and felt sure that when the time was right her problems would surface. She had a quiet word with the others.

'Poor Roz. You'd never guess. She seems happy most of the time. You never know what folk have to put up with, do you?' Amy nodded sagely.

'I wonder if she'd like to borrow my new Ruby Murray record?' Sandra had her own brand of kindness.

Rosamund never realised how her friends cocooned her that day, but Mr Archer could see that something was wrong, and respecting the group's protective attitude, made no demands on her.

After supper Rosamund locked herself in a bathroom. It didn't have one of her favourite blue baths – they were all in cubicles – but she sank into the comfort of the steaming depths with relief. Always in the past she had been able to find privacy and never valued it. She and Pa had had plenty of space at the Old Rectory, and there were numberless boltholes out of doors where she could find solitude. Her mind visited again those beloved places: the stables where all the garden tools and machines were stored, with its smell of earth and sacking; out in the woods where she found loamy nooks under trees, among bluebells in spring, and later among ferns; beside sparkling streams where, surrounded by birdsong she could watch water voles going about their business; in the lee of the Jubilee Stone – a carved granite rock on the moor – her and Francis's special place, where the scent of wild thyme blew on the wind and skylarks tumbled from the sky in a torrent of song, and the circling shadow of a buzzard overhead. Francis knew them all too, and would seek her out if he thought she had been missing for too long. Here at the hospital this was the only place she had yet found to be alone. Francis. I miss him so. It didn't get any better. It seemed more than a year, another lifetime since she'd found the broken ivory wing at the bottom of the Chinese cabinet, and spied the yellowing scrap of paper. Why had she put it in her pocket to read later? How she wished she had just screwed it up and thrown it away. That wouldn't have altered the dreadful facts, but she would never have known that Francis was her half-brother. They would have been married now, living together in the farm cottage, closer even than they had been before in their lives – if that were possible. She relived the sureness of Francis's presence, the muscled firmness of his arms as they held her; the outdoor scent of his skin against hers; his kisses that last time in the wood, felt them hot and urgent on her face. She stirred her legs, swirled the hot water about her body. I wish I'd let us make love then. Before I knew. At least we'd have had that… No I don't, of course I don't. I feel guilty enough as it is. But oh Francis – would we have fallen in love if we had been brought up as brother and sister? How could we know? Was it like that for Uncle Edgar and Mother? But they knew. There was no excuse. I'm glad she died. No I'm not. I miss her even though I never knew her. Did Uncle Edgar know I was his? He obviously didn't get her letter. I loved Uncle Edgar. He was funny and kind and playful and – matter-of-fact. Steady. He treated Francis and me the same – like brother and sister? Could he have known? No, of course he didn't. He and Aunt Maud, and Pa… Rosamund was in an agony of pain and confusion, going round and round in her mind until nothing made sense. The only absolute was that she loved Francis, and she missed him and she wanted him and it was wrong. She was back where she started. In a new life that was exciting and fulfilling, filled with friendships and new experiences. Without Francis. And that was how it was going to be for the rest of her life and she had better get used to it and make the best of it. Make a success of her life. She'd have a damned good try anyway.

The water had cooled and she stood up in a great flurry of indecision and stepped out onto the cork bathmat. She wrapped herself in an enormous towel, and when she had rubbed herself dry there were still tears on her face.

***

She managed to keep going, but only just. The old 'glass bowl round her' feeling had returned, and for some time everything that happened seemed at a great distance, nothing to do with her. But end of PTS exams loomed. The class was getting jittery, and even Sandra's blasé faith in herself was shaken.

'Will you test me on enemas?' she was heard to ask Amy. Unprecedented.

'Ay, I'll do that, if you'll test me on physiology. Ah'm all right on straightforward stuff, but all this scientific argy bargy has me beat.'

Helen laughed. 'Nonsense, Amy. I'll bet you're top.'

Rosamund worked quietly and steadily. She was still feeling low. Once she had let herself think of Francis in the way that she had done, she had trouble in pushing him to the back of her mind again. Revising for the exams helped. A bit.

Muriel's gloomy outlook became even more gloomy. 'I'll never pass. I don't know how I got accepted on the course in the first place. Me mum set so much store by me being a nurse that I had to have a go, but I'll not pass.'

'Course you will, we all will.' Helen had gone through this before. 'They don't want you to fail. Besides, we all did well enough on the tests. Just keep your nerve, girls.'

They did all pass, even Muriel, but she decided to leave anyway.

'I don't think her heart was in it,' observed Rosamund.

'No, Ah don't think it were. But she stood up to that mother of hers, didn't she? Med up her own mind.'

Then they were trying on new uniforms, blue and white striped dresses and starched collars and cuffs which scratched their necks and arms unmercifully. They pinned crisp white aprons round their waists and perky butterfly caps on their heads. A new school of first year student nurses was launched on the wards.

**

'Ooh my feet.' Rosamund threw her cloak on the bed and collapsed across it. 'They're on fire.' She pulled off her sensible black shoes and rubbed her aching toes.

'You'll get used to it.' Helen, at her dressing table in her housecoat, was brushing her hair.

'I'll never get used to late duties,' wailed Rosamund, 'and going on early is just as bad. I couldn't do a thing right today. I knocked over a bottle of gentian violet. Sister was not pleased. Then Mrs Carstairs called me a cow just because I couldn't give her a bedpan in the middle of dressings. After that Sister sent me over to E ward for a long stand. 'Just wait over there, nurse,' Staff told me. I must have been there about quarter of an hour before I plucked up courage to remind her I was waiting, and she said, 'Well that's what you came for, isn't it? A long stand.'

'Oh Roz, you didn't fall for that old chestnut, did you? You poor old thing.' Helen laughed sympathetically as Rosamund peeled off her black stockings and tottered off to the bathroom.

She stopped in the doorway and smiled. 'Mrs Aykroyd took two steps on her artificial leg today. You should have seen her face when she realised she had done it on her own.'

Rosamund had never worked so hard in her life, and being tired was just something she would get used to. Her depression gone, she loved her work with her patients, and was glad to be sharing a room with Helen and a couple of third years whom they rarely saw. All in all life was good. It would soon be Christmas again, and this time she would not be lying in bed listening to carols, she would be one of the scarlet-cloaked nurses singing their way round the wards.

9

'Helen, once and for all I do not want a boyfriend. Will you please stop trying to matchmake?'

'It's not normal – not normal at all. You can't dislike men or you wouldn't be like you are when you're nursing them. I sometimes think you're only half alive when you're not on duty.'

'And just what do you mean by that?' Rosamund lifted her chin in indignation, eyes flashing blue sparks.

'Don't take offence, Roz. You're all right when it's just us – the girls I mean. But in mixed company you're so – wooden, stiff. I don't know how to put it. You're all defence, armourplated, and no man can get near you.'

'What's wrong with that? I dont want them to get near me. And talking about defences, what about yours? Do you have any? You get through boyfriends like hot cakes, not one at a time either. How many is it just now? Three? Surely that's not normal either?'

'But it is, precisely. It's called playing the field, being young, having fun. Oh Roz, you're missing such a lot. You're fun when you let yourself be, but you're so prim and proper at times.'

'I can't help that.'

'I don't know whether you can or not. I know you had a broken engagement, then that bad experience with Ace, but you should be over all that by now, surely? You're not going to let it cramp your style for ever, are you?'

'It's not just that, Helen. If only it were. It's – oh, I can't talk about it. For heaven's sake shut up or go away. Just leave me alone.'

'Don't let's fall out over it. I hate to see you stuck in the nurses" home with your nose in a book while the rest of us are out having a good time. You'll end up an old prune like Miss Garbutt.'

Rosamund giggled. 'Do you really think I'll end up like her? What a prospect. I do hope not. Seriously Helen, I do not want a boyfriend. Okay?'

'What're you two up to?' Amy just off duty, came into the sitting room where Rosamund and Helen, the only occupants, toasted themselves in front of a blazing fire. She threw her cloak across the back of a chair, stretched her spine, rubbed her back, eased herself into a chair and stuck her feet towards the hearth.

'That Mr Thomas'll be the death of me. He's so fat it's unbelievable. His breathing's that bad he can't do nothing for himself, and he wanted a bedpan urgently. You might guess Miss Hoity Toity Sandra wasn't in sight when she were needed. So I had to put him on it by myself.'

'Amy, you've hurt your back!' Rosamund was alarmed. A back injury was every nurse's dread. In spite of correct lifting being drummed into them, they were all familiar with situations like the one Amy was describing, where they were left with no choice but to do what had to be done.

'Not this time.' Amy flexed the biceps on her thin arms, then held her back again. 'It just aches a bit. I fetched Sandra out of 'tlinen room to help me take him off t'bedpan. *And* I made her wipe his bum. She didn't like that, but I gave her no option. I just went round far side of the bed, and rolled him off it. You should have seen her face.'

'Poor Mr Thomas,' gasped Rosamund when she could for laughing.

'There you are,' pounced Helen. 'It's all right when they're patients – you really do care.'

'What's all this?' Amy looked from one to the other, serious now.

'Oh nothing,' said Rosamund airily. 'But you are right about Sandra. She loves to take the medicine trolley round, but she doesn't like the dirty jobs.'

'You should have to share a room with her,' groaned Amy. 'It's our Wendy this, our Wendy that; or Daddy says, or Daddy does, or Daddy knows a man… She's more airs and graces nor Miss Garbutt.'

Rosamund and Helen exchanged grins.

Amy went on. 'She's worse nor ever since our Wendy's been going out with yon anaesthetist. I think she'd like to catch a doctor herself, but our Wendy doing it's the next best thing.'

'Is it that bad? It's not like you to go on about people.' Rosamund was sympathetic.

'Aw it's all right really. I get a bit fed up now and then. She looks down 'er nose at me because I come from Shutt End and my father's a miner. She forgets her father and mine worked down t'pit together when they were young men, only mine stayed where he belonged. Not like hers marrying into trade and making brass. Enough to send her and our Wendy to Greenfield Academy, while Shutt End Secondary's good enough for the likes of us.'

Helen poked the fire, dark head lowered, while Rosamund smoothed the pages of the open book lying on her lap. Amy looked from one to the other and grinned, her freckles crinkling.

'I'm not jealous, if that's what you believe. She knows what I think, and there's no love lost between us. I like to take her down a peg or two when I get the chance, that's all. Now I've got that off me chest I feel better.' She stood up carefully. 'Me back's better too. Coming for supper? I'm starving.'

Rosamund scraped up the last of her treacle pudding and custard with relish and looked at Amy, who now held herself awkwardly on her chair. 'If you'd like, I'll come along to your room and give your back a rub.'

'Thanks. I'd like that.'

'I'll just pick up a bottle of wintergreen, then I'll be with you. It'll smell the place out. That all right?'

'Aye. Ah don't mind t'smell. Her Highness might though, I expect she'll be there.'

Amy started slowly up the stairs to her room, and Rosamund, her mind on easing Amy's ache, caught up with her as she opened the door to the room she and Sandra shared.

Sandra whirled round, an armful of clothes clutched tightly against her chest. Rosamund and Amy, surprised, looked from her to the open suitcase on the bed, the open wardrobe and drawers.

'Going somewhere ni…?' Amy bit back her quip as she saw Sandra's face swollen, blotchy and full of misery. Rosamund closed the door and leaned on it. Amy crossed the room and sat down slowly on her own bed. 'What's happened, Sandra?'

'You don't know? I thought everyone would by now – specially you. You're always the first to think badly of me and mine.'

Rosamund, not wanting to be party to a row, turned to leave.

'You might as well stay now you're her,e Roz.' Sandra looked at the floor as though contemplating diving through it. Rosamund felt the panels of the door at her back and tried to make herself invisible, the bottle of rubbing oil unheeded in her hand. A shoe dropped from the armful Sandra still clutched, and she made no move to retrieve it.

Absently Amy reached out, picked up the black lace-up duty shoe and balanced it carefully back on the pile. 'We've 'eard nowt. Are you in trouble?'

Sandra ignored the question. 'If you don't know I'll not tell you.' She turned and dropped the clothes into the suitcase.

'You're going 'ome? Leaving?'

'Yes.' Sandra continued to gather her belongings and dump them in the suitcase, head bent and shoulders shaking. Rosamund, moved by her distress, took a step forward. Amy shook her head at her and cautiously addressed Sandra's dejected back.

'Look – er. Can we help, or would you rather we went? Leave you to it like?'

Sandra, resigned, looked up. 'No. I'll tell you myself. I expect it'll be well embroidered by the time it gets to you from anyone else.' She sagged on the bed, and whispered, 'I'm so ashamed.'

'Why? What have you done?' Amy was blunt.

'It's not me – it's our Wendy.'

'O-oh, I might have known our Wendy'd be in it. It can't be anything very terrible then. Go on.'

'Miss Garbutt sent for me. Said I should hear the truth before the gossip got about.' Sandra twisted her hands in her lap. 'You know Eric – Dr Hall, the anaesthetist Wendy's been going with?'

'Ye-es.'

'Well – he – they…' She started again with a rush. 'She's on Theatre you know, and Eric used to visit her of an evening when she was on late duty. When there're no operations it's just cleaning up and preparing dressings for sterilizations, and things…'

'I know, I've been on Theatre. Get on with it.'

'Last night she sent the Junior off early when Eric came for her, and they were on their own in the Theatre block. Later, when Night Sister came on duty there was still some lights on, and she went in to turn them off.' She gulped, then went on in a strangled voice. 'She found – in an anaesthetic room – on the floor – Wendy and Eric – with no clothes on. Naked. They'd been using the anaesthetic machine you see. Nitrous oxide – laughing gas. And they were absolutely stoned. Laughing and helpless, just rolling around together on the floor. Our Wendy!'

Sandra was crying now. Amy gaped in awe, Rosamund was dumbfounded.

'Night sister fetched Matron out of bed. They've both been on the carpet this morning, with Matron and the Chairman of the Hospital Management Committee, and they've both been dismissed immediately. Ooh, the disgrace. Mummy'll be heartbroken, and Daddy'll be that mad. She's ruined my career, has our Wendy. I can't stay now.' Sandra threw herself onto the pillow and sobbed.

'How are the mighty fallen,' murmured Amy, catching Rosamund's eye with a twitch to her lips. She stared down at the quivering blonde curls. 'Oh my god, what a sensation!' She picked up a crumpled skirt, folded it. Sandra looked up and watched her lay it on the bed. Another skirt then a cardigan followed.

'What're you doing?'

'That's no way to pack a case, you'll ruin all them expensive clothes. If you're set on running home with your tail between your legs for no good reason that I can see, I can't stop you. I think it's a shame to throw up a perfectly good job you like just because your sister's been stupid. I know, I know,' as Sandra started to protest. 'There'll be a lot of gossip, but it'll be a nine days wonder. Folks'll have forgotten about it in a couple of weeks. You'll be the centre of attention for a while, but then you like that usually, don't you?' Amy cast a sly glance at her, and continued folding and refolding until the bed was stacked high with all Sandra's clothes and other belongings. 'Now then, which is it to be? Into the suitcase or back in the drawers?'

After a long moment Sandra rose, snatched up a pair of shoes and hurled them into the bottom of the wardrobe.

'Damn, damn damn our Wendy.' She started refilling drawers in a great hurry as though to complete the task before changing her mind.

'Here, steady on. You'll unfold 'em all again,'

'I've always worshipped our Wendy. Mummy always liked her best, so I tried to be what she was, and do everything to be like her, and now…' Sandra's chest heaved.

'And now the rose coloured spectacles are smashed and you can start being yourself. Mummy'll have to like it or lump it. And Daddy,' she added with a grimace.

Sandra stared, unseeing. 'Yes,' she said at last. 'Yes, you're right. Maybe our Wendy's done me a good turn. Still, she must be feeling awful. I think perhaps I ought to go home and see how they're all taking it. But not tonight. Tomorrow.' She looked directly at Amy, apprehensive. 'What shall I do now?'

'What *we* will do, Sandra Clegg, is show a bit of Shutt End grit and go downstairs to t'sitting room and watch a bit of television with the others.'

'Right,' said Sandra, and locked the wardrobe door with a snap.

***

Later when she was getting ready for bed, Rosamund recounted the tale to Helen, who was propped up in bed, filing her nails. 'Poor Sandra,' Helen observed. 'You never know what makes people tick.'

'You should have seen Amy, she was really something. Good to have as a friend, though she'd make a formidable enemy, I should think.'

Helen put her nailfile down and slid down the bed. 'S'not likely is it?' She pulled the blankets over her head. 'I'm on early tomorrow. G'night.'

Rosamund switched out the lights from beside the door and climbed into bed herself. Helen's voice came sleepily out of the darkness.

'Did you get to rub Amy's back?'

'No, but I left the wintergreen in their room. Perhaps Sandra'll rub it for her.'

'Stranger things have happened.'

***

A year went by and they entered their second year of training. Night duty came round, and the four friends moved into night staff quarters, which were supposed to be quiet. The central heating pipes were so noisy that the transition to sleeping by day was made more difficult. As their bodies adjusted to the new routine, the pipe noises became a lullaby and their sleep was undisturbed. The hardest part was getting up to a breakfast which was an evening meal to the rest of the staff, but after about three weeks they became used even to that. Sandra was on Women's Medical and Rosamund on Gynae. Helen had Boys and Amy Men's Medical. They met one morning at the breakfast table before going to bed.

'Just porridge for me this morning. I can't face bacon and egg to sleep on.' Helen slung her cloak across a chair and dropped her bag on the floor. 'I'm dead beat this morning. I nearly didn't get finished in time for day staff.'

'What happened?' asked Amy from the middle of a bacon sandwich. 'It's usually quiet on Boys.'

'That little devil Peter Bailey had been round in the night while I was out of the ward, and put toothpaste in the ears of all the boys asleep. I had to wash every one's ears myself, or Sister would have had my guts for garters.'

Sandra spluttered into her coffee.

'You need laugh. He scared me to death the other night. He hid behind the screens at the far end of the ward where it's dark, then leapt out at me covered in a sheet. It's time he went home.'

'My lot behaved themselves last night. Quiet as a graveyard, 'cept for the snores.' Amy spread butter and marmalade on toast. 'I got a kip myself on a spare bed. Took me shoes off and propped my cap up so it wouldn't squash. Dropped right off too. One of the patients woke me when Night Sister arrived early to do the round. I managed to clap my cap on, but she never noticed all the way round the ward that I was in my stocking feet.'

'You get away with murder, Amy,' said Sandra. 'I've been hard at it all night. How about you, Roz?'

'Busy. It always is on Gynae. There's always a wardful of women suffering because of what men do to them.'

'Don't be cynical, Roz.' Sandra was shocked.

'It's true if you think about it. Women losing babies, losing uteruses, having prolapses repaired – all conditions caused by men. Most of our patients are married. One of them last night was a Miss. A sixteen-year old girl who got engaged yesterday evening and had intercourse for the first time to celebrate. Celebrate – she nearly died. Started to haemorrhage and didn't stop. By the time she was admitted, you could practically see through her. Her fiancé was there with her parents. You could see he was scared to death, it was his first time too. Oh she'll recover, we pumped umpteen pints of blood into her, but they'll forget and do it all over again. Then in two – ten – twenty years' time she'll be back with something else.'

'It's really upset you Roz, hasn't it?'

'Yes it has. You get used to seeing the older women, the used up, worn out ones. But a girl of sixteen!'

'You've got it all out of proportion. The ones who end up in our gynae ward are only a tiny number of all the women who live in this city. Hospital's for healing the sick. We don't see people who are well.'

'Don't preach, Helen. You didn't see her.'

'It's Nights getting you down, Roz. It'll look different when you're back on days.' Amy pushed her chair back from the table. 'I'm for bed.'

'Didn't you get enough sleep in the night?' Sandra teased as they went off together.

Rosamund stood up straight and pushed her hair back. 'I'm not ready for bed yet, Helen. I'm going into town. You go on with the others.'

'Are you sure, Roz? Would you like me to come with you?'

'No thanks. I just need time on my own. Try to sort out my feelings – you know. And I need some more black stockings and other odds and ends. See you this evening. Sleep tight.'

10

Rosamund put on her outdoor uniform and caught the bus into town with her mind still on the night before. The ward had been full when the girl had been admitted as an emergency, packed up with bloodied towels; she'd been all eyes in a transparent face, weak and scared. Her parents waited in the corridor with the boy while Sister and Rosamund put up a drip. There was an atmosphere of anger and fear between the parents and the boy, and he visibly shook. Later he'd sat beside his fiancée holding her left hand and twisting the single diamond on her finger, as they gazed mutely at each other. Was it worth it? Rosamund wondered. She hadn't realised how upset she was, and had been as surprised as her friends at how she'd sounded off about her women patients. Perhaps Amy was right, and she wouldn't normally have reacted so strongly. Night Duty did tend to distort reality. There was something else she'd discovered about nursing. She'd been taught how to cope with practical situations, but had not been prepared for her responses to other people's emotions, tragedies, and to death itself. Nurses talked to each other, but it wasn't always enough.

Rosamund made her few purchases mechanically. Weary now, her mind was still too active for sleep. She went into a teashop, and seated at a window table with her elbows on the table and a cup of comforting hot chocolate between her hands, she gazed at the church opposite. Not very old – Victorian Gothic she judged – its stone stained black with industrial grime. Not at all like the church back home nestling into the landscape, square granite tower worn by six centuries of Cornish weather. She hadn't been in a church since she left Treblissick over two years ago. Francis was chapel and she church, but they'd both attended either, depending on what was going on. Village life had centred round St Hyldroc's and the Methodist chapel, and their activities had been part of the pattern of her life. This was another place, another church, another life.

Her drink finished, she gathered her shopping and paid her bill. Then dodging the stream of traffic she crossed the road to the church, pushed open the heavy door and stepped into the faint smell of incense mingled with wax and metal polish. She took a prayer book from the ledge on her left and walked round the church with it comfortably in her hand. There was a Roll of Honour and a memorial to past citizens, a shiny brass eagle lectern and an east window that glowed with blues, purples and scarlet. Everything in the church looked lovingly cared for. The pews were polished and the lectern gleamed, the flowers freshly done. Rosamund sat in a pew and rested for a while, the prayer book fallen open on her lap at the General Confession. She slipped to her knees on a plush hassock.

***

'Are you all right, my dear?'

Rosamund raised her head to see a pair of penetrating grey eyes looking into hers with concern. Stiff and cramped, she lifted herself back onto the seat.

'Sorry. I must have fallen asleep.'

The grey eyes relaxed and she saw that they were set in a seamed, much lived-in face topped with a bush of iron-grey hair. She looked further and saw a clerical collar, a cross and a belted cassock.

'You'd been there such a long time without moving that I had to make sure there was nothing wrong,' he said.

Rosamund rubbed her eyes. 'I was on duty last night and didn't realise how tired I was. It was quite a night.' She found herself telling him what had happened and its effect on her, of how she felt that the women she nursed on the gynae ward were there because of what men had done to them.

'I wonder how many of those women would agree with you?' he queried. 'You are seeing just the pain, not the love that brought them where they are. Loving is giving, and that means bodily giving too. If it means wearing out our bodies as part of that then it is part of the sacrifice that *is* Love.'

'No!' Rosamund cried. '*Denial of love* is a sacrifice. It has to be, or everything is wasted. No. No.' She was white and tense. 'And I haven't been able to deny it – not fully. I'm guilty however hard I try.' Her distress shredded the silence.

'Can you tell me? From the beginning?' His voice was gentle, eyes compelling.

There was no sound in the church. A shaft of scarlet and blue light bathed a pillar.

'It's a long story.' The priest nodded. She dredged up her courage and told him. Of her motherless early life with Edith and Pa; of Aunt Maud and Uncle Edgar and Francis their only son, childhood friendship and burgeoning love between herself and Francis; its flowering into adult passion. Pa's death and their marriage plans. Her eyes misted, remembering. 'We were so in love, Francis and I.'

'What went wrong?'

For a long moment she struggled to find the words.

'After Pa's funeral we made plans to marry the following spring. Then, after Edith had returned to South Africa I discovered something shocking about myself.' She choked back a sob. 'Something so shameful that I couldn't tell Francis, or Aunt Maud, and it meant that Francis and I could never marry. I couldn't stay and ruin all our lives, so I got on a train and found myself here.'

'What was the shocking thing?'

Wordlessly Rosamund drew the letter from the dark recesses of her purse, and the fragment of broken ivory wing lay on her palm as she offered the letter to the priest. As he read the flimsy page, his face filled with compassion. He said nothing as she told him of her determination to build a new life; how Francis found her and how she'd used Ace to deceive him; how Ace attempted to rape her; of her road accident; her recovery and entry into student nurse training.

'I've tried to forget him, push him out of my mind – but he's part of me, in every breath I take. Helen, my friend, says I should get to know other men, but something holds me back. I know I should put the past behind me, but it's always with me. How can I forget that I am in love with my bro-o-ther?' The last word became a wail, and Rosamund covered her face with her hands and bowed her head.

When her sobs subsided the priest spoke.

'My child, you haven't sinned in loving this man, nor he in loving you. You fell in love with each other in all innocence. Remember this. Love is never wasted. You need to channel yours into a sister's love for her brother. A love which is natural and right. That way you'll be relieved of your guilt, and the way will be open to make relationships which will satisfy your sexual needs and through which love may blossom again. One love doesn't exclude another. Indeed, the more you love the greater becomes your capacity for loving.

'You make it sound so easy, but I don't believe it's possible. You can't suddenly turn feelings like this round.' She felt as if she was spinning in space, her heart in tumult. For so long she had clamped it tight, trying to deny all thought of Francis and home. Now it quivered, ready to blossom into new life, if only it were possible.

'It will happen if you let it. Open up and allow your feelings to flow. Part of the guilt you feel now is tied up with your feelings of anger and betrayal in the circumstances of your birth. Think of your mother, your uncle – and the innocent ones, your father and Aunt Maud. Let yourself be angry if you need to, but try to see what it might have been like for them too. You can't possibly know the whole story from a short note.'

'I never thought about them – just about Francis and me.'

'Francis and you. That's what has been troubling you most, isn't it?' The priest sat back, palms together on his lap. 'Remember the companionship and friendship you had with Francis? With time, if you concentrate on memories of that side of your relationship you may be able to satisfy your other needs in another direction.'

'You mean other men?'

'Yes. There's no need to look for love. Your friend was right. Have fun – like you do with your girl friends. Like you did with other boys you used to know.'

'I see.' Thoughtfully Rosamund pushed the flop of hair away from her forehead. 'You really think it's all right to think of Francis? I've tried so hard not to.'

'I do, but in a new way. It won't be easy. But you've done so much to rebuild your life already that I'm sure you'll win through in time. And it wouldn't hurt to ask the Good Lord to help now and again.' The grey eyes smiled into hers. 'You may even be able at some time to go back and make your peace with Francis and his mother.'

'I doubt it. They'll never forgive me for running away.'

'There's nothing to forgive. At the time you did what you felt was right, and it cost you dear.'

She gulped, but lifted her chin.

'As for your feelings about the women in your ward, you're angry with them for having what you denied yourself, and see their ills as punishment. Look at them now as you do all your other patients – simply as sick people whom you help to heal, whatever their personal circumstances.' His eyes searched hers as he stood, and they walked together up the aisle. 'Go home now, Rosamund, and sleep. You'll find that telling someone will have lightened your load straight away. But be kind to yourself. Let life and opportunities come to you. You won't escape being hurt – no one ever can. It's part of life.' They were through the heavy studded door and in the porch. 'If you need me again you'll find me here. God be with you.'

He gave her a last encouraging look and turned back into the church, leaving Rosamund with the city pavement under her feet and the din and rush of traffic streaming by.

***

The priest was right. Rosamund did feel that her load was lightened. It was a relief to acknowledge her love for Francis if only to herself, but it was going to take a long time before it felt like brotherly love, she thought to herself wrily. She returned to the ward and heard her patients talking about their husbands and boyfriends, and recognised that her attitude had been cynical to say the least.

She looked at Helen's boyfriends with new eyes. She looked at men allowing herself to believe they might be attractive, and eventually saw that some of them *were*. Next time a group of student nurses, including Helen, were planning a night out at the local dance hall, she found herself saying she would go too. There were gasps of astonishment.

'You wouldn't know what to do with a chap if you fell over one, Roz,' challenged one of the girls.

'Maybe, maybe not,' replied Rosamund, 'but I can dance.'

'Betrayed,' wailed Amy, who didn't go out with boys either.

'Come too, Amy,' urged Rosamund.

'No fear. Dangerous creatures, boys. I'll be a midwife and come and deliver all your babies.'

Rosamund bought a midnight blue dress with layers of stiff petticoats, and shoes with high heels. It felt good to be bathed and perfumed, fine nylon on her legs and mascara on her lashes.

'You look super,' Helen told her, looking good herself in a cherry red dress that glowed against her dark hair.

Rosamund felt nervous as the group of friends entered the dim cave of the dance hall. She followed them to a table at the edge of the dance floor where couples drifted by to a slow dreamy number, and looked around spellbound. This was not in the least like the dances in the village hall which she'd known. The band stood on a low platform at the other end of the long room, where a spotlight played on maroon and gilt uniforms and bounced bright gleams off their instruments as they dipped and swayed to the music they made. A blonde girl in a figure-hugging dress of flame clutched a tall microphone as she huskily crooned the words of Smoke Gets In Your Eyes, sending the notes floating out into the cigarette haze above the dancers' heads. The girls' full skirts swayed and swirled under the low lights, green and blue and crimson and purple, while the mirror-faceted revolving ball in the centre of the ceiling sent flakes of irridescent light across the faces and kaleidoscope clothes of the dancers. The warm air smelled of perfume and promise.

'May I have the pleasure?'

Rosamund looked up to see a fresh-faced young man with dark straight hair and a bright yellow tie standing before her.

'Yes, I think so,' she said uncertainly. She smiled at him and stood. 'Yes. Thank you,' and placed her left hand gingerly on his shoulder. She had a wild moment of panic when he placed his hand on her back, a vivid sense of Francis which she frantically pushed away – then he swung her expertly into a quick-step, steered them swiftly into the revolving crowd. He was a good dancer and led well, and she was able to relax and enjoy the movement and rhythm, matching her feet to his. It had been a long time since she had danced, but her feet remembered. They turned, reversed, and it really felt as if she had 'twinkle toes' as her skirts swung against her legs to the strains of Glen Miller's Little Brown Jug.

'I haven't seen you here before,' he murmured as he steered her down the long side of the hall.

'I haven't been here before. I've come with a group of friends.' She nodded towards their table.

'Ah, the nurses,' he grinned, and squeezed her lightly. 'I hope you'll come again.'

The music stopped and they stood to clap before he led her back to her seat. Helen was already there, breathless from an energetic dance with a tall young man with a large adam's apple pushing a laundry trolley in the hospital corridor.

'And the next dance is an Excuse-Me Waltz.' The bandleader's smoochy voice came over the microphone, and Rosamund's previous partner claimed her again. Not for long though. Five times she found herself with a new partner as a succession of different young men with a quick 'Excuse me!' whisked her away, laughing.

The evening passed in a tide of sound and scent and movement, glowing with colour.

Rosamund didn't want it to end, but eventually the band finished with a flourish, playing a jazz version of a Chopin Polonaise with a wild solo on the double bass that had the whole room stamping and whistling, before swinging into the Last Waltz and The Queen, and everyone tumbled out onto the wet pavements shining in the gas light before breaking up into couples and groups with a chorus of good nights.

Rosamund and Helen refused offers to walk them home, and walked arm in arm through the lamplit streets, rain gurgling in the gutters and dripping off the edge of their rain coats to run down their legs. They arrived laughing at the hospital gates at the same time as the rest of the gaggle, and were waved in by a sleepy porter to report to Night Sister on their late night passes.

Safely in their own room, Helen shrugged off her wet things and asked 'How was that, Roz?'

'Super. I should have done it ages ago.' She kicked off her shoes and viewed her legs ruefully. 'That was a new pair of nylons, would you believe? Look at them now. Ruined.' She gave a tired grin. 'But it was worth it.' She flung herself full length onto her bed, arms behind her head. 'It did feel good to dance again.'

So good that if she was off duty she joined the girls whenever they went to the dance hall. She often danced with the same partners, and occasionally let a boy walk her home. Some of them expected to kiss her, but she allowed no intimacies. She found that Francis was not so often in her thoughts now she did not have to struggle to keep him out. It still seemed absurd to have to think of him as a brother, but she did try.

11

FRANCIS

Treblissick, Cornwall 1956.

They were carrying hay high on the slopes overlooking the river valley. The mid-summer greens of native woodland revealed here and there glimpses of shining blue, and the glint of silver where the river wound its way alongside the single rail track. At noon the whistle of the little train carrying clay up to the dries at Wenbridge sounded through the valley. As one, the band of workers who had been hard at work since the sun had evaporated the dew from the drying hay, stopped what they were doing, and eased aching muscles. Time to eat. They gathered at the edge of the field where Maud had left a barrel in long grass beneath the shade of an elderberry tree heavy with creamy blossom. Francis pulled up beside them on the grey Ferguson tractor. He turned off the ignition and jumped off. Floss bounded up to him from where she'd been investigating an interesting smell in the edge of the field.

Alan handed him a mug of homemade lemonade. Francis grinned his thanks and drained it in one. 'I needed that.' He wiped his chin with the back of his hand, poured water from a bottle into a bowl for Floss and flung himself down on the grass. 'Weather's holding.' He looked up at the cloudless sky, and bit into the golden crust of a pasty. 'Wonder where Eli's to this month.' He chewed with relish and swallowed. 'You never know when he's going to be around.'

Dan nodded, and pushed his dilapidated cap to the back of his head before unwrapping his own parcel of food. 'Handy sort o' person, Eli. Well used to beasts, I'd say.'

'Mm. We'd have lost Pansy without a doubt, as well as her calf.'

Francis remembered a drenching wet, cold day during April when he'd struggled for hours to help a heifer in labour with her first pregnancy. After vainly trying everything he knew himself she was fast losing her strength, and he'd just decided to call the vet when Eli appeared at his elbow. He hadn't seen what Eli did, but Pansy had a safe delivery and quickly bonded with the calf who soon suckled with vigour.

Alan joined in. 'Remember the cow with ringworm, Francis?'

'Do I? We'd tried everything, hadn't we, and her yield had gone right down. I'd swear Eli charmed her, and it worked. She milks as well as she ever did now.'

Jimmy, not to be left out, volunteered with a cheeky grin and bulging cheeks, 'P'raps it's along of him being a Gyppo.'

'Gypsy, young Jim.' Dan corrected him, as Jimmy knew he would. 'It might well be. He certainly has a way with livestock.'

'That's not all he has a way with.' Jimmy swallowed hard and grinned even more cheekily. 'I heard tell he has a way with the girls an' all.'

'What if he has. Good luck to him. It'll be your turn soon enough, Jimmy Curnow,' teased Alan. He stretched, leaned back against the rough trunk of an ash tree. 'I'm sick of grey skies and rain, rain, rain. I've been looking forward to this all week and crossing my fingers for good weather. Much better here than sticking in the old office preparing house details, wasting the sunshine.'

Thirteen year old Jimmy examined the inside of another thick sandwich. 'Huh, just jam again.' Bit into it anyway. He turned to Alan. 'Better'n boring old school, with Old Chalky droning on about the Hundred Years' War, and such.' He was not known for his devotion to learning. 'I wish it was holidays all year round.'

'You'll be back behind your desk like me on Monday, young Jim. Back at the grindstone.'

'You gets paid for un.'

'Don't you be cheeky to your elders, boy.' Dan finished eating, and folding the greaseproof paper his pasty had been wrapped in, his veined brown hands stowed it carefully in a battered tin with a picture of King George V on the lid. 'What'ye saving up for this time?'

'Dynamo. Mr Crabb at cycle shop in Bodmin says Miller Dynamos's good, but I fancies Lucas King of the road meself.' Jimmy's eyes shone with enthusiasm for the thirdhand bicycle he was gradually rebuilding into the most up-to-date machine on the road.

'Hmm. They're good too,' Alan reflected. 'Pricey though.'

'They're thirty shilling, but Mr Crabb says he'll let me have one for twenty-five. We only needs five shilling more. After I've got me dynamo, I'll go for a new saddle bag. But I might ask for that for Christmas,' he finished thoughtfully as he bit into an apple.

Francis lay with his eyes half shut, a little apart from the rest. Breathing in the honeyed scent of elder blossom, he was only half listening to the conversation and the shimmering song of skylarks. Overhead a buzzard circled lazily, dark against the intense sapphire of a midsummer sky. He wondered what it was seeing with its extraordinary vision. A field mouse deep in the hay, waiting for it to make a dash across the open field perhaps? A rabbit? Rosamund had always been full of compassion for these creatures, prey to predators. He'd explained at length about the food chain, and the dependence of one species upon others. She'd argued hotly about it, but he knew she understood really. She was just being Rosamund, and he loved her for it. Where is she now, he wondered. It's one year and ten months since she left. Does she still look the same? Will she ever come back? It doesn't seem likely. I can only live in hopes that one day… He brought his thoughts back with an effort to the present scene. God, it was hot. But he mustn't grumble. They'd finished Middle Field this morning, and now half the hay in this field lay in even swathes, and the rick by the gate was only half built. There was still a lot to be done, heat or no heat, and he wanted to do as much as possible before dusk.

'Let's get back to it then.' He swallowed the last mouthful of lemonade, uncurled to his feet, and stretched. Then pausing to relieve himself in the hedge, climbed back on to the tractor without looking to see whether the rest of them were following. He switched on, and the roar of the engine drowned out the skylarks. Dan, Alan and Jimmy got to their feet with varying degrees of alacrity, lined up likewise against the hedge, then pitchforks in hand, spread themselves across the field. Floss stayed where she was in the shade, panting, pink tongue lolling.

***

Francis guided the tractor along the edge of the swathes, chasing the bitter after-tang of lemon round his mouth with his tongue. The scent of the dusty green-gold grass filled his nostrils as he dropped each raked load in a heap. The men, joined now by friends and neighbours, forked the hay into the wagon to be carried up the field to where Dan, atop the unfinished stack, skilfully continued to build. It was still very hot with the sun blazing onto the hillside and little or no wind. Francis wiped the sweat from his face with his forearm, tempted to take off his shirt, but knew he'd regret it later with a blistered back. He contented himself with opening another button and pushing his rolled-back sleeves higher.

He drove on through the afternoon, riding the bumps of the uneven field with practiced ease, up and down the steep slope. They started at last on the Top Field. Shadows had started to lengthen, and trees in the valley bottom were turning a hazy blue, although the sun still blazed on the slopes where they toiled. The Fergy grumbled into low gear as Francis climbed the steep hillside and, rounding the top corner trundled across the top of the field where the lichened gate opened onto a lane.

Francis could see a bobbing row of heads above the hedge, and a group of girls with carrier bags and baskets appeared in the gateway. They stood watching, coloured dresses bright against the green behind them. Francis couldn't hear above the noisy tractor the banter that was going on between the girls and the field workers, but he gave a friendly wave as he passed, then took no further notice. They were village girls he had known all his life. Probably Rosamund would have been among them if she hadn't already been in the field, helping. He knew she wasn't there – one glance had told him that. He knew it was daft, but he still looked for a sight of her wherever he was.

Up the field once more, then down towards the valley, and a right hand turn across the bottom.

As he came up the field again, a figure separated from the rest and stood alone looking down the slope towards him. He saw a bright red dress and long black hair. As he drew nearer, features appeared. A wide red mouth, pale skin and huge pale eyes like water, fringed with sooty lashes. Eyes that fixed their gaze on him, watched him all the way up the row. Her expression didn't change as the tractor approached, kept those pale eyes fixed on him. He'd never seen her before – probably a visitor, or a friend or relative of a local, from up country. Feeling distinctly uncomfortable he concentrated on driving straight, and when he turned up the hillside again the girl was gone, along with all the others.

***

Later his mother appeared in the Land Rover. Dan was nearest, and took a heavy basket from her and carried it across to a shady bank. Jimmy bumped the Chariot, a large box on wheels Francis's father had converted from his old bogey cart over the ground and parked it beside the basket.

'Hope you've brought plenty, missus.'

'Mind your manners, boy.' Maud swatted at him affectionately, flopped down beside the basket and began to unpack. 'Tea everybody – as if you didn't know.'

Francis was last to arrive. He switched off and jumped down, just missing Floss. 'Mind yourself, lass.' He patted her flank. Contented, she returned to supervising the unpacking of tea. The sun now slanted across the hillside, as the opposite side of the valley came into shadow. He took off his shirt, wiped his face and neck as he sat down beside his mother.

Maud held out a large mug of tea. 'Mind you don't get sunburnt. I don't want to spend my time dabbing you with calamine tonight.'

'Dreadful stuff,' Francis murmured, then louder, 'Don't fuss, mother. Sun's not so hot now, and 'put it on when we start again.' He rolled his shirt up and wedged it behind his head, then reached for a generous slice of yeast cake and bit deep into its fruitiness. 'All right then, Dan?'

'Ay. Warmish.' Dan's jaws were busy too.

Everyone clustered round Maud and her tea, extra helpers too. She sat in the grass like a queen distributing largesse, plump arms freckled, auburn hair tucked under a spotted head square, dark patches of sweat under the arms of her yellow blouse. She reached out to offer apple pasties to this one, saffron buns to that one, wielded the enormous enamel teapot to fill and refill the generous mugs with sweet refreshing tea. There were meat pasties and thick home cured ham sandwiches, and scones with cream and strawberry jam. Maud was famous for her harvest teas, and it ensured there were always willing helpers in the fields. Francis smiled to himself. He loved her generous spirit, and she was in her element in this setting.

'What were they maids doing up here?' someone asked. 'I notice they didn't stop to help.'

'Goin' picnickin' up the moor, they said.'

'Come to eye up the talent here, no doubt. Us all being so handsome like.'

'It's Jimmy here's the attraction. They likes 'em young.'

Jimmy blushed scarlet and buried himself behind an enormous bun.

'Leave the kid alone. He've more important things to think about, ha'nt 'ee, boy?'

Francis laughed with the others, and leaned back, watching the moving branches above. Good, a bit of a breeze had got up. It'd be cooler now. They'd start on the next field before dusk. His eyes moved to the field beyond that where barley was rising green, silvered where the early evening breeze stroked the bending stalks like a hand across velvet. The more sheltered fields were already tinged with gold… His attention was nudged back to the present.

' … that pretty maid with the girls then – who's she? Never see'd her before.'

New landlord at the Ring o' Bells, his girrl.'

'Didn't know we 'ad a new landlord.'

'You been neglecting your hobby then, Bill.' There was a guffaw from some of the lads. 'Moved in last week, from down West, I believe. Somewhere near Penzance.'

'Looks a bit of all right to me, the daughter.'

'I don't think your Eva'd like to hear you say that. 'Sides, it rather looked like she'd have her sights on a chap already.'

'Oh. Who might that be?'

Francis rose to his feet and threw his apple core into the hedge.

'Let's get back to it, folks. Time's getting on. Thanks, Mother.' He shrugged his shirt on and tails flying, jumped onto the tractor and started the engine.

'What's got into him then? Slave driver.'

They swallowed the last of their tea, and went back to work.

***

'Put it there will you, Francis?' Maud tied on an enormous red and yellow flowery apron as she indicated the middle of a white cloth embroidered with the WI emblem. 'That's right. If you put them all in the middle I'll sort them out directly.'

Francis went back to the van, to return with a tower of cake tins propped under his chin, then staggered over again, this time with a heavy cardboard box filled with jars of jams and chutneys.

'That's the lot, Mother. Is there anything else you want me for?' He hovered, not wishing to be drawn into anything.

'No, thank you, dear. You'll come back for me about half past five?'

'Okay. I'll get home now.' He jingled the keys to the van.

Maud waved, and turned to speak to some new arrivals who were inspecting each other's offerings for the stall. This was St Hyldroc's Feast, one of the most important events of the year, and competition was fierce among the ladies.

'Hey Francis.' Alan hailed him across the green where stalls of all shapes and sizes were springing up. There was a Church stall, a Chapel stall, Mothers' Union, Young Farmers, Scouts, Guides, all jostling for the best place to sell homemade pincushions, knitted cardigans and baby clothes, cards and calendars, vegetable produce, household crockery on sale-or-return, and a wealth of other delights. 'You're not going yet, are you?'

''Fraid so. I came down earlier to the Beast's Fair, and I've just brought Mother down now with all her things for the stall. I must get back or the work won't get done.'

'Come on, the pub's open. The farm'll keep for half an hour. Come and have a drink. I hardly see you when you're not working these days.'

Francis hesitated. It was true, he hardly ever took time off. It was easier that way.

'All right then. Just a quick one.'

They threaded their way with Floss in attendance, through the melée of half-set-up stalls, dodging laden men, women and children and excited dogs, to a bench in the sun outside the Ring o' Bells overlooking the green. Alan disappeared immediately into the dim interior.

Francis settled on the bench with the knot hole in one end where Rosamund used to stuff her sweet wrappers, while Floss made for the shade underneath. The sun-warmed stone wall beneath the mullioned windows of the old inn was comfortable to his back, and his feet rested in the dusty patch worn by innumerable feet in front of the bench. There was a murmur of voices from inside, and the smell of beer mingled with the scent of dry trodden grass from the green. Elm trees, dotted about the green gave shade to many of the stalls, which were now a kaleidoscope of moving colour, and beyond, he could see the top of the Big Wheel where the fairground, which would be thronged with revellers tonight, lay. The square granite tower of St Hyldroc, whose

Feast this was, presided over the scene, while the tiny school where he and Rosamund and countless children over the years had chanted their times tables, nestled close by. He closed his eyes, felt the warm pressure of her thigh against his, the smell of her new-washed hair.

As Alan emerged from the wide doorway with two foaming glass mugs, Francis's eyes jerked open to the empty space beside him. He blinked.

Alan sat down and passed him a mug. 'Get yourself outside that then, boy.' He gazed across at the busy scene. 'Things are hotting up out there.'

Francis sank his mouth deep into the dark brown brew. 'Aah!' he said when he came up for air, wiped the froth from his upper lip with the back of his hand. 'I got out before I was press-ganged.' He made a face. 'Your mum coming?'

'Mmm. Later.'

'How are they both? Your dad liking retirement?'

'They're both fine, thanks. Dad does like retirement strangely enough. I really thought he wouldn't be able to keep out of the office and leave me to it.'

'That's good. How's it feel being the boss?'

'Okay. But you know I'd always wanted to go into the business, so working with Dad after I left school just seemed natural.'

'I know what you mean. Same for me really. But I still find myself wanting to ask Father about things, and it's been six years now. The farm seemed to get bigger after he'd gone.'

They fell silent, each remembering when Francis's father had gone over the edge of a ravine at the bottom of Long Meadow on his recently acquired second-hand Fordson tractor, the first he'd ever had. Alan had been there with Francis at the time, and they'd both watched the awful unbelievable slow motion with which the tractor had toppled over and disappeared from view. The dreadful silence after. Francis wouldn't have another Fordson. He'd replaced it with the grey Ferguson.

A group of men came out of the dark doorway of the inn into the sunlight laughing noisily, and when their voices faded into the distance Alan said, 'Luckily I can still ask Dad, but I try not to. He was glad to give up, and I want him to enjoy himself – and Mum too.' He took off his thick rimmed spectacles, polished and replaced them before saying, 'You know I've been going out with Gwen Trethewy? I'm thinking of getting engaged.'

'I didn't know. Good for you, Alan. She's nice. I can see you two bringing up a couple of dozen kids…'

'Don't rush us,' interrupted Alan. 'I haven't asked her yet, but I don't think she'll say no.'

'I really have been out of touch, haven't I? Give me a bit of notice when the wedding's fixed, won't you? I mustn't miss that.'

'You'll have to know all about it. I want you to be Best Man.'

A bald man with a red face and a tea towel wrapped round his corpulent middle came out of the pub, and collected several empty glasses from the windowsill the other side of the doorway. He nodded at them and went back inside.

'New landlord,' explained Alan. 'You'll not have seen him before.'

'Someone did say.' Francis remembered the hay field and how the strange girl, the new landlord's daughter, had stared at him. He stood up. 'Time I got back. I've plenty to do this afternoon before I fetch Mother with all her paraphernalia, plus anything else she's bought. I enjoyed that Alan, thanks.'

'Why not come back this evening to the fair?'

'I don't know…' He stuck his hands in his pockets, jingling change.

'What's to stop you? There'll be a crowd of us, the usual gang. It'll be like old times …'

Francis glared at him. 'No it won't, and you know it.'

'Sorry, I didn't think. Look Francis, you can't wait for ever, let life pass you by. Come on out with us. There's nothing to commit you to anything more than a good night out.'

Francis rubbed his hand round the back of his neck. He took a deep breath.

'D'you know, I think I will. Yes, I'll come.'

'Right,' said Alan quickly before Francis could change his mind.' Meet you at eight thirty by the Hoopla stall.'

12

There were lights in the caravans where the fair folk lived, drawn up at the side of the field backing onto the churchyard. Francis felt strangely reluctant as he walked past the roar and diesel smell of the generators, and stepped over the black snaking cables to commit himself to the exotic world beyond, that throbbed in a riot of colour and smells and music. What was the matter with him? It was only St Hyldroc's Fair. He'd been to countless ones before – probably in his pram, and certainly when he and Rosamund had been small enough to dodge through the legs of the crowd and crawl under the backs of sideshows, only to be hauled out by an irate showman.

Drawn by the sugary smell of candyfloss, the salty smell of roast potatoes and chestnuts, he plunged into the blaze and heat of multicoloured lights and threaded his way among the crowd bent on pleasure, shouts of invitation from showmen ringing in his ears and a good-humoured hubbub all around. The merry-go-round whirled and dipped, a blur of scarlet, gold and blue. Barley sugar poles and gaudy cocks and horses, double-decker buses, racing cars and elephants pranced up and down to the rich jingly strains of the Carousel Waltz on the steam organ. 'Da-da-di-dah, di-dah didi-di-dah. 'The tune burned itself into his brain and lured him into the heart of the fair. The carousel slowed, a prancing white and vermilion horse came to a halt beside him, and he remembered he was supposed to be meeting Alan and Gwen and the rest of the gang at the hoop-la stall.

They were all there – Alan and Gwen and about a dozen other young people. As he approached, the group opened to include him, to greet him with smiles all round. 'Here's Francis,' 'Hey, Francis,' 'Good to see you, boy,' they chorused.

He looked at the welcoming faces. A warm feeling washed over him and a lump came to his throat. Why had he shut himself away for so long eaten up with grief? Nothing could change his feelings for Rosamund, but perhaps this was the start of something new, something good.

'It's good to be here.' He cleared his throat. 'Anyone won anything yet?'

He took change from his pocket and counted out pennies in exchange for a handful of hoop-la rings from the Gypsy woman behind the stall, an array of gaudy prizes clustered behind her. She laughed at him with yellow stained teeth, and the gold hoops in her ears shook against her neck.

He selected a flat blue ring from the coloured bunch he'd hung on his wrist.

'Come on, Alan, dig deep. You're usually first to win a prize.'

'Oh, but he has.' Brown-eyed Gwen with her fresh open face grinned at him and held up a plaster figurine of a dancing lady with spread skirts. 'Look.'

'I might have known. You always were a jammy devil. How did you win that?'

'Sheer skill, of course – rolling pennies.' Alan struck a pose. 'But I saved the big one till you came. Always fancied yourself shooting ducks, didn't you?'

'You're on.' Francis tossed the ring towards the nearest object, a glass tumbler. It hit the top and bounced away.

There was a burst of laughter from the group.

'You're supposed to throw the ring right over it, you know.' Betty Sandey took the sting out of her reproof with a twinkle and a bubbling laugh.

'I'm out of practice, that's all.' Francis smiled down at her. 'I'll have another go.'

This time the ring fell plumb over the glass, and the Gypsy handed it to him.

'Here you are, Betty. Have this one on me.'

'Thanks, I'll put it in my bottom drawer. Want to win the set for me?'

'Cheeky. No thanks, that's your lot.'

They ranged among the stalls and side shows, trying this one then that. They always 'did' the fair this way, first stalls and side shows, with things to munch – toffee apples, ice cream and clouds of foamy candyfloss.

Francis enjoyed himself. He hurled wooden balls at hairy coconuts balanced on slender stands with gusto, to knock one off eventually and win it. Others won things too. Mick clutched a striped ball, and Lofty a tiny pack of playing cards from a slot machine. The fair was getting busier. Parents with sticky children and babies fast asleep in pushchairs, still clutching bobbing balloons in fat little hands were leaving. More young people crowded the trampled grass, and jostled round stalls and rides. The noise of the crowd rose and the tempo of the music increased.

They were at the rifle stall about to have the famous duck shooting competition between Francis and Alan. Francis picked up a gun from the counter at the front of the stall. He raised it and looked along the sight. Straight away he replaced it, and picked up another and another. He knew the guns were rigged to shoot inaccurately – so did Alan, who was doing the same – and they chose their guns with care.

The young Gypsy chivvied them. 'Come on, guvs. You're holding everyone up. Give someone else a chance.' He knew an experienced punter when he saw one, and these two could win too many prizes.

'Okay, I'll take this one. Ready, Alan?'

'I'm ready.'

The metal cutouts of yellow ducks, dented and pitted with old shots, slid jerkily on wire across a faded scene of sky and reeds. As the rifles began to crack, pellets thwacked against the metal background. They were both good shots, soon had the measure of the air rifles and hit a duck with a ping most times. Each failed to tip one over until Francis managed two in succession to cheers from the gang. Alan set his jaw and took steady aim, leaning low over the counter. Ping. Another duck lay flat. Two – all. The Gypsy's eyes narrowed, and almost invisibly the ducks speeded up across the scene.

Francis paid for another set of shots, wiped the sweat off his face and hands and dried them down his sides. He had picked up the gun to take aim again, when his arm was suddenly jostled by someone standing close beside him. Involuntarily he turned, and looked straight into the pale eyes of the girl who had stared at him in the hay field. The landlord's daughter. She wore the same red dress with a wide neck, and her black hair flowed over her shoulders.

'Sorry,' she murmured in a curiously harsh voice, her eyes unwavering on his.

'It's okay.' Francis turned back to his shooting just as Alan bagged another duck.

'That makes us even,' he crowed. 'Next one down's the winner.'

Francis gripped the gun with damp hands and squinted along the sight, the wooden stock hard against his cheek. His heart unaccountably thudded, his mouth dry. A duck began its erratic progress and he followed it with the rifle tip, squeezed the trigger. Crack. The pellets thwacked uselessly against the background. After that every shot went wide, and it wasn't long before Alan's triumphant cry came.

'Got it.' He waved his rifle in the air.

Francis laid his rifle on the counter, and grinning, punched Alan on the shoulder.

The low harsh voice was right beside him. 'Bad luck. Sorry if I spoilt your aim.'

He turned with reluctance. 'No, I just lost it,' he replied. 'Alan deserved to win.' He dragged his gaze away from hers to where Alan and Gwen were giggling over his prize – a goldfish in a round bowl.

'I'll just nip over to the car with this, and your dancing lady,' Alan told Gwen, 'then we'll have a go on the Dodgems, shall we?' He gave her a quick kiss on the top of her head and dashed off.

'The Dodgems!' cried the group as one, and surged towards the enclosure where the stubby two-man cars buzzed about the metal floor. They all watched as the drivers struggled to steer the vehicles, and cheered at the many crashes. A blue car with two girls in it couldn't get going at all, and were buffeted and bumped on all sides by madcap males.

The cars were slowing as Alan returned minus his trophies. The friends, with the rest of the waiting crowd, dashed onto the floor to grab a vehicle as the previous drivers left.

Francis had hopped neatly into a battered yellow car, folding his long legs into the low seat, when a flurry of red skirts slid in beside him. The car set off with a crackle of electricity where the top of the pole sparked blue against the metal mesh ceiling. The fairman stepped onto the bumper and leaned down to Francis, money pouch slung at his waist and one arm round the pole.

'Two, guv'ner?'

Francis hesitated, taken by surprise. 'Er. Yes. Two.' He paid up, and the fairman swung away to the next car. Francis grabbed the wheel. He'd always been good at this, twisting and turning through the chaos. He wasn't one to do the bumping if he could help it. He enjoyed steering adroitly to use any gaps he could, and avoid those intent on colliding at any price. He didn't look at the girl beside him, but was acutely aware of the press of her thigh against his as they were thrown from side to side, zigzagging and corkscrewing in the melee. Even over the rumble of the cars on the uneven surface he heard the small gasps she made each time there was a jarring crash, and saw her long fingers grip the rim of the car as they swerved. Francis didn't care. He felt the vibration through his body as he spun the wheel, feeling it slide back through his hands as he threw them into yet another tight turn. He would give her as rough a ride as he could, and see if that would put her off.

When the cars slowed and the ride was over he got out and walked away, thoughts in turmoil. What was she up to? He didn't even know her name, and he was not going to be lumbered with her, that was for sure. He felt angry. It seemed that he was being manipulated into something he had not asked for, and for which he had no desire. But when they all climbed into the carriages of the Waltzer, despite his manoeuverings to avoid the girl, he found her by his side again, and a sick feeling gathered at the pit of his stomach. The fairman snapped the safety gate onto their lap and there was no going back.

The circular carriages on the end of huge spokes began to move in an undulating circle, slowly at first, then gaining speed. Faster and faster they went and the carriages began to rotate, first this way, then that way. He was flung against the girl, squashing her against the side of the spinning carriage, then as it turned the other way she fell across him, black hair flying in his face and the musky scent of her strong in his nostrils. The machine thundered, music blared, coloured lights blurred into an encircling rainbow. All around in the other carriages people yelled, girls shrieked, skirts flew up as waves of air rushed up from the floor. Again she was flung across him and her skirts bellied up in a gale of white petticoats revealing long pale thighs. Francis closed his eyes and pushed her upright, then stretched both arms forward to clutch the rail so that she couldn't fall across him again. But he couldn't avoid the heavy heat of her body pressed against him.

When the ride came to an end at last he staggered down breathless, on rubbery legs and escaped to the Gents. When he came back she was nowhere to be seen, and the rest of the gang had congregated round the hot dog stall.

'Where's your new girlfriend, Francis?' Mick inquired with a wink as Francis approached.

'Quiet, you.' Lofty nudged Mick.

Francis glared at Mick.

'You all right, Francis?' Gwen, who hadn't heard the exchange, looked concerned. 'You're ever so pale.'

'I'm okay,' he growled. 'Be better still when I've had a hot dog.' He didn't really feel like one, but it seemed best to stay with the crowd.

He bit into the smoky sausage wrapped in a soft roll, tucked a stray piece of fried onion into his mouth and found that he did feel better. His head had stopped whirling and his stomach stayed in place. The usual banter was going on around him. Something about the Americans leaving more behind than hot dogs when they left at the end of the war, not just nylon stockings and chewing gum either – or some such nonsense. Shall I call it a day and go home now? Francis wondered. Then someone said 'Let's finish on the Big Wheel, and then go over to the Ring o' Bells for a nightcap.'

So that was what they did.

Betty tucked her arm into Francis's. 'Can I come on the Big Wheel with you? I'm not so keen on heights, and I know you won't laugh at me.'

'Of course you can, Bets. We'll just take it gently and admire the view.'

Betty was no threat. Nothing disturbing about her. Then his memory flashed a glimpse of long thighs and the feel of cloudy black hair brushing his face. He sighed and stifled a groan. Oh, Rosamund, where are you?

***

They had been in the Ring o' Bells for some time, gathered round a long scrubbed pine table in the window opposite the bar. The low beamed room, its white-washed walls yellowed by tobacco smoke and blackened by oil lamps, was full. There were outbursts of noisy laughter and the scrape of chairs on the slate floor. Someone was playing a mouth organ in the saloon bar through a door at the end. Francis, feeling happier in the friendly atmosphere, sat with his back to the bar, and several rounds had been consumed before it was his turn to buy one. He pushed his way to the bar, and had to raise his voice to give his order to a short woman he didn't know, with an expressionless pale face and black hair pulled back into a low bun. She looks as if her face would crack if she smiled, he thought. The landlord, serving further along the counter sported a red spotted scarf round his neck now, since Francis and Alan had seen him that morning. His red face was even redder and beaded with sweat. His podgy hands deftly pulled pints, a cigarette stuck in the corner of his mouth. He didn't look too happy either. Francis wondered how long a couple like that would last in the village. There was a cheerful babble among the customers and a haze of cigarette smoke hung under the ceiling.

The door stood open to the comparative coolness of the late evening, and music from the fairground in the distance filtered through. He nodded and spoke to several people while he waited, and was just gathering the first glasses to take to the table when a door behind the bar opened, and the landlord's daughter came through. Francis nearly dropped the glasses. *Christ, how could I have forgotten who she is? What a fool I am.* He stood transfixed, right in front of her.

The short woman spoke. 'Ruth. Will you finish this order for me. I have to go out the back for Father.'

'Yes, Mam.' She looked straight at Francis, and her harsh voice sent a shiver through him as she took her mother's place.

'What is it you want?' She tilted her head provocatively, her tone of voice belying the innocuous words.

Francis repeated the order distantly, as though he had never seen her before. He succeeded in carrying the drinks to the table without mishap and returned with reluctance for the rest.

So Ruth's her name, he thought. *She must have left the fair to do a stint in here. That's where she disappeared to. So what? She's nothing to me – but I wish I'd never set eyes on her.*

She leaned forward on folded arms across the bar. Her eyes glinted as she looked at him sideways with a half smile. Francis ducked his head, then wished that he hadn't as he found himself looking down the cleft between her breasts. He turned and pushed through the crowd, glasses clinking wildly on the tray, and knew she was laughing at him.

'Hey, Francis. Leave some in the glasses, boy. The tray's swimming.'

Alan good-naturedly rescued the drinks and packets of crisps and pork scratchings, and passed them round.

'Sorry.' Francis flopped down again next to Betty with his back to the bar, and hid his confusion in the head on his mug of beer. He couldn't leave, and he didn't want to stay. Or did he? He didn't know. It was easier to stay where he was and take the drinks put in front of him. Gradually the music and laughter, the friendly voices round him merged into one as he slumped lower into his seat. He didn't have to do anything, and everything would be all right if he just stayed put.

The landlord rang time on the big brass bell at the back of the bar, and the wide oak door was closed and locked after only a few people had left. Lights were lowered and curtains drawn against prying eyes. The smoky atmosphere became even thicker, and the drinking went on until even the landlord had had enough and drove them all out. Francis and his friends were the last to leave. As they stepped unsteadily into the muggy semi-darkness of the midsummer night his friends staggered off in ones and twos, leaving him swaying outside the door. Francis vaguely saw Alan setting off with both arms round Gwen, looking back to see where Francis was. At that moment his arm was taken, and he found that he was being led firmly down the path. Alan, apparently satisfied, waved and turned away.

'Goo'night ole man.' Francis attempted a wave with the arm that was being held.

'Ssh. Come with me,' the low harsh voice commanded quietly.

She steered him lurching wildly down the path, around the side of the pub and into a yard lit murkily by the light from a small square window high on the back wall of the pub. Across the yard lay the outline of a low shed with a yawning black patch of a doorway. Francis paused, lined up and launched himself across the cobbles, unaware of the guiding hand in the small of his back. He arrived at the doorpost and sniffed.

'Tha's good. Hay.'

'Come on, sit here.' He was pushed gently but firmly until he was sitting, then lying in the sweet smelling hay. He closed his eyes. There was a rustling beside him and something soft brushed his face.

'Ooh, that tickles.' He pushed it away and tried to sit up. 'Da di-di dah... Ping. 'Nother duck down.' He giggled and subsided into the hay. There was someone beside him. Rosamund? No, it wasn't Rosamund. Didn't smell like her. Didn't feel like her. He felt hands on his face. Lips touched his softly, opened. The kiss deepened, and a tongue probed. Francis lay helpless. The hands moved to the buttons of his shirt, lingered over the curls on his chest, then crept down to unfasten his belt and fumble with his trouser buttons. He felt cool air on his chest and belly, then the pressure of hot flesh against his. A musky scent.

13

Early next morning Dan found him in a heap in the barn.

'What're you doing here, you silly bugger?'

Francis opened one bloodshot eye. 'Go to hell!' he croaked.

Dan hauled him to his feet and shoved him, not unkindly, through the barn door and across the cobbles still wet from earlier rain.

'Get in there.'

He pushed him into the scullery, turned on the tap over the stone sink, and held Francis's head under the full force of the icy stream of spring water, until he finally allowed him to come up spluttering and gasping. Francis shook his head like a dog scattering silvery droplets around, and winced at the splintering pain.

'That'll teach you, my 'andsome. You don't do things by halves, do you? It's all or nothing with you.' Dan's brown eyes danced, grey stubbled cheeks creased in a sympathetic grin. 'I just hope you had a darn good time getting into that state. Maud,' he called up the stairs.

'Just coming.' She emerged ready for anything in a large pair of ex-Land Army dungarees that did nothing for her figure, and a check shirt. 'What is it? O-oh,' as she set eyes on Francis.

'Look what I've found in the hay barn.'

'A drowned rat by the looks of it,' she observed drily. 'Good night was it, my dear?'

'Not you as well.' Francis groaned and clutched his stomach.

Maud chuckled. He stood there in his soiled and rumpled finery. Hollow blood shot eyes, hair plastered to his forehead, with water dripping down to darken his shoulders. She dropped a rough towel over his head. 'Never mind. Soon be breakfast time.'

Francis tore the towel from his head. His face had turned green, and he stumbled into the yard to empty his guts in a muddy corner.

Dan laughed. 'I'll go and start milking.' He clumped off in the direction of the cowshed.

***

Francis spent a truly miserable day, sickened and angry with himself, but he struggled through his work with dogged determination. There was a cold drizzle and his head ached abominably. What was worse was that he didn't know what had happened to him. Not properly. He remembered the fair – the fun and excitement, being with friends – until that darned girl started to chase him. Ruth. That was her name – he remembered her serving at the pub later. He hadn't been drunk then, but from there on his memory became confused. What had he done? It couldn't be anything very terrible. He'd been drunk before, not often, and never as badly as this. Why did he feel ashamed, guilty? It was something to do with Ruth, he was sure. But what? He wasn't attracted to her, didn't want her attentions. He didn't think he actually had done anything – could have done anything. The early part of the evening had been good, would have been even better if Rosamund had been there too. Until that girl appeared. Surely he could go out on his own without getting involved with anything else, always had done before with no question. He'd have to stay out of Ruth's way, keep his head down. He thrust away hazy recollections of sights, sounds, sensations. Best forget the whole thing.

He went into the pighouse and let the sow and her piglets through the low wooden door connecting with the sty. They all tried to rush through at once, with squeals and grunts, the little ones getting stuck in the narrow entrance. At last they had all squirmed their pink bodies through, and the sow rooted happily in the mud. Francis turned the tap on in the yard, and dragged the hose over to the piggery where he turned the full force of the jet onto the walls and floor with ferocity, flushing the mess of dung and urine out into the drain in the yard, the pungent pig smell strong in his nostrils. His stomach churned, but he swallowed hard, gritted his teeth and carried on. The spray splashed over his boots and felt cool on his face, but the activity did nothing to relieve his headache.

He'd skipped breakfast and barely touched dinner, but gulped mugful after mugful of cold spring water. By early evening began to feel more like himself and came to the table with a ravenous appetite.

Maud put a generous helping of pie in front of him, and ladled out cabbage and carrots and mounds of potato. He knew she'd been shocked at the state of him this morning in spite of her apparent equanimity, and raised an apologetic eyebrow.

'Sorry about this morning, Mother. I must have been a real mess.'

'You were,' she agreed, pulling a face. 'It must have been quite a night. I've never seen you like that before.'

'I hope never to get like it again,' he declared. He picked up his knife and fork. 'This looks good. I could eat a horse.'

'Mutton will have to do.' Maud clattered the serving spoon against her own plate to shake off the potato. She knew he wasn't going to tell her what had happened last night, but felt in her bones that that wouldn't be the end of it.

Francis ate two helpings, followed by treacle pudding with lashings of custard and several mugs of dark sweet tea.

'What it is to be young,' Maud observed as she cleared the plates away. 'You must be feeling better.'

'I am, specially with that inside me. Thanks, Mother.' He smiled at her.

He did feel physically better, but was still bothered by being unable to remember. The vague feelings of guilt wouldn't go away. He felt that somehow he'd let Rosamund down, which was nonsense. If she cared she'd be with him now, and last night would never have happened. He sat by the hearth and picked up the Farmer's Weekly. After only a few minutes he realised he hadn't taken in a word, and threw it onto the dresser.

'I'm going out for a while. I'll check round when I get back,' he said to no one in particular.

Maud, washing dishes in the scullery hummed 'Guide me O thou great Jehovah, o'ver the suds.

He pulled on his boots, tightened his gaiters and armed himself into his coat. Whistling for Floss he went out into the yard. The rain had stopped and a watery sun shimmered through thinning clouds. Floss followed him out of the yard, tail aloft. The lane they took was deep and dark, little more than a stony path which rose between mossy boulders and ferns, where overhead leaves dripped onto sodden grass. Francis climbed steadily up to a gate which opened onto the moor where the air was clean and fresh, still laden with moisture from the Atlantic. His wiry legs took him up a long grassy slope littered with granite boulders and mazed with bracken and stunted hawthorns to Jubilee Stone, carved by a Durrant ancestor two hundred years ago with royal and Cornish emblems to commemorate a bygone celebration. From here on a clear day you could see the distant sea and a glimpse of the river Camel estuary, yellow or blue according to the state of the tide. Today low clouds obscured the horizon, but he could see sheep spread across the moor, and a herd of Fred Curtis' shorthorns grazing across the valley. A patchwork of tiny fields merged fold over fold into the grey distance. Up here the moorland grass was still bent with raindrops and the air smelled sweet and good. He took in great lungfuls, stood tall facing the wind, and felt it fill his being and clear the last remnants of a fuzzy head. Renewed, at last he turned homeward. Slipping and sliding on the wet grass he pelted back down the long slope, as he had done ever since he was old enough to climb up here.

They'd come often to Jubilee Stone, he and Rosamund, regarding it as their own place. Sometimes they'd bring a picnic, and explore rocks and hollows. Or just lie in the sun, lazily chewing grass, as they watched the buzzard riding the thermals. He remembered one time when they were lying side by side on a sunny day. They'd been talking – then gradually fell quiet, heads turned toward each other. They looked deep into each other's eyes, and Francis felt again the sensation of utter belonging as he'd submerged deep in the blue depths of her eyes. Her pupils shone, her irises iridescent with streaks of different blues, speedwell, cobalt and violet, and here and there a hint of gold, all enclosed in a clear grey circle. Then she'd blinked, scrambled to her feet and run off into the heather. What had she seen in his eyes? he wondered.

Francis regained the track winding among bracken, and gorse heavy with golden blooms. 'When gorse is out of bloom, then kissing's out of fashion,' Rosamund always said. She was his life, and he wouldn't knowingly do anything to hurt her.

Floss had gone off on her own, but emerged now, bounding from the bushes to lead him to where a rabbit crouched quivering, with the clouded festering eyes of myxamatosis.

With compassion he put the creature out of its misery and hid the body under bracken. 'Good girl,' he told Floss and smoothed her wet coat, stroked the white patch under her chin. She grinned, pulling her gums up and back to bare her teeth, and wafted her plume of a tail in pleasure. He swung easily on over familiar ground, descending to the farm tucked into the hillside beneath its sheltering elms. As he shut the yard gate behind him, his mind was already busy with next day's work.

***

It was the second week in August. June had crashed out in yet another thunderstorm, but farmwork had gone on as normally as possible through a cold wet July into a cold wet August. It's a strange year for weather, Francis thought, as he loaded tall shiny churns containing the day's milk into the trailer hitched onto the back of the Fergy. The corn harvest'll be light, like the hay harvest. There aren't many good days when we can carry what the rain hasn't flattened. He threw a spade into the trailer as well. The stream, which ran close to the lowest part of the farm track had over-flowed, and he intended to clear it on the way back.

The track lay deep between high Cornish hedges, and the tractor crunched over leaves and the twigs and branches torn from overhead trees during the terrific gale which had ravaged the county on Bank Holiday Monday last week. Jouncing along on the rough surface and ploughing through deep mud in places, he whistled to a cock blackbird who answered him with a burst of afternoon song.

It's time I did something about this track, he thought. Get a decent surface on it. It shakes vehicles to bits, and Mother can't walk anywhere in decent shoes. That last batch of heifers fetched a good price at market. Even with indifferent weather we should be able to afford a few improvements soon. Electricity. That's high on the list. It'll make life easier in the house and cottages. Electric lights in the barns and yard would be good too. And maybe one day we'll be able to milk by machine, have a proper milking parlour, and extend the stock. I'll talk to Mother about it when I get back.

He was approaching the two farm cottages on the right at the end of the lane where he and Rosamund had planned to start married life. Dan occupied the cottage nearest the junction, and as Francis changed down to negotiate the corner he heard the chink of a spade on stone and smelled tobacco as he passed. Smiling, he turned left to pull into the open space beside the stone churn-stand.

There was someone on the platform, sitting on her hands at the edge and swinging her legs. Ruth. Damn. Francis stopped beside the churnstand and switched off the engine. He waited a moment, and stare down at the metal floor of the tractor before he swung his legs round and jumped down. He strode to the back of the trailer and undid the tailgate.

'I'll need to put the churns on there,' he said without looking at her.

She didn't reply, and stayed where she was.

'Please move. It'll only take a couple of minutes,' He rolled the first churn towards him, about to lift it off the trailer.

'I'm going to have a babby.' The harsh voice scratched at his brain. 'It's yours.'

It took a moment to register, then shock flared through him and lodged in a molten lump in the base of his chest. Quickly it cooled and settled, hard and heavy. He turned to face her.

'What did you say?' he demanded through white lips.

'I said I'm going to have a babby, and it's yours. Francis.'

'Rubbish. I don't even *know* you.'

'Oh, you do. You know me all right.'

'I know your name – err – Ruth. You chased me at the fair. But as for anything else…'

His voice tailed off as with mounting horror, hazy recollections began to emerge. The feel of her thigh against his on the Waltzer, her slanted smile across the bar, her hand on his arm as they walked down the path from the pub. Lying in hay. But surely not…?

'I can see you're remembering, Francis.' She slipped off the platform and stood in front of him, eyes large in her narrow face. 'Well. What are you going to do about it?'

'You must be joking. What do you take me for?'

'It's yours.'

'Come off it. I've never touched you. Couldn't have.'

'That's not what I remember.'

'I was drunk, for God's sake. How could I?'

'Oh, you could, and you did – drunk or not. Fine vigorous boy you are, Francis. I couldn't stop you. Not that I wanted to, mind.' She paused, a half smile hovered. Then with assurance. 'You'll have to marry me.'

'*Marry you?* Not likely. If you're expecting it's nothing to do with me. How do I know who you've been with?'

'Babby'ss yours.'

'You're lying.'

'Why would I lie? I never done it before.'

Francis ground his teeth, a flush staining his neck. He clenched his fists at his sides. 'I'm not in the habit of seducing virgins – especially ones I don't know.'

'I'm pregnant, and you're its father.' Her eyes were like ancient glass.

'I'm not having that. Not at any price. Get out of my way.'

As he heaved the first churn out of the trailer and onto the churn-stand he caught her shoulder with his elbow, and knocked her sideways.

'Now look what you've done.' She rubbed her shoulder.

'You should have moved.' In angry jerks he heaved the next churn and the next, until they were all on the platform.

Ruth stood to one side while he worked, looking mulish.

'When we getting wed then?'

Francis ignored her, continued to load empty churns for tomorrow's milk into the trailer, snapped the tailgate shut and climbed onto the tractor. He looked down at her.

'We're not.'

He switched on and drove off.

As he jerked the Fergy round the corner she shouted after him.

'It *is* yours, Francis Durrant, and you can't deny it.'

***

The hard lump still lodged in his chest, but white rage blazed in his head. He drove furiously down the uneven track. The tractor jolted and lurched from bank to bank, the trailer and its contents bucked and banged, and his teeth shook in their sockets. He nearly didn't stop when he got to where the stream was blocked and the overflow had pooled across the track, but he needed to do somehting physical. With the spade grasped in both hands he waded in, and dug and scraped and hacked until, splattered with mud, he dragged out a dead branch clogged with soggy grasses and a drowned vole. The muddy water swirled, bubbling and sucking, then broke free with a viscous glug and a gurgle. Immediately the stream escaped, chuckling between the raw earth banks where Francis had dug, as though glad to be free. Calmer now, he leaned on the spade and got his breath, watching the flow as it glided on into the green shade of fern fronds and bent grasses, heavy with seed heads. In the frenzy of digging he had almost forgotten what it was that had driven his anger. He remembered now.

Back at Pennygarra, Francis put the tractor in the barn and unhitched the trailer. Before leaving the empty churns beside the cooler in the dairy, wet and muddy, he cleaned himself at the tap in the yard – there was always a dry pair of trousers hanging in the scullery. Everything he did felt unreal, exaggerated. He made his nightly rounds, smelling the familiar farmyard smells of beasts and manure, deisel oil, and the scent of new stubble blowing in from the cornfields. Cows in the field next to the farmyard mooed gently, and gazed with soulful eyes at him over the gate, bony flanks sharp against the darkening sky. Mother had shut the hens in the ark already, safe from foxes. The piggery door was rough to his hand, the metal bolt smooth and cold. All was fast. It needed to be – pigs could escape anything, and fequently did, snouting their way through and under the stoutest barriers. Sukey, the marmalade cat, stalked silently across the cobbles with twitching upright tail, to make her evening inspection and sum up the night's possibilities. Floss looked hopefully up at Francis, then slunk to her kennel. He could put it off no longer, and made for the lights of the house.

Maud was darning socks, a pile of mending and her workbox on the table beside her. Her needle flashed in and out through the heel of Francis's sock, drawn tight over a wooden mushroom. She looked at him in the lamplight, her closework spectacles slipped to the end of her nose.

'You all right, my dear?'

'Mmm. Just going to take a look at the accounts.'

Maud looked quizzically at him, sighed and returned to her darning.

He lit a taper at the fire, padded in stocking feet over the slates and across the passage into the dim parlour, which smelled faintly of damp and lamp oil. When the lamp was lit and the wick turned up he sat down at his father's desk. The accounts book lay already open, and he slid a pile of invoices towards him. But instead of the page before him he saw Ruth's figure on the churn-stand, legs swinging. Her harsh voice, 'I'm having a babby, and it's yours – it's yours – it's yours,' echoed through his brain. He clasped his hands to his head and leaned his elbows on the desk. Stop it. Stop it. It wasn't true. It couldn't be true. How dare she? Some whipper-snapper of a girl newly come to the village, accusing him of getting her into trouble? It was ludicrous. Absolutey ludicrous. He'd have nothing to do with it.

Francis raised his head and looked round the room, where as a boy he'd lain on the red turkey hearthrug to listen to aunts and uncles and grandparents putting the world to rights on high days and holidays. It was here that as children, he and Rosamund had lain on that same rug, reading comics together by firelight. Now the room was mainly unused except as an office for the ever increasing farm paperwork. Incongruous in its elegance, a carved sofa on tapering legs and woven cane back and arms, the seat cushioned with slippery maroon stripes, stood between homely leather armchairs. A dark oil painting of the twin hills of Brown Willy and Rough Tor painted by grandmother Durrant, presided over the room above the centre of the mantlepiece. Below it a pair of Staffordshire dogs guarded a heavy Victorian clock. The desk where he sat had been grandfather's before his father's. Now it was his. He thought of the two men, and wondered what they would have made of his predicament. But they weren't here to ask, and he would have to sort it out himself.

Sort out what? There was nothing to sort out, was there? Then Francis recalled the feelings of shame and guilt he'd had after his binge on the night of the Midsummer Fair. There was nothing to feel ashamed and guilty about getting drunk once in a while. So why…?

He struggled with what he could remember of that night, but it was hopeless. He didn't even know how he'd got home. No. He could safely deny everything. Ruth might have been the town tart where she came from for all he knew. But she said she'd never done it before. Perhaps he had…? She had been pestering him at the Fair, that's for sure, so it couldn't have been all his fault. If he *had*. He groaned. This was getting him nowhere. Plainly, if the child was his he'd have to marry her, like it or not. The odds were it wasn't, but he couldn't be sure either way.

To hell with it. He closed the ledger and rose to his feet. Beside the desk, lamplight gleamed on the inlaid Chinese cabinet rescued from her old home that he'd bought as a wedding present for Rosamund. He'd arranged with Alan to store it at the auction rooms for him to surprise her with, but she'd never known about it. After she left he'd brought it here anyway, perhaps in faith that one day she'd return. He stroked a mother-of-pearl dragon, smooth and delicately carved. He wouldn't part with the lovely piece of furniture, and no other woman would possess it, he vowed.

14

He didn't sleep, and a grey fine dawn saw him herding cows into the cowshed. He was halfway through milking when Dan appeared in the yard.

'Mornin' Francis. I seed 'ee cleared that stream.'

Francis lifted his head in its disreputable old milking cap from against the cow's side.

'Yes. Storm debris it was. It's running all right this morning, is it?'

Dan nodded. 'You're bright and early. Got enough churns for today, have 'ee?' He glanced at the group beside the cooler.

'What…?' Comprehension dawned. 'You heard.'

''Fraid so. Bit of a problem?'

'Hope not. I'll sort it out,' he said with confidence he didn't feel. 'I haven't told Mother yet, maybe won't need to.' Clarabel moved restlessly. 'Steady girl, mind the pail. Looks like being a fine day, Dan. Think we can risk getting the combine out – start on Bull Field?'

'Probably. I'll go hitch it up as you're on with milking, shall I?'

Okay. I'll finish here. I'm giving breakfast a miss, so I'll go straight up to the field. The dew should have dried by then.' He was beginning to feel more cheerful. Just a little. 'See you up Bull Field later.' He started to whistle just a little too nonchalantly.

***

Halfway through cutting corn during the late morning, on impulse he jumped down from the combine beside Dan, who was lugging a bale in each hand up the field.

'Take over, will you? I have to go into Bodmin.'

Dan put the bales down and rested a foot on one. 'You're not going to do anything rash, are you, boy?'

'No. I need to talk to Alan.' His tone was brusque, his face set.

'All right then. Take care, mind.'

Francis was already halfway to the gate.

***

It was a little before noon when he arrived at the estate agent's office in Launceston Road. Alan was with a client.

'Ask him if he'll join me at dinner time at the Market Cafe, please. It's Francis Durrant,' he asked the young receptionist, who sashayed away on high heels to enquire.

She returned to say 'Mr Phipps says he'll be with you in about twenty minutes.' She gave him a dazzling smile, and Francis beat a hasty retreat.

***

From a corner table under a print of Land's End, Francis watched Alan thread his way towards him among the crowded diners in the cafe.

He arrived at the table and sat down. 'What's all this then? I'm not usually invited out to dinner.'

'I need to talk to you Alan. Look…'

A waitress appeared at his elbow. 'Are you ready to order, sir?'

Francis handed him the menu. 'What'll you have?'

'You paying?'

'I am.'

'It must be serious. Double egg and chips please, with bread, butter and tea.' He smiled up at the waitress.

'Make that twice,' Francis growled without looking up.

Alan looked askance at his friend. Francis wasn't usually so offhand. 'What is it?' he asked.

Francis passed his hand across his chin, realised that he hadnt shaved, then grabbed the left side of his neck in the absence of anything more solid to hold onto.

'Well, it's like this. I – er – umm.' There was no easy way to say it, so he plunged on. 'You remember the night of St Hyldroc's Fair – midsummer?'

Alan nodded.

'Ruth – the new landlord at the Ring o' Bells – his daughter? She chased me on the rides and things…'

'We all noticed.'

Francis didn't pause. 'Then after, at the pub…' His neck reddened.

Alan helped him. 'We all got drunk as lords – even the girls.' He grinned in reminiscence.

'Yes, that's just it.' Francis leaned forward and gripped the edge of the table. 'Ruth says she's pregnant. That it's mine, it happened that night, and she wants me to marry her.'

Alan whistled in disbelief. The egg and chips arrived, and a plate of bread and butter and a brown pot of tea for two. Francis sat back and balled his fists on his thighs. He was beginning to feel angry again. He must not, he must stay cool.

'That's a fast one.' Alan's face was a picture. '*Is* it yours?'

'That's the trouble. I don't *know*. I was so plastered I can't remember what happened. Can you remember? Did you, or Gwen, notice anything?'

'Well.' Alan reached for the HP Sauce bottle. 'She certainly set her cap at you at the fair, and you seemed rather flustered. But you weren't responding…'

'But at the pub? What happened there?'

Alan screwed up his eyes, his jaws busy with chips. He swallowed. 'Let's see. After she'd served you, you seemed to be all of a doodah, spilled the drinks. But you didn't go back to the bar.'

'Mmm. I do remember that.'

'You were very quiet the rest of the time, and you really put it away. I don't remember seeing you with Ruth in the pub after that. But I might not have done anyway – Gwen was being particularly fascinating that night.' His eyes sparkled.

'I can remember Ruth coming out of the pub with me.'

'That's right, she did. We were just in front of you, and I looked round to see if you were all right. I could see you both with the light from the doorway behind you. You were standing very close together, so I assumed you were okay and doing what you wanted to do, so… You don't mean to say?'

Francis nodded.

'Oh my God. But you've never looked at anybody since Rosamund… What do you *think* happened? You must have some idea?'

'Honestly I haven't. I've a hazy recollection of lying in hay, and some sensations – you know. She was there, but I can't remember doing anything.'

'Have you ever done It? I mean – I know Rosamund wouldn't let you near her, she made no secret of that.'

'Oh sure, I played about some when I was at Upavon. We all did. Didn't you, when you were in the forces? We RAF boys were fair game for the local girls, and not unwilling. There was nothing serious. I was just getting to know my way around.' He picked up his fork and drew patterns on the tablecloth. 'Rosamund and I hadn't got together then, she was still just a kid. More like my sister, really, with Mother having a big share in bringing her up. When I was demobbed things were totally different. I've never looked at anyone else since.'

'Until now?'

'No!' Francis was vehement. 'Ruth chased me. It was not what I wanted, but I can't deny she disturbed me, even at the Fair. God knows what I did that night.'

'I'm not surprised, after all those years of being celibate,' Alan observed.

'Yes, well.' Francis paused. The egg and chips were congealing on his plate, and Alan was mopping up the last of his egg yolk and HP Sauce.

'I know I lay in hay somewhere with her. I know it was Ruth, because I remember what she smelled like – sort of musky. And she was doing things to me – don't ask what. But that's all I remember. Either I did the deed and don't remember, or… She seems very certain.'

Alan poured two cups of tea and pushed one towards Francis, who automatically spooned three sugars and stirred it round and round.

'No one knows much about the family. Only that they came from near Penzance. They keep themselves to themselves here. It's a long way away, Penzance.' He attacked the bread and butter. 'Do you want those chips?'

Francis pushed the plate towards him.

'Thanks. Here, have this last piece of bread if you won't have anything else. What do you think you might do?'

'I don't want to marry at all unless Rosamund comes back. I don't even know this girl.' He covered his eyes with his hands. 'But if the baby *is* mine – I suppose I shall have to stand by her. The trouble is I don't *know*. It could well be. I couldn't bear it if there was a child walking about the village the spitting image of me, and I'd let it be born a bastard, poor little devil.'

It was the first time he had thought about the end result of all this. A real live baby. There was a tightening in his chest.

'What in God's name shall I do?'

The words hung between them. Alan pulled out a packet of Woodbines and lit up. Francis tipped back in his chair, hands deep in his pockets. He gazed unseeing at the yellow check tablecloth. Alan blew a stream of blue smoke, which drifted above them to mingle with smoke from a dozen other cigarettes.

'She can't be very far on. What is it – six weeks, maybe a bit more since midsummer?'

'She didn't say. Long enough to have missed a period, anyway.'

'Still, it's a bit early to know for definite.' Alan flicked ash into the thick white ashtray.

Francis was thoughtful. 'Could be.' He tipped the chair level. 'You might have something there. I'll not give her an answer yet. See what happens.'

'Take avoiding action, you mean?'

'Yes, but it'll be difficult. She can find me whenever she wants.'

'Put her off as long as possible. Maybe it'll all fizzle out.'

'Oh, I hope so.' Francis sigh was heartfelt.

Alan put down his empty cup. 'And if it doesn't, would it really be so bad?'

Francis, surprised, stared at him. 'I hadn't thought about that.' He ran his hands through his hair.

'Lots of people get married because they have to. Maybe you should think about it, just in case.'

'What a bloody mess.'

'Look, I'm here when you want me, but I've got to get back now.'

'Thanks for listening, Alan.' He signalled for the bill. 'I'll hope for the best for the time being.'

Alan scraped back his chair and looked at his watch. 'I'm going to be late,' he said. 'Thanks for dinner. Keep your chin up, and keep me posted.'

'So long,' Francis said to his retreating back.

***

'What's on your mind. Francis?'

It was later that evening when he looked up with a start to meet his mother's worried brown eyes fixed on him across the table.

'You've been stirring that tea for at least two minutes, and your plate's still half full. So what's on your mind?'

He stopped stirring and put the spoon down. There was silence, then Sukey wound herself round his leg and began to purr.

'You know.'

'Yes.'

'Dan? I hoped he wouldn't.'

'Dan and half the village. You and your friends woke Annie with your racket when you left the pub that night. She sleeps over the shop, and her window overlooks the 'Ring o' Bells. Annie doesn't miss much and she saw you and Ruth go together round the back of the pub when the others had left.'

Francis, bound in misery, couldn't speak.

Maud nodded. 'I knew no good would come of that night, the state you were in next morning, but I never dreamed you'd be as daft as this.' Her voice softened. 'Oh Francis, what have you done?'

'I don't know what I've done, Mother. The child might be mine, and it might not.'

'She wants you to marry her, of course.'

'Yes. But I haven't agreed. I'll hold her off for a while, she might find she's mistaken and change her mind.'

'And pigs might fly.' Maud snorted, stood up and began to clatter dishes about.

'I've talked it over with Alan today – that's where I went this morning. She can't be very far on if it's true, so there's no great rush.'

'There'll be a rush all right when her family get to hear about it – if they don't know already. You'll find yourself hitched in a trice.'

'Look, I don't want to marry this girl, but if I have got her into trouble, then I suppose I must,' he exclaimed with bitterness.

'What about Rosamund? She might still come back.'

Francis's look of agony wrenched her heart, but she had to ask.

He laid his head on his arms on the table, and his shoulders shook. Maud remained silent. After a while he lifted his head and looked at her with such pain in his expression that her eyes filled with tears.

'Don't you see, Mother. If Ruth *is* pregnant, I can't prove that the child isn't mine. Could you see a bastard of mine and not want to claim it?'

'I do see. I'm just so very, very sorry this had to happen to you, my poor boy.'

'Well, it has.' He took a deep breath and gave her an uncertain smile. 'It'll work out somehow. I'm still hoping it'll be a false alarm. I'm going to try and keep out of the way for a while.'

***

It was just three days before Ruth found him.

He was in Low field chopping up a fallen ash tree where it had lain in long grasses since the spring storms. He swung the axe with powerful even strokes into a thick branch, severing it from the trunk. He had been in the field since milking and there was already a neat stack of logs and a pile of twiggy branches to show for his industry. It was a blue and gold morning and he had taken off his shirt, enjoying the stretch in his muscles and the feeling of air across his skin, able through activity to push his troubles to the back of his mind.

'So this is where you're hiding.'

Her voice jolted him. He paused, the axe poised over his head.

'Well, Francis?'

He finished the stroke, and leaving the axe buried in the raw wood, turned to face her. She stood just a few feet away beneath an oak at the edge of the field, her flowered skirt and white sleeveless blouse bright against the deep greens and gold of dappled shade. Francis reached for his shirt and wiped the sweat from his face and neck before putting it on, conscious of her gaze on his bare torso.

'Ruth,' he said.

'Soon to be Mrs Francis Durrant.'

It took his breath away – the audacity. He'd known that when it happened it would not be an easy meeting, but...

'It' s polite to wait until you're asked.' He spoke mildly, determined not to be rattled.

'Oh, I think we're way past that, don't you? It's not a case of 'will you?' It's 'when?''

'Ruth.' He struggled with rising temper. 'Ruth, look – come and sit down – over here. Let's talk about this sensibly.'

She picked her way across the sawdust on the grass and sat carefully on the tree trunk, her face pale. She arranged her skirts with composure and shook back her hair to look up at Francis with glinting eyes.

'There in't a lot to talk about really. Just setting the date. I've told you before, I'm having your babby. Nothing's changed – 'cept I'm a bit further on.'

He had been going to sit down beside her to be gentle, reasonable, but decided against it. Too intimate. Stepping away from her he stood to one side, half facing her with arms folded and legs astride.

'We've been over all this. I've told you. It's not my baby.'

'And I know as it is.'

'How do you know?'

'Because of what happened after St Hyldroc's Fair.'

'That doesn't mean anything – it could still be someone else's.' He narrowed his eyes. 'How far on are you?'

'Six weeks. You know when it was.'

'It's too soon to know for sure.' He felt on firmer ground now.

'I've got all the signs. I'm definitely pregnant.'

'What signs?'

'I'm sick every morning. You should've seen me this morning – I can't even keep me cornflakes down. I'm all right now, it passes off by about half past ten.'

'You don't look all right – you're as pale as a ghost. What else?'

'Me titties is swollen, and they're that sore.' She pressed her breasts gently. 'And I've missed a period. Mam says it's certain.'

'You told your mother? Already?'

'Course, what else should I do when – *that's* been done to me?'

Francis put up both hands, palms facing her in denial, and backed away.

'*That's* been done to you? Oh no. Not me. It must be somone else's. It can't be mine. No.'

'Why not, Francis? Course it's yours, after what we done together in the hayshed on St Hyldroc's Fair. Remember?'

'Not clearly.' He knit his brows together. 'Surely it didn't go as far as…? I was…'

'You can't fool me. Not the way you was enjoying yourself. I tell you, we'll have to get wed. Give the babby a name.' She paused. 'Wonder which one of us it'll take after.'

The baby. His heart lurched. A skylark pelted into the sky and showered them in song, and he could smell the nettles in the hedge. Berries on the hawthorn were turning red already. Funny how you could still notice things like that, even when your world had turned upside down.

'Marry you?' Could he do it?

'Yes, and quick too. My dad doesn't know yet, but he'll have to soon. I'm the apple of his eye, you know – his little darling. But he'll kill me when he knows. Well – more likely you. But if we tell him we're going to get wed, it won't be quite so bad. At least I hope so. He"ll be mad anyway.'

Francis groaned. If only he could remember properly what had happened that night. But he couldn't.

Ruth rose from the tree trunk and stepped close to him. She was nearly as tall as he was, and she reached out to cup his face. Her musky smell filled his nostrils and, as her mouth closed over his it opened, and her tongue probed his. With a shock his senses recognised her. He stood still, not returning the kiss, fighting rising desire until it subsided and cold inevitability won. He broke the kiss, and unclasped her hands from his face and holding her wrists, took a deep breath. He let it slowly out and it was as if he would never ever take another breath again. With that breath went his last hope of Rosamund, and of his present freedom.

15

'All right.' He looked her full in the face and straightened his back. 'I'll marry you. I don't know you, and I don't love you. But there's a child in this, and I can't prove it's not mine. So I'll take you both and do the best I can. With a bit of give and take maybe we'll rub along all right. If we can't, then heaven help us all.'

Ruth gave a strangled gasp, and buried her face in his neck. Francis sensed genuine relief as her shoulders shook and his shirt became wet with her tears. He hesitated, then put his arms round her narrow back, her hair soft over his hands. He rocked her to and fro, gazing over her head into the white noon sky where swallows darted and swooped, and with a heavy heart thought his first tentative thoughts of the future. After a while her sobs subsided, and he lifted her chin, taking charge.

'Ill tell my mother today. It won't be such a shock to her, we've already spoken about the possibility.' He gulped. 'When will you tell your father?'

'I don't know.' She rubbed her eyes with a childish gesture. 'P'raps Mam'll do it – or… You wouldn't like to do it yourself would you? Ask his permission, like?'

'Not likely. I'll ask his permission, it's only right. But it's up to you to tell him about the baby, however you want to do it. Then I'll come and see him. When's the best time?'

'After half past four, I should think. When he's had a rest from dinnertime opening, and before evening hours. I'll tell him then, tomorrow – he should be in a good mood.'

Francis considered the little he knew of Ruth's parents – the red-faced abrupt man behind the bar, and the black-haired stony-faced woman, and realised with surprise that Ruth was like her mother in features, except for her eyes. He gave a bleak sigh, and leaned on the axe where it was embedded in the raw branch. Ruth sat beside him a little distance away. She plucked a leaf from a twig and began to shred it nervously between her fingers.

'Tell them Ill come tomorrow at quarter to five.' He had mentally rearranged the day's tasks, trying not to think of Ruth's father's likely reaction. 'Are you sure this is what you want? There's no other way out you want to take?'

She looked at him, puzzled for a moment, then understanding, shook her head.

'You're right, of course.' Oddly Francis was relieved. He'd not want to be responsible for ending a child's chance of life, and many mothers didn't survive abortion either. It was against the law and dangerous.

'Anyway, my mam says you're a good catch, owning your own farm and being young and healthy. Good stock for a babby to take after, that's what she says.'

It wasn't worth pursuing the subject. He had set his hand to the plough now, and there was no going back.

'Do you think you'll like being a farmer's wife?'

She looked forlorn and very young. Overwhelmed, not triumphant as he might have expected.

'I don't know.' The harshness of her voice was muted, as though saturated by her tears. 'I don't know anything about it.'

Her face was even paler and there were dark circles under her eyes. This was going to mean big changes for her too, he realised.

'I'll try to make it as easy as I can for you, and Mother'll help I know. You'll need time to get used to being a mother yourself, won't you?' She didn't reply. 'Come on.' He pulled her to her feet. 'I'll walk up to the road with you.'

They set off through the long grass, and climbed together towards the field gate.

***

Maud didn't say much, but her sorrow and disappointment were evident.

'I'll do all I can to help, you know that. You'll bring her here of course. It was always going to be the plan that I moved out to one of the cottages when you married, but as Ruth is such a stranger to farming, what do you think if I stay until things are more settled?'

'It'd be a relief if you would, Mother. I know you'd hoped to ease off a bit when we – when I got married, but if you feel you can stay I think it would make all the difference. My marrying Ruth will change things tremendously for you, I know that, and I'm truly sorry that it's worked out this way.'

'Well, least said about that the better. Now.' She gathered herself. 'I've been thinking. I shall move out of the big bedroom, there's plenty of room for a cot in there, and I shall do very well in your room. No protests. My mind's made up.'

'Thank you.' His voice was unsteady, then in an effort to console, 'You'll have the grandchild you've longed for at least.'

They each knew the other was thinking of Rosamund.

***

As Francis parked the van on the edge of the Green and crossed over to the Ring o' Bells, he was conscious of curious eyes on him. Annie was craning her neck behind the Post Office counter of the village shop. Gwen was serving a customer in the general part of the store, and was trying not to look and failing. The gossips would have a field day. He pocketed the car keys without locking up – no one ever did, and made his way round to the back door of the pub as he had been bid, trying not to look at the open doorway of the hay-shed. Ruth opened the door immediately.

'You've told him? How did it go?' he asked in a low voice.

She was whey faced, with red-rimmed eyes.

'Like I thought, but he's calmed down now. I got Mam to tell him this morning – give him a bit of time to get used to it. She's told him we're getting wed.'

She led him along a narrow slate-flagged passage to a dark painted door at the end. Inside Bill Nankivell waited sitting square in a large Windsor chair at one side of a central table, and facing the door. At the other side of the table in a slightly smaller chair, Beryl Nankivell twisted a handkerchief between her hands. There was nothing on the table except a mustard coloured cloth. The room held no other chairs, boasted no pictures on its dingy white walls, and only a battered model of a sailing ship graced the sideboard opposite the window overlooking the yard. There was clearly little time, or perhaps inclination, for comfort in the lives of the landlord and his family. Ruth took his clammy hand and drew Francis into the room.

'This is Francis Durrant, Dad, Mam, that's going to marry me and be a father to our babby.'

Bill Nankivell placed each beefy hand square on the arms of his chair, his mouth set in a hard line in the folds of his face.

'Well, young man. What have you to say for yourself?'

'Good afternoon, Mrs Nankivell, Mr Nankivell. I – er…'

'Well?'

Francis cleared his throat, but none of the carefully prepared words he had rehearsed emerged from his mouth.

'Er – er.' The china blue eyes bored into him. 'Yes. Ruth and I are going to get wed – er – married. Just as soon as we can.' Then with a rush of courage. ' 'Though it's by no means certain I'm the father of her baby.'

Ruth looked at him with alarm. She had pulled out a stool from under the table, and was sitting close to her mother.

'What do you mean, boy? By no means certain? Ruth's a good girl. If she says you are, then you are.' The bright blue eyes were flinty.

'Well, I – er I. We… I was drunk…'

'You certainly were. I know that.'

'… and I don't really know whether we – or even if I could… You know.'

'He did, Dad, he did.' Ruth's face was tense.

'You need a thrashing. Me only daughter ruined.' Bill's hands gripped the ends of the chair convulsively, his neck bulging over his collar and tie. Ruth's mother shrank back in her seat.

'Do you know how old she is?' he barked.

'No. I haven't known her long enough. She hasn't said…'

'Sixteen.'

'July 17th,' supplied Ruth. 'It isn't too late to buy me a birthday present, Francis.'

He ignored her.

'Do you mean to say that – in June – St Hyldroc's Fair – she was…?'

'Under age. Still a child.'

Francis was horrorstruck.

'But she didn't look... She looks at least nineteen. Oh God.'

And behaved it, he thought. But he couldn't tell them how she *had* behaved. He pulled himself together and lifted his chin.

'You took advantage of her, you drunken savage,' Bill snarled, rising.

Although his face burned, with an effort he kept his voice calm. 'It wasn't like that at all.'

'Well what was it like? Tell me.'

'With respect, Mr Nankivell. Whatever did or didn't happen that night, or how old Ruth was at the time, isn't the present issue.' He couldn't resist adding, 'Ruth was...' He caught her eye, but carried on. 'The fact is that she was as much responsible, if not more than I was for what happened that night. I don't believe that Ruth's baby is mine, but I can't prove it, so I've accepted responsibility for her and the child, and we plan, with your permission, to marry as soon as we can.'

'...before me bump shows,' added Ruth smoothing the front of her skirt.

As Francis spoke, Bill deflated and dropped his shoulders.

'You can't say fairer than that, boy. Accidents can happen, and you're willing to put right what you can. Be good to my little maid.'

Francis took the proffered hand and, with his heart in his boots promised, 'I'll do my best.'

Ruth threw her arms round her mother. 'I told you Mam, didn't I? He's a real smasher.'

'Come here and give your old Dad a kiss then.' Bill pulled Ruth onto his knee and she planted a kiss on his pink pursed lips.

Beryl, without a word or a look threw a white cloth over the mustard one, and produced tea and shop bought cakes. Francis managed a cup of tea, but only crumbled a piece of swiss roll on his plate while wedding plans were discussed. He'd been to Bodmin that morning and the simple amethyst and silver ring which was all he could afford was burning a hole in his pocket. He hoped it would fit.

***

It was a small wedding party that congregated three weeks later outside the Registry Office in Bodmin, Francis with stiff back and set face, and Maud in her church-going navy coat and hat. Ruth wore a blue costume with a pencil skirt, and a white hat with veiling and a white rose. She stood awkwardly with her parents, who were in stilted conversation with Alan and Gwen, now engaged themselves, who were to be witnesses.

That outfit doesn't do anything for her complexion, Francis thought, and her eyes look like glass.

When she smiled at him though, her teeth were white and even.

'Thank you for my flowers, Francis.' She touched the spray of pink roses on her lapel with long slim fingers.

'I'm glad you like them.' He made an effort and smiled back. 'Nervous?'

'Yes. Aren't you?'

'It'll soon be over. Come on. Let's go inside.'

It was all over quickly and, after an uneasy lunch in the back room of the Bull's Head, Mrs Francis Durrant, wearing a shiny new wedding ring, caught the afternoon train to Newquay with her husband and arrived at Beach View Guesthouse for her one night honeymoon.

***

Francis hadn't quite known what to expect of their first night together, but he was hopeful. Maybe if they got off to a good start to this side of their life they could build something from it. It seemed to be something that Ruth was keen on, and he certainly wouldn't be averse to a good sex life. But when he returned from the bathroom at the other end of the landing in a state of anticipation, part excitement and part apprehension, Ruth was already in the high white bed with brass knobs, and fast asleep. She lay curled up like a child facing the wall with one hand under her face, her hair spread on the pillow behind her. Surprised to find he was relieved that she *was* asleep, Francis turned off the overhead light at the switch beside the door and tiptoed across the lino. Cautiously he lay down beside her, startled by the sudden 'ping' of the bedsprings. In the semi-darkness, a hint of her musky smell and perfume reached him. He lay on his back, hands behind his head, and watched the light from passing cars fan across the ceiling, listening to the sounds of fellow guests creaking along the landing, the murmur of voices next door, and Ruth's quiet breathing. She didn't stir, and eventually he turned on his side to the sloping edge of the bed and fell into an exhausted sleep, leaving a cold white hollow between them.

The first thing Ruth did when she woke next morning was to reach for the chamber pot from the cupboard in the nightstand beside the bed, and lean over it groaning and retching.

'My wife won't be down to breakfast,' he told the landlady, the word strange on his tongue. 'Do you mind if I take a cup of tea up for her?'

'Yes do take her a cup. Feeling poorly, is she?'

'Just a bit sickly. Yesterday was a bit too much for her – the wedding, you know.'

'Ah yes. Poor lamb.' The landlady gave him a wink. 'There's no rush to vacate your room. I've no one coming into it till next weekend. Midday suit Mrs Durrant, d'you think?' she cocked her head on one side.

'That's kind of you. It had better suit her – we've a train to catch this afternoon.'

Later in the morning Ruth felt better, and they crossed the road and descended to the beach where rocks fringed the sand and a granite mole threw a protective arm around a few fishing boats. It was a soft grey day, the sea calm as polished metal, retreated in small waves curling onto the foreshore. Only a few families were entrenched in striped deckchairs in the scuffled sand above the high water mark.

'Let's climb on the rocks Francis, and look in the rock pools, there's sure to be some.'

'Do you think you should?'

'Course, I'm fine now,' and she skipped away to clamber on the nearest rock, scrabbling with her fingers in lichened cracks, until standing, she danced from one rock to another until she stopped at the edge of a tide-filled pool, her hair blowing across her face. Francis with a tingle of pleasure followed and took her hand, steadying her.

'Oh look – sea anen-namies.' She dabbled her fingers in the pool, and the red anemone obligingly curled up. Ruth darted from pool to pool, exclaiming and stirring up tidal waves until the sea creatures in each took refuge in crevices and fronds of weed.

Then, changing mood, 'Let's go down to the sand now,' she demanded.

When they approached the edge of the rocky area Francis slithered to the beach and turned to hand her down, but she jumped to land close in front of him. He put his hands out and caught her by the elbows, to find her eyes inches from his. They stood for a long moment without moving, her breath soft on his face. Then for the first time of his own accord Francis kissed her, very gently. When he felt her lips begin to part he drew back.

'Let's walk,' he said.

Hand in hand they walked at the tide's edge across the ribbed sand. Ruth chatted happily, looking up into his face, her steps light. For the first time he felt easy with her. The smell of seaweed was sharp in their nostrils and gulls cried and wheeled above. They stopped to watch a tiny girl in a ruched pink bathing costume drag an enormous trail of seaweed up the beach towards a group of deckchairs. Ruth put her hand to her stomach, momentarily shy, and he squeezed her hand. At last Francis looked at his watch and they turned their steps back to the town and the station.

***

Back at Pennygarra Farm, Maud had one of her famous teas waiting for them. Francis watched Ruth's face as she gazed at the laden table, the blue and white bowl of marigolds touched by slanting sunlight through the deepset window, the glow of polish on the sideboard and flicker of flames on the hearth.

'Oh my,' was all she could say.

Maud laughed and embraced her.

'Welcome Ruth,' she said, and drew her in. And there was Dan with a grin as wide as the table, with a bottle of wine in one hand and a corkscrew in the other.

'Hello Mother,' Francis hugged her, 'and Dan, you old devil.' He shook hands, then turned to Ruth. 'Sit here by the fire while I take the bags upstairs.'

He was back in a moment. 'Ruth, come upstairs and see our room.'

She followed. She had seen the room before when she had come to meet Francis's mother and look round the house, but 'Oh my' was all she could say again. Against fresh cream coloured walls the big bed glowed with the gay colours of a patchwork quilt. Soft blues, creams and purples in the rug echoed flowered curtains, and on the dressing table a posy of late sweet peas was reflected in the swing mirror. On a low chest under the window lay a modest pile of gaily wrapped parcels.

'Wedding presents.' She couldn't believe her eyes. She turned to Francis and flung her arms round him. 'It's beautiful, just beautiful.'

'Steady, girl, steady.' She had nearly knocked them both over. 'Tea'll be ready by now, and you can thank Mother yourself – she's done everything except the painting. I'll fetch the presents down afterwards and we'll open them downstairs.'

Tea was splendid. There was even an iced cherry cake with a pre-war china figure of a bride and groom on top. In the warmth and comfort, replete with food and wine Francis relaxed. He felt a tiny part of the cold knot which had been with him since Ruth's announcement of her pregnancy begin to loosen. Her animated face shone with delight. Perhaps he could allow himself to recognise the celebration which Maud had created for them, except that it wasn't for… No. He shut all other thoughts firmly away.

They opened the presents. There was bed linen from Gwen and Alan, and they were touched to find smaller gifts from Francis's friends and friends of his mother. The patchwork quilt on the bed was from Maud, made by herself years ago in anticipation of another wedding, and one of the new Premium Bonds for twenty pounds. Beryl and Bill Nankivell were to buy the pram later, and Dan had fashioned a low nursing chair of elm wood for Ruth. She tried it out.

'It's lovely Dan, thank you. And thank you for the quilt, er… What shall I call you?' Shy now, she looked up at Francis's mother.

'Maud, of course.'

Ruth nodded. 'Maud. And thanks for making me welcome, and for all this.'

'I wanted to give you both a good homecoming. Now.' She looked at them both seriously. 'I've arranged to stay at night with Vera Martin for the next week. I'll come up each day to do all my normal chores, and give you any help you want, Ruth. But you'll need time to yourselves for a while without me tramping about the house as well.'

'Mother, please don't feel you have to do this.'

'Nonsense. Do you think I want to have young lovers drooling all over each other around me?' Ruth went pink, and Maud's eyes twinkled. 'No, it's mostly self-preservation, believe me. Really, it'll be fine.'

Francis found he couldn't take his eyes off this new, softer Ruth with shining eyes, her long face flushed in the firelight, the glint of his ring on her finger. When at last Dan went out to do the milking before going home, and Maud had hugged them both and set off down the lane, he straightaway put his arms round a responsive Ruth and kissed her thoroughly.

When they came up for air he said, 'Bed time, Mrs Durrant,' and pushed her towards the stairs. At the bedroom door she hesitated.

'What is it?'
'It won't hurt the babby will it?'
'I shouldn't think so. I'll be as gentle as I can.'
He drew her into the room and shut the door.

16

'Do I really have to do this?' Ruth followed Francis unwillingly to the cowhouse.

'Of course you do, it's not difficult once you know how. I've saved Bessie for you, she's nice and quiet.' Francis handed her a dairy coat from a hook just inside the door.

Ruth eyed the cows' enormous red speckled flanks, back to back in their stalls, with distaste. Bessie turned soft brown eyes towards her and drooled a string of saliva as she chewed sideways. Ruth viewed her swollen udder with apprehension.

'Here you are, girl.' Francis scattered handfuls of concentrates into the trough in front of the cow, then to Ruth, 'This should keep her quiet while we milk her.' He patted her neck and fetched water and a cloth to wash the udder.

Ruth watched in uneasy fascination as he placed a clean bucket under the cow and hooked the low stool with his foot to where he could comfortably reach to milk. He pulled the filthy-looking milking cap which they all wore for the job low on his forehead, and sat down, leaning his head into the cow's bulging side.

'Like this, see?' He spoke soothingly to the cow as Ruth watched his fingers rhythmically pull the teats, and thin streams of creamy milk spurted into the bucket. 'Good girl.'

Ruth started forward to see better, and she flinched back as Bessie shifted slightly. 'Steady, girl, stand still now,' Francis murmured, more to soothe Ruth than the cow. Her tail swished and there was a splatter from her rear. Ruth wrinkled her nose.

When there was quite a bit of milk in the pail, Francis looked up at Ruth.

'Your turn now.'

She took over the stool, and he put the cap on her head. She shook it in irritation, but butted against Bessie's side as Francis had shown her, and reached for the udder. Gingerly she held two of the smooth warm teats between her finger and thumb. 'Does it hurt her?'

'No,' Francis laughed. 'Don't be afraid to hold firmly.' He leaned down, one hand on Bessie's flank, the other guiding Ruth's hand. She pulled. Pulled again and again. Nothing happened.

'Keep trying, you'll get the hang of it.'

He could see Ruth was hating every minute. 'Don't jerk, Ruth. Keep it smooth.'

Bessie stood patiently as the clumsy hands tugged and tugged.

'I can't do this,' Ruth screamed suddenly, and kicked the bucket over, catching the cow's foreleg. She lifted her foot and the edge of her hoof caught the side of Ruth's foot.

'Oww! She kicked me!'

Ruth leapt to her feet, flung the despised cap into the puddle of milk, and limped with a howl from the cowhouse.

Francis cursed and set about restoring order. Bessie took some soothing and didn't give as much milk as usual, but eventually he turned her out into the yard with the others and fetched the next lot in. It all took longer than usual, and the yield was down. Cows didn't like to be disturbed. It looked as if this was yet another farm job Ruth wasn't going to cope with – or didn't want to cope with. He turned the cattle out into the field, then swept the cowhouse floor and hosed it down with more than his usual vigour.

When he went into the house prepared to comfort and encourage Ruth, he found her upstairs in their room stretched out on the bed while Jerry Lee Lewis belted out 'Great Balls of Fire o'n the transister radio her parents had given her for Christmas.

Francis's good intentions flew out of the window. He strode across the room, snapped off the radio, and stood over her, red-necked with anger.

'What the hell do you think you're doing?'

'I'm having my rest like I'm supposed to.' She lowered True Romances and spread the magazine protectively over her bump. 'Besides, my foot hurts.' She challenged him with a pale look.

Lips pouting like a stubborn child, he thought. Of course, I keep forgetting – that's what she is. He turned away from her to stand at the dusk-filled window, fists thrust in his trouser pockets, and struggled to keep his temper.

'That's the third rest you've had today, Ruth.' Tight jawed, he tried to keep his voice reasonable. 'We're all supposed to work together on this farm – me, you, mother and Dan. You agreed that when you came here.'

'I wasn't seven months pregnant then.' She sighed. 'I do try, Francis.' Her voice was small, contrite.

'So do I. Try to keep you happy. We go to the pictures when I can manage it, you see your parents when you want. I spend all the time I'm able to with you, try to make life easy for you in any way I can. But the farm has to come first. It's our livelihood.' He went over to the bed, sat down and ran his hands through his hair. She might behave like a wilful child, but she was still his wife. 'I know farming's not what you've been used to, but I'd hoped you would be taking to it a bit by now. I don't ask you to do anything heavy, of course I don't, but it's only fair to do your share when you can.'

'Rub my foot for me will you Francis? Where that cow trod on it.'

'You haven't been listening to a word I said, have you?' He picked up her foot and began to massage it.

'I was listening to you, but when I do things they always go wrong. So whats the use? Like when I was looking after the hens. The fox got in the ark and had them all.'

'Mmm. That was expensive.'

'You see what I mean?'

'Mother had no egg money till we'd replaced them. All it would have taken was to make sure the door of the ark was fastened properly. Does that feel better now?'

'Thanks, it does.' Ruth giggled. 'Endless chicken we ate, didn't we? Roast chicken, fried chicken, cold chicken, chicken pie, chicken stew.'

It was no use getting angry with her. He stood up. 'I have things to do now, but how about if we go down to the Ring o' Bells for an hour, this evening? See your mum and dad – if they're not too busy.'

She looked at him from under her lashes.

'Will I have to have another go at milking?'

He hesitated. 'Not for now anyway.'

'All right then. I'll get ready.'

***

It was raining hard when they arrived back at the farm. It slanted through the light shed by the naked bulb over the barn door and dripped down slates and off roof edges, and puddles pocked with drops spread widening circles chasing each other to their rims. Water gurgled and rushed in all the drains and gullies. Ruth made a lumbering dash for the lighted doorway. Francis sat on alone and allowed his thoughts to roam in forbidden pastures for a few moments, then shook his shoulders and blinked hard. I should have known better, it never works if I let my thoughts stray. He climbed out of the van and checked the stock and the outbuildings before he flipped the generator switch by the door, and the yard was plunged into darkness.

Downstairs was dark too, and no light shone under his mother's door. Dispirited and longing for oblivion for a few short hours, he climbed into bed beside Ruth. She snuggled up to him. 'I'm glad you didn't have any of Mam's raw onion with your bread and cheese,' she said, and pulled him to her.

Later, lying on his side with Ruth folded close behind him, he felt a light pressure in the small of his back.

'Mmm?' he queried, half adrift.

Ruth was asleep. He wriggled closer and felt it again. Yes, he knew what it was, and fell asleep smiling.

**

There was a loud banging on the bedroom door.

'Pigs're out!' Maud shouted, and Francis heard her clatter down the stairs. He leapt out of bed and followed as quickly as he could. 'Pigs're out!' was a cry to be dreaded, especially on wet dark nights. They got everywhere, and every last one must be found if the fox were not to feast that night. He heard their squeals of terror (or could it be pleasure?), and the grunting of the sow; his mother's swearing and yelling as she chased them. He pulled on his wellingtons and plunged into the rain to join the hunt.

Maud had switched on the generator on her way past, but there were still countless dark nooks and crannies, and there were muddy pink piglets running all over the place. Francis swooped about, picking up squealing slippery bodies, and tossed each one over the pigsty wall. Maud had already herded the sow back into the sty and blocked the door under which they had escaped, and was darting back with two more in her arms. The two of them ran hither and thither. They slipped in the mud, splashed through puddles, shouted and whooped, making as much noise as the pigs.

Gradually Francis became aware that another figure had joined them, and a succession of growled swearwords mingled with Maud's whoops and his own yells. One last pig made a dash through the newcomer's legs, and he bent to grab the slippery body.

'Got ye, ye varmint!'

Francis stood still. Dan. He looked at his mother. She stood with her hair hanging in straggles round her shoulders, with a piglet under each arm. Her soaked nightdress clung to her, muddy and ripped where she had trodden on it with her wellingtons, and there was a beatific grin on her filthy face.

He looked from her to Dan. His bare chest and stubbled chin were plastered with mud, his hair stood on end and his good flannel trousers stuck to him as he clutched the last pig in front of him like a talisman. His expression was equally beatific.

'Blasted little buggers,' he said.

'Mother? Dan?'

They looked at each other and broke into gales of laughter. Francis took the pigs from Maud, tipped them over the pigsty wall and returned to relieve Dan of his. The two of them were helpless with laughter, bent over with mirth and pointing at each other.

'Wha – what?' stuttered Francis in astonishment as they turned to point at him.

He looked down at himself – at his muddy pyjamas, soaked and sticking to him, one leg hanging over the top of his boot. He ran his hands through sodden hair and felt it slimy with mire. He began to chuckle, then to shout with laughter. The three of them staggered about, slapping each other's backs. Francis grabbed his mother and danced a jig, grabbed Dan and swung him. They joined hands and were kicking up their legs and singing when a harsh voice from the doorway stopped them dead.

'Are you lot crazy?'

There was silence except for subsiding squeals from the pigsty. Francis, Maud and Dan dropped their arms and turned to Ruth where she stood in the doorway, her inadequate dressing gown clutched over her bulging abdomen. Francis took a step towards her.

'You're disgusting!' she said, turned her back and shut the door.

Maud and Dan looked at Francis.

His shoulders drooped. 'Let her go. She doesn't understand.'

***

Francis looked sad as he came into the kitchen, clean now and dressed.

'She doesn't want to come down,' he said.

He looked at his mother and Dan with affection and not a little envy. Maud, in a voluminous plaid dressing gown, red-gold hair streaked with grey hanging loose down her back, looked pink and downy like a child newly awake. She spooned cocoa into mugs at the table. Dan, in a pair of Francis's trousers, legs rolled up and gaping at the waist and one of Maud's jumpers tight across his shoulders, knelt at the hearth, busy with a toasting fork.

'Leave her be then, my dear. Come by the fire.' Maud's eyes shone with compassion.

He sat in the Windsor chair and stretched his stocking feet to the glow.

'Mind the toast.' Dan looked up at Francis under grizzled brows. 'Don't let her rule you, boy. It don't do her no good, nor you neither.'

Francis shrugged.

'You needs to keep your head on your shoulders not in your britches. She'm only a young maid. You'll find maybe you've more in common when she's had chance to grow up a bit.'

'I wonder.' Francis stared into the fire. Maud stirred vigorously and Dan turned a piece of toast.

Francis lifted his head. 'What about you two then? You dark horses. Why didn't you say something before, instead of sneaking round like a couple of guilty teenagers?'

Maud went even pinker and shot a look at Dan. 'We didn't like to with everything else that was going on. When the baby's born, we…'

Dan put down the toasting fork and sat back on his heels.

'You probably didn't know, Francis, but your dad and I both courted Maud when we were young. She chose Edgar and I've respected that. I've never looked at another woman, and she's just as beautiful to me now as she was then.' He turned to face Maud. 'Seeing as I'm already on my knees, for the second time of asking – Maud, will you marry me, my lover?'

'Oh Dan, you great lump. Of course I will.' She pulled him to his feet, then held his face between her hands and kissed him with great tenderness.

Francis felt tears start in his eyes as he watched them. How Rosamund would have loved this. He rose and put his arms around them both. 'You should have done it years ago.'

'Well, I thought seeing as how you'd found out about our hankypanky, I'd better make an honest woman of her.'

They drank a toast in cocoa and ate toast dripping with butter, and there wasn't much of the night left when Maud and Dan turned towards the stairs.

Francis sat on until milking time, thinking his own thoughts.

17

'Hard work that mister.'

Francis looked up from the trench he was digging to the new septic tank, and thinking of Rosamund. 'Eli! Haven't seen you since last spring. How're you doing?'

He stuck the spade in the earth and sprang from the trench.

Eli's teeth flashed white as his grin spread, dark eyes snapped and long black curls bobbed as he nodded. 'Getting by, getting by. Had a good summer last year. Plenty work down west.' He put a finger along his nose and winked. 'Pretty maids too.'

'Good for you,' Francis laughed. 'We missed you at harvest. Are you staying? Lambing's started.'

'Might, might not. You all right? Heard you were wed.'

'Last August. She's…' A distant figure emerged from the back door carrying a bowl on her hip, and made for the pigsty.

'That's Ruth.'

The two men regarded her. The March wind moulded her smock to her pregnancy, large and low on her narrow frame. She shifted the bowl from her hip and tipped its contents into the sty. Hand in the small of her back, she stretched and pushed her hair from her face, then lumbered back to the farmhouse.

Eli removed his pipe from between his teeth.

'Near her time.'

'Three weeks. We'll both be glad when it's over.'

'Near her time she is.'

A gust of wind blew down from the moor, and a door banged in the yard. Muddy grey clouds bore down on them from the north and a sullen yellow tinge rimmed the horizon.

Eli knocked out his pipe against his boot, and put it away in the depths of his ex-army greatcoat. He sniffed. 'Plenty a' wind up there. And snow.'

'You'd best stay then.'

'Naw, Mister. Get off the moor and go down one of the coast valleys. No snow there.'

Francis nodded, and looked down at the heap of fresh earth from the trench, mentally checking what he would need to do to secure the farm against the pending storm. When he looked up to offer him dinner, Eli had gone.

***

By the time all the jobs were done and the stock sheltered, the wind had strengthened, blowing colder. The yard was full of noise. Wind howled through gaps, blew hay and straw whirling into the air. Every door rattled and groaned, and a loose piece of corrugated iron on the haybarn roof flapped and slammed in each increasing gust. Coming out of the cowhouse after milking, Francis dodged a shower of rooftiles which missed his head by inches, to shatter on the cobbles. Maud and Dan had gone off to the cottage into the darkness half an hour ago, heads down into the gale. As Francis crossed the yard sleet knifed into his face, and he shut the door against the clamour with relief, looking forward to an evening by the fire.

'Francis!' Ruth called urgently from upstairs.' Bring a bucket, quick!'

'What is it, a leak?' He grabbed a bucket and raced upstairs. 'Where are you?'

'In our room. Hurry!'

She stood on the rug with fluid dripping from beneath her skirt.

'Is it the babby? I haven't just wet meself, I know it.'

He pushed the bucket under her and helped her to lower herself onto it.

'I'm not sure. Didn't they tell you at those classes of yours?'

He knew about sheep and cows and pigs, but not a lot about babies. 'Where's the booklet they gave you?'

He searched frantically in a drawer.

'It's in the top of me suitcase.'

He riffled through the pages. 'Here it is.' He read on, then looked up, eyes wide. 'Your waters have broken. The baby's definitely on the way, and you should go to hospital immediately, it says.'

'Oh!'

They stared at each other.

'I'm scared.'

'Try not to be. I'll get you there as quickly as I can. Pad yourself up with something, and I'll fetch the van up to the door. D'you think I ought to carry you downstairs?'

'Just get the van.'

It was snowing. Big sticky flakes whirled in the light from the doorway, and the wind drove them into his face as he ran to the van. It started first time, for a wonder. She waited by the door, bundled up against the cold, her face full of fear. He tucked her in as comfortably as he could, and set off down the farm track. Trying to miss the worst of the bumps and ruts, he fought the wheel, struggling to see past windscreen wipers that scarcely coped with the wet snow piling against them. The rear doors rattled, and the wind howled and blew gales round the unheated vehicle. They shivered in their thick coats.

Hurtling down the dip they heard a loud creaking and splintering that seemed to go on for ever. The trunk of a huge tree loomed in the snowy headlights – falling towards them. Francis had no chance to avoid it. He slammed on the brakes and the van slithered sideways into the hedge. The tree landed across the roof with a splintering, ear-splitting crash.

Silence. Broken by the tinkle of shards of glass falling to join the rest of the windscreen which had already showered them. Where Ruth sat, the roof had caved in inches above her head. The rest of the trunk stretched forward over the bonnet, the vast splay of roots and earth completely blocking the lane. The headlights blinked once and went out.

'Ruth?'

He reached for her in the darkness. 'Are you hurt? The baby?'

'I – don't think so.' Her voice was shaky. 'Francis, what are we going to do?'

He cradled her in his arms, and his mind began to function again. There was no way they could get through. Ruth couldn't possibly try to climb the hedge and into the fields to go round. Even if he left her here and reached Dan's cottage himself, he had no transport, no telephone. Already the snow had settled onto the bonnet of the van, and blew through the gaping windscreen onto them, wet and chill. They couldn't stay here – but they weren't far from home.

'We'll have to go back. Do you think you can walk ?'

'I think so.' She tried the door handle and it wouldn't budge. 'I can't get out!' she shrieked.

'Wait a minute.' Francis tried his door and it opened. 'You'll have to climb over to my side.'

He got out of the van, pushed his seat back as far as it would go and brushed away the broken glass with his hand. Ruth tried to lift herself across.

'It's no use. I'm stuck on the steering wheel.'

'Go back and start again. If you turn round onto your knees you'll do it. Hold on to the back of the seat. I'll help.'

She was halfway there when she stopped, rigid. 'Oow. My belly.'

The pain passed. She managed to scramble out, Francis half lifting her onto the muddy snow. He reached into the back of the van for the suitcase.

'I expect you'll need this.'

'Can't do without it,' she gasped.

Francis half carried her up the steep lane, arm under her shoulders and the suitcase in his other hand.

'I can't go no further.' She sagged against him.

'Take the case then, and hold tight.'

He swung her into his arms and attacked the snowy slope at as near a run as he could manage. Slipping and sliding, arms nearly out of their sockets, at last he reached first the gateway then the door, staggered up the stairs and rolled them both onto the bed.

For a while Francis lay gasping. Gradually his breathing eased and the tight pain in his chest released its grip.

'Ruth?'

Lost in a pain of her own, she groaned and clutched her abdomen. He didn't know when the last pain had been, but it was obvious things were moving fast, and with a thump of his heart he knew they were on their own.

When she was quiet again he said, 'You realise we'll have to deliver the baby ourselves?'

'I know,' she croaked. 'How long will it take?'

'Could be hours, could be quick – so we'd best start getting ready.'

'I should be in hospital.'

'Well you're not, but we'll manage. We'd best clean ourselves up first, then read your booklet.' He touched the scratches and cuts on her face from the broken windscreen. His own face smarted too.

As he read the booklet aloud to her, his confidence grew. It couldn't be so different from animal birth. Then doubts returned. There was the accident she'd just had, and she was only sixteen – how would she cope? Well, it'd happen somehow. He'd do his best and trust in Mother Nature – and he'd soon know whether the child was his or not. But he mightn't be able to tell – never know who was the father. What would he feel when he first saw the baby? He thrust the thoughts away. There was a job to do first.

'You should keep busy, and move about as long as you can,' he told Ruth slumped in the chair.

'Are you sure? Will it be safe?'

'Sheep and cows do. It's natural.'

'Me belly's so big I'm scared it won't be able to get out,' she wailed. 'I want me Ma-a-m!'

'Come on, get up.' He heaved her to her feet. 'Even if we did nothing, the baby'll come,' Please, he prayed.

***

'Here comes another.' Ruth sagged at the knees and clung to the bedstead. Francis rubbed her back. He cupped her belly with his other hand, felt the muscles harden. Contractions were every ten minutes now. He looked round the room. All was as ready as they could make it. The bed was piled high with pillows, and the carrycot stood near the fire where the glow of flames flickered over tiny white clothes warming on the hearth. This pain was lasting a long time.

'O-o, ow, oo…ow.' It turned into a shriek. He felt the taut mound relax. She buried her damp face in his shoulder. 'Can I get into bed now? I'm that tired.'

Francis helped her into bed, where she sank onto the pillows. He'd not seen her eyes look so dark against her chalky face.

'That were bad.' Her brow was beaded with sweat.

He mopped her brow and took her hand. This child-woman, the wife he scarcely knew, giving birth to a child he couldn't be sure was his.

'Can I have a drink of water?'

She sipped, wiped the dribble from her chin with her hand, and lay back with her eyes closed.

Not for long. 'Ooo-oo-oh!' She hung on to his hand squeezing and digging in her nails. 'U-uh. Want to push – u-uh-uh.'

'Try not to yet. You're doing fine. It won't be long now, I promise.'

'Ma – a – am.' Ruth grabbed the bedrail and screamed.

Francis peered between her legs.

'It's nearly here. I can see the head, with black hair. This is where you have to pant through the next contraction, remember?'

She nodded.

'Here it comes. Ready? Pant.'

They panted together. Slowly the disc of black hair grew and the baby's head emerged.

'Next time give a really big push.' He wiped the tight shut eyes.

There was a slither and a rush of fluid, and he found himself holding a tiny warm body.

'It's a girl! Oh, it's a girl!'

As if in response to his voice the baby opened her mouth and yelled, tiny pink tongue a-quiver.

'Oh, you little darling.'

She stopped crying and opened eyes of the darkest blue and fixed them on Francis's face. He fell in love.

'Here, let me see.' Ruth struggled to sit up.

He laid her tenderly on Ruth's empty belly.

'Eyugh! She'm all slimy and bloody, and what's that white stuff?' She drew back.

Francis picked up the infant, wrapped her in a towel and returned her to her mother. She took her this time and peered into the baby's features.

'Her face's all squashy – and look at her dear little nose. Are you sure she's a girl?' She opened the towel and closed it again quickly, horror-struck. 'There's a horrible twisty rope thing hanging out of her belly. What's wrong?'

Francis laughed. 'That's just the cord. I'll cut it in a minute. It won't hurt her.'

As soon as he was able, he cut the cord and dealt with the afterbirth. It was like an animal birth after all – it only needed someone else to help. They'd been lucky, though. Supposing something'd gone wrong?

He washed the baby by the fire, delighting in the feel of her silky skin and the scent of baby talc on his hands.

'Do you want to dress her, Ruth?'

'No, you do it. I'll watch.'

All went well until he got to the nappy. However he folded and pinned the terry square it fell off her tiny hips.

Ruth clutched her stomach. 'Don't make me laugh, it hurts. Just wrap it round and put the plastic pants on. I'spect they'll be too big too.'

He laid his daughter in the carrycot and caught his finger in her outstretched hand. His daughter. She was his now, whatever her beginnings had been. The baby's fingers closed round his, and he stayed like that for a while, too moved to speak.

Later, when Ruth was clean and comfortable and the room tidied, Francis became aware of the lowing of cows from across the yard. He yawned and stretched.

'Milking time.'

He peered through the curtains into a black and white world. 'It's stopped snowing, but it's deep. I'll have to clear a path to the cowhouse. No one'll be able to reach us for ages.'

He moved the carrycot near the bed. 'I'll do the milking, then I'll have earned a rest.' He leaned and kissed the sleeping baby's forehead, then took Ruth's face between his hands and kissed her on the lips.

'I'm proud of you, Ruth,' he said.

***

'Francis, she ain't got a name yet, ' Ruth greeted him when he returned.

'I've been thinking that, too.' He'd brought a breath of cold air in with him, and made up the fire before warming his hands at the flames. 'What would you like to call her?'

'Well, there was this story in True Romance, and the heroine was called Meriel. I think it's ever such a pretty name. But p'rhaps you fancy something better?'

'Meriel?' He looked down at the baby, snug in her shawl. She gave a little snort and he smiled. 'I like it. Yes. Meriel it is.' He picked her up, she opened one eye and blew a bubble. 'Do you like that, Meriel Durrant?'

'Give her to me, will you, and fetch me the paper bag in the top drawer there, please? We've got a surprise for you, me and Meriel.'

He came back with the package.

'Happy birthday, Francis! Go on, open it.'

'I'd forgotten all about my birthday. That's something we'll always share on the twelfth of March, my little maid,' he told the sleeping infant.

He opened the bag. There was a card decorated with golden glitter and fat satin roses. Inside in violet ink in big round letters was written *'To My Darling Husband, from your own wife, Ruth Durrant, xxxxxxxx.'*

'You chose this for me?'

'Yes, but it's from both of us. I didn't know Meriel was going to be here, so I couldn't put her name, even if I knew it. Open the present, go on.'

He drew from its tissue wrapping a porcelain figure of a foal. Golden brown with a white blaze, it stood on splayed legs each tipped with a tiny black hoof, its mane flopped over one bright eye. The foal looked as if it had just scrambled to standing for the first time, slightly startled, and ready for life.

'It's perfect, Ruth. Thank you doesn't seem enough.'

He stood the card and foal on the mantelpiece before turning again to Ruth and the baby. His heart was full as he gathered them both in his arms.

***

On a fine April day when Meri was six weeks old, Francis dressed her warmly in a knitted suit of white wool and pulled a bonnet over her black curls. He tucked her inside his coat and buttoned it close. It was Sunday afternoon, the quiet time when the farm was least busy. Maud and Dan, after helping with the morning chores had retired to their cottage to eat roast beef and apple dumpling. Ruth lolled on the big double bed, True Romances propped against her knees, with Tommy Steele belting out Singin' the Blues from the transistor.

Floss came running and they left the farmyard together. Francis strode surefooted up the deep wet lane which rose between moss-encrusted boulders and uncurling knubs of fern to the gate which led out onto the moor. The air was clean and fresh and Floss's black and white rump led the way over the springing grass. The baby jounced against Francis's chest and he could feel the warmth of her over his heart as he bounded up the long slope among stunted thorn bushes and golden flowered gorse.

'Gorse in bloom, kissing's still in fashion, Meri.' Remembering the old country saying, he bent his head and kissed her forehead under the white bonnet, and felt his lips bounce off her as he slipped on a tussock. One eye shone up at him from the nest where her cheek was creased against his shirt and her head braced by the firm fabric of his coat. She was quite safe, but he slowed his pace, glancing down now and then at the rosy face peeping out. Breasting the rise, he circumnavigated the bulk of the Jubilee Stone and stepped off the turf above onto its granite top.

Although the sunwarmed breeze still had a tingle in its edge, he unbuttoned his coat and released Meri into the protection of his arms.

'Here we are, my little maid.'

Standing tall on the ancient rock he could feel the springiness of new life in her body, and an answering surge of energy in his own. She waved her mittened hands as if trying to catch the sky, and wrinkled her face.

Francis laughed out loud, turned his back to the wind and sheltered her with his body, facing the landscape below. He knew she couldn't see far, but he told her about it all the same.

'Look, Meri. There's the sea – that wide bit of blue beyond the snaky yellowy river. It must be low tide, and we can see the mudbanks. Look at all those fields, laid out like little hankies, between the hedges. We'll look for primroses there soon, and cobnuts too in the autumn – if the squirrels don't get there first.'

At the sound of his voice she turned her head and watched his face and he believed she understood every word.

Warming to his theme, he continued. 'It's true, my little maid. We'll do all those things and more. We'll come up to the moor often, and you'll have all sorts of adventures like I did when I was a young 'un.' And when Rosamund was a little maid, a small voice reminded him. He nudged it away and continued. 'Sometimes it's cold and wild and cruel, others when the sun shines like today, there's no place better on earth.'

A buzzard hung in the sky, spread pinions sifting the air as it surveyed the ground.

'That's old man buzzard looking for his dinner. And there's the skylark. Hear his bubbly song? There he is – that tiny speck up there.'

He pointed, and Meri screwed up her eyes at the brightness. A tremendous feeling of love swept over him. He hugged her close, then grasping her firmly under her arms, swung her high into the sparkling air.

'Rosamund! Wherever you are, Rosamund,' he called. 'Do you see her? Do you see my beautiful daughter? This is Meri. Meriel Durrant.' He turned in each direction.

Only the song of the lark cascaded on the limitless sky, and the wind carried his voice away over the moor.

He caught the baby to him and buried his face in her coat. 'Perhaps you'll know her, one day,' he breathed into the milky warmth of her and the smell of wet wool where she had dribbled. Her eyes grew big, her mouth turned up at the corners, and he knew it wasn't wind.

He lowered himself into a familiar cranny in the rough surface of the rock, and propped Meri against his crooked knees, her feet in his lap. Rummaging in his pocket he brought out the penny whistle that had been silent since the last time he and Rosamund had been together on a different part of the moor, and put it to his lips. Floss returned from her explorations to curl beside them, and lilting notes of a Cornish tune went dancing over the moor. Meri watched his face and fingers until she blinked twice, and fell asleep.

***

That night, lying beside Ruth in the bed where he had been born, Francis thought about that afternoon. He hadn't planned to take Meri up to the moor, least of all hadn't planned to invoke Rosamund. Had he been disloyal to Ruth? Undoubtedly he had, but he felt no shame. He'd known as soon as he saw her face when she was half born that he had not fathered Meri. But she *was* his. She was his because she bore his name; because he had delivered her; because he changed her nappy, fed her, got up to her in the night; because he delighted in each fold of her satiny skin and the scent of her babyhood. And because he had fallen instantly and irrevocably in love with the little scrap. He had grown fond of Ruth as one might grow fond of a capricious child and tried to be a good husband, but by trapping him into marriage Ruth had stolen his hopes that one day he still might marry Rosamund, and in his heart he couldn't forgive her. But he would never regret Meri.

18

At last! Francis put the grease gun down beside the tractor and listened. The sound of a vehicle over-revving to change gear, and a few moments later Bill Nankivell's pre-war black Standard chugged in at the farmyard gate and pulled up in a scatter of squarks and hen feathers.

Shielding his eyes from the early evening June sunshine, Francis crossed the yard towards the car, and nodded at Bill. He, not offering to get out, sat with his window rolled down and reached a podgy hand out to remove a sprig of ash leaves caught on the wing mirror.

Francis could see Ruth in the back with three month old Meri bundled in her arms. He wiped his oily hands on the front of his overalls and opened the door for her. Ruth's face and legs emerged and he reached into the car to help her out.

'What happened? It's nearly six o'clock. Is something wrong?' he asked and peered anxiously among the folds of Meri's shawl. His daughter broke into a toothless gurgle at the sight of him.

'Hello, my little maid.' Reassured, he kissed her button nose.

Ruth hitched her bundle awkwardly in her arms, one corner of the shawl trailing in dusty. Floss lifted her nose to Meri and drew back her lips in a doggy grin.

'No, naught's wrong. I just didn't fancy pushen' the pram back up th'hill, an' up that horrible lane, so Dad give us a lift.' She extricated a lock of her hair from Meri's fist. 'Here, you take her.'

'I can't, I'm filthy.' He took a step back. 'You've left the pram at your mother's?'

Bill leaned out. 'Stands to reason. That lane id'n fit to drive a car up, never mind a 'spensive pram like that.'

Francis bit his lip. He didn't tell Bill that Ruth had spent all morning rubbing Mansion polish on the pram. She'd buffed it up with more vigour than he'd seen her use on anything in a long time, until she could see her face in it. Ever since the pram, the long awaited wedding present from her parents, had arrived soon after the birth, she'd been eager to show it off in the village. Until today it had only been used for a daytime sleeping place for Meri, its only outings round the farmyard. He'd planned to concrete the lane before the baby's arrival, but how was he to know it was going to be early? Since that snowy March day, bad weather and lambing had held up the work, although he'd managed to get almost half of the lane done. Today Ruth had been set on going down to her mother's with the pram.

'Just wait another week,' he'd begged her 'It'll be finished by then.' But she'd tossed her head, wouldn't listen. He'd worried all afternoon, with visions of the overturned pram, an injured Meri – even an injured Ruth – with no one near to help. It was a relief when he'd driven the tractor home up the lane just now not to find them lying there helpless.

'You coming in, Bill?' he asked with indifference as he picked up Ruth's bag.

'Naw. 'Tis nearly openen' time. Bye bye, maid. Come and give your old dad a big kiss.'

Ruth obliged with a wet smack. There was a wail of protest from Meri, squashed in the process.

Francis turned away in distaste. He supposed it wasn't fair, but he hated Ruth's visits to her parents, especially when she took Meri, which was mostly. He sighed. She was still only sixteen, and a young sixteen at that – in most things.

He followed her into the house.

'…Mam said as how I'd got the pram lovely, an' Annie at the shop saw me and waved. Oh, and I saw Gwen. She was some taken with the babby. She's beginning to show – due in October she is. She said Alan's thrilled at going to be a dad. And… Oh!' Ruth stopped in the kitchen doorway. 'Where am I supposed to put babby?'

Francis sighed. He seemed to be doing a lot of sighing these days.

'I'll fetch the carrycot down, but you'll have to hold her till I get cleaned up.'

The baby began to make small whimpering noises. Ruth sat in the big chair and looked about.

'Where's Maud to? I was hopen' she might have a bottle ready.'

'They went home ages ago.' He went into the scullery where he dragged off his overall. 'Didn't you take a feed with you?'

'I didn't think. Put the kettle on will you, before you go upstairs?'

That was another thing, thought Francis as he scrubbed his hands and arms. After the first few days Ruth wouldn't feed Meri herself – said it felt dirty. Besides, it hurt. He towelled himself dry, went back into the kitchen to pull the kettle onto the Rayburn hotplate to boil. Meri was crying properly now, and Ruth jigged her vigorously in her arms. When he brought the carrycot down, Ruth was trying vainly to mix a feed one-handed with the kicking screaming infant in her other arm.

He took the baby and put her up to his shoulder. 'Shush, shush my darling. Supper's coming.' He walked the room with her but unusually, she didn't quieten.

Ruth carefully measured scoops of National Dried Milk powder into a blue and white striped jug and poured on boiling water.

'Phwarghh! Ruth, when did you last change this child?'

She stopped stirring and wrinkled her brow. 'I don't know. Must 'a been afore I went to Mam's.'

He knew it was useless to comment, fetched a clean nappy and washing things and laid his daughter on the rug. He sponged the sore little bottom as gently as he could and smeared on zinc and castor oil cream. All the while he talked to her as if he were gentling a horse, and sang scraps of nonsense until she was all smiles again. He blew raspberries on her tummy, then tucked the terry napkin round in spite of her vigorous kicks, and pinned it firmly before pulling on frilly pink plastic pants. He'd got the knack of that now, but Ruth didn't always get it right still – then there were complaints about extra washing.

Most of the time she did try, but was easily discouraged. It didn't help that Meri often cried when Ruth was holding her, and seemed to sense her mother's lack of confidence. Francis had hoped that she would take to the baby in time, but it hadn't happened yet. He could usually find a surrogate mother when a ewe rejected her lamb, but he'd had to do his best himself for his daughter. Not that that was any hardship. From the moment she'd opened her eyes to the world and looked into his he'd adored her. Ruth had no idea what she was missing.

'Francis, will you feed her while I get us somepn' to eat?' Ruth called from the scullery where she was shaking the bottle of milk under the cold tap to cool.

He took the baby in the crook of his arm and settled in the Windsor chair. Comfortable now, she took the teat and sucked frantically at first. Her jaws worked and a dribble of milk ran from the corner of her mouth. Francis chuckled and eased the teat when she clamped too hard and stopped the flow of milk, to fill again with a rubbery swoosh. Soon she settled into a steady suck, and looked up into his face with serious eyes, and her tiny hand patted his big one where it curved round the bottle.

When Meri was asleep, Ruth and Francis finally ate their meal of cold ham and fried potatoes. Afterwards, Francis pulled his overalls on again and went back into the yard to finish greasing the tractor and do the evening rounds. He returned to find Ruth curled in the big chair with one of her interminable True Romance magazines, the carrycot beside her.

He stood wide-legged and stretched his arms up to the blackened beams, and yawned hugely.

Ruth laid down her magazine and came to stand in front of him. She put her arms round his waist and snuggled into his neck.

Francis snapped out of his stretch.

'Can't a man even have a good stretch? What d'you have lined up for me now?'

He held her shoulders and looked into provocative pale eyes almost on a level with his, her head on one side, wheedling.

'Nothing, Francis. I know I don't always do things right, an' I couldn't manage without you, but I do love you, you know.'

'I know you do, but I shouldn't have to be thinking of the things you should be doing for Meri as well as all my other work. I don't ask much of you on the farm – it's the least you can do.'

He linked his hands behind her back and rocked with her from side to side.

'I do try, honest. But I thought Maud would have been here more – to help me like.'

'That's a bit thick, especially when she and Dan are newlyweds. Besides, she's already done her duty raising me.'

And Rosamund, he thought. I know Mother would have helped more, she loves having a granddaughter, but she also believes in not interfering, letting Ruth find her own way. Only she isn't, he thought with a touch of bitterness. Dan doesn't want Mother too involved either. 'Let the young folk get on with their own lives. I waited too long for you to share you now, my 'andsome – and they've got longer than we have, God willing', he'd said.

Ruth twisted a copper curl in the open neck of his shirt round her finger and rubbed herself against him like a cat.

Francis suddenly felt unutterably tired. He took her wrists and pushed her from him.

'I'm going to have half an hour with a book, then I'm going to bed.' He picked up The Cruel Sea from the dresser and settled in the chair she had just vacated. 'How about making some cocoa for us both?'

He looked at the cover with its illustration of heaving sea and livid sky. 'I feel like a bit of escapism,' he said as he opened the book at the page he'd marked, and began to read.

Soon the book drooped in his hand and his eyes closed.

19

ROSAMUND

Leadersfield 1957.

Rosamund went with Helen to stay at her home near Whitby for a week, and was welcomed into a warm noisy family who accepted her easily. They played cricket in the garden with Helen's younger brothers, went for picnics on the moors, and spent a glorious day on a beach backed by high bare cliffs, with a sparkling sea and the familiar cry of gulls. They returned to Leadersfield bronzed and happy, Rosamund feeling more carefree than she had done for years.

At breakfast before their first duty after the holiday, Sandra was bursting with news.

'Amy's fallen in love with a patient.' She sat back to watch the effect of her words.

'Never!'

'She hasn't!' Rosamund and Helen chorused.

'Hook, line and sinker. He was an emergency appendix brought in last week. Sister sent Amy to shave him for theatre, and she came out all starry eyed.'

'I can't believe it. Amy in love. What's he like?' Helen wanted to know.

'Quite nice actually. Dark hair with a quiff, pale skin, dark eyes. He's fallen for her too. It's Amy's day off today, so you won't see her till tomorrow.'

'It's lucky I'm on the same ward. I must inspect this young man – it'll be very interesting,' chuckled Rosamund, swinging her cloak across her shoulders as she made for the door.

Rosamund pushed the dressing trolley down the ward looking for the next name on her list. She hadn't had a chance to go round the patients yet, as she'd had to relieve on B ward until coffee break. Ah, here it was. Cyril Bottomly, Appendicectomy. Remove Sutures. Perhaps this was Amy's beloved.

It was. Just as Sandra had described him. The young man with a dark quiff lay with headphones over his ears, eyes closed. Rosamund stood at the foot of the bed, unbelieving. The dark lashes fluttered and his eyes opened. Recognition dawned and his eyes mirrored the shock she knew was in her own.

It was Ace.

She looked away and checked the bed chart, her heart pumping wildly. 'Cyril Bottomly?'

He nodded.

She felt sick. What on earth should she do? This man had all but raped her. She didn't know if she could bear to touch him, remove his sutures. And Amy, her friend, had fallen in love with him. What a mess.

'Your stitches are due out today.' She forced herself to speak to him.

He didn't reply, and she could feel him watching her as she parked the trolley beside the bed and went to fetch the screens. She would behave as if she had never seen him before, she decided. But could she? Her flesh crawled as she remembered the cruel buckle, and the weight of him on her. She turned down the sheet quickly, before she lost her nerve.

'Will you undo your pyjamas please?'

He obeyed, fumbling the cord, to reveal the dressing on the right side of his lower abdomen. She loosened the dressing.

'I'm just going to wash my hands.' No reply.

She adjusted her face mask and stood at the sink with trembling knees, then soaped and scrubbed her hands and arms over and over. He had recognised her too. Whatever else, he must be worried that she might tell Amy. She felt a sudden surge of confidence. He was the vulnerable one, lying there uncovered. He'd have to submit to her scissor-wielding hands. If she didn't look at his face she could manage. He's just a patient who had an appendectomy, she decided.

Before her resolve could waver she returned to his bedside, elbowed the screens together and picked up the forceps. He lay with his head averted while she set to work with only slightly trembling fingers. Black stubble was beginning to grow across his pubic area, and she felt her cheeks grow hot as she remembered what lay beneath the dressing towel across his groin. It's harmless now, she told herself severely. She was careful not to cut him, but it did cross her mind as she snipped away at the stitches that she didn't have to be particularly gentle – could pay him back – just a little. Don't be stupid, she chided herself, do it properly just as you always do.

It was done at last, and he hadn't winced once. She laid the sutures, looking like a collection of dead flies, on a piece of white gauze on the locker beside him.

'Just a memento, Mr Bottomly,' she murmured, and took the dressing trolley away.

***

'You seem glum, Roz. What's up?' Helen pulled her cloak closer about herself as the two of them walked over to the Nurses' Home for dinner, their caps bobbing in the wind.

'I'm not glum really, but…' Then with a rush, 'I've met Amy's boyfriend this morning. And you'll never guess. It's Ace.'

'Ace? You mean the one who…?'

'Yes. The one who… Alias Mr Cyril Bottomly. No wonder he had to find a fancy name for himself.'

'Roz! What did you do?'

'I took out his sutures, just like I was supposed to. I don't know how I did it. I was shaking inside, but there was nothing else I could do.'

'No, I suppose not.' Helen was thoughtful. 'Hey, you didn't 'accidently' nick him, did you? I think I would have done.'

'I thought about it, believe me. No, I thought it'd be better if I acted as if I'd never met him before.'

'Did he recognise you?'

'Yes. He didn't speak at all. I should think he'll be worried about what I'll tell Amy.'

'What will you tell her? She's bound to ask.'

'I don't know. I don't want to burst her lovely bubble when she's only just found her Prince Charming, but I can't let her think I like him, can I? I'll have to wait and see what happens.'

'I can't get over how you coped. I think I'd have gone to pieces.'

'I would have in the past. I nearly panicked, but having a job to do helped.' Rosamund's voice faltered. 'I was sick afterwards, and my stomach's still churning.' They had arrived at the dining room door, and Helen went to push it open. Rosamund hung back. 'Go on in, I'm not hungry.' She turned away towards the stairs. 'At least I don't have to face Amy until tomorrow.'

***

'What do you think, then?' Amy demanded the next day. She looked almost pretty, Rosamund thought, with sparkling eyes, and even her freckles seemed to have taken on a glow.

'I've met him before, Amy,' Rosamund said. 'At the Jester. He used to come in with a bunch of other boys and girls. I knew him as Ace.'

'Oh.' Amy was taken aback.

'Yes. They used to come in for coffee and play the jukebox. He was leader of the gang.'

'I'm not surprised. He's a grand chap is my Cyril, none better. But what do you make of him?'

This was the difficult one, but she had to tell the truth somehow. 'He's not my cup of tea, but he's obviously yours. I'm happy for you, Amy.' Rosamund knew it sounded lame, but it was the best she could do.

Amy looked at her closely. 'I've no competition from you then?'

'None at all. He did take a bit of a shine to me once, but I was never interested.'

She looked directly back at Amy, who after a moment seemed satisfied.

'That's all right then. I expect he'll tell me about it.'

***

Cyril was discharged next day, much to Rosamund's relief. The romance continued to grow, followed with bemused fascination by friends and colleagues, who couldn't have imagined man-hating Amy in this state.

'How are the mighty fallen.' Helen laughed.

'I think she really loves him.' Sandra, who spent a good deal of her spare time with Rosamund and Helen, now Amy was otherwise occupied, commented earnestly. 'She clucks after him like a mother hen.'

'Have you seen how his eyes shine when he looks at her?' asked Helen. 'I saw them in a clinch last night when he brought her back. Passionate it was.'

'She certainly seems to have tamed him.' Rosamund spoke without thinking, and the others looked at her, surprised.

'What do you mean?' Sandra jumped on her words. 'D'you know something we don't?'

'He has a bit of a reputation, that's all. He was a great one for the girls before.' She caught Helen's eye. 'And look what he's done to Amy. Britain's last bachelor girl bites the dust.'

They all laughed.

'I have to let her in through the fire escape most nights now. She used up her quota of late night passes ages ago.' Sandra paused. 'I wonder how long it'll last?'

But within a month Amy sported a sparkling ring on her left hand, and on a blue and gold day in late October she and Cyril were married in a blaze of chrysanthemums at Shutt End church, while Rosamund was unavoidably on duty. Amy moved out of the Nurses' Home and came to work each day from the terraced brick house they rented in Shutt End Road. There was a warm welcome for her friends at the little house in their off duty hours, and on the whole Cyril got on well with them. None of them noticed how little Rosamund visited, and when she did it was always with others. She and Amy were not entirely comfortable with each other now, although nothing was ever said, and she took care to go only when she knew Cyril would not be there.

***

It was 1958 and springtime, the third one of their training, and love was in the air again. Rosamund and Helen were sitting in the sun on the grass outside the nurses' home, ostensibly revising for a test.

'Have you seen the new houseman on surgical?' Helen sounded excited.

Rosamund looked up from her paediatric textbook. 'No. What's he like?' She was used to Helen's enthusiasm for a new male face.

'Absolutely gorgeous.'

'Aren't they all – for five minutes? What's special about this one?'

Helen considered. 'I don't really know. He just is.'

Rosamund put her book down. 'Is what?'

'Oh, he's not what you'd call handsome, but there's something about him' She paused. 'He's got really nice shaped ears. I noticed because I was standing near him on the ward round. And when I dropped the casenotes he helped me pick them up, and gave them back to me with a smile that went right through me.'

'What's his name?'

'Doctor Wheatley. He's got fine fairish hair that falls in his eyes, and looks to have a rather sporty shape under his white coat.'

Rosamund chortled. 'You did have a good look. Anything else.'

'Sister kept giving me dirty looks, so I had to try and seem interested in the ward round. I did notice he needed a haircut. He smiled at me again when they left the ward.'

'Do you think he'll ask you out?'

'I hope so.'

***

He did, again and again. Helen talked of nothing but Philip, and Rosamund saw that this might indeed be 'it' for Helen. She had never seen her like this and was glad for her. She scarcely saw her these days.

'What are you doing tonight, Helen?' she asked hopefully. She hadn't had a night out for ages.

'Playing tennis with Philip. Why?'

'I wondered if we might have gone to the pictures.'

'Sorry, but it's arranged. I'll come next week maybe. We'll fix something when Philip's on duty and we're both off.'

Rosamund said nothing. She wasn't jealous, but was beginning to feel lonely. She and Helen had been close for a long time, and she missed her.

'Look, Roz,' Helen said after a moment. 'Why don't you come too? Philip and I don't have to be on our own all the time. Yes, do come. I'll get Philip to bring along Dr Smith's new houseman to make up a foursome. He's called Neil something or other, and Philip says he's rather a charmer – we could all go for a drink afterwards. What do you think?'

'That's when I get left with the charming Neil, is it? Okay, I'll give it a try. It's years since I played tennis, though. Be warned.'

***

The four of them met at the tennis courts in the hospital gardens.

'Roz, this is Neil Sinclair. Neil, Rosamund Hambly, my best friend.'

He was tall and thin, and as she looked up into his face she caught a sudden flare of interest in his eyes. Then as suddenly it was gone and the grey eyes were mild, his handshake firm and dry.

He smiled down at her. 'Hello,' he said in a light pleasant voice, 'You're on Women's Surgical are you no'? I've noticed you coming back from theatre.'

Rosamund relaxed. He seemed unthreatening, with irregular features and an already receding hairline. He looked a bit older than the other housemen.

'That's observant of you. I haven't played tennis for years, so I hope I can give you a decent game.'

'Och, I'm sure we'll get on fine. I shouldn't think those two love birds'll care anyway, but we'll give them a run for their money.'

She enjoyed the game. She had never been a wonderful player (Francis had been the one with all the crack shots), but she didn't disgrace herself. Neil was pleasant and friendly, and they settled into a reasonable parnership, in spite of which in the end, Helen and Philip won easily.

'No doubt due to their prior experience as partners,' Neil observed to Rosamund as they collected their sweaters.

'I heard that,' called Philip with an embarassed laugh. The remark produced a deep blush from Helen, much to Rosamund's amusement.

***

'What did you think of him? Neil, I mean.' Helen asked later as they prepared for bed.

'He seems okay – easy to get on with. It's quite refreshing to go out with someone who doesn't make a pass at me. He was fun, in a quiet way.'

'That Scottish accent's attractive, isn't it? I think he rather liked you.' Helen looked sideways at Rosamund.

'You're matchmaking again, Helen. Stop it.'

'All right, all right. He's only being brotherly, that's what it is – I don't think!'

Rosamund choked. If you only knew, she thought.

***

A few days later Rosamund was washing black stockings in the bathroom after supper.

'Ha-a-mbly,' a voice called from the hall below, 'Telepho-o-ne.'

She dried her hands and rushed downstairs. She had never had a telephone call before in all the time she had been here. Whoever could it be? Her hands were shaking as she picked up the phone.

'Hello?' she said cautiously.

'Rosamund. Neil Sinclair here.'

She subsided against the wall in relief. She'd had the wildest, impossible thoughts. But it was only Neil.

'Rosamund? You still there?'

'Yes. Hello Neil. What a surprise.'

'I hope it's a nice one. I was thinking – it was good to meet you and play tennis last Tuesday.'

'Yes. I enjoyed it too.'

'Well. I wondered if you'd like to go for a drink sometime. There's a wee pub just down the road I like the look of. I haven't had chance to get about at all since I arrived, so I don't know what it's like. Would you care to try it with me?'

'Oh, I don't know…'

'When are you off next? I'm wondering about tomorrow evening?'

'I am on early, but I've promised to visit Mrs Wilson – a friend of mine. No, definitely not tomorrow.'

'How about next Wednesday then? I've got time off in the evening again.'

'The off-duty isn't up yet for next week. If you could ring again tomorrow after nine-thirty…'

'Better still I'll meet you off the ward. You're still on Women's Surgical, aren't you?'

'Yes. How did you know?'

'Aha. I've seen you around. Well, what about it?'

'All right.'

'See you tomorrow then.'

***

Helen was not surprised when Rosamund burst into their room to tell her.

'I thought he'd taken a shine to you. Are you going?'

'It looks as though I am. I seem to have agreed to meet him to arrange a time. How peculiar.'

'Do you want to, that's the thing?'

'Ye-es. I think perhaps I do – 'though I hope he's not going to be pushy. It'll put me off if he is,' she reflected. 'Goodness, I've left my black stockings in the bathroom sink. I'd better go and rescue them.'

***

Neil met her at the hospital gates and they walked together down the hill to the Talbot Inn.

He seated her at a small round table and went to the bar for their drinks. It was a working man's pub, with a plain wooden floor and an assortment of yellowed photographs and prints, mostly of greyhounds, on the walls. She was the only female there, and was the subject of covert glances from the half dozen or so men with pale coal-pocked faces who were drinking and playing dominoes in the smoke filled room.

'Here you are. Lemonade you said?' Neil put a glass in front of Rosamund and sat down beside her with a pint of beer.

Rosamund felt shy. She realised she had never done this before – sat in a pub with someone she didn't know. She fiddled with the toggle on her duffle coat, not knowing what to say.

'It's quite a nice little pub, isn't it?' Neil took a drink. 'I'm glad they haven't done it up. At least it's past the spit and sawdust era.' He glanced at Rosamund, who still felt uncomfortable. 'Is your drink all right?'

Rosamund managed a smile and took a sip. 'Yes, it's fine thanks.'

'I remember being in bars in back streets in Edinburgh a bit like this.'

'Is that where you're from, Edinburgh?'

'No, but I was at med school there. I'm from Dunoon. My parents have a croft on the hills near there.'

'I was brought up partly on a farm in Cornwall,' she volunteered, then wished she hadn't.

'So that's the pretty accent. I couldn't place it. You've only a trace though.'

'What brought you to medicine?' she asked, not wanting to be drawn into conversation about her past.

'When I was a wee lad, my dad was ill for a while and the doctor had to call often. When he'd finished with Dad, he used to take me with him on the remainder of his rounds. I'd wait in the car while he made visits, and between calls he told me stories about his work. It made me want to be a doctor too. I particularly liked the stories about the high jinks the medical students got up to during their training.' He lifted his eyebrows and rolled his eyes. When Rosamund didn't respond, he went on. 'He was canny, was Doc Henderson. I reckon he set out to brainwash me.'

'What did your parents say?' Rosamund had relaxed against the settle back.

'Och, it wasn't easy. Mum was all right. She read doctor and nurse romances so it all sounded glamorous to her. But Dad wasn't keen. I used to practice on our animals. Dad said I should be a vet if I was going in for curing. I'd be more use to him with animals, he said. He really wanted me to work on the croft with him, and we had words about it. He came round in the end, and he's proud of me now.'

'But why come all this way for a job? Surely doctors are needed in Scotland nearer home.'

'That's just it. I wanted to get away from crofting. It's hard frustrating work, and the weather's mostly against you. I'd had a taste of Edinburgh life and thought I'd try my luck further south. Look for somewhere I liked enough to settle. How about you? Why did you come north?'

'I came to Leadersfield after a broken engagement, and started nursing when I recovered from a road accident.'

'Don't you miss Cornwall?'

'Of course I do, but I'm fine here. I have good friends and I love my work.'

'I can see you do.' Neil looked at her intently. He held her gaze for a moment then picked up his empty glass. 'Another drink?'

She hesitated.

'Why not try something different, a Babycham or something. You know, the one in the advert on television where a baby deer drinks out of a champagne glass…'

'And when it drinks a bubble bursts on its nose – "ting".' They both laughed. 'Yes, I'll try a Babycham.'

They sat on in the pub and talked. More people arrived, some of them she recognised.

'You do realise that the whole hospital will know by tomorrow that we've been here together?' Neil asked.

'If not before! The grapevine's very efficient. The truth will be distorted, no doubt.'

'The truth being…?'

'That we're just out for a quiet evening's chat, and that's all there is to it.'

'Ah,' he said.

***

It was the first of many such evenings. Sometimes Helen and Philip came with them and they were partners at tennis from time to time. Sandra was going out with a radiographer, and Amy of course was at home with her Cyril, so Rosamund was glad to have company.

She was sitting on her bed darning black stockings and listening to Radio Three on her portable radio. She smiled to herself as she remembered the previous evening. She had taken Neil to the Jester after the pictures, and she could see that Susan was impressed. A new bunch of young people clustered round the jukebox, and she regaled him with stories of her time there to the tune of, 'One o'clock, Two o'clock, Three o'clock, Rock,' and endless Elvis records, with the familiar hiss of the Gaggia in the background. It had been raining, and the smell of damp clothes mingled with the aroma of coffee. She'd felt her cheeks glow in the steamy atmosphere, and had become aware of the gleam in Neil's eyes as he listened and watched her face. And chose to ignore it.

There was a knock on the door and Sandra's head appeared.

'You busy? I've brought your book back.' She put a purple-and-yellow-backed copy of Doctor Zhivago on the bed. 'I don't know how you can listen to this classical stuff.' She covered her ears in mock horror.

'A dose of Dr Mozart never did any one any harm.' She chuckled as she picked up the book and added it to a stack of others. 'Thanks. What did you think of it?'

'Couldn't make head nor tail of it. It's a bit long for me anyway, so I didn't finish it. I'd sooner have Red Letter any day. I like a nice romance.' She prowled about Rosamund's dressing table, inspected her face cream, squirted herself with Blue Grass, then picked up the post card tucked into the edge of the mirror. "Table Mountain',' she read. 'From your sister?'

'Mm,' Rosamund bit off a thread. 'They're on holiday there – or were. I expect they'll be back in Jo'berg now.' She turned the wireless down. 'What do you want, Sandra? It's obvious you didn't come just to return my book. You've had it for months. There must be something else on your mind?'

Unable to prevaricate longer Sandra blurted, 'How are you getting on with your new boyfriend?'

'I might have guessed. If you mean Neil, he isn't my boyfriend.'

'You'd have fooled me.'

'He's just a friend,' she insisted.

'It looked more than that the way he was dancing with you at the students' hop.'

'Oh come off it, Sandra,' she laughed, 'and what were you doing with your tame radiographer – James isn't it? Seriously, there's nothing between us.'

Then she coloured as she remembered the kiss he had given her on her cheek when he said goodnight after the dance. A gentle kiss, but lingering.

***

Soon she found herself daydreaming about him. Going about the hospital she hoped she would meet him – in the corridors, on the wards, anywhere. Stacking clean laundry in the linen room she saw in her mind's eye the way his hair swept back from his temples. Cleaning bedpans in the sluice, she remembered the wiry tuft that showed in the open neck of his shirt. After a game of tennis she sniffed for the scent of his sweat when she saw the damp patch down the back of his shirt, and sitting beside him in the gloom of the cinema she was aware of his thigh muscles under the taut material of his trousers, and felt the warmth of his breath on her hair as he spoke.

***

'When are you off duty next, Rosamund?'

They were leaning over the parapet of a bridge watching a froth of industrial waste float into the murky depths under the bridge, while traffic roared behind them.

'At the weekend. Why?'

'Would you like to go to Haworth?'

'Where the Bronte sisters lived? I've read about it, but I didn't realise it was near here. I'd love to go.'

'It's not too far away, and Philip says we can borrow his car. I don't think I could run to a restaurant as well as petrol, but we could take a picnic and go on Saturday for the day, if you'd like that.'

'I've not much money either, but I could probably manage a cup of coffee and a bun for us. Yes, I'll really look forward to it. It's a place I've wanted to visit ever since I read Wuthering Heights. There are moors there, aren't there? Oh, it would be good to smell moorland air again.'

'Haworth on Saturday it is. Let's hope for good weather.'

20

She nearly called it off, said she had to go to Mrs Wilson's or Amy's, anything. In spite of the fact that he had made no move, Rosamund was aware that tension had built between them. She knew that this day out with Neil would change their relationship.

Do I want this to happen? she asked herself. It would be losing faith with Francis. But what was the point of saving herself for something she could never give him. What was it the priest had said? Think of Francis as my brother and allow myself other relationships? Something like that. She sighed. I won't fight it, she decided in the end. 'Que Sera Sera' as the song says, whatever will be, will be. And if nothing does happen it won't be the end of the world.

***

They arrived safely at Haworth in Philip's old Morris, and parked at the bottom of the village near the station. Neil took a knapsack out of the boot and slung it on his shoulder.

'Lunch,' he explained as Rosamund eyed it.

'Perhaps we'd better have that coffee I promised us first,' she said.

They climbed the steep main street with its grey stone houses and old fashioned shops. Near the top where the sign for the Black Bull came into view they found a café, and Rosamund kept her word.

'That was good coffee, not to speak of the Yorkshire parkin.' Neil put down his empty cup. 'What would you like to do first, Rosamund?'

She said promptly, 'Visit the Parsonage where the Brontes used to live.

It's a museum now. Did you know that Mrs Bronte was a Cornishwoman from Penzance?'

'Was she really? Is that where you're from?'

'No, it's miles away.' She didn't want to talk about home.

'We'll get a guide book at the museum, for the walk to the moors afterwards.' Neil slid her a long look. 'That is – if you still want to go there.'

Rosamund didn't answer.

At the Parsonage at the top of the hill they lingered in all the rooms, Rosamund moved by the personalities and inner lives of the Bronte children shown in their childish writings and pictures, and the artifacts of their daily lives.

'Think of them clustered together round this table and beside the hearth on those bleak Yorkshire evenings, Emily, Charlotte and Anne, and brother Branwell.'

'What an imagination you have.' Neil put an arm companionably round her shoulders.

'When our house was sold after Pa died it felt empty, soulless. Even though the Brontes have been dead and gone for years, their imprint is still here. People are still interested in the family, and want to know how they lived.' She saw him looking at her with raised eyebrows. 'I suppose it's not the same really. But it reminds me.' She heard herself chattering, trying to keep everything normal.

'Och, come on. Don't be so serious.' Neil laughed and gave her a squeeze. 'Let's look at the church, then walk up to the moor. See if we can find Charlotte by the Bronte Waterfall and Emily at Top Withins. No doubt brother Branwell will be at the Black Bull, but he can wait. The sun's shining.'

She wasn't in the mood for the church. It seemed dark and gloomy to Rosamund after the brightness outside. The Parsonage was much nicer, even with all those gravestones crowded up to the garden wall, she decided.

A narrow paved path led across the field behind the Parsonage in the direction of the moors.

'Can you imagine the three sisters in crinolines and bonnets dancing daintily from stone to stone like this?' she said taking exaggerated steps.

'You mean from cowpat to cowpat?' Neil caught her as she overbalanced trying to avoid one.

She laughed up into his face. 'I expect they wore stout boots, even if they were unladylike.'

Neil held on to her, and held her gaze for a long moment. Feeling suddenly shy, she broke his hold and leapt ahead crying 'To the moors.' In the distance a curlew echoed her call.

The track curved round the hillside away from the village, and soon all signs of habitation were left behind. The track descended to a steep narrow valley, where a stream chuckled and gurgled silver between bracken banks and berried rowan trees. They stopped to consult the guide, Neil standing close behind Rosamund to look over her shoulder, his head close to hers.

'There's the Bronte bridge.' He pointed down the path. 'We go over it and take the path up the hill.'

They crossed the stone bridge and started to climb towards the heather clad heights. Rosamund flung back her head and breathed in the moorland air, feeling her hair lift in the breeze. Her eyes sparkled as she recognised familiar scents. She spread her arms and broke into a run up the steep track towards the ruined building she could see just below the skyline.

Neil slung the knapsack over his shoulders and followed at a lope, caught up in Rosamund's excitement. She had to stop to get her breath, laughing, and turned towards the sun to wait for him to catch up with her. In the brightness her vision blurred, and for an instant, it was Francis who was climbing towards her. Her heart missed a beat, then he stumbled as a stone skidded underfoot.

'Damn!'

It was Neil again. A cloud shadow passed over them, darkening the hillside, and Rosamund felt cold. A wave of homesickness broke over her. These were not the moors of home. She looked up and around at the purple hills, and thought of Heathcliff wandering these heights in his hopeless love for Cathy. A yearning and a wildness filled her, a restlessness that made her leap away again, breaking away from the track across the open moor, where heather scratched her legs and the clean wind blew in her face. She could hear Neil behind her, feet pounding the peaty ground. On and on she went, running towards – she didn't know what. The yearning grew and grew, and light splintered into a myriad colours as blood drummed in her temples.

He caught up with her in a turfy hollow fringed with bell heather and cotton grass. She turned to face him, breathing hard, feeling her hair cling damply about her face as sweat beaded her top lip. He halted in front of her, panting, grey eyes looking deep into hers. Slowly he reached out and drew her into his arms. She closed her eyes as his head blotted out the sky, and he lowered her onto the springing turf.

When at last they drew apart, Rosamund began to weep. Great tearing sobs wrenched her as she rolled away and lay face down on the grass. Her tears dripped between the leaves and slid down tawny stalks into the earth.

'My God, this was your first time? Why did you no' say?' Neil was bewildered. He knew girls often wept the first time they made love, but this was something different. 'Have I hurt you, Rosamund?'

'No. I mean, yes a bit. But it's not that.'

'Then what is it?' He leaned over and stroked her hair. She looked up with a red and swollen face.

'I don't know. I can't explain. Please leave me alone.'

Neil looked hurt, but he left her and climbed a little way up the hillside and stood with arms folded looking out across the valley.

Rosamund sat up where he had left her, still crying quietly. She was conscious of a strange feeling of relief, overlaid too with sadness and regret. This was not how it had been meant to be. She looked at the flattened grass where they had lain, and felt she had written the last words of a chapter. Neil was sitting now, profile outlined against the sky, elbows on knees, chin in his hands, and she felt a tingle of excitement at the thought of what had just happened between them. He had been ardent and exciting, and she felt no wrong in what they had done. This had to be the beginning of a new chapter. She dried her tears and climbed up to kneel beside him.

'Sorry, Neil,' she whispered in his ear. 'I'm all right now.'

He turned with relief, put his arms round her waist and buried his head in her breast.

'Thank God. I thought it must be me. Oh Rosamund, that was wonderful. You've no idea how I've longed for you, but you seemed untouchable – until today.'

'Yes, well…' a smile hovered round Rosamund's lips. 'Today is another story, isn't it?' She tugged at his hands, 'Let's go on, up to Top Withins and see if we can lay any more ghosts.'

Neil looked puzzled, but allowed himself to be pulled to standing.

They climbed hand in hand to the ruin which legend had was the inspiration for Wuthering Heights. It was as bleak and lonely as the the book described, and they didn't linger in the deserted landscape. They had meant to picnic there, but Neil suggested going back to the hollow where they had made love.

'No. I'd like to eat by the Bronte Waterfall. It's somewhere near the bridge I think.'

'Right you are. We'll go back to the waterfall. On one condition.'

'What's that?'

'I'll tell you when we get there.'

They found a spot further upstream from the waterfall, but where they could still hear its music. It was hot, and bees hummed in the heather, and after they had eaten Rosamund drowsed in the sunlight.

Something tickled her face and she brushed it away, then opened her eyes to see Neil laughing down at her. He was lying on one elbow with a piece of bracken in his teeth, and it was with that that he was touching her face.

'About that condition.' He transferred the bracken to his hand and began to stroke her with the tip. He stroked first her cheek, her neck, then her arms with the frond. Rosamund sighed with pleasure, and he leaned over to kiss her deeply. The bees still sucked nectar in the heather, larks quivered overhead and time stood still as they lay together in the languid afternoon. There were no tears this time, and she stayed in his arms relaxed and sated. She revelled in the scent of his body and the feel of the sun on her skin, and the long line of his flank, which was all she could see without moving.

They lay until bracken shadows reached out to rouse them, and the heat haze turned to violet smudges on the edge of the hills. Arm in arm they followed the stony track back to Haworth, and past the Parsonage.

Rosamund murmured, 'Poor Emily. How could she have written with such passion and never have known it herself?'

'Maybe she did,' said Neil. 'Who knows.'

***

Rosamund could scarcely believe what had happened to her. It didn't take long for Helen to spot it though.

'So Neil finally came up to scratch did he, Roz?'

Rosamund managed to look puzzled.

'Oh come off it, Roz – it's written all over you. It took him long enough. Phil and I were practically laying bets on how long it would take. That day when you went to Haworth was it?'

'How did you guess? I didn't even know for sure that anything would happen at all. But I'm glad it did.'

'Are you, Roz? Are you really? You've got over your Cornish boyfriend?'

Rosamund stilled, looking inwards. 'It's not like…' she ventured with caution. 'This is different.'

'How?'

'Just – different.'

'Hiya, you two.' Amy slung her bag on a chair and sat down beside them. 'What's for dinner today?' She inspected their plates. 'Dumplings, goody goody. What's new then?'

'Rosamund's got a boyfriend.'

'O-oh, that balding houseman? The patients were talking about him.'

'Stop it Amy, he's not bald.' Rosamund protested, flushing scarlet.

'Like that, is it? Well, you know what they say about bald men.'

'What do they say about them?' Helen spluttered over her greens.

Amy gave them a wicked look. 'You'd better ask Rosamund. No doubt she's found out for herself by now.'

So the cat was out of the bag, and Rosamund didn't try to hide how she felt. She spent all the time she could with Neil, she didn't care how her friends teased her. She had discovered a new world, a world of the senses which she believed existed, but had given up all hope of exploring without Francis. Now Neil filled her with an intensity of pleasures, new and exciting.

Both of them waited anxiously after that first time for her next period, but all was well. After that they took precautions. So she floated through the weeks on a tide of desire and fulfilment, scarcely noticing any time spent away from Neil eating and sleeping, and the work she loved was now done in a dream.

***

'It's the Finals in three weeks, Roz.' Helen sounded worried.

'Is it?' she answered dreamily.

'And I haven't seen you doing much studying.'

'Thanks for your concern, but I really don't want to know, Helen. I do look at my books – sometimes. I'm sure it'll be all right.'

'But you spend so much time with Neil … .'

'So what? Stop fussing. I know what I'm doing.'

'Do you?' Helen muttered under her breath. 'I do hope so.'

***

'Helen's been on at me about the exams,' Rosamund told Neil. Early autumn scents drifted through the blue September evening as they strolled, arms about each other, in a country lane near the hospital.

'Mm,' he murmured and nibbled her ear. 'What about them?'

'They're soon, Neil, and she thinks I should be revising.'

'Oughtn't you to be, then? Helen's usually right.' He transferred his lips to the back of her neck.

'I have a peek at a book now and then. What I don't know now I'll never know, as they say.' Rosamund halted, twisted round in his arms and looked up at him. 'What's more important is – do you realise that…'

'When did you say your exams are?'

'In three weeks. October the…'

'October? Good Lord. My housemanship's up soon. I thought I had ages yet.'

Rosamund went cold.

'You'll be leaving!'

'Not necessarily. I could go back to Scotland , but there's a place for a gynae man coming up here. Maybe I'll try for that.'

'I could come with you to Scotland – after I qualify, of course.'

'Och, we don't want to have to think about that yet.'

'What's going to happen to us, Neil? I couldn't bear to be parted from you.'

'Silly wee goose, you know I can't do without this,' and he touched her lightly so that she quivered and melted into him.

After a while he said, 'If I get the gynae job, we'll be able to stay together here. If I go back to Scotland – well, we'd have to see about that one.'

Rosamund was reassured, and wondered if he would ask her to

marry him. She didn't think she was ready for marriage anyway, so it didn't really matter. Life was good as it stood.

***

The Finals arrived, the culmination of their three year's training. The nurses in Rosamund's school filed into the examination room and found their places. Rosamund looked at the question paper placed face down in front of her and knew a moment of panic. What had she done? Suppose she didn't know enough. Suppose she should have spent nights revising. After all, it was what most people did before exams. Suppose she had wasted all those years. She looked across to where Helen sat across the aisle, but she was busy with her own thoughts and she couldn't catch her eye.

'You may turn the question paper over.' The invigilator's quiet voice cut in on her thoughts.

There was a quick rustling sound, like leaves before a storm, then silence as each nurse began to read the paper. One by one pens were picked up, heads leaned over desks and the room became full of the scratching of fountain pens and the occasional rustle as pages were turned.

At the end, when the papers were handed in and they left the examination room, Sandra said with relief. 'That's the first paper out of the way. It wasn't too bad was it?'

'You speak for yourself.' Amy's dark eyes looked huge against her pale freckled face. 'I can't abide writing at any price. Give me summat to do and I'm all right.'

'You'll be all right anyway, Amy,' Rosamund told her. 'I'm glad that one's over, though.' She gusted a sigh.

'I hope I've done well enough to pass,' wailed Helen. 'I couldn't face all this again.'

'So do I.' Amy was grinning now. 'I'll be much too busy to tekk it again. I'm expecting a bairn.'

'Amy, you dark horse,' cried Sandra.

The girls crowded round her with cries of surprise and congratulation, then bore her away for a cup of coffee and to hear all the details. Rosamund at the back of the crowd, marvelled. Amy, of all people to be the first to be a mother. She chuckled, and a warm glow spread through her. A baby. Would it look like Amy, thin and spiky, or be a little Cyril, solid and dark? A baby. A feeling stirred in the pit of her stomach, and suddenly she was filled with yearning. What would it be like to have a baby? A soft bundle of tiny limbs, huge eyes and an ever-open mouth. She had a brief vision of Aunt Maud, red-gold head bent over her darning, and the sound of her voice – 'You'll fill this kitchen with bairns like as not in years to come. You and Francis.'

She wrapped her cloak round herself and hurried after the others.

Thinking about it later, she realised of course this was not the time to have a child. How could she be so stupid as even to consider it, she was going to qualify and become a staff nurse, then after that who knows? If I pass… She supressed a flutter of doubt. I definitely mustn't go all soppy and start thinking of babies. She sighed and resigned herself. But the longing persisted.

***

One evening soon after, Neil met her at the ward door, as he often did when she was coming off duty. Straightaway he hugged her close, pressed himself against her and kissed her hungrily. The stethoscope in the pocket of his white coat dug into her hip.

'Ouch. Stop it, Neil,' she said when she had chance. 'Someone will see us.'

'What's the matter, don't you want me?'

'Of course I do, but not here. You're not that desperate, surely?'

'Och but I am. If you only knew. Come back to my room, then.'

'What's the great rush?' Rosamund laughed.

Once there he snatched her to him, and kicked the door shut.

'Neil, what's got into you? I've just come off duty, I'm dead beat. Give me a few minutes.' She pushed him away. 'How about making a coffee for us?'

He peered suspiciously at her, a frown creased between his eyes. She kissed him on the cheek. 'Go on. I need reviving – give me energy.' Smiling at him, she plumped herself in the easy chair and kicked her shoes off.

He shrugged off his white coat, put the kettle on and became busy with cups and Nescafe.

Rosamund lay back with her eyes shut. She did want to make love, but he was impatient, demanding. She'd be ready for him in a minute. She smiled to herself, anticipating.

'Here you are, sweetheart.' He put the steaming cup beside her and sat on the floor, leaning against her knees to gaze up into her face. Rosamund touched his cheek. Something was wrong. Perhaps he was worried about his job.

'Have you applied for that gynae job yet?'

'No,' he said shortly, tipped his head back and drained his cup. He took Rosamund's cup from her and pulled her to her feet and steered her towards the bed.

'Now!' And he stopped her mouth with his and made love to her fast and hard until she was gasping. His touch felt desperate and his whole body tense and unyielding, so that her own desire ebbed. At last he rolled away and lay silent.

Rosamund felt numb. He had never treated her like that before. She got off the bed and reached for her clothes. Standing by the bed, she pulled on her blue and white striped uniform dress and looked down at him.

'What was all that about?' she asked.

He turned his head. 'I'm sorry. I don't know what came over me.' He sat up and held her round the hips, his head against her belly.

Rosamund said slowly, 'That didn't feel in the least loving. Why?'

His voice was muffled. 'I don't want to lose you.'

'Why would that happen?'

'It just – might.'

She sighed and held him. 'Not as far as I'm concerned.'

They stayed like that for a long while.

'It's late.' Rosamund stirred. 'I must go, I'm on early tomorrow.'

He stood, and when he kissed her his cheeks were wet.

21

The telephone rang in the office of Women's Medical. Rosamund, Staff Nurse in charge that evening, finished recording the temperature of the last patient and clipped the chart onto the foot of the bed before she dashed to answer it.

'There's an admission on the way – acute broncho-pneumonia. A Mrs Wilson,' she told the two juniors. 'Wright, will you get the bed ready please? Collins, you and I'll carry on with the routine stuff until the patient arrives.'

Rosamund worked with her usual competence, half her mind on the new patient. There were lots of Wilsons, she knew, but her Mrs Wilson had been sneezing and red nosed last time she had seen her about ten days ago. She hoped it wasn't her, but remembering how she wheezed when she climbed stairs, feared it may well be. She'd soon find out.

Neil had done his evening ward round earlier with a smile and a word for each patient, and a quick squeeze for her behind the office door on his way out. She smiled at his audacity. He'd ordered an enema for Mrs Simpson and written up some sleeping tablets for Miss Cartwright. She'd sent for the prescription straight away, and the enema would be to do after supper. She looked round the ward. Most of the patients were in bed, counterpanes turned back, red blankets cheerful against white sheets. She paused at the foot of Mrs Murgatroyd's bed. She was sitting upright, dozing with her mouth half open. Her grossly swollen legs hung down against a rubber sheet, tubes sticking out from small dressings to drain into jars on the floor. A messy and thoroughly unpleasant procedure, Rosamund thought. Her dressings'll need changing, but I'll let her rest for a while longer. She moved on. There was Theresa, bright red lipstick illuminating a face grey with pain. There was little to be done for the tumour that was consuming her stomach, but she had begged for a chip butty for supper. Rosamund had made sure there would be a portion of chips at suppertime for Theresa's chip butty, even though she knew it wouldn't stay down five minutes.

'Looking forward to supper, Theresa?'

'I am that, nurse. It'll be worth being sick. Don't forget the tomato sauce, will you.'

It was staggering how brave these people could be. Bed tables were drawn up and Nurse Collins was setting up for supper. How was Nurse Wright doing? The admission bed was ready – good. She watched her drag the heavy oxygen cylinder into place.

There was a stir in the corridor as Rosamund adjusted Miss Butler's saline drip, and two ambulance men and a trolley came into view.

The patient was propped up, the blanket drawn up to her chin. It *was* her Mrs Wilson, with a blue frightened face and staring eyes, breaths harsh and gasping.

Rosamund took her hand and kissed her cheek. 'You'll be all right now, m'love. You'll soon be comfy. Try to relax,' she soothed. 'Wright, will you ring Dr Sinclair and tell him Mrs Wilson's arrived?'

The ambulancemen transferred Mrs Wilson's bulk smoothly to the bed, and one of them handed Rosamund the customary letter from the GP.

'You'll be wanting this, luv.'

"Re Mrs Adeline Wilson," she read, and smiled to herself. Adeline was it? Just wait till she's better.

They soon had her tucked in, propped high and warm. Rosamund took her pulse and respiration rate, observed the blueness round her nose and mouth, and her panting rapid breathing.

'Doctor's here now,' she said to Mrs Wilson as Neil appeared round the curtain. He grinned and winked at Rosamund, and Mrs Wilson opened her mouth in a greeting which turned into a fit of coughing.

'Don't try to speak,' Rosamund told her. But her folds of flesh shook, and her chest heaved and rattled in paroxysm. Rosamund held a sputum cup for her until she sank back, turning her head from side to side, mumbling.

Neil took her hand. 'Hello, Mrs Wilson. I'm Dr Sinclair. You are having a time of it, aren't you? Let's see what we can do about it.' He reached into the pocket of his white coat. 'I'd like to listen to your chest first.'

As he withdrew his stethoscope, a white card fell to the floor. He bent over Mrs Wilson, and Rosamund, behind him picked up the card. It was a photograph of a young woman and a toddler, who looked back at her with the unmistakeable features of Neil.

The world receded as Rosamund gazed at the image, and a cold fist clenched inside her chest. She looked at the back of Neil's head as he reached across to turn back the covers, saw the curve of his skull and the place where his hairline finished in an off-centre point. Nurse Collins rattled the supper trolley past at the other side of the curtains, and the world swam into focus again. Rosamund pushed the photograph into the bib of her apron and moved to the other side of the bed to unbutton Mrs Wilson's nightdress for the probing stethoscope.

'Get the oxygen going, Rosamund – try fifty per cent – and we'll start her on penicillin straight away.'

Neil had finished his examination and was speaking to her.

She saw his mouth move, and his words reached her ears from a distance as she obeyed like an automaton.

Mrs Wilson became more agitated as the rubber mask was placed over her nose and mouth, and Rosamund had to hold it there until the oxygen reached her lungs and her breathing eased a little. But she still struggled and repeatedly plucked off the mask, and the effort made her cough even more. She muttered and moaned, and her chest rose and fell in ever more rapid gasps.

Rosamund's fingers found her pulse. 'It's racing more than ever.' She lifted anxious eyes to Neil, seeing a stranger.

'This is doing no good,' he said as he adjusted the oxygen valve. 'She's delirious. The oxygen can't help if she won't keep the mask on. We'll have to put her in an oxygen tent.'

'I'll organise it. Take over here, Nurse Wright, please.' And Rosamund was able to escape – for the time being.

The rest of the evening passed in a blur. It was a long time before Mrs Wilson's breathing was under control although still rapid, and she could rest behind the celluloid windows of the rubber oxygen tent erected over her as she lay in bed. Long after night staff had come on duty Rosamund still sat in the office writing the report, weary head resting on one hand.

Neil came in and closed the door. He stood behind her and enclosed her in his arms. She could smell the clean antiseptic smell of him as he bent over to kiss the ear that was visible.

'Nearly finished?'

'Yes.' She carried on writing.

'Come to my room,' he murmured.

'No. I have to finish this, then I'm going straight to bed.' The photograph was burning a hole in her apron front.

'Come to mine.'

'Go away.' She lifted a shoulder and carried on writing.

***

Back in her room Rosamund pulled off her cap, threw it onto the bed and unfastened the stud in the sharp edged collar of her dress. Automatically she rubbed the sore red line on her neck. She sat down on the dressing table stool and slid the photograph out of her apron. With a sharp intake of breath she handled it with the tips of her fingers as though it really had been burning her ribs all evening, and propped the black and white photograph against the mirror.

It was an ordinary snap taken in what looked to be a sitting room. In the light of a standard lamp a young woman sat on a sofa in front of leaf-patterned curtains. She was very pretty with dark hair curling over her ears and a tip-tilted nose, and her hand round the toddler's waist bore wedding and engagement rings. The little boy in shorts buttoned onto a short sleeved blouse perched on his mother knee, clutched a toy car in a fat hand and gazed solemnly out at Rosamund with Neil's eyes.

She flinched as though from a blow. This was what his anguish had been about. A wife and child. She raised her eyes to her own reflection in the mirror and saw features darkened with fatigue and shadowed with – what? Sorrow, regret? She looked again at the young woman. Her mouth was curved as if she was about to burst out laughing. Was it something the child had said? About his daddy perhaps? What would she feel if she knew about me? Rosamund felt shame stain her cheeks. I never thought to ask if he had a girlfriend, was married. I was naive enough to assume he was free, she thought with immense sadness.

She turned back to the photograph. This little boy, so like Neil – without his daddy to play with him and sing to him, cuddle him and tell him stories. Instead his daddy... She choked.

She thought of all the times they had made love, how she had enjoyed his body, his passion, his fun. Things she had no right to and he had no right to offer. She laid her head down and wept bitter tears. He had deceived and lied to her, just when life had opened up for her again. Now she had found out the truth, she was stricken with humiliation and remorse.

Lifting her head she stared at her tearstained reflection. She might be stricken, but she wasn't going to lie down and die. Anger flared. Who did he think he was?

She washed her face, stormed down the stairs to the hall and picked up the telephone receiver on the wall.

'Dr Sinclair's room please.'

'Sinclair.' He sounded sleepy.

'Neil. I want to talk to you.'

'Rosamund, I'm glad it's you. I thought it was the ward wanting me. You're coming over after all?'

'No. I'll see you tomorrow – I'm on split duty. You're off in the afternoon as well, aren't you?'

'Yes I am. You sound a wee bit fierce Rosamund. What's the matter?'

'Be at the gate by the ploughed field at the top of Back Lane at two thirty.'

'It's a bit damp and cold for a field. Why don't you come over here?'

'Be there.' She slammed the phone down, and slumped against the wall, tears running down her cheeks.

***

Deliberately she made him wait. Instead of flying along as she usually did, she walked up the lane at a steady purposeful pace. It was a grey drizzly day. The colours in the hedge were muted and a few dead leaves lay sodden at the edge of the lane. Rooks dotted the sky over the ploughed field behind Neil, their raucous calls mocking. He leaned with his back to the gate, arms hooked over the top rail, one leg crossed over the other.

Rosamund fingered the curling photograph in her pocket. Her head came up and her chin jutted. Neil lifted himself from the gate as she approached, and a shower of raindrops fell from the spiders' webs which festooned the bars, and the metal latch rattled. He went to take her in his arms, but his eyes were wary.

She stopped in front of him just out of reach, and held up the photograph.

'Oh.' His arms dropped to his sides. 'I wondered where that had got to.'

'Well?'

'Where did you find it?'

'You dropped it in the ward last night.'

'Why didn't you say anything then…?'

'We had a job to do. Well?' she demanded again.

'I suppose you've guessed.'

'You tell me. Who are they?' She thrust it at him.

He took the photograph with unsteady fingers and touched the two faces with his forefinger.

'It's Jeannie and wee Hamish.' His face crumpled, the colour of putty. 'My – wife – and little boy.' His eyes met Rosamund's stony gaze. 'It's not what you think.'

'How do you know what I think? Tell me about it.'

'I never meant anything to happen between you and me. I didn't want to be unfaithful to Jeannie.'

'Huh,' she said. 'I saw the flash in your eye when we met. But you had me fooled.'

'I wasn't going to do anything about it, but – things just happened.'

'You could have told me you were married. You can't have told anyone else either, or I'd have heard. If no one knew, it left you free for a bit of you-know-what wherever you could find it, didn't it? Was that what you planned?' Anger flared, and she heard her voice rising.

His eyes fell. 'It must look like that, but I didn't plan it consciously. Look, I don't have to explain myself to you.' He stowed the photograph away in the recesses of his coat.

Rosamund watched the pert features of the girl and the solemn eyes of the child disappear with a lump in her throat. She struggled to stay calm.

'Oh, but you do. Go on.'

'I fell for you as soon as I saw you. I could see you weren't wanting more than companionship, and at first it was okay, it suited me too. I enjoyed being with you and it didn't hurt Jeannie.'

'But it didn't stay like that, did it?'

'No. I should have realised it was too dangerous. But by the time I did you were involved too, and what happened was inevitable.'

'Oh, no it wasn't. Even then you could have told me you were married. But you didn't. You went ahead, and deceived both Jeannie and me – and that dear little boy. How could you – you – unspeakable, filthy – coward. You absolute TURD!'

She sprang at him and raked his cheek with her nails. He grabbed her and held her close to him, fingers digging into her arms. She hammered his chest with her fists, horrified to find that in spite of her shame and rage heat kindled deep down and threatened to overwhelm her. She wanted him to kiss her hard and tell her it was all nonsense, to take her there and then in the muddy gateway.

Breathing hard and heart pounding, she struggled until she broke his hold. She wrenched herself out of his grasp, fists still clenched as she backed away from him. Blood ran down his chin and she could see by the look on his face that he wanted her too, and if she had stayed in his arms it would have begun all over again.

She felt sick and dirty.

'Get out of my life,' she said.

Rosamund turned her back and walked away.

***

That evening, she dragged herself back to the ward with a heavy heart. To her relief, Sister was on and Rosamund was not in charge.

After she had walked away from Neil in the lane, shaking, she had stared in horror at the skin and blood under her nails. She had never in her life done anything like that before, never been so angry, never used such violence – and hated herself for it. She scrubbed her hands sore and filed the nails as short as she could, wanting no scrap of Neil's flesh embedded in hers.

She had calmed down by the time she was back with the patients, and thankfully turned her mind to them and their needs. Mrs Wilson looked a little better, although she was still in the oxygen tent.

'How are you now?' Rosamund asked her friend.

'Middling, Rosamund, but I don't like it in this here tent,' she gasped.

'Most people don't. You won't be in it longer than's necessary.'

'I was badly last night though. I'm right thankful for what you did for me – and that nice Dr Sinclair. Is he the one you're going out with?'

'Not any more. I finished with him this afternoon. I'll tell you about it when you're better. Now, do you think you can manage this medicine, or do you want to be higher?' She pushed her hands through the rubber seal to offer the medicine glass.

'No, I can manage, lass. I'm right sorry to hear that. He seems such a nice young man, and he was right good to me.' She drank the medicine and pulled a face.

'He'll be round later to see how you are,' Rosamund told her.

But it wasn't Neil who came into the ward after supper.

'He's gone off sick,' the other houseman told Sister when she asked. 'I don't know what's the matter.'

Rosamund was relieved she wouldn't have to face him just yet. She wondered what excuse he would give for the scratches on his face. Serve him right, she thought. Why should he get off scot free?

***

Helen was back from Days Off when Rosamund returned to the Nurses' Home that night.

'What, you're not seeing Neil tonight?' she asked.

'No, and I won't be seeing him again.' She flung herself into a chair and stayed huddled in her cloak.

'Oh-oh. What's happened while my back was turned?'

Rosamund told her.

'The rotter! What did you do?'

'Scratched his face and told him to get out of my life, to put it shortly.'

'You didn't actually go for him, did you?'

'I was so mad. To think that he'd been hoodwinking me all this time. And his poor wife, sitting there in Scotland looking after their child, waiting for him to find a future for them. I wonder if he'll tell her.'

'Probably not. Do you know, I really thought you two'd make a go of it.'

'I thought we might too, but I was just living the present as it was, and loving every minute.' Tears squeezed out of her eyes and trembled on her lashes. 'I'm going to miss him, Helen. I really am.'

The girls were commiserative when they heard.

'You can never tell with men,' said Sandra.

'Oh you can, mostly,' said Helen. 'But I would have said Neil was a hundred per cent okay.'

'I never thought to question him,' Rosamund was rueful. 'But I've thought and thought to see if I can remember anything that might have given him away. There was nothing. Or perhaps there was and I missed it. Maybe I'm to blame somehow.'

'Of course you're not to blame. You mustn't think like that, Roz.' Helen was adamant. 'He should at least have told he was married, and then it was up to you whether you went along with it.'

'I don't know what I'd do without you girls.' Rosamund's voice shook.

'We're here to help each other, you know.' Sandra gave her arm a squeeze. 'It'll be nice to have you back, Roz. We've missed you.'

'What do you mean? Oh I see. I suppose I haven't been around much, have I?'

'Don't worry about that. We're all changing – different boyfriends, new experiences. And it'll change again once we're qualified.' Helen looked at them both. 'Whatever happens, let's always keep in touch.'

'Don't forget Amy,' Sandra reminded. 'I wonder what she'll make of this.'

'She'll be sympathetic, I'm sure. But she's living in a dream of impending motherhood, and nothing much else gets through to her.' Rosamund smiled again at last, and the conversation turned to other things.

***

Neil was still not back from sick leave in time for the next consultant's ward round. Rosamund wondered why. She found out when Helen returned from the cinema with Philip.

'Roz, have you heard?'

'Heard what?'

'Neil's gone.'

'Gone?'

'Yes, his room's been cleared and no one knows where he is or anything.'

'Oh.'

'Roz, are you all right?'

'Yes, of course I am. I was just thinking – I did tell him to get out of my life. That's a bit drastic though. Still, I won't have to see him any more, and I can start again.' Her chin went up and she nodded. 'Yes, I'll pick up the pieces and start again.'

22

Rosamund's period was late.

She didn't tell anyone at first, but after two weeks she was really worried, and she told Helen when they were in bed ready for sleep.

'Neil did take precautions, didn't he?'

'Faithfully.' She pondered. 'Well, not always. I mean there was the odd accident, but not the last few times I think.'

Helen looked hard at her.

'You're not sure, are you?'

'Not really.'

Helen lifted up onto one elbow and looked across at Rosamund in the next bed. She lay on her back hands behind her head, eyes on the ceiling.

'Have you thought what you'll do if you are – you know?'

'I've thought of nothing else.' Rosamund's voice was calm, flat. 'I know that after a shock a period can be late, but it's a long time now and it looks as if I'm going to have a baby.'

'Perhaps you're wrong and it'll happen after all.'

'It's ironic, I've been longing for a baby even though I knew it wasn't a good time to have one. But if it happened and Neil had asked me to marry him, I'd have said yes.'

'Even if you could tell him now he wouldn't be able to do anything about it.'

'I wouldn't ask him to. I'd rather he didn't know. As it is, I'll make my own way.'

'What will you do?'

'To start with, they'll throw me out of the hospital. So with no home and no job those will be the first things to tackle. Mrs Wilson would probably find me a room though she doesn't normally take children. But without an income…' Her voice strengthened. 'I'll manage somehow. I'll have to.'

After a silence Helen said, 'How do you feel?'

'Physically, just the same yet.' Her tone was sardonic. 'Emotionally, wretched.'

'There must be something you could do. Have you tried hot baths?'

'I've sat in enough hot baths to boil a lobster twenty times over. It just makes me sick and dizzy when I get out. I've no access to anything stronger except perhaps gin, and I can't afford that. Besides, where would I get drunk? I'd just be thrown out sooner.'

Helen was thinking. She sat up and hugged her bent knees. 'Perhaps Amy could help. Look after the baby with hers while you come back to work?' She saw Rosamund's look. 'Perhaps you could go to my mum for a while – until you've had it at least.'

'Helen, you're an angel, but I have to sort it out myself. I don't want this baby. After all, I don't know whether I could love a child of Neil's in the circumstances. Maybe I'll have it adopted when the time comes.'

'The curse might come yet.' Helen got out of bed and put her arms round Rosamund. 'Nobody said life should be easy, but you seem to have more than your fair share of trouble.'

'I expect I'll get over it, I have before.'

But she knew she hadn't. Part of how she felt was to do with what she had lost in the golden days when Francis was the future and Aunt Maud's prediction about filling the place with bairns could have come true.

***

Rosamund, Helen and Sandra stood on Amy's doorstep, lit from through by small panes of stained glass set in the door, and waited for their ring to be answered. They all sheltered under one umbrella, each trying to avoid getting drips down her neck. Rods of rain sparkled in the light from a gas lamp, roofs and downpipes burbled and gurgled, and a sneaky wind slapped gusts of rain against their legs.

'Come in, all of you.' Amy stood at the open door and drew them into the warmth and the glow of a small Christmas tree, to stand dripping on her sitting room carpet. 'Let's get them wet things off you before you catch your deaths.'

She had their coats off their backs in a trice, and soon kitchen chairs in the red and white back kitchen were draped, rain hats perched on top of the cooker and the umbrella was propped in the sink to dry.

The three girls laughed and chattered as they kicked off their wet shoes and lined them against the hearth to dry in front of the coal fire. They arranged themselves round the room, Sandra and Rosamund on the couch while Helen perched on a fireside stool.

'The room looks lovely.' Rosamund admired the coloured streamers and tinsel ornaments hung from the ceiling, casting glints of sparkle round the room.

'Cyril had to hang that lot up,' said Amy, 'but I did the tree.'

'You look well.' Sandra told Amy, relaxed in a rocking chair opposite Helen.

'I am an' all, now I don't have to get up at the crack of dawn to trek to the hospital and do a day's work. My legs can have all the rest they want now I'm at home – and my back.' She eased herself against the cushions.

Her sharp features had filled out, her fine sandy hair was soft and shining. She wore a green and yellow flowered smock over the neat mound of her pregnancy. Rosamund couldn't take her eyes off it.

'What have you done with Cyril?' asked Helen.

'It's his regular darts night, and they're having a bit of a Christmas do afterwards. I've told him not to hurry home. He said he didn't mind, it was worth having to have an extra pint to miss all the chattering.'

There was a general laugh. This domestic Amy was still a novelty to them, and it still amazed Rosamund that flashy Ace had taken to the role of a conventional married man. Perhaps that was what happened to everyone in the normal course of things.

'Don't you miss work?' asked Rosamund.

'No, funnily enough I don't, but I've hardly had chance to get used to it yet – it's only been a fortnight.'

'What do you do all day?'

'I've my home to keep clean.' Amy looked proudly around the shining room. 'Then there's shopping, and going round to see my mam.' She ticked things off on her fingers. 'I do a lot of knitting, and there's getting the room ready for the baby. Then I have to go to the doctors and the hospital for check-ups, and I'll be going to ante-natal classes soon…'

'Stop, stop, it's worse than casualty on a Friday night.' Sandra raised protesting palms. 'How did you find time to go to work?'

'It was very tiring.' Amy shot Sandra a sharp look. She got up and opened a sideboard cupboard. Rosamund could see pink, blue and white garments neatly stacked on the shelves. Amy lifted out a tissue wrapped package which she carefully undid.

'Look what my Gran made.' She shook out the delicate folds of a white lace shawl.

A concerted 'A-ahh' gusted from the girls. Helen reached out and held it up to the light.

'How fine it is. Beautiful.' She passed it to Sandra, who touched it in reverence before silently handing it to Rosamund.

She spread out the shawl, felt its feather weight across her lap and filled her hands with the snowy folds to press them to her cheek. She smelled the clean new wool, and imagined a tiny infant wrapped in its softness, then gathered the shawl to cradle it in her arms.

The others watched her.

'I do believe Roz's getting broody,' declared Amy.

Rosamund caught Helen's solicitous eye and smiled her reassurance.

'It's gorgeous,' she said, handing the shawl back to Amy who wrapped it back in the tissue paper. 'What a lucky little baby. Your Gran's very clever – the work's exquisite.'

'She's had plenty of practice. This is the seventh one she's done.'

'Let's have a look at the other things,' Sandra suggested, and soon the room was strewn with bootees and matinee coats, bonnets and tiny vests.

'It'll never wear all this lot.' Sandra was amazed.

'And more. You'd be surprised. Ooh!' Amy put her hand on her bump.

'What's the matter?' Sandra sprang up.

Amy's grin was wide. 'It kicked,' she said. 'It often does. Feel.'

Gingerly Sandra touched her abdomen. 'I can't feel anything.'

'Not there. Here.'

'Oh, yes. I felt it – just a tiny movement. Helen, come and have a feel.'

'Do you mind, Amy?'

'No. It'll have to get to know its Aunties.'

Helen touched Amy, but the foetus didn't move under her hand.

'What about you, Roz? Come and say hello to your godson – or daughter.' Amy sat back, expansive and smiling.

Rosamund hesitated, then knelt beside Amy, who took her hand and laid it firmly below her ribs.

'There. Leave it a minute, and it'll give you a kick.'

Rosamund's heart fluttered. There it was – a gentle bump against her palm. Then again. There was a slight squeezing in her own womb, a tiny nudge of not-quite-pain. She sat back on her heels. 'Imagine, that's a little foot or a hand!' She was filled with wonder.

'Or a knee or an elbow,' said Amy. 'He or she's going to be strong. Cyril's convinced it's a boy. But either way I'm going to be black and blue by the time I'm nine months!'

There was a moment of quiet.

'Time to go to sleep now, little one.' Amy stroked the mounded green and yellow flowers. 'Now. Who's for some supper?'

She heaved herself up to the table under the window where she uncovered laden plates and dishes hidden beneath a checked tea-towel.

They crowded round the table exclaiming at the wonders of Amy's baking – the tastiness of her meat patties, the lightness of her sponge cake. Amy bustled from kitchen to table and back, boiled a kettle and served coffee in the china cups and saucers from the tea-service the girls had given her for a wedding present.

They loaded an enormous plateful for Cyril to eat when he came home, which Amy with great tenderness, bore off to the kitchen to cover with a tin plate and keep in her tiny pantry.

Much later, having exchanged Christmas gifts, and sated with food and conversation, they spilled out onto the still wet pavement into a starry night, calling goodbyes and thanks to Amy as she stood silhouetted in her doorway.

***

Sleep did not come straight away for Rosamund that night, although she was tired. Her mind was full of the sights and sounds of Amy's happiness, and her joy in her pregnancy. She cupped her hand across her lower abdomen. Do I really not want this child? she wondered. It'll be a struggle on my own, and the stigma won't help. She'd seen how a 'Miss' with a child was regarded. I won't care, she decided. I can outface them all. I will manage for money somehow – I'm sure it can be done. She remembered the faint but solid thrust of Amy's baby against her palm. How long before mine will quicken? The first flickerings of love crept into her heart as again the nudge of not-quite-pain settled deep in her abdomen.

***

Women's Medical was frantically busy next day, and Rosamund had no time to think of anything else.

She and Nurse Wright did beds and backs, and helped a thinner Mrs Wilson into her enormous blue dressing gown to sit beside her bed,

'That's better. I reckon nowt to lazing in my bed all day. Did you know I'm going home tomorrow?'

'That's smashing news. Though this place won't be the same without you.'

'Well, there's a few folks in here as needs a bit of mothering and such. You have to do what you can, don't you?' She folded her hands in her lap and regarded the ward with a proprietorial air.

Rosamund turned to Wright, who was trying not to laugh. 'She's just the same at Sebastopol Road – mothers everyone.' She sobered. 'You just about saved my life when I first arrived.'

Mrs Wilson went pink with embarassment.

The two nurses spread clean sheets on the bed, and pulled up the blankets. The houseman who had taken Neil's place swished through the double doors, and nodded to them before going into the office.

'Our Dolly'll fetch me to their house at first – till I can manage by myself. You remember Dolly, the daughter as I babysit for? She's right good to me.'

'That reminds me.' Rosamund wagged a finger at her in mock remonstration. 'Your secret's out. I can't go on calling you Mrs Wilson now I know your name, can I – Adeline?'

'If you can't call me Mrs Wilson, I'll not be Adeline. There's too many funny stories attached to that. Just call me Addy.' She chuckled, and managed not to cough.

'Right, I'll do that, Adel – Addy!'

'Come on Roz, we'd better get on, there's heaps still to do.' Wright was pushing the trolley to the next bed.

'All right, I'm coming.' She turned. 'Are you comfy, Addy? Got your blackcurrant pastilles, yes? See you later then.' And she moved on to where Wright was already pulling the sheets off the next bed.

'Theresa Grey's morphine is due, Staff Hambly. Will you give it, please? I'll get it and check it with you in just a moment.' Sister was everywhere, working just as hard if not harder than the rest of her staff.

Rosamund set a tray, and signed in the Dangerous Drugs book for the small clear ampoule of morphine. She had the glass and metal syringe already fitted with a needle, lying in a kidney dish. She flicked the narrow top of the ampoule with her finger and thumb until all the precious fluid had drained into the base, picked up the tiny file to saw at the neck of the bottle. It snapped off cleanly and she drew up the morphine smoothly into the syringe. She carried the tray out into the ward to where Theresa lay white with pain, wearing her scarlet lipstick like a defiant flag.

'My saviour.' Her sunken eyes greeted Rosamund. 'It's bad today, Nurse. I'm glad to see the needle.'

'This'll ease it soon, Theresa.' Rosamund swabbed her wasted arm with spirit, and deftly injected the drug. 'There, how's that?'

'Never felt a thing. I'll be all right now for an hour or two. But – could you get me a bedpan before I settle down, Staff?' She managed a faint smile.

'Of course, right away.'

Rosamund slipped the warmed bedpan under Theresa's bony buttocks, supporting her with her other arm.

'I'm going to be sick, Staff. Quick!' Theresa gagged, and Rosamund just had time to grab a vomit bowl from the locker when she heaved and retched. But it wasn't vomit. It was bright red blood. It poured from her mouth and nose in great gouts. Theresa heaved again. Blood flooded the bowl and flowed over Theresa's pretty pink bed-jacket and Rosamund's hands, the metallic smell clogging her nostrils. Rosamund shouted for help, someone whipped the curtains across, and in no time Sister and a bunch of white coats were round the bed. Theresa clung to Rosamund with terrified eyes as the blood continued to pour from her mouth, tainted now with pus and stained with black. On and on it went. By the time a transfusion had been set up it was too late, and Rosamund lowered Theresa's lifeless body back onto the pillows, and slid the bedpan from under her.

***

Nurse Wright helped Rosamund to lay her out, and they worked quietly, remembering Theresa's bravery and her quirky humour. As they washed her body and laid her in clean linen, Rosamund was conscious that the not-quite-pain she had had low in her abdomen since last night now most definitely was pain. It grew and smouldered deep and heavy in her pelvis, and the weight of it felt as though her insides would drop out, and an ache spread down her thighs.

When at last their task was done, Theresa lay white and serene with no sign of the horror in which she had died. There was still a trace of scarlet on her pale lips, and Rosamund hoped that there would be chip butties in heaven.

She straightened and rubbed her aching back. Wordlessly the two nurses moved away from the bed, and as she moved Rosamund at last recognised the pain, and as it gripped tighter she knew without a doubt that there was no baby, and never had been.

23

FRANCIS

Treblissick.

It was late February in 1960. Francis was hedging in Bull Field in the mild damp 'Cornish' weather he liked, when the air was soft after the harsh winds of winter, and fine drizzle spangled the twigs and breaking green buds on the hawthorn, and the scent of spring hovered over burgeoning primroses. Another armful of small branches tossed into the trailer, then with the billhook he began to bend pliable stems of young hazel, layering them sideways one above the other where they grew. Taught him by his father, it was already a dying craft, and time consuming.

I don't begrudge the time, but it could be done in half the time by machine, he thought. But then machines I can't afford would make a lot of jobs easier and quicker. There's never enough money for everything we need, and with that new load of cattle feed delivered yesterday, there'll soon be another bill to add to the pile. Then there's…

The drizzle turned to rain, but he worked on, worrying.

…the tractor breaks down so often it needs mending with a new one, and I still owe the tractor man for last time. Better equipment would soon pay for itself, then I might be able to take on another man. Dan struggles sometimes, and I know his arthritis plays him up. The old boy's stubborn as a mule. Swears he'll go on for ever, but…

Hair plastered to his head, he threw his tools into the trailer and headed for the farm.

He splashed into the yard and disturbed Ruth's ducks paddling in the puddles like plump matrons from the WI on a seaside outing.

Dan wheeled a barrow across the yard. 'You'm lookin' dampish, boy. Forget your umbrella did 'e?' Grinning, he continued into the barn.

Francis laughed and called, 'You could say that…'

'Aargh!'

Francis was off the tractor in a trice and into the barn. Dan lay doubled over a sack of feed half in and half out of the barrow, clutching his back.

'Take it easy, Dan.'

'Damn back!' Dan's face was grey and sweat stood out on his forehead. 'I'll be all right in a minute.'

After a while, with Francis's help he tried to stand, but sank back in agony.

Maud's anxious face peered round the door. 'What have you done to yourself now, you old fool?'

'Don't you start a-fussing' Dan growled. ' 'Tis only that old back of mine playing up again. I'm right as rain now.'

Again he attempted to stand, but his face twisted with pain, and he swore and groaned. Francis scooped him up in his arms and dumped him as gently as he could in the wheelbarrow.

'Shut up, Dan and keep still.'

He wheeled him unceremoniously over to the kitchen and lifted him into the Windsor chair. Maud had already filled a hot water bottle and stuffed it into a red cover before before she slid it behind Dan's back.

'Tha's better, my lover.' Dan managed a thin smile.

Ruth finished buttoning an already booted and wriggling Meri into her yellow raincoat ready to take her down to the village. Free at last, Meri darted forward and planted a kiss on Dan's ear.

'Never mind, G'andan. Meri kiss it better.'

'Thank you, it's better already, little maid. Go with your mammy now, she's waiting.'

'Okay, G'andan. Mammy's going the pub an' me's goin' to play wiv Jane. Jane's going to have a baby brother or sister. She wants a brother, 'cos she's already got me to play with, an' I'm a girl.' She sat on the floor to pull on her wellington boots.

His expression bleak, Francis looked at Ruth as she picked up her raincoat. Nineteen now, she still wore her hair about her shoulders. Pale eyes rimmed with dark lashes accentuated the pallor of her skin, which never tanned even in the strongest sun. Her figure had filled out after

Merry's birth, and her short black skirt clung to her hips and her tight white jumper left little to the imagination.

'Are you helping in the bar again, then?'

'Yes.' She pushed her arms into the coat sleeves and stared back at him.

'It's a bit early to be going down.'

Ruth looked stubborn. 'There's things to do afore the pub opens. Meri's going to Gwen's.'

'You know I...'

'Da-dee.'

Meri dived for Francis and grabbed him round both legs. He bent to smile at the elfin face looking up at him, eyes like blackberries, her baby teeth white against skin that glowed rosy brown. She climbed onto his boots, a foot on each and reached for his hands.

'Walk me, Daddy. Walk me wiv giant strides,' she commanded.

Even Meri couldn't lighten his mood, but obediently he stalked round the kitchen to peals of her laughter.

'Look a' me, G'annie. Look a' me G'andan.'

'Come on, Meri. Stop that foolin'.' Ruth made for the door.

'Say goodbye, Miss Giant.' Francis walked her to her mother and prised her off his feet.'

'Goo' bye ever body.' She blew kisses in the direction of Maud and Dan.

Ruth took Meri's hand, but she tugged it loose and dashed back to where Dan sat, his face still creased with pain.

'You be good boy now, G'andan, an' you soon be better.' She peered into his eyes. 'G'annie'll make you better.'

'Meri, come o-on.'

'Okay, Mammy. S'all we find some puddles and make big splashes?' She ran out of the door, still doing giant strides in her red wellies.

'Don't be late back, Ruth. Dan needs to be in bed, and I'll take Mother too when I take him home, so there'll be no one else to see to the poultry and do tea.'

With a mutinous look, she pushed past him and started across the yard after Meri. 'See you,' she flung over her shoulder.

***

The doctor didn't come until the following dinnertime, and left precise instructions on Dan's care. Francis went down to the cottage before he started his afternoon work, with a set of planks to put under the mattress. The old boy's not going to like this, he thought, as he helped his mother to make up the bed.

Maud tucked the sheet firmly over Dan, stretched out on his back in clean pyjamas in the spare single bed.

'There, let's see you get out of that, you old devil.'

'I shall be out of it soon enough and back in our feather bed with you, my girl.' He untucked her handiwork with an impatient tug. 'These boards are some hard, Francis, there's no need to torture me.'

Francis laughed. 'I'll think of something even more fiendish if you don't behave yourself. The doctor knows what he's doing.'

'Flat on my back on planks and out of my mind with painkillers for three weeks, can't even get out of bed for a pee? I hope he does.' He paused and looked up at Francis with concern. 'I know an old bugger like me's not indispensible, but how will you manage?'

'That's all taken care of. Jimmy Kernow's starting tomorrow.'

'Oh.' The lines between his eyes deepened. 'We could do with yon Eli turning up. Good worker he is. Experienced.'

'I know. Haven't seen him for – what? – nigh on three years though. No, Jimmy'll be fine.'

'I'll be back on the job before you know it.'

'Dan,' Francis's voice was gentle. 'I've taken him on full time. Permanent. He's always wanted to farm, we all know that. But he's only just left school, he needs a good man to train him.'

'And that good man's me?'

'Who better, and you've always worked well together when he's helped before.'

'I can't say I'm not relieved, it'll make a big difference. But it'll be years afore I'm ready to hang up my hat, boy' he warned.

'And you'll keep going longer with Jimmy alongside.'

'How're you going to pay him?'

Maud interrupted from across the bed. 'Never you mind. I'm sure Francis has thought it all out, haven't you, Francis?'

His eyes steady and his fingers crossed behind his back, 'Of course I…'

The telephone rang in the kitchen below.

'I'll go, Mother,' and he bolted down the stairs.

He picked up the heavy black handset.

'Francis?' It was Ruth. 'Is Meri with you?'

An icy hand gripped his chest.

'No. She was in the dairy with you when I left. But that was an hour ago.'

There was silence, then a sob and Ruth's voice tiny down the line.

'I can't find her anywhere. Francis, she's lost.'

**

Francis burst into the farmyard, grim faced. 'Where have you looked?'

'The house, barns, cowshed, linhay – everywhere. All the places she plays.' Ruth snivelled and wiped her nose with the back of her hand. 'I dussen't go no further lest she come back and no one here.'

'You should have called me sooner. How long's she been gone?'

'I don't kno-o-w,' she wailed.

Maud put an arm round her shoulders. 'Where's Floss? She's not with Francis.'

'I ain't seen her.'

Maud and Francis exchanged looks of fear. With as steady a breath as he could muster Francis took charge.

'Someone has to stay here. Ruth, go inside and start ringing round for helpers to search. Ask anyone you can think of. Try Tregenna's first – they're nearest. Can you do that?'

Ruth gulped and nodded.

'Mother. We'll search the nearest fields, and when the others arrive I'll break off and organise them. Oh, and Ruth,' he called after her. 'Ask them to bring torches, and a whistle if they have one. It might be dark before we find her.'

'Right.' She entered the house at a run.

'Better take another look around the outbuildings. Ruth might have missed something in a panic.'

Francis plunged into the old stables, now housing farm machinery. There was so much that could damage young flesh – sharp teeth, cutting blades, wheels to crush, places to fall from, places to get wedged in. He'd not realised what a dangerous place a farm was. Meri was a sensible child for three, but she was still only a baby. She was nowhere in the outbuildings or the yard. He breathe a sigh of relief and banished thoughts of her lying mangled in a dark corner – there anyway.

'She could be anywhere by now,' panted Maud, catching him up in Home Field. 'I can't understand why Floss isn't around.'

New lines round Francis's mouth deepened. He knew that with Meri *and* Floss missing, one or both was in trouble.

'We'll find them for sure.' But under his breath he was praying.

One by one, friends and neighbours by car and tractor rumbled up the lane, and soon a dozen or more were combing fields, poking into hedges, along streams and ditches, beating bramble brakes and along woodland paths, calling Meri's name, and Floss's.

The early dusk lay eerie among the scattered stones of the ruined chapel in Poley's Field. Francis had searched every inch here where, as he and Rosamund had done in years past, Meri loved to clamber and play her pretend games while he worked nearby. He stumbled in long grass between half-hidden stones, and felt despair settle on him, cold and heavy as a sodden cloak. Another blue-black cloud loomed over the nonexistent sunset, and he felt the first drops of rain streak his face. Suppose she'd found her way out onto the road, been snatched by someone in a car, along with Floss: someone driving along the main road out of the county. Fear curdled his throat. It was time to call the police.

In a panic he set off across the curve of the hillside, his feet finding their way through muddy depressions and uneven tussocks as he ran towards the farm. Hoping against hope that she would have been found, was even now sitting before the open doors of the Rayburn with a mug of cocoa and telling the tale of her adventures, word tumbling over each other in eagerness, he scrambled over the last stile.

There, etched black against the farm lights he saw a small moving figure. No, *two* small figures. Meri appeared to be helping Floss who was limping badly.

Thank God! He gulped great gouts of air, then found enough breath to call out: 'Meri!'

She turned and waited, her face a pale blur in the near dark. Floss lay down.

'Sweetheart. You're safe!' He knelt and gathered her to him.

Meri clung, both arms round his neck. 'Daddy, I knew you'd come.' Her chest heaved, and a hiccup turned into a sob.

He let her cry, holding her close, then held her away to wipe her tears with his thumb. Even in the dim light he could see mud and bloody streaks on her cheeks.

'Sweetheart, what's happened? Are you hurt?'

'I's not hurt, but Fossie's got a poorly paw. Look. It's all messy and bleeding.' She stooped and hugged the dog. 'It's all right now. Daddy's here.'

He took the paw gently in his hand. 'What is it, old girl? Let me see.' Floss had licked the wound, and he saw torn flesh and white splinters of bone.

Meri squatted besid him and stroked the wet fur. 'It's nasty, idn' it? Do you think she needs the vet?'

'Yes she does, and I'm sure he'll be able to help her. Like to tell me how it happened?'

'She got stuck in a metal thing in the grass down by th' ole chapel. She cried and cried, but I couldn't pull her paw out. Then the man came.'

'What man?'

'The man 'at lives in the woods, course. He peeps at me sometimes, but he don't know me sees him.' She giggled and covered her eyes.

'I see,'said Francis, although he didn't. 'What did the man do?'

'Undood the metal thing and took her paw out.'

'Then?'

'He did this.' She put her finger to her lips as though to shush or keep a secret. 'An ' then he wented.'

'Where to?'

'Jus' wented. So we came home. We couldn't come quick 'cos of Flossie's paw.'

'You've been a brave girl. Come on, then, let's get you both home.'

***

He squatted and tenderly lifted Floss, who yelped and licked his face. 'Good girl,' he murmured and bent his head. 'Hop on, my maid and hold tight.'

She put her legs astride his neck. He braced his thighs and stood, Floss in his arms and Meri on his shoulders, fingers clutching his hair as she was used to doing. Mingled with relief at Meri's safety, Francis's stomach churned at the thought of someone setting traps on his land. It happened occasionally, but not for a long time, and it made him furious. It could so easily have been Meri who was hurt – bad enough that it was Floss.

And who was the mysterious 'man in the woods' who had come to their rescue?

***

Francis was a long time at the vet's. He'd stayed and stroked her silky head until her eyes closed under the anaesthetic.

***

Meri was asleep in the narrow bed in the room over the porch which had been Francis's until his marriage. She lay on her back with the grey lumpy shape of Lawwie, the sheep that Maud had knitted for her first Christmas clutched to her chest like a woolly shield. The mud and blood had been cleaned away, and a trickle of tears ran from the corners of her eyes into the tangle of curls that lay across the pillow. Francis lowered himself cautiously onto the edge of the bed. Her lips puckered and she screwed up her eyes, but didn't waken. It was hard for a little girl to be put to bed without knowing what had happened to her beloved companion, and she'd obviously tried to stay awake until he came back.

Meri's breath came soft and even. Francis felt the soothing warmth of her small body through the eiderdown, and stayed to think and rest, absorbed in the peace of the quiet room.

What a day it had been. Most of the time he shouldered his responsibilities with equanimity, but today had overwhelmed him with a rollercoaster of emotions since he learned that Meri was lost. Helpless in his love for the child, he'd floundered in a morass of fear, panic, guilt, loss. Relief at her safety turned into wonder and pride in the three year old's stoicism and compassion. Then there was his anxiety about the identity of the man in the wood, Floss's mystery saviour, still niggled at the back of his mind. And anger and sorrow at the suffering and mutilation of his old friend.

Now he must go downstairs to Ruth.

Abruptly he stood. From long custom, he ducked his head under the low beam as he crossed to the window and opened the curtains and unlatched the window. The night was starry, and the smell of rain lingered in the air. He leaned out and breathed deeply, taking in energy for what he knew was next to come.

Downstairs Ruth was curled in the Windsor chair watching television.

'There's a chop in the bottom of the Rayburn,' she said, without taking her eyes off the screen.

Francis retrieved the dried-up meal, wrinkling his nose at its unappetising smell, and sat at the table with his back to the flickering black and white figures on the screen. The dried up potatoes and mashed swede were tasteless and the chop like leather, but he forced most of it down, then took his plate into the scullery to run it under the tap. Ruth was still glued to the television screen when he returned and took the chair opposite.

'Well? Don't you want to know if Meri's all right?'

'She must be. She din't call out or anything, after I put her to bed.'

'Is that what happened this afternoon? She was out of sight and quiet, so you never noticed she'd gone?'

'No. She was in the dairy wi' me while I was packing eggs for the eggman, making a bed for her doll in that ole washing up bowl and singin' to herself.'

'And?'

'Then this man come in the yard in a blue car. He be selling a new sort o' pig feed, he said. Wanted to see you. I told him you were expected soon, an' he said he'd wait. So I give him a cup of tea while he waited.'

'He's been round before, and I told him I wasn't interested. We always deal with Bibby's, like my Dad did.'

'Well, we had a chat, and when he'd finished his tea he said he wouldn't wait no longer. Left you that card.'

Francis examined the calling card, opened the doors of the Rayburn and threw it into the depths.

'Yes, that's the one. I told him not to call again, but you weren't to know that. So what about Meri?'

'She din't come in the house with us, and when I went to look for her I couldn't find her.'

'Aghh, Ruth!' he groaned, hands over his face.

For a few moments he sat ominously still and tried to control the anger which bubbled and churned inside him – the pressure of years of useless trying to please her; trying to understand and make allowances for her; the years of resentment for trapping him into a marriage doomed to fail; for her indifference to her own child: now for the neglect that had threatened her safety. It was no use. He couldn't contain his rage, and in a red blur he leapt up and switched off the babbling TV.

Ruth, surprised, stared up into his livid face as he stood over her.

'What sort of a mother are you, eh? Suppose Meri'd been hurt or even died?' He thrust his face close to hers. 'You aren't fit to have a child, d'you know that? You don't even love her.'

'I don't get much chance wiv you around.' Her gaze was defiant. Then she crumpled. 'There's none of you wants me here. I can't do nothen' right.'

'Stop whining. You're lucky I do treat her as my daughter. Which you know full well she is not,' Francis ground through clenched teeth, then forced himself to turn away. Tremors of rage rolled through him like peal after peal of thunder, and he strode to the wall and hammered the painted surface with clenched fists.

'What you'm getting yourself in a tizz for? She'm safe now.'

He turned to face her, hands hanging by his sides. It had been festering for too long, and like pus from a burst abscess, his pain erupted.

'If you'd taken better care of her she wouldn't have been lost,' he roared. 'All you cared about was entertaining a pair of trousers while you got the chance. Don't think I don't know why you enjoy helping in the bar at the Ring o' Bells so often, all come-hither eyes and mysterious. I know how you operate, remember?'

Ruth's face was blank. He'd never got used to her pale cold eyes which stared back at him now without expression. Angry as he was, he could see she didn't care.

'You don't even bring any money back from your so-called job, and you know how hard up we are,' he yelled.

he came to life at last. 'Me Dad don't pay us no wages, but I sometimes gets a tip. You never give me no money, so I keeps it.'

'A tip!' he scorned, 'And what do you do to earn a tip, might I ask?'

Ruth kicked him. Hard.

'Owww!' Francis hopped about rubbing his shin. 'You bitch!'

'What am I supposed to do. You don't love me. You never comes near me in bed no more, an' I'm human jus' like anyb'dy else. If someb'dy's kind to me, what am I supposed to do?'

Francis gasped. 'You – you – whore. You cheating whore!'

Grabbing her by the shoulders, he hauled her out of the chair and shook her like a terrier shakes a rat, her head jerking backwards and forwards. Shook her until her teeth rattled.

Suddenly he realised what he was doing and, horrified, opened his hands and dropped her. She fell back into the chair, breathing hard. He stared at her wild eyed, his heart still hammering with anger.

After a long moment she wriggled upright and grinned.

'See,' she crowed. 'There ain't nuffing you can do about it. An' I'll soon have me Dad up here if you tries that again. I s'll take Meri down the pub an' I shan't bring her back.'

Like a bucket of cold water, her words drenched his temper, and he plummeted into despair. From the moment he'd agreed to marry Ruth, he'd made tremendous efforts to make the marriage succeed. Often his resolve had worn thin, but now for the first time he felt defeat.

Francis turned away from her taunting face, and said with infinite sadness, 'Don't be ridiculous, Ruth. You don't want Meri – you never did. Now for God's sake get out of my sight and go to bed.'

***

That night he slept in a spare room, and for two days they scarcely spoke to each other.

The morning of the third day started as usual.

Francis broke off from forking hay for the cattle when he heard noises of departure, and came to the haybarn doorway to say goodbye. Ruth, wearing a tight skirt and jacket, and showing more than a hint of cleavage was just about to leave with Meri to drop her at Gwen's before continuing to the Ring o' Bells. Francis took a step towards her, but she turned away. Before he had time to call out the post van chugged up the lane and drove into the farmyard.

'Postie, Postie,' sang Meri. She ran up to the van when it stopped by the door.

'Here, maid, take these.' Alf leaned out of the open window with a bundle of letters. 'There's a good girl.'

Meri took the bundle and twinkled up into his weatherbeaten face. 'I's take them for my daddy.' She skipped off into the house.

'Lively little maid she be, Missus.' He called to Ruth who was already at the gate.

'She be too lively sometimes, Alf. Come o-on, Meri!' she snapped, her harsh voice full of impatience. For a long moment she looked directly at Francis, the cold depths of her eyes unreadable, before she swung round, long black hair swirling about her, and went through the gate.

Meri banged the scullery door behind her and ran across the yard.

"Bye Daddy.' She rushed over to Francis, flung her arms round him, planted a kiss on his cheek, then scampered after her mother, who was already out of sight down the lane.

"Bye sweetheart' he called to empty air

***

At four o'clock Maud, out in the pigsty, was summoned by the double burr of the telephone rigged to ring loudly in the yard as well as in the house. She hurried through the scullery and wiped her hands on the bib of her dungarees before she picked up the heavy black handset. She listened.

'Hold on, I'll ask him.' She rested the phone on the dresser and hurried out to find Francis in the cowshed preparing to start milking.

'It's Gwen.' she told him with a puzzled frown. 'Ruth was late picking Meri up, and when she rang the pub they told her Ruth wasn't there. She wants to know what she's to do.'

'Blast that woman, what's she up to now? Tell Gwen I'll be right down.' He shrugged off his cowgown and hung it on the peg by the door. 'Sorry to ask you, Mother, but will you carry on milking?'

He went to the pub first.

The big oak door was closed, and he went round the back. He cast a sideways glance across the yard into the shadows of the open shed where Ruth had lured him, almost senseless with drink, on the night of the fair four years ago.

Bill Nankivell let him in on a waft of old beer and stale cigarettes, and stood foursquare in the gloomy passage, hands on hips.

'She bain't 'ere.' There was satisfaction in the set of his shoulders, the spread of his legs, and triumph in the harsh tone.

Francis gaped. 'What do you mean, not here? Where is she?'

'Gone. Left. Skidaddled.'

'Ruth?' Francis was bewildered. 'She can't have.'

'Went this afternoon, after closing time.'

'Bill, what is this? She didn't say anything to me. Where is she? When's she coming back?'

'I doubt you'll see her again.'

'For Christ's sake, Bill, tell me what's going on.'

'She'm gone with a man.'

It was like a punch on the nose. Francis reeled. He shook his head, tried to clear the mist before his eyes, unclog his brain. Then through the haze comprehension dawned. He didn't need to ask. He knew.

'A pig feed salesman with a blue car.' The bitter words dragged from him.

'It's what she wants.'

'What about Meri?'

'She don't want Meri. Says you can 'ave her.'

Francis nodded. There was something to be salvaged. 'So that's it?'

'That's it.'

Bill closed the door, and Francis turned away, ashamed to admit there was no point in trying to find Ruth, relieved to have to let her go.

***

Later in the warmth of the farm kitchen with the chores all done, Francis sat in the Windsor chair with Meri on the rag rug at his feet busy with her crayons, and tried to get used to the absence of Ruth at the other side of the hearth. The pile of letters the postman had brought that morning lay unopened on the table, and the Western Morning News lay unread on his lap. Maud had insisted on giving them tea at the cottage when he had called to tell them the news, so he hadn't had to get a meal for himself and Meri tonight, but what he was going to do in the future he didn't yet know. What surprised him was how calmly he was taking Ruth's defection. He still felt numb, but knew there was anger and pain rumbling in the background ready to catch up with him. Hang on to that calm for Meri's sake, he told himself, until you've had chance to think things out.

He clenched his fists on the newspaper, and a picture of Ruth as he had last seen her that morning filled his mind. That's what that last long look had meant. She knew she wasn't coming back.

He couldn't ask his mother to take Meri on now, especially with Dan still confined to bed with his back, and he needed to make long term arrangements. Perhaps Gwen would look after her every weekday. It was a lot to ask, and he'd have to pay her of course – how was another matter! Then there was the house, and washing and ironing, and cooking and thousands of other things he felt sure. It wouldn't matter if it were just himself, but a little girl of three took a lot of looking after.

He looked down at Meri. Still unknowing that her mother had abandoned her, she lay on her tummy in red dungarees, knees bent, feet in the air, a rainbow of wax crayons scattered about her on the rug. With her tongue sticking out, she was vigorously colouring a piece of paper. There was a strip of bright blue across the top, and now her fist worked up and down to create an expanse of jerky green.

'Daddy, d'you think Flossie's all right?'

'Yes, we went and settled her down, remember?'

She nodded and carried on crayoning. Francis returned to his thoughts.

It wasn't altogether Ruth's fault things had gone so wrong. They had never been right in the first place. She hadn't been capable of being a farmer's wife, and their marriage was doomed from the start, founded on deception as it was. He'd done his best, and knew it hadn't always been good enough. Ruth had obviously thought so too. He felt a sudden surge of anger as he thought of the way she had gone, but he wasn't altogether surprised, she'd always seemed…

D 'you think she'd rather be in here with us?'

He came to with a start.

'Who?'

'Flossie.'

'No, I think she prefers to be in the stable where she's always had her bed.'

'She's good at walking wiv only three legs. D'you think it hurts now?'

'Probably a bit, but it'll be well soon.'

'I'm drawing her.'

'Are you, sweetheart?'

His mind came back to the practical problems. I'll close most of the rooms in the house, just keep the ones we use clean – if possible. I really need to get someone in to look after the house, do Ruth's jobs and look after Meri. He thought in a panic of the pile of bills on his desk in the parlour.

'Look, Daddy. Look at my picture.'

She held the paper up towards him.

'I like that, Meri. That's Floss with her poorly paw, isn't it?'

'Yes. I did lots of blood. Can you see it on the grass as well?'

'I see – that lovely bright red. And is this you standing by Floss?' He peered at the figure with a brown face and round black eyes, and black scribbled hair.

'No, silly. That's the man in the wood.'

But Francis was suddenly distracted. 'What's that paper you're drawing on?'

'E'velope.'

'Let me look. It's not been opened. Must have fallen off the table.'

He put his finger under the flap and ran it along, then slid out the contents. He read. Then read again. And again.

'Well, I'll be damned. It's a cheque from Ernie for one thousand pounds! A Premium Bond's come up!' He picked her up and hugged her tight. 'Not a lot, but the first luck I've had in ages.'

'Put me down, Daddy, you're squeezing me.' Then when her dignity had been restored, 'What's a Peemyum Bond?'

'This Premium Bond, Meri, is Grannie's wedding present to your Mammy and me. Wouldn't Ruth be mad if she knew she'd missed it!'

24

ROSAMUND

Leadersfield, 1960.

'Try to be quick this morning, nurses. I want all the patients comfortable and the ward spick and span for Dr Grainger's ward round.'

As she spoke, Rosamund closed the casenotes she had been reading and placed the red folder on the glass-topped trolley beside her. She stood at the cabinet in the centre of the ward where she was preparing for the consultant's weekly ward visit. Patients' flowers were displayed on top of the cabinet, and a vase of daffodils stood nearby. She moved it to make more room, and its remembered fragrance flooded a part of her mind with memories of Francis's birthday, when there were always drifts of daffodils in the garden at Pennygarra Farm, and primroses clothed the hedges in the lane…

'Yes, Sister Hambly.' The two first year students pushed the 'beds and backs' trolley close to the next bed and swished the curtains round.

Rosamund picked up another folder, skimmed its contents, and placed it in bed-order with the others on top of the trolley. She deciphered the scrawl on the notes in front of her with difficulty. It looked as if an army of giant ants had trekked across the page, and she wished for the umpteenth time that doctors had handwriting lessons as part of their training. A wave of fair hair fell across her forehead and she pushed it back, feeling the still unfamiliar Sister's triangular cap resting lightly across her shoulders as she leaned once more over the casenotes. It still took her by surprise to look down and see her dark blue uniform instead of the light blue of a Staff Nurse's, and her stiff white cuffs were nearly always sitting on top of the filing cabinet in the office while she worked in the ward with sleeves rolled up.

Satisfied, she put the last notes on top of the pile. She was ready now for Dr Grainger's round, but was the ward work all done?

Mrs Fowler the orderly, cap perched precariously on her frizzy new perm, was still tidying locker tops and giving out glasses and jugs of fresh water, and Bradley and Sykes were more than halfway round with 'beds and backs'. The ward looked good, she thought with satisfaction. Bright sunlight slanted through high sash windows and lay like treacle across the polished brown floor. The recently-made-up fire crackled, and its sooty smell mingled with the scents of spring flowers. Patients lay to attention after Bradley and Sykes's ministrations in readiness for the consultant's visit. Beds looked cheerful with scarlet blankets and crisp white sheets, and there was an atmosphere of anticipation, for all hoped for encouraging news of their progress, and after the round some patients would be making plans to go home.

Rosamund moved to the foot of Mrs Todd's bed and loosened the counterpane over her feet. She smiled at the little woman with a faded blond fringe lying pale against the pillows.

'That's better, Sister, thank you.' She wiggled her feet. 'Do you think Dr Grainger'll let me go home this time?' she whispered.

'You'll be home just as soon as you're well enough, Mrs Todd. Let's wait and see what he says.' She spoke gently, knowing that Mrs Todd was unlikely to see midsummer, home or not.

Miss Crowther crept by in her pink dressing gown, sponge bag over her arm.

'I have got time, haven't I Sister?'

Rosamund glanced at her watch pinned above her apron bib. 'Yes – so long as you don't want a bath.'

She had time to spare herself too. She could start checking the lotion cupboard for the dispensary order. Bradley and Sykes had a few more beds to go. A remedial gymnast in his whites and navy blue belt was making Nurse Dunn blush as she washed her hands at the sink near the ward door. Another romance blossoming? Rosamund smiled to herself.

She knelt at the lotion cupboard in the cabinet, unlocked it and began to make a list. Bottles clinked, and there was a distant hum from the corridor where the ward cleaner was polishing the floor. Dunn was still talking by the sink. Rosamund hoped she would get on with her work soon or she would have to be told and the gymnast sent packing. But another minute or two wouldn't hurt. Patients chatted quietly to each other. There was an occasional rustle of newspapers, and a tinny crackle from un-switched-off headphones hanging above an empty bed. Laughter erupted behind the curtains where Bradley and Sykes were rubbing Mrs Simpson's behind with enthusiasm, judging by the accompanying giggles and gasps.

Rosamund chuckled into the cupboard. She liked her patients and staff to get on with each other, but the nurses sometimes needed checking. Nurse Sykes was one – she didn't always pull her weight. She'd had to speak to her last week when she'd left someone on a bedpan for too long. The poor woman had been very distressed. Rosamund sighed. It wasn't easy being a Sister, but she wouldn't have it any other way. She examined a ridged bottle containing purple liquid. Methylated spirit was low. The next, smaller bottle was dark brown, and she uncorked it to peer in. And tinct. benz. She added them to her list.

The two nurses moved to the next bed at the other side of the cabinet from where Rosamund knelt, and drew the curtains round.

'We're just going to make you comfortable and tidy for the ward round, Mrs Lewis. Can you roll over so we can rub your bottom?' Nurse Sykes sounded business-like.

***

Rosamund reached into the back of the cupboard and emerged with a sticky glycerine bottle. The hum of the polisher in the distance stopped.

'…think she is – the snooty bitch? Talk about Ice Maiden.' Sykes's voice was low but clear from behind the curtain. There was a stifled snigger.

'What she needs is a man.' It was Bradley this time.

'She wouldn't know what to do with one. Dig your heels in Mrs Lewis, and we'll lift you up the bed. Oops-a-daisy. For such a good looking woman, she's a cold fish!'

Rosamund stuck her head back in the cupboard. What poor soul was being pulled to pieces this time, she wondered. The hospital was full of gossips. Carbolic acid. When did we last use this for goodness' sake? She put it with the other empty bottles.

'Yes, quite comfy, thanks, Nurse. She's been ever so good to me, and when Mrs Smith was dying and no relatives here she sat and held her hand as if she was her own mother.'

With burning cheeks, Rosamund suddenly realised who they were talking about. She started to get to her feet.

'Oh, I grant you that. She's good to the patients, but we're only the nurses.' The scornful voice persisted. 'That right, Bradley?'

'Come off it. Sister's not as bad as all that. She's strict, but fair. You can't skive on this ward.'

'Don't I know it! I still say she needs a man. That'd soften her up.'

Bradley was making warning faces when Sister Hambly wrenched open the curtains, eyes glittering like chips of blue ice.

'*When* you have finished, Nurse. Dr Grainger is on the next ward. We should be ready for him *now*.'

'Just one more, Sister,' was Nurse Bradley's studiously innocent reply. Sykes didn't say a word.

Rosamund closed the curtains firmly, grasped the sides of her trolley and swept out of the ward, the wheels drumming over the polished floor like a swarm of angry bees.

The nurses finished the beds just as the consultant and his team reached the ward, and retreated into the sluice, dragging the trolley behind them. Rosamund emerged from the office still smarting from the words she had overheard, but her face and demeanour were calm as she pushed her cuffs over her wrists and greeted the consultant.

'Good morning, Doctor Grainger.'

'Good morning, Sister. Shall we go in?'

He moved with dignity into the ward. The sun glinted on careful black and silver waves swept back from a broad forehead. With high cheekbones and an aquiline nose set between dark eyes, he was a handsome man. Not tall, he moved gracefully but, Rosamund thought, with a curious restraint. She liked the way he looked intently into the patients' faces as if each one really mattered.

'Ah, Miss Simpson. How are you feeling today?' He took her hand.

'A bit better, I think, Doctor. Only – I've still got this pain here.'

'Have you indeed? We'll have to see what we can do about that. Let's have a look at your tummy.'

His fingers searched gently. Miss Simpson winced. 'Tender, is it?' He looked up at Doctor Batty, his houseman. 'Here, feel this again and tell me what you find. Are the results of the last blood tests back yet, Sister?'

So the round continued, moving from bed to bed. Afterwards, the procession filed out of the ward and into the office. Nurses Sykes and

Bradley scuttled back into the ward, Rosamund could hear Dunn rattling bedpans, and Mrs Fowler wheeled a trolley from the kitchen to set up for dinner.

In the office Rosamund waited until everyone was settled, then poured coffee into china cups. This was all part of the ritual while Doctor Grainger discussed his cases and made further plans for his patients' care. Rosamund handed round biscuits, then bit into a bourbon herself. She enjoyed this part of the round – the pooling of ideas, the planning, being part of the team. Doctor Grainger had the knack of making each person's contribution valued, although he had been at the hospital for only a few weeks. His predecessor had been very different, charging round the ward, and speaking to each patient as though she were deaf. He'd sat in the office, legs splayed and a china cup fragile in his beefy hand, looking as though he would be more at home in a rugby club bar. He regarded all nurses, including Sisters, as underlings – and that put up Rosamund's professional back. He had been everything Doctor Grainger was not.

As they were leaving the ward the registrar, Ron Smith, who was a friend of Philip's, stopped to have a word.

'Is Helen ready for tomorrow, Rosamund?'

'Yes I think so. She's rather nervous, but determined to enjoy herself. Once the ceremony's over she'll relax. How's Philip?'

'Bearing up, you know. We'll make sure tonight that he's well prepared.'

'Don't go and give him a sore head for tomorrow,' warned Rosamund. 'Helen would never forgive you.'

He laughed. 'A man's got to enjoy his last night of freedom. We'll look after him, don't worry. When are you going up to Whitby?'

'I'm finishing early and travelling up with Sandra this afternoon. We bridesmaids are staying at Helen's parents.'

'Right. See you at the church.' With a wave he turned to catch up with the rest of the team.

***

'There, I think that's everything.' Rosamund pushed back her chair and stood up. 'They're all yours for the weekend.' She reached for her cloak from the back of the office door.

'Don't worry about a thing.' Staff Nurse Daly closed the Report

Book and slid her cuffs off her sleeves. 'Just go, and have a wonderful time. I'll want to hear all about the wedding when you get back.'

'It seems half the staff are off to Whitby this weekend. It leaves you a bit thin on the ground.' Rosamund hovered in the doorway.

'We'll manage. Let's just hope there won't be too many emergencies. Helen and Philip deserve a good send off. Now, go, go, go!' She rolled up her sleeves and shooed the laughing Rosamund into the corridor.

The telephone was ringing as Rosamund pushed her key into the door of her room. It was Helen, fizzing with excitement.

'I can't believe it's happening at last.' Rosamund could hear the happiness in her voice all the way down the phone line. 'My dress and the bridesmaid dresses have arrived today, and they're gorgeous, Roz.'

'I thought they would be. I'm dying to wear mine.'

'We'll have a trying on session this evening. Just you, me and Sandra. And Mum of course.'

'That'll be lovely. How's your mum coping?'

'She's dashing about like a whirling dervish. I think she's more nervous than I am. The dogs and the boys keep getting underfoot, even though she finds jobs for them to do – the boys, I mean – not the dogs. And when it all gets a bit too much for Dad he escapes to the bathroom with the Yorkshire Post. You know what he's like!'

'I do.' Rosamund pictured Helen's slight, shy father with wispy brown hair and gentle eyes. He was no match for her mother, who was rosy and energetic. She had got to know them well over the last few years, and smiled to imagine the scene. 'You haven't seen Philip, have you? It's bad luck if you do, you know.'

'No, of course not. He was travelling up this morning. Should have arrived at the Grosvenor by now with his Best Man. You'll have a chance to get to know David. He's not a bit like Philip – you'd never guess they were brothers. I think you'll get on with him, Roz.'

'You never give up, do you Helen. Forget it.' She laughed. 'I saw Ron this morning after the ward round, and he says the gang are taking Philip out tonight.'

'I hope he doesn't overdo it. I don't want a bridegroom with a headache!'

'Ron promised they'd look after him.'

The line went quiet for a moment, then, 'Roz, I wish you were here already.' There was the slightest quiver in her voice.

'I'll be with you soon. I'm just getting ready to catch the train. Does your dad know you're ringing me? This call must be costing the earth.'

'Probably, but who cares today. He won't mind anyway. I won't hold you up any more, though. So – so long, safe journey.' And she hung up.

Rosamund unpinned her cap and stepped out of her uniform. Five years she had known Helen. All throughout their training – and several months before. It would be strange not to be sharing their lives in the same way. She would carry on here in her solitary room, while Helen retreated after work to the brand new house on the outskirts of the city which she and Philip had bought when he became a Registrar. They would still see each other, of course, but it would never be the same. No more gossip over a cup of tea in the evening in one or the other's room; no borrowing of stockings or earrings; no popping off to the shops together; no letting off steam when she was fed up or sharing the good things that happened; no dashing next door to read out the latest letter from Edith. Even though she would see her most days, there were countless ways in which she would miss Helen.

She stood in her petticoat and looked at her reflection in the wardrobe mirror. How much had she changed in these last six years? Certainly she was not the innocent young girl who had arrived in Leadersfield overwhelmed with shock and grief, pitchforked out of a life of love and security into a bewildering new world of loneliness and struggle. Did it show? She touched her face, feeling the hard edge of her cheekbones, traced the sculptured hollows of her cheeks and the line of her jaw. The ring finger of her left hand stroked the curve of her lips. Would Francis recognise her now? Her nose was still long and straight, but there were shadows in the blue depths of her eyes that had not been there the last time he saw her. Life had taught her a lesson or two since then. She ran her hands over her breasts and hips, slender still, but fuller than her teenage figure had been.

An ambulance siren wailed in the distance. You have a train to catch and a wedding to go to, she told herself with a shake. Stop this daydreaming and get dressed.

Rosamund turned to where her travelling clothes were laid out on the bed and picked up a nylon stocking. In spite of her intentions her thoughts ran on.

Do people really see me as the 'Ice Maiden'? she wondered as she fastened a suspender and twisted round to adjust the seam. Am I such a 'cold fish'? Could the protective skin she had grown over her wounded self have obscured the warm and loving person she knew herself to be? She had picked herself up after blow after blow, determined to find fulfilment in her work as a nurse, to do the job to the best of her ability. Damn this zip, it always sticks. She tugged until it ran free, then pulled a honey-coloured jumper over her head. Perhaps Nurse Sykes had been right. Maybe she *was* too hard on the juniors. She felt so passionately about the care of her patients that probably she expected too much of the students. No, I don't think I do, Rosamund decided as she pulled a comb through her hair and ran a coral lipstick over her lips. Maybe it's the way I go about it that gives the wrong impression.

She shrugged and slung her toilet things into her holdall, slipped on her jacket and folded her raincoat over her arm as she looked around the room. Yes, I've got everything...

'Are you ready, Roz?'

Sandra was at the door.

'Perfect timing. Have you got our wedding present?'

'Right here in my suitcase. Let's go.'

25

Whitby, 1960.

In the blue and gold ballroom at the Grosvenor Hotel, the bride's father and the best man had delivered their speeches, while Helen and Philip, the most photogenic of bridal couples, sat starry-eyed between them, no joke or anecdote too embarrassing for their enjoyment. The wedding cake had been cut and shared, and now the room was cleared for dancing. The dance band, at the far end of the room under a huge mirror and flanked by a bank of flowers, made quiet toots and tunings, rustled their music sheets, and shook surplus moisture out of their instruments. The leader nodded to the drummer, and a drum roll crescendoed round the room, silencing the crowd.

'Ladies and gentlemen. Take your partners for – the Palais Glide!' the band leader announced with a flourish, several chins wobbling against his white tie.

Helen grabbed Rosamund and Sandra. 'Come on. We *must* do this together. Where's Amy?'

She looped her wedding gown unceremoniously over her arm and dashed across the floor to where Amy sat beside Cyril, with two-year-old Sally on her knee.

'Amy, you can't sit this one out.' She lifted a surprised Sally onto Cyril's lap. 'Here you are, poppet. Sit with Daddy, and watch Mummy dancing.'

'Naw. I'll slow yer down.' Amy hugged her seven month pregnancy.

'No you won't.' Helen took her hands and pulled her onto the floor where Rosamund and Sandra were poised like butterflies in their full-skirted lilac bridesmaid's dresses. Amy gave in. She straightened her green smock and grinned at them.

The band were already into the number, and dancers swarmed onto the floor. Several colleagues from the hospital – nursing sisters, registrars and consultants, were clustered around a large table near the open French doors, and most of them got up in a burst of laughter to join in the dance. Helen and Philip's parents linked up together, and a gaggle of nieces and nephews jostled each other for places. The four girls found a space and cross-linked their arms behind to girate round the dance floor.

When the dance ended after a last triumphant 'stamp, stamp' that shook the floor, laughing and breathless the four girls returned to where a glowering Cyril juggled Sally and his almost empty beerglass.

'Dance, dance.' Sally clapped her hands and swung her legs.

Amy plumped down heavily and fanned her face. 'Eh, they'll be the death of me, these girls,' she said to Cyril.

'The exercise'll have done you good.' He plonked Sally back on Amy's lap and drained his glass. She hugged the little girl and kissed the top of her dark head.

Philip and David pushed through the crowd and stood before them side by side.

It was true, thought Rosamund, they didn't look in the least like brothers. Philip's fairish hair was straight, and flopped over twinkly blue eyes. He was always having to flick it back even though he plastered it down with Brylcream, and his fresh round face gave him a deceptively boyish look. David had unruly curls, a long chin and high forehead, and Rosamund thought he looked like a wild professor with a wicked gleam in his eye.

'May I have the pleasure, Mrs Wheatley?' Philip bent over Helen's hand with playful courtesy.

'Certainly, husband mine.' Helen put her hand in his and rose with a loving look.

Sandra looked up at David with a flutter of her long lashes. It worked like a charm.

'May I have the pleasure?' He smiled at her and winked.

Sandra flashed a triumphant glance at Rosamund and glided into his arms. Rosamund chuckled. She didn't mind a bit, expected it of Sandra, in fact. She turned to her tiny god-daughter, who was jigging about in Amy's arms.

'Come and dance with me, Sally.' She held out her hands.

'Just for a minute or two.' Amy set Sally on her feet. 'I must take her up to our room to bed soon. If she'll settle.'

The toddler held out her arms. Rosamund waltzed her round like Ring o' Roses, then scooped her into her arms and whirled into the melée of dancers. Round and round they went, weaving in and out of the throng. Couples smiled at them as they passed, and Sally clung to Rosamund's neck and squealed and giggled, her eyes screwed up in delight, until Rosamund gradually slowed the pace and they returned gently to her parents. Rosamund rocked her on her knee, and hummed to the music until she relaxed and put her thumb in her mouth. Feeling her weight on her arm, Rosamund looked down at her godchild, sprawled in sleepy abandon across her lap. She was a solid child, more like Cyril than Amy, with straight dark hair and brown eyes, but her sunny nature was all her own. Thick lashes fringed closed eyes, translucent lids faintly blue in the subdued light of the ballroom; the curve of her cheeks, and dimpled chin made Rosamund's heart swell with love. It didn't matter that Cyril was her father.

'Bed-time now, sweetie.' Amy reached for her.

Sally jerked awake. 'A'ntie Woz. More dance.' She tried to scramble down.

'No love, it's your bedtime now. Daddy'll dance with Auntie Roz. Now, kiss goodnight and let's go find Teddy.'

Rosamund panicked. He mustn't know that the very thought of him made her flesh crawl, that she loathed him with all her heart. It was for Amy's sake and little Sally's that she ever visited their house, when she made as sure as she could that Cyril would not be there. Since the day when she had discovered that the man who had tried to rape her six years ago was Amy's beloved, she had been in his company only a handful of times, and had always been able to avoid being alone with him, and she wasn't going to dance with him now. She stood up.

'I'm just going to…'

'No, Roz, I always do as Amy says.' Cyril slanted dark eyes at her and slicked back his hair, and before she could prevent it he had steered her into the dance.

She couldn't break free without making a scene, so she swallowed her misgivings and without looking at him, concentrated on following his lead. They danced past Amy with Sally in her arms, and as soon as she had lumbered out of sight into the foyer, Cyril adjusted his hold and clasped Rosamund more firmly.

'I haven't forgotten you,' he whispered. His beery breath on her neck made her shudder, and she felt him looking down the front of her dress.

She didn't reply, but stiffened and tried to hold herself away from him.

'Oh no, you don't.'

His hand moved down from the middle of her back. He pulled her closer until they were hip to hip and she could feel the hardness of him against her belly. The more she tried to move away the tighter he held. She could see a hungry glint through his lashes, and a deceptively bland smile played about his wet lips. Rosamund closed her eyes. Ace. Fear and revulsion filled her, as memory of the night when he had attempted to rape her flooded back, and the scent of his hair oil brought bile to her mouth. Anger flared and spread, and threatened to explode. I don't want to make a scene on Helen's wedding night, she worried, but I'll have to do something. Then she realised with horror that he was going to steer her through the French windows into the darkness of the terrace. She stopped abruptly, and with no further thought stamped the stiletto heel of her satin shoe with all her force on top of his foot.

'Aa-argh!' His mouth opened wide in a strangled yell, and Rosamund just had time to register his look of agony, closely followed by disbelief, when there was a polite 'Excuse me', and she was swept away from him into the arms of…

'Dr Grainger!'

She gasped, and missed a step.

'Sister Hambly.' He chuckled and whirled her round. Brown eyes twinkled as he led smoothly round the dance floor, his hold cool and correct.

Still shaking, Rosamund caught her breath and her eyes filled with tears. She couldn't tell whether she was still angry, or whether they were tears of relief. Determined not to shed them, she met his gaze.

'Thank you, Dr Grainger. That was getting rather tricky.'

'My pleasure, Sister. I am glad of the opportunity to dance with you. You dance well, if I may say so – given the chance.'

She managed a wry smile, and decided to enjoy herself.

When the dance finished she returned with him to the nurses' and doctors' table. She wasn't going to let what had happened with Cyril spoil things. She saw Amy come back from putting Sally to bed and sit down with a glass of orange in her hand beside Helen's grandmother.

There was no sign of Cyril, thank goodness. Drowning his sorrows in the bar, she guessed. The evening flowed on. She didn't lack for partners and danced several more times with Dr Grainger, surprised to find the dignified consultant such good company.

After the interval, Helen threaded her way to where Rosamund stood talking to Ron and his girlfriend, and Maggie Dale from paediatrics and her husband.

'We want to leave for our honeymoon in about half an hour, Roz. Will you come and help me change?'

'Course I will.' Rosamund put down her glass. 'Shall I get Sandra too?'

'I wouldn't bother looking. She's not been around for ages – neither has David.' They exchanged knowing looks and laughed.

'Ladies and gentlemen – the Gay Gordons!'

Sweat stood out on the bandleader's shiny face, the band swung into the Scottish tune and there was a multicolour surge as dancers took their places. The rising babble of people who had been enjoying themselves for hours and fully intended to go on doing so, became muted as the two friends entered the foyer.

'Just a minute.' Rosamund stopped. 'Look.'

Two of the male guests were trying to help another up the stairs. He was almost incapable, with buckling knees and lolling head. Amy stood by looking mortified, a large key with an ornate tag clutched in her hand.

'Come on, Cyril. Help yourself, lad.' Urged one of the men.

Cyril lurched to the bannister and draped himself over. He hung there with collar awry and slack mouth, looking down on the small crowd which had collected. Rosamund turned away in disgust, but he spotted her.

'Tha'sh 'er,' he slurred, swung his arm and pointed an unsteady finger in the general direction of Rosamund. Athough he could have been pointing at any one of the people who were giggling or staring with distaste at the scene on the stairs, she knew it was meant for her. She was right.

'That's the whorin' bitch 'at attacked me. Stabbed me in the foot, the teasing cunt.'

'Cyril, stop that.' Amy faced up to him, face chalky. 'Get up to our room. Right *now*!'

'An' you're as bad. Nivver let a man 'ave a good time, yer mingy bugger.' Amy took a step towards him and he attempted to shoot off up the stairs on all fours, but went sprawling on the next step. With a sigh of resignation, Amy shoved from behind and the two men half dragged, half carried him the rest of the way, mumbling and cursing as he went. The onlookers lost interest and dispersed.

Amy dropped back, and clapped her hand to her mouth.

'They can't tek him to our room. Our Sally's asleep in there. She'll be terrified.'

'I'll take her, Amy.' Rosamund put her arm round her. 'She can come back to Helen's with me until morning. We'll take her with us into Helen and Philip's room for now,' with an enquiring look at Helen, who nodded agreement. 'If she wakes up she can help. She'd love that.'

'We'll fetch her now, when you go in to Cyril.' Helen hesitated. 'Unless you'd rather come with us as well?'

'Nay, Helen. He'll expect me there when he wakes up. He's allus vile when he's drunk. I've got used to it.' She grimaced. 'It's never been in public before though. Sally's never had to see him, and I don't want her to. Yes, thanks, you'd better take her – though I expect she'll miss me in the morning.' Amy turned wearily towards the stairs. 'Come on then. They can't get in without the key.'

'He doesn't deserve her,' Helen muttered to Rosamund as they followed.

Rosamund carried the sleeping Sally wrapped in a blanket along the corridor to the room where Philip had slept the night before, grateful that Helen hadn't questioned her about Cyril's ravings.

'Wait there and I'll make her a nest.' Helen moved her headdress and veil from the bed where she had abandoned them earlier, and laid them across the back of a chair. She bunched up the eiderdown and a pillow to make a child-sized hollow where Rosamund laid down her burden. Sally didn't stir. Rosamund tucked a blanket round her, kissed her forehead and stepped back.

'There. Snug as a bug in a rug. She's fast asleep. With a bit of luck she'll stay that way.' She looked at Helen. 'Now, what do you want me to do?'

Helen stood in the middle of the room in her wedding gown. Philip's blue and white pyjamas lay in a lump on the floor; his hairbrush and open toilet bag stood on the dressing table beside her wedding bouquet of white lilac and pink roses, whose perfume spilled over a rumpled heap of yesterday's clothes and a scatter of confetti. A wet towel laid a trail to the bathroom. Unheeding, she moved to look in the mirror and gazed at her image, eyes large in the golden light from the bedside lamp.

'It's funny, there's all that planning and panicking for months and months to get everything just right. There's temper and tears and excitement and 'oh God what can go wrong next?' And it feels like forever. Then all of a sudden the day's here. Your wedding day. It's happening, and it's wonderful. Then just when you've realised that, it slips through your fingers, and all you're left with is a blur. I've only worn my wedding dress for a few hours, and I may never wear it again.'

'I thought you were going to keep it as a ball gown?'

'I was, but it wouldn't be the same. It'd be obvious it was my wedding dress.'

'You could always have it altered.' Rosamund waited, wanting like Helen to prolong the moment. Eventually she went on. 'Look Helen, I don't want to rush you, but Amy's problem and poppet here have delayed us, and Philip'll be here to collect you soon.'

'I don't really want to take it off.' Helen still gazed at her reflection. 'But I must, of course.' She raised her arms behind her head. 'I can manage the hook and eye at the top. Can you undo all those buttons down the back?'

Rosamund was all fingers and thumbs, her mind still in turmoil from the evening's events. Tongue between her teeth, she concentrated on pushing the tiny covered buttons through the loops.

'There, that's the lot.' She stood up and eased the dress over Helen's shoulders, and helped her to step out of it billowing folds.

Helen went into the bathroom, and Rosamund heard taps running and the swish of water in the bowl. She picked up the dress, heavy with its stiff underskirt, hung it on the end of the wardrobe, and stroked the drift of snowy lace.

'It's a dream of a dress,' she said as Helen came out of the bathroom in a cloud of Coty L'Aimant. 'And you looked wonderful in it.'

'I felt wonderful in it – just as I always imagined I would feel as a bride. Did you see Phil's expression as I came down the aisle?'

'Yes, and I wanted to cry.'

'A memory to treasure. But there's our honeymoon yet. No surprises there I'm afraid.' She arched her eyebrows in mock regret, reached into the wardrobe to bring out a scarlet dress and jacket.

'That's smashing, it sets off your hair perfectly. Here, let me help.'

Rosamund lifted the pencil-slim dress over Helen's dark head. 'I'm so pleased for you, Helen.' She hugged her friend with tears in her eyes.

'It'll be your turn one day Roz, just you wait and see.'

Rosamund turned away, chasing the fleeting image of another church, another wedding, never to be.

26

Leadersfield.

Back at Leadersfield life settled into its usual pattern. Nothing dreadful had happened on the ward while she was away, and Rosamund gave Staff Daly a lively account of the wedding. But she said nothing about dancing with Dr Grainger, nor about Cyril.

She felt sick when she thought about what had happened, and was still angry that he had tried to take advantage of her, especially at the wedding. She remembered with satisfaction the feel of her stiletto heel as it slammed into the bony tissue above the tongue of his slip-on shoes, and the howl of anguish as he let go of her. It serves him right. I don't know how Amy puts up with him. She ought to know the truth about Cyril and me before she met him – how he attacked me in my room at Mrs Wilson's. I've always felt guilty that I didn't tell her. Rosamund made up her mind. I *shall* tell her, even if it means I can't see Sally again. Sadness slid over her like a cloud over the sun.

On the way off duty she went to see if there was any post for her in the pigeonholes outside Home Sister's office. It wasn't that she ever had much post, but there just might be a letter from Edith. There was no blue airmail envelope, but there was a post card with a view of Ambleside from Helen and Philip saying that the weather was good and they didn't 'wish she was here'. Rosamund smiled and picked up an elegant grey envelope with firm sloping writing in a vaguely familiar hand. She took it back to her room to open. Where had she seen that writing before? She slit the envelope with her nail-file, pulled out a single piece of notepaper and sat down on the bed to read it.

My dear Miss Hambly, she read.

I so much enjoyed your company at the wedding last week, and would very much like to see you again. I do not know your tastes, but if you are free on Wednesday next week, the Liverpool Philharmonia Orchestra will be playing at the Town Hall. If you would like to go I should be delighted to take you.

I do hope you will say yes.
Yours sincerely
Laurence Grainger.

Astonished, she realised where she had seen the writing before – on casenotes.

There was a tap on the door and Sandra's head appeared.

'Oh sorry, you're busy... Are you okay? You look a bit shell-shocked.'

'I am. Read this.' She held out the letter with an embarrassed laugh.

'Oh my, aren't you the lucky one?' Sandra was all agog. 'How did you manage this?'

'I didn't *manage* anything. At Helen's wedding, while you were so discreetly out of view with the dashing Dave Wheatley, I was doing the usual things, like dancing. With Dr Grainger, among others.'

'You don't say. Shall you go?'

'I don't know. I haven't had time to think about it yet, I've only just opened the letter. Don't you breathe a word about this Sandra, I really don't want it to get out. Promise.'

'I suppose so, if I must.' Sandra was thoughtful. 'The letter seems a bit starchy, but he's rather a dish, even though he is a bit old. I wondered how long it would be before someone snaffled him. He's not married, is he?' Their minds went back to Rosamund's disastrous affair with Neil.

'I don't think so. He doesn't seem the type somehow. I don't want to get into anything like that again.' She shuddered. 'You mustn't jump to conclusions, though. He's only asked me if I 'd like to go to a concert, for heaven's sake, not jump into bed.'

***

Dr Grainger was polite and attentive as he settled her into her seat. Rosamund, who had never been in a proper concert hall before, looked round excitedly at the rich mouldings on the ceiling; the gilded organ pipes which soared above the formal black and white figures of the orchestra as they took their seats on curved tiers above the conductor's rostrum. Sheets of music fluttered on music stands, and the gleam of instruments winked out at the audience as it flowed into the auditorium. Their murmurings mingled with the toots and twiddles as instruments were tuned. Dr Grainger leaned towards her, sharing the programme. He smelt fresh and clean, of a citrusy cologne. There was a ripple of applause as the conductor took his place on the rostrum. Then the woman soloist entered and cradled her cello lovingly against spread skirts, bow poised.

A magical moment of hush, then the first quiet chords of Elgar's cello concerto stole through the dimness. Rosamund sat entranced as the rich chords soared and swooped, filling the hall with thrilling sound, and she was transported in imagination over moorland hills and wooded valleys. She could feel the wind of her going, and the surge of the sea was in it. There was a wildness in her heart, and the scent of grass and green leaves in her nostrils, and flying clouds were all around her. Then, as the music drew to a close and applause swelled and died like rain pattering on leaves, she turned to her companion. He was looking at her intently with a look she couldn't fathom. It was a look that didn't threaten, and she smiled and turned back to applaud the cellist again.

Afterwards, they lingered for a while in a nearby bar. He asked her to call him Laurence, and they talked easily of music and Helen and Philip, until he took her back to the hospital, purring up to the gates in his dark green Jaguar car. She asked to be put down outside the gates, and he did as she asked without fuss.

***

Helen and Philip returned from their honeymoon. Rosamund looked at the gold band on Helen's finger, and the unmistakeable glow of happiness she wore like a garment, and was glad for her. It wasn't long before Rosamund told Helen about Laurence, but swore her to secrecy as well as Sandra.

'It's not as if there's anything to hide,' she told her 'but the gossips'll have us married off in no time if it gets out.'

'Do you think so? I wondered if he was a bit precious. You know – not the marrying kind.' She looked at Rosamund with her head on one side.

'Of course not, it's just his 'olde worlde charm'.' Rosamund laughed at the suggestion. 'He *is* courteous and considerate. Perhaps it's because he's older. I don't have to fight him off like I do younger men – they always want more. It's good to have a man friend – and a social life!'

'I'm pleased for you, Roz. You deserve to have someone nice in your life.'

***

It was three weeks after the wedding before Rosamund decided she couldn't put off talking to Amy any longer. She had meant to go before, but with the surprise of Laurence's invitation, then Helen and Philip coming back from honeymoon… You're just making excuses, she told herself. Go and do it.

It was a cold April morning but the sun shone, slanting a long chimney-topped shadow across the setts of the street where Amy and Cyril lived. Rosamund shivered waiting for her knock to be answered, not sure whether she was shivering with apprehension or cold. It was a while before the door opened, and Sally rushed out and grabbed Rosamund round the knees.

'Auntie Roz. You've come!' she cried.

'I have come, Sally.' She picked up her god-daughter, laughing, and kissed her cheek. 'Hello Amy.'

'I was upstairs doing the bedrooms,' Amy panted. 'Come in Roz.'

'I want to talk to you,' Rosamund followed her friend into the room.

'Aye, I thought you might.' Amy gave her a level look. 'Later, when Sally has her rest, mebbee?'

'That's fine by me.' She sat down on the sofa. 'How are you?' Amy's thin face was even thinner, and there seemed to be nothing of her behind the bulk of her pregnancy.

'I'm middling. There's only five weeks to go, so I'm slow and clumsy. But I can't complain.'

Sally brought a book and climbed on Rosamund's lap. 'Read it, p'ease.'

'What have we here?' She cuddled the little girl against her. 'Ginger's Adventures. Who's Ginger then?'

'Doggie.'

Rosamund read the story. Sally listened, leaning back against Rosamund, enthralled with the pictures.

'You'll stay for some dinner, Roz?'

'Yes, please. I've brought some boiled ham and plain teacakes, and bananas for a treat. Sally and I could get it ready, couldn't we, Sal?'

'I'll leave you to it, then.' Amy took her knitting out. 'There's some nice tomatoes in the pantry that me dad brought up yesterday from his greenhouse.'

Rosamund cut bread and butter and set slices of ham on plates. Sally put tomatoes in a green bowl and with her tongue stuck between her teeth, carried it carefully to the table. She went back for the salt and pepper, chatting all the time, oblivious to the tension that was mounting between the two women.

After the meal Rosamund tucked Sally into bed with Teddy in her arm and her thumb in her mouth, and went downstairs to where Amy waited, her feet up on a stool.

They looked at each other for a long moment. Rosamund spoke first.

'There's something you should know, Amy.'

'Is it about what went on at the wedding?'

'Yes, it is.' Rosamund composed herself. 'But it's more than that.' And she told her from the beginning when Ace pursued her at the Jester coffee bar.

Amy sat back, eyes closed and a taut expression on her face, even paler than she was before. When Rosamund got to the place where she was knocked down by the bus, Amy opened her eyes.

'I allus knew there were more than either of you said.' Rosamund's eyes widened. 'Oh, yes, I asked Cyril, and he told me same as you did – that he took a shine to you, but you weren't interested. It were over and done with before I met him, he said, so I reckoned it were none of my business.'

'I wanted to tell you at the time. You were so happy, I couldn't. I've felt guilty ever since.'

'I were happy. We both were. I don't think I would have believed you then.'

'I tried not to think about what had happened when I knew him as Ace, only to see him as Cyril, your boyfriend and then your husband. And I took good care only to come to your house when I knew he wouldn't be here.'

'Things were never quite the same between you and me after I met Cyril, were they? Then he said those things to you when he were drunk at the wedding. I didn't take much notice at the time, I were that mad with him anyway. Something else happened that evening, didn't it?'

'I'm afraid so.' She told her about the dance Cyril had forced her into, how she had stamped on his foot, and of Laurence's rescue. 'It can't go on, Amy. That's why I've told you the whole story. I'm sorry it's come to this, and the last thing I want to do is upset you.'

'I'm not all that surprised,' Amy said. 'I've seen glimpses of what he can be like.'

'Amy?'

'I respect you for telling me, but I can't pretend it won't make difficulties.'

'I was afraid of that. What will you do?'

'I sh'll tackle him about it, never fear. Tell him straight. Now we all know what's what, he'll have to behave.' She struggled to her feet and began an ungainly pacing backwards and forwards from the hearth to the kitchen door, one hand to the small of her back and the other supporting her bump. 'Bye, this child's being a little bugger today!'

Rosamund started to get up.

'No, it's all right – he quietens down if I move about a bit.' She paused. 'Rosamund, none of this is your fault, I can see that. Though I've had my doubts at times. You were the first person that spoke to me when we started at Leadersfield Hospital, and I'm not going to lose your friendship just because my husband's a stupid fool. Besides, you're our Sally's godmother.'

'I hoped you'd feel like that. You and Sally – I couldn't bear it if I lost you both.'

'D-don't.' Tears rolled down Amy's cheeks.

'Oh, I'm sorry, I've been clumsy, I *knew* I'd upset you.'

'No, it's not that. We've cleared the air between us, and I'm glad about that. It's – well, to tell the truth, things haven't been too good between me and Cyril anyway lately.'

'Why, what's the matter?'

'I've not been so well with this little one.' She stroked her abdomen. 'Sally's at an age when she needs a lot of attention. She wears me out. I've been more sickly this time, and I've no energy. It seems when Cyril comes home from his work that I've nowt left over for him, and I haven't been as attentive as I ought to be. He's taken to coming home later and later via the pub. So he's not in a mood to be patient when he does get here. And – he's inclined to be a bit forceful – at times.'

'Amy, I'd no idea.'

'It's all right. I expect it'll be better after the baby's born.'

Have you told your mother how you feel, asked her to help?'

'No, I've managed for myself.' She sniffed, and felt for a handkerchief up the sleeve of her jumper. 'I feel better for having let some of it out anyway.'

'I think you should tell your mother and the midwife how tired and anxious you are. I'll have Sally on my days off if that would help.'

'I suppose you're right. I expect it's just end of pregnancy blues, but a bit of help would put me on.' She knuckled her eyes like a child. 'I will tell me Mam – but not about Cyril – that's between me and him.'

'You haven't had any rest this afternoon, with me here. How about if I make us a cup of tea now. When Sally wakes up I'll take her out for an hour, then you can get a proper rest in bed.'

'That'd be grand, it'll be nice to be pampered a bit. If you don't mind I'll not wait for her to wake up, I'll go up now. I'm exhausted.'

'I'll bring your tea up to you, and an aspirin. All you need is a little t.l.c.'

She left the little terraced house well before teatime with mixed feelings. Amy looked more rested after her nap, although there were still purple shadows under her eyes. They'd hugged each other before she left, and Rosamund had promised to return on her day off the following week to look after Sally. It was good to be back on their old footing, but she was saddened and a little apprehensive about how things would turn out for Amy and Cyril. What Amy had learned today might make things worse – just before the new baby's birth, too. Rosamund sighed. Still, she'd been honest with her, and the rest was up to them.

***

The restaurant was on the first floor up thickly carpeted stairs. Rosamund and Laurence were shown to a table in the window, with a view of Victorian municipal buildings across the road, rosy pink brick in the evening sunlight. The white damask cloth was set with gleaming cutlery, and pleated napkins fanned out of wine glasses. There was a posy of cream rosebuds and a tall candle. Rosamund hoped no one could tell that this was a new experience for her, that she had never before dined in this style. There was a murmur of polite conversation, and a mingled smell of fine cooking and subtle perfumes. She accepted a large menu from the waiter.

Laurence took out a pair of half spectacles and perched them on his nose. He ran his eyes down the ornately printed page, looked across at her over his glasses.

'What will you have, Rosamund?'

She was still immersed in the menu.

'It's a good thing there's an English translation,' she murmured. 'My schoolgirl French isn't up to these culinary terms – although I can guess some of it. Just listen to this. *Buisson de Goujonnettes, Sauce Remoulade.* That's fried fish fingers with remoulade sauce – whatever that is.'

Laurence raised his eyebrows and chuckled.

Encouraged, Rosamund continued.

'*Supreme de Carrelet Tartarin* is fried fillet of plaice with tartare sauce. And *Consommé en Gelée...*' she looked up, saw Laurence trying to smother laughter, and blushed scarlet. 'Sorry. I'm showing my ignorance, aren't I?'

'Not at all. The menu's extremely pretentious. But I think we should choose, don't you? The waiter is hovering.'

'I'd like prawn cocktail. At least I know what that is. Then roast beef with Yorkshire pudding – or *Aloyan de Boeufroti à l'Anglaise* if you'd rather,' she decided with a mischievous twinkle. 'With *Pommes Persilées et Petits Pois*.' She closed the menu with a snap. 'And I do know that persil is parsley! What are you having?'

'Mm – *Hors d'Oeuvre Grand Vatel* – and I've no idea what that will turn out to be.' He entered into the spirit of the game. 'And I'll join you in the roast beef.'

The waiter swooped, and Laurence gave the order in impeccable French.

'Where did you learn French like that?'

'My mother came from a very good family, and she made sure I knew my way around.' He perused the wine list, and she didn't interrupt.

The food was good, as was the one glass of wine she allowed herself. They had more fun with the pudding menu. After several agonising jokes, in the end they both plumped for blackcurrant pie.

Coffee arrived, and two glasses of brandy. Rosamund cupped her brandy glass in both hands, and swirled the golden liquid as she had seen it done in films. Laurence took a leather cigar case from his inside pocket, smoothed and moulded to the shape of the body against which it had nestled for many years.

'Do you mind?' he indicated.

'No, I like the smell of cigars. Pa used to smoke them occasionally – on special occasions.' She craned her neck to read the worn gold letters along the side of the case. He pushed it across to her. 'My mother gave it to me on my thirtieth birthday.'

'E.L.G.' she read. 'What does E stand for?'

'Ernest. It was my grandfather's name, my mother's father.'

'Not your own father?'

'No.' He blew a column of blue smoke into the air, and leaned back, one hand resting on the table. You could see the elegance of his breeding if you looked, she thought, seeing the fine wrist, the broad palm with tapering fingers. The gold of a cufflink gleamed in the candle flame. 'He and my mother – all the family in fact, but he was the intractable one – were estranged. She fell in love with my father, Sam Grainger, who was an Able Seaman in the Merchant Navy. He wasn't considered good enough for the family, and her father forbade them to marry. However, by that time she was pregnant with me, and they turned her out.'

'Just like that?'

'Just like that. The proverbial 'never darken my doors again'. She and her father had always adored each other, and she had believed he would forgive her.'

'The poor girl. What did she do?'

'She and Sam married immediately. They found lodgings in Southampton, but very soon he had to go back to sea.'

'That must have been hard for your mother. Was he back in time for your birth?'

'He never came back. Two weeks after he sailed he fell between the ship and the quay in Marseilles and was crushed to death.'

'How awful. So you never knew him'.

He shook his head. 'Mother had a hard time of it. She found work cleaning in the offices of a shipping agent, while her landlady looked after me. She couldn't afford to be proud, even with her upbringing. After a while the manager, who was a widower, took her on as his housekeeper, and eventually they married.'

'What a story. So you did have a father in the end.'

'A stepfather – for a while, although he was never very interested in me, would have preferred to have my mother to himself. He did very well for himself, and became rich. He wouldn't have succeeded so well if it hadn't been for Mother. She was decorative, very good at entertaining and popular with his clients. She never forgot that she was a lady, and she brought me up accordingly.'

Rosamund was fascinated. 'You had a stepfather – for a while. What did you mean?'

'He had a stroke and died when I was twelve. He was a lot older than Mother, and fond of good living. I was away at school, and mother sold the house at Southampton and bought a cottage in Warwickshire a long way away from the sea. It has been our home ever since. Naturally Mother and I have always been close, and I go back whenever I can.'

'Why medicine then? It was bound to take you away from home?'

'It was something I'd always wanted to do, ever since I can remember.' He had been gazing into the winding wisps of cigar smoke, when he suddenly blinked and smiled across at Rosamund as though only then remembering she was there. 'But I've done too much talking. What about you? Tell me about yourself.'

Immersed in Laurence's story, feeling relaxed and dreamy from the effects of the brandy, she was suddenly catapulted into panic. This was something she usually avoided – talking about herself. There was so much she couldn't tell, and remembering was always painful.

She took a sip of brandy, felt the fiery liquid burn its way down her throat, glad of the gasps and coughs that gave her time to think.

'I'm not nearly so interesting,' she said when she could speak. 'My father came back from the First World War with shrapnel in his back, a semi-invalid for the rest of his life. He managed to go back to teaching, but only in the school in Treblissick – the Cornish village where we lived. He was a brilliant man, and should have had a brilliant career. My mother died soon after I was born, and my sister Edith, who's ten years older, lives in South Africa with her husband and twin sons. Father got worse, and after he couldn't work any longer I nursed him at home until he died. The house was sold, and as I'd had what you might call a disappointment in love, I came north and found myself nursing. That's about it.'

She knew it wasn't much, but it would have to do.

'And now?'

'I love my work, it's my life – and I have a circle of good friends. I'm happy.' She ran her finger round the edge of the brandy glass and looked at him. 'Let's put our skeletons back in the cupboard and talk about something else, shall we?' she said with a brightness she didn't feel.

'Of course, I didn't mean to pry.' He laid his cigar in the glass ashtray. Ash glowed red and grey against the dark brown of the stub, and he reached across the table and laid his hand over hers. 'I know you are not keen on people knowing about you and me – our friendship. Why should it matter so much? People gossip anyway, and it doesn't mean anything for long. We could do so much more together if it were not all a big secret. I should like us to make up a set at tennis, and badminton maybe; and to invite you to supper in the doctors' dining room – be part of the hospital scene. How about it?'

Rosamund looked down at where her hand lay unresponsive beneath his. Shall I pull it away? Or…? I will not let myself be hurt again, she determined, and I don't want to spoil our friendship.

He waited, one eyebrow slightly raised, head cocked. 'Well?'

She disengaged her hand gently and returned it to her lap.

'I'd like that, Laurence. It's time I came out of my shell.' She chuckled. 'And I've a fancy to start by sweeping up the drive to the Sisters' Home in your super Jaguar.'

He grinned back at her, and gave a mock bow. 'With the greatest of pleasure, mademoiselle. I'll be proud to be seen with you.'

Although determined to enjoy this new social life, Rosamund at first waited to see if Laurence would behave any differently towards her. She could see not the slightest difference. He was still polite and attentive but their relationship was more relaxed. If there was going to be gossip, she decided to relish it. As Sandra had said, a consultant was quite a catch, even if the situation was not as people would think. Let them talk.

She went to Amy's at least once a week to look after Sally as she had promised. Sometimes she took her out – to the river or to the swings in the park, or a ride on a bus, which she loved – and revelled in the company of her lively little god-daughter. Amy's mother and sister came to help her several times a week as well, and Amy lost her pinched look. She said nothing of what had transpired between herself and Cyril, and Rosamund didn't ask.

On the sixth of May, Amy's son was born at home. It was the day of the royal wedding, when Princess Margaret married Anthony

Armstrong-Jones, and Amy watched the ceremony on the television while pacing her sitting room in the throes of labour, a far cry from the grandeur and music at Westminster Abbey. The baby was a skinny scrap with a tuft of sandy hair and a yell you could hear for miles. Rosamund held him in her arms and, looking down on the crumpled determined little face, a replica of his mother, felt a surge of longing. Amy called him Joseph Anthony, after Princess Margaret's new husband.

That summer, Rosamund came out of her self-imposed social exile, and it became a time to look back on with pleasure. Work was no longer all-encompassing, and for that was all the more fulfilling. She and Laurence maintained their formality on ward rounds, and the patients would never have believed what fun staid Dr Grainger could be in private.

Summer rolled into autumn, and it was nearly Christmas when Laurence announced: 'I'm going to give a Christmas party.'

27

Dr Ron Smith's Morris Minor was bursting at the seams. He and Sandra's latest, a burly radiologist with a Desperate Dan chin and amazing blue eyes, were in the front. Crammed in the back in their party clothes were: Sandra, wearing scarlet lips and a frock to match; in the middle Ron's girlfriend, Brenda – a cuddle of a girl with a throaty chuckle, and Rosamund. Squashed up against the car door behind Ron's seat, she tried not to crease her new wool dress of parma violet. She had only recently had her ears pierced, and the amethyst earrings found in a junk shop felt deliciously sophisticated as they swung against her neck. With a white mohair stole borrowed from Helen she felt glamorous and glowing, despite her uncomfortable seat.

She peered out of the window to see an unfamiliar part of town, with tall unlit office buildings on both sides of the road. The Morris turned a corner into a square of Regency houses enclosing a church with a dome, where a tall fir tree dressed with white lights and an enormous star sparkled a welcome. To Rosamund's surprise, the car drew up at the pillared entrance to one of the houses. The chatter and laughter in the car faded to silence.

'Crikey!' Sandra was the first to recover her breath. 'This is *posh!* Roz, you never told us Laurence lived in a mansion!'

'I didn't know where he lived. I certainly didn't know it was here. It's not the whole house, though. He lives in a first floor apartment.'

'Well, don't sit there all night.' Ron had got out and folded down the back of the front seat. He reached in to help Rosamund first out of the car onto the pavement. 'Let's go and find out.'

They were admitted by a young man in a dinner jacket, into a carpeted hallway and through double doors into a swirl of colour and conversation. Over the heads of people Rosamund could see tall windows full of reflected candlelight, and a vast Christmas tree glowing with jewelled lamps stood near a marble fireplace, its high mantel garlanded with voluminous swags.

The familiar scent of citrus cologne, and there was Laurence to greet them.

'Welcome, all of you. Do have a hot toddy to warm you up.'

A waiter with a tray of steaming glasses stepped forward. Each took a glass and moved forward into the room to mingle in the throng.

Laurence turned to Rosamund. 'Mother's been looking forward to meeting you. Come, let me introduce you.'

It had to be accidental, but it seemed to Rosamund that the crowd parted, and she found herself looking across the room into the sharp, dark eyes of an old woman seated in a wing chair by the fire. The resemblance to Laurence was almost shocking. The same waves of snowy hair (although Laurence's as yet was mostly dark,) swept back from a broad forehead; the same high cheekbones and aquiline nose. Her bearing was regal, although Rosamund saw immediately the twist to the spine that told at what cost she maintained her posture. She wore a gown of burgundy velvet, a pearl choker at her throat, the hands resting on the arms of the chair bare of rings, gnarled and swollen. A silver-topped stick rested within reach against the chimney breast.

Laurence led her forward, hand under her elbow.

'Mother, this is Rosamund Hambly. Rosamund – Alicia Grainger, my mother.'

Her voice was vigorous, still low and firm.

'How do you do, my dear? I've looked forward to meeting you.'

Rosamund took the proffered hand, saw the steely shine in the depths of her eyes, the lines of pain round them, and the curve of sweetness in her smile.

'I'm glad to meet you. Laurence is always talking about you.'

'Now what could he have been saying, I wonder?' Alicia cast a roguish glance in Laurence's direction.

'Just what an ogre you are, of course.' He rocked on his toes, hands in the pockets of his charcoal grey slacks, a lilac cravat tucked into the open neck of a pale grey shirt.

'Nothing of the kind,' laughed Rosamund. 'He's full of your life in Warwickshire.'

'Ahh, the village. It is a charming place, not far from Warwick. There's just a church, a post office-cum-shop, a public house, my garden, old friends, and peace and quiet. It's…'

'Oh hell*o*! You just *have* to be Laurence's mother!' Sandra swooped among them, hand outstretched. 'I'm Sandra Clegg, a friend of Rosamund, and this is…'

But her burly radiologist had made his escape, the back of his neck scarlet with embarrassment. 'Oh, never mind.' She sank onto the sofa beside astonished Mrs Grainger. 'I'm *so* pleased to meet you. Tell me…?'

Rosamund raised amused eyebrows at Laurence, and moved away. She collected a glass of something amber from a tray offered by a waitress, and wandered off in the direction of a group of young doctors whom she knew.

'Rosamund.' Helen and Philip came up. 'There you are. We've only just arrived. Isn't this magnificent? Why didn't you tell us Laurence lives like this?'

'Why do people assume I'm intimate with Laurence's living arrangements? I've never been here before either. It's a surprise to me too.'

'Sorr – ee.' Helen put up her hands.

'It's okay. I expected that he'd live in an ordinary place like most people, but this does seem to suit him. Have you seen Sandra?'

'Couldn't miss her.' Philip rolled his eyes. 'Leadersfield's answer to Marilyn Monroe. She's been at the peroxide again.'

'Don't be horrible, Phil. She looks stunning.' Helen dug her husband in the ribs. 'Definitely out to make an impression, though.'

'Don't worry. I'm sure Mrs Grainger is more than a match for her.' Rosamund chuckled. 'Look.'

Sure enough, Sandra left the sofa, and teetered away to return immediately with a full glass and a meek expression. She handed the glass to Mrs Grainger, then came over to where they were standing.

'Met your match, have you, Sandra?' Philip mocked.

'Not at all.' She tossed her curls. 'She's too frail to fetch her own drink – she might get knocked over in the crush. Has anyone seen signs of food yet? Rosamund, I expect you know where it is? Lead on.'

Rosamund shook her head and sighed in exasperation.

'Looking for supper? It's through here.' Laurence pushed open folding doors and led them into the next room where, beneath an array of fine watercolours a massive pedestal table with clawed feet groaned with party fare.

'You've really gone to town, Laurence. What a spread. I can see why you turned down my humble offer of help. My cheese straws wouldn't have been a patch on this.'

'I'm sure they would have been perfection, Rosamund. No, I got in caterers to do the whole thing – food, drinks. And they serve and clear up, too. That leaves me free to entertain my guests. Much the easiest way. Do help yourselves. I'll circulate and round up some more people.'

'I'm impressed.' Helen picked up a plate, and the others followed suit.

Mrs Grainger came to the table, leaning on her silver-topped stick, and chose a small assortment with relish.

'Come and eat with me, my dear,' she said to Rosamund, lifting her plate with swollen knuckles.

'Of course I will, Mrs Grainger. Let me take your plate.' She carried both plates back to the hearth.

'Thank you so much. And do call me Alicia.'

Seated companionably beside the fire, conversation flowed easily between them. Rosamund was enchanted to hear about Alicia's life in Clavercote, and shared some of her own memories of village life at home in Treblissick, unvoiced for years. Laurence brought his plate and sat on the hearthrug at their feet, listening.

'That was delicious. What a clever boy you are to have found such good caterers.' Alicia dabbed her mouth with her napkin.

'Word of mouth, Mother. I was lucky.'

Rosamund tasted the hot spices and felt the last crumbs of mince pie melt in her mouth. Laurence lit a cigar from the now familiar leather case and held out a hand.

'Come and mingle with me, Rosamund. You don't mind do you, Mother?'

'Of course not. I shall be content to sit and watch the scene. But don't keep her to yourself for too long, we still have a great deal to say to each other.' She raised a conspiratorial eyebrow in Rosamund's direction.

Laurence's smile included them both. 'Women and their secrets!'

They moved together about the crowded room. Laughter and conversation flowed. Occasional phrases of dance-band music could be heard from the radiogram in a corner, where a few couples swayed in each other's arms. Noise and temperature rose in equal volume to the moulded ceiling.

'Do these windows open?' Rosamund lifted her hair from her sweating forehead.

Laurence pushed up the sash windows. Cold night air and the sound of a brass band flowed into the room.

'Carol singers!'

There was a rush to the windows to see the band and cluster of figures gathered round the Christmas tree by the church. Faces and instruments and touches of red and blue and green clothing glowed in the light from the tree, and the bold notes of 'Good King Wenceslas' rose into the night. The partygoers joined in, and tossed down coins to fill the wooden collecting boxes held up to them. When the last carol had been sung and the carol singers departed, Laurence's guests turned again into the room, where the candles guttered and ashtrays overflowed. Coats and wraps were gathered, and goodnights and thanks, interspersed with Merry Christmases filled the air.

Ron herded his crowd for the return journey in the Morris.

'You ready yet, Roz?'

Laurence took her arm and drew her to him. 'I'll take Rosamund home.'

'Okay. Goodnight then, and thanks for a smashing party.'

Rosamund suddenly felt tired. Her throat was dry and scratchy, and she had the beginnings of a headache. Cigarette smoke and several glasses of wine, she thought. It's been worth it. She leaned her head against the green leather car seat and closed her eyes. The Jaguar purred through the quiet streets, turned into the brightly lit hospital drive and drew up silently in front of the door of the Sisters' Home.

He turned to look at her.

'Tired?'

'Yes, but happy. It's been a wonderful evening Laurence, thank you so much.'

I think it was a success. It felt like it, but...' He hesitated. 'Perhaps that was because you were there,' he added quietly.

Not knowing how to answer, she said nothing.

'Come and have lunch with Mother and me.' The impulsive words jolted her. 'I'm taking her home on Saturday – Christmas Eve, and staying on for Christmas, so I won't have another chance to see you before the holiday. Besides, she wants to meet you again.'

'I'm on early tomorrow, it would have to be Thursday – the day before you go.'

'Perfect. Just the three of us.'

Laurence helped her out of the car, and they stood together on the path. He tucked the stole closer round her shoulders, and kissed her lightly on the cheek.

'Good night, Rosamund.'

He got back into the car and drove off. Rosamund stared after him, her fingers on the cheek which he had kissed – the one and only kiss since they met.

***

Rosamund did not go to lunch with Laurence and his mother.

The tickle in her throat which had started at the party turned into a furnace of broken glass, her back ached abominably and drums beat a tattoo in her head. After a sleepless night she was coughing and sneezing, her temperature soared, and by lunchtime she was in isolation in sickbay with raging influenza.

'Early,' the doctor observed. 'It doesn't usually start until January, but flu nevertheless.'

Rosamund didn't care what month it was, nor that for the second time in her life she would spend Christmas in hospital. She just wanted to die.

It was a week before her temperature came down, and she was exhausted after her first foray down the corridor to the lavatory, on marshmallow legs. With the risk of infection high she had not been allowed visitors, and had seen only nursing and medical staff, and for the first time in many years she was swamped by loneliness. Because of the Christmas holiday many people didn't know she was ill, and it wasn't until just before New Year that she had her first visitor, Helen. She brought a pile of Christmas parcels for her to open.

'I haven't even wrapped any,' Rosamund wailed when she saw them, and burst into tears.

'We'll have a special session when you come out.' Helen passed her her handkerchief. 'Phil sends his love, and Amy says she'll come and see you when you're discharged. I haven't had a chance to let Addy Wilson know you're ill yet.'

'She'll be worried. I always see her at Christmas.' Her eyes filled again.

'And Laurence is coming to see you this evening. You don't want him to see you with red eyes, do you?'

'He'll have to take me as he finds me. If my eyes are red, my eyes are red.' She sniffed and dabbed at her nose, which was still sore from sneezing. 'I know he's been away, but after seeing him so often I feel deserted. I've missed him.'

'Have you now? I thought he was only a friend.'

'Well, he is. You're my friend, too, and I've missed you.'

'It's not quite the same is it?'

'Of course it is,' she said quickly.

***

The sitting room in the Sisters' Home was empty except for Rosamund.

With her slippers kicked off, she sprawled listlessly on a settee in front of a blank-eyed television. She couldn't even be bothered to get up and turn it on to see if there might be something worth watching – probably wasn't anyway. Even the copy of Lady Chatterley's Lover beside her which Helen had given her for Christmas held no appeal, though she knew that Helen had had to queue for ages to buy it.

It was early in January, and Rosamund was still convalescing from her bout of flu. Always slender, now her clothes hung off her; the face that greeted her in the mirror was pale and drawn; and eyes that usually sparkled back at her were a dull cloudy blue like faded flowers. Amy had been to see her that morning with the children and, much as she loved them, Sally and Joe, who was now seven months old and a real wriggler, had exhausted her. Addy, shocked at Rosamund's appearance the week before, had pronounced that she needed a holiday – that would soon put her right. All very well, but where would she go at this time of year – except home.

She looked round the impersonal room. Comfortable enough, but it was clearly just a place to pause in the middle of busy lives.

Home.

Pa sitting close to the Aga, in a shapeless tweed jacket, feet in old brown slippers with the toes out resting against the tiled plinth. He'd have a book on his lap, round glasses on the end of his nose, and call out in ringing tones to wherever she was to read an amusing passage or some splendid verse. He had a warm deep voice, like Gregory Peck's, and she used to tease him that he could have been an actor in another life. She wouldn't be far away – never was, apart from her mornings at the Post office, and the occasional night out with Francis. He mostly came to her, now Pa was too infirm to go out. She'd perhaps be mopping the hall where her bicycle was propped against the hallstand, or dusting in the sitting room where the Chinese cabinet gleamed and glimmered in the shady room.

She could hear Pa now…

'…listen to this, Rosamund,' he declaims. "The splendour falls on castle walls And snowy summits old in story: The long light shakes across the lakes, And the wild cataract leaps in glory."

She joins in. "Blow, bugle, blow, set the wild echoes flying, Blow, bugle; answer echoes, dying, dying dying… 'Before you ask, it's Tennyson.'

Back into the kitchen, she leans over to kiss his bald spot, makes tea and toast to share as the grey afternoon fades to dusk. The thin sweet notes of a penny whistle outside in the darkness, footsteps in the porch, and Francis comes in laughing and shaking diamond drops off coppery hair. She is enveloped in the smell of cattle feed and beasts and diesel, which clings to the sack he wears over his shoulders to keep out the rain. Breathes his own wholesome outdoor scent.

He releases her, takes the chessboard from the dresser, sets up the carved black and white pieces, sits down opposite Pa. She's at the table writing to Edith. Her leaky pen flies over the thin blue sheets until the clock whirrs ready to strike. She rises, switches on the wireless. The stroke of Big Ben signals the Nine O'clock News. She makes cocoa, reaches the battered blue biscuit tin from the pantry shelf, and the smell of homemade ginger biscuits fills the room. The news finishes. Francis stands, without speaking pulls the sack over his head hiding his face. She picks up two empty milk bottles from beside the sink, carries them out to the cold and draughty porch where she sets them side-by-side on the cracked tiles. Francis looms above her as the chill air blows in her face. She grips the ridges of the doorframe and watches as he strides away down the path of light slanting from the doorway, until she sees him no more in the darkness under the dripping trees…

***

A coal settled in the grate, and Rosamund started up with a cry to find her cheeks wet. A flurry as footsteps passed the sitting room, and the outside door banged. She looked at her hands, half expected to see her fingers stained with ink, then got up to heap more coal on the dying fire. She flopped back on the settee, the feeling of the dream still about her. Rosamund had never forgotten her home, but it was impossible to think of it without Francis being somehow involved, so she seldom allowed herself to remember.

Home. Pa was dead and gone, the Old Rectory sold seven years ago. And Francis? Would he be married after all this time? She ignored the empty space in her heart. Probably he was. Such a loving man needed a woman, even though it couldn't be her. She tried to think who it might be. Betty Sandey used to be keen on him…? No use going down that lane.

It was funny how life turned out. I'm still the girl who lived that other life, nothing can take that away. I don't for one moment regret the career I have. Maybe I would have been a nurse even if I'd stayed in Cornwall. Oh, stop chasing rainbows, Rosamund Hambly, she told herself. But Rosamund Hambly wouldn't listen. What I do need is a home of my own and – and children. All these years I've been living in rooms and nurses' homes, reasonably contented for a long while now, but I know there's something missing. Even with all my friends around me – it's not like having family.

She sat up and pushed her feet into her slippers. Stop wallowing, my girl, it's only a touch of post-flu blues. You've a lot to be thankful for – all gained by your own efforts. Go and find a cup of tea. There'll be someone to talk to in the dining room now.

She put up the fireguard and left the room.

28

During her convalescence, Laurence took her for a run in the country in the Jag, and back to his apartment for tea. It was the first time she had been there since the Christmas party when it was crammed with people and it looked quite different now – no Christmas tree of course, and the furniture rearranged. The dark blue velvet sofa deep with cushions, and a worn leather chair as well as the wing chair where Alicia had sat, enclosed the hearth. A Georgian side table held a white vase of early narcissi's and a silver framed photograph of Laurence's mother, and a bookcase on the side wall was filled with medical tomes among a wide range of other titles.

Laurence paused in the doorway. 'Make yourself at home, and I'll get tea. Would you like some music?'

'No, I'll come and help. Where's the kitchen?'

He showed her.

'How do you manage here?' Rosamund wondered, looking at the minute work surface, ancient gas cooker and chipped enamel sink squeezed against a shining refrigerator.

'Not easily. It was made from a housemaid's linen cupboard when the house was converted. I have to be very organised.'

'I can see that.'

'The kitchen's not ideal, but it's not worth doing anything about it. I shan't be here for ever, and it's adequate until I leave. You've seen the bathroom?'

'Formerly a former broom cupboard?'

He laughed. 'Look, there really isn't room for two of us in here. Do go and sit down. Put some music on the radiogram. There are LPs in the cupboard underneath.'

After tea Laurence let down a hinged arm of the sofa, and installed Rosamund with her feet up, then settled himself in the old leather chair. The strains of Debussey's Claire de Lune and the scent of spring flowers flowed over them, and she gazed into the caverns of the fire and felt at peace. She thought of other hearths where she was welcome. Amy's, overhung with Cyril's shadow, but where she always had armfuls of children; Helen's house, busy with the comings and goings of their many friends; Addy's living-kitchen with the old fashioned range from where she kept a motherly eye on her tenants, and where Rosamund found affection and common-sense advice. But oh, Addy could talk the hind leg off a donkey! Here in this beautiful room, Rosamund relaxed with Laurence in easy companionship, only exchanging a few quiet words when he got up to change a record. The evening flowed on until Rosamund yawned and stretched.

'You're tired! I hope you haven't overdone it.'

'Not a chance. Just sleepy.' She struggled to her feet. 'Time I went.'

***

She was half asleep as he drove her back to the hospital, the street lights flicking red across her closed eyelids.

'I had a letter from Mother this morning.'

'Mmm?'

'Wants to know when she's going to see you again.'

'Really? Why would she do that?' Rosamund opened her eyes and sat up. She looked at his profile outlined against the street lights. 'I hardly know her.'

He overtook a toiling cyclist with a dim rear lamp.

'She likes you.'

'Oh.' She thought for a moment, recalling her conversation with the old lady with the straight back and swollen knuckles. 'She's nice. We got on well.'

'I hoped you would.' Laurence slowed for a woman with a dog on a Belisha crossing.

'Why? Why's it important that I get on with her?'

Without replying he pulled up under a kerbside tree. His hands gripped the steering wheel.

'It *is* important. It's about you and me.' A pause, a deep breath, then he spoke almost in a whisper, and she caught a whiff of his citrus cologne. 'I haven't met a woman I felt so comfortable with before, who shares my interests and whose company I enjoy. Women have pursued me, and I never liked that, but you're different.' His eyes were large and dark as he turned to face her. 'I've been happy since I met you. Rosamund? Could you – will you be my wife?'

Shock, amazement, and a twitch of hope burst through Rosamund's mind, and her skin prickled all over.

'I- I don't know, I never thought… For Heaven's sake, I had no idea you were going to *propose* to me!'

'I hadn't planned to do it yet. I was going to wait until you were properly well. Arrange a special dinner, and flowers and…' He hesitated. 'I know there's a big age difference between us, but I'm sure we could be happy. Please think about it.'

This was a Laurence Rosamund hadn't seen before. Unsure, pleading. In the street light the shadow of bare tree branches swayed across the bonnet of the car. She took a deep breath and turned to him…

Torchlight flashed in her eyes, and a policeman bent to peer into the car.

'Tcha!' Laurence snatched at the handle and wound down the window.

'Is everything all right, sir?'

Everything's perfectly all right, Constable.' Tight with frustration.

'Very good, sir. Sorry, only it seemed a funny place to park. Thought you might be having a spot of bother. Is the young lady all right?'

'I'm fine thanks.' Rosamund leaned across to smile up at the policeman.

'Well I'm blessed if it isn't Nurse Hambly. She was an angel to me, a right angel, sir, when I had my hernia done.' He bent closer. 'Remember me, Nurse, four years ago, Bill Riley?'

'Of course, Mr Riley,' she lied. 'This is Dr Grainger.'

'How do you do, sir? Well I'll be getting along if you're all right. Goodnight to you both.'

They watched him walk away down the street. Rosamund couldn't hold back any longer. She burst into giggles. Laurence looked outraged, then saw the funny side of it. They laughed uproariously until Rosamund had to wipe her eyes and blow her nose.

'Talk about timing,' she gasped, remembered what had been interrupted, and sobered.

'It was a damn nuisance, but you can't blame the man for doing his job. He couldn't have known that he was interrupting a proposal of marriage.'

Rosamund felt laughter bubbling up again, but forced it back when he continued.

'Let's be serious, Rosamund. What were you going to say? Something important, I hope.'

Laughter died, and she took a few moments to reassemble her thoughts.

'I've had two serious relationships – I was engaged to one man – and both times I was badly hurt. I've been assaulted as well – by someone I knew. So I vowed never to put myself in a position to be hurt again, and since then I've avoided close friendships with men. Did you know the juniors on the ward call me 'The Ice Maiden?''

He shook his head.

'Then you came along, and I haven't ever felt you were a threat.'

He caught his breath, but she carried on.

'I've really enjoyed the times we've spent together, and all the new experiences I've had. It's been good to have a friend and companion who never pushed for more. But marriage – I'd be vulnerable again, and I don't know whether I would cope.' She covered her face with her hands. 'Oh, Laurence. Why did you have to complicate things?'

'I understand. Take all the time you want. I'll wait – but don't take too long, please?' He cupped her face between his hands, and for the first time kissed her – chastely on the lips. Then he started the car and let in the clutch.

The car move smoothly forward, and Rosamund gave a convulsive chuckle.

'What?' he asked.

'I didn't really remember him, you know. That policeman!'

***

It took her two weeks to make up her mind.

She had never thought of Laurence as a suitor, and it took time to adjust to this new view of their relationship. Her work was done in a dream, and it took all her waking moments to work it out, a little at a time.

How do I feel about Laurence? I like him, am fond of him even, but love? Surely I'd have recognised it by now. It isn't like the instinctive total love for Francis I've been trying to deny for seven years, and will do for the rest of my life. It isn't like the searing physical passion I felt for Neil in those few crazy weeks. Maybe love's different each time. Her thoughts flew off at a tangent. If I were married it wouldn't matter if I met Francis again, unlikely though that is. Forget that, it's a stupid reason for saying yes. Maybe I should stay single. Then she glimpsed the sterile future that would mean, and quailed. What do I really want? A home; someone to cherish as well as be loved myself; a sexual relationship; children. Longing swept over her so strong that her breasts tingled and her arms ached. And I thought I'd avoid being hurt again, she thought. Sure as eggs is eggs children make you vulnerable, but I'm willing to risk it. With Laurence? Wondering, she found that she was, wanted to even.

'I'm not sure that what I feel for you is love,' she told him when eventually when she said yes. 'Affection certainly, and who knows what it might grow into.'

'That's good enough for me. Many marriages founded on less turn out well.' He hugged her and looked anxiously into her eyes. 'How do you feel about children?'

'I yearn for them.'

'It's what I'd hoped, but I'll be fifty this year.'

'Still in your prime. I'll give you sons, and daughters too if you want them. Although I'm nearly twenty seven, old to be starting a family.'

They laughed into each other's eyes, and went to town in the green Jag to buy an engagement ring.

***

Sandra was effusive in her admiration. 'What a rock! What a super ring!' She hugged Rosamund. 'You lucky thing. A consultant's wife, Roz. I *thought* you'd snaffle him, but you took your time.'

Rosamund turned her hand to see the rainbow sparkle of the square-cut solitaire diamond on her left hand. When she felt Laurence slip it onto her finger, she'd had a moment of déjà vu, remembering the garnet and seed pearl ring she had worn all those years before. Sometimes she wished she'd kept it, but knew in her heart it was right to have left it behind.

'I'm so pleased for you, Roz.' Helen beamed with warmth. 'It's what you really want?'

'Yes,' Rosamund answered quietly. 'It was time.'

'You'll have a big wedding with all the trimmings, of course.' Sandra bounced with excitement.

'Oh, no. We want a quiet wedding with just a few friends. No fuss.'

That had been the idea, but the girls had their way in the end. Besides, Edith and family insisted on coming over from South Africa and, as Sandra said, if they were coming all that way they had to give them something to come for. Rosamund and Laurence, feeling shy, gave in with good grace, and the girls took Rosamund shopping to choose a wedding dress and trousseau. She asked Sally to be bridesmaid, and Helen Matron of Honour.

'Yes. But please have the wedding in the afternoon, because I'm being sick in the mornings at the moment.'

'You aren't! Oh, that's wonderful news. You're sure you'll be all right?'

'Absolutely. Wouldn't miss it for the world.'

***

The wedding was set for July the twenty seventh. They booked the church in the centre of Leadersfield, where Rosamund had talked to the priest who had given her hope to start afresh. He was no longer there, and Rosamund was sorry. She'd always meant to go back, and never had. Still, if she couldn't get married in St Hyldroc's, here was as good as anywhere.

At Easter, Laurence took her to visit his mother in Warwickshire. She immediately fell in love with the village of Clavercote, and the old red brick cottage opposite the church where Alicia lived. She looked out of her bedroom window under the eaves to see Laurence walking with his mother in the garden. He wore old flannel trousers, a baggy brown pullover with the elbows out, and muddy wellington boots, his hair still in its usual immaculate waves. She hadn't seen him dressed so informally before, and realised there was a great deal she didn't know about him. Still, plenty of time to learn.

Laurence, as though hearing her thoughts, looked up.

'Come and join us,' he called. 'Mother's potty about her garden, and wants to give you the grand tour.'

She threw on a jacket, and ran down to where they surveyed burgeoning daffodils under apple trees.

After a leisurely circuit of the garden in pale sunlight, Alicia sank onto the seat near the sundial. 'That's far enough to walk today. I think it's warm enough to have our coffee out here, don't you, Laurence? Would you go and prepare it, dear? I want to have a chat with Rosamund.'

The two women watched as he walked away up the path, and Rosamund felt a tingle as she thought of future intimacies. Alicia interrupted her thoughts.

'It's hard to believe he's nearly fifty. He looks very much as his father might have done at that age. Laurence has told you our history, I gather?'

Rosamund nodded, and Alicia continued.

'I know you'll make him happy, my dear. I so want to see him settled before I die. You see, we've always been close, and I was afraid he would be lost without me. With you beside him, he'll cope.' She turned to Rosamund and took her hand. 'But – you may not have an easy time. Laurence is an only one, a bachelor and set in his ways. He may find it difficult to share his life.'

'We've talked about that. I've had to fend for myself for years too. It won't be all sweetness and light with me either. I'd been a solitary being for a long time when I met Laurence. I hope we'll start a family soon, that should help.'

'That is my dearest wish – to see my boy with his own child.' Her eyes were far away as though seeing that child. 'Rosamund – my dear. If you're ever worried, or there are – difficulties – I will help all I can. I may not find it easy to share him, I know. I'm just a selfish old woman, but he's all I have, and his happiness means everything to me.' Her eyes were bright with tears.

Rosamund kissed her cheek. 'I'll do my best,' she murmured.

***

It was her wedding day tomorrow, and today was her last duty on Women's Medical. As she climbed the stone stairs and turned into the long corridor she heard shouts and howls coming from the main ward. Swiftly she shed her cloak in the office and rolled up her sleeves.

'What's up?' she asked a junior as she passed.

'Patient's gone bonkers.' The junior scuttled off into the safety of the sluice.

Staff Daley was behind the curtains round the corner bed, where a young woman rocked wildly, kicked and struggled with flailing arms against the three nurses who were trying to hold her.

'Thank goodness you're here,' gasped Daley. 'Help to keep her still so I can get this injection into her.'

Rosamund grabbed the threshing hands and held them tight, while the nurses leaned on the woman's legs. She looked into a face young in years, but ancient with agony, and eyes that held only blankness. The moans turned to screams as Daley swabbed her upper leg, and the woman tried to wrench her hands out of Rosamund's.

'Hush, it'll be over soon,' she soothed, the sickly sweet smell of the largactil injection filling her nostrils.

Soon the young woman became quiet. While the other staff cleared up Rosamund kept her hands in hers until she slept.

'Thanks.' Daley pushed in pins to secure her cap which had been lost in the struggle. 'You came at the right time. Puerperal psychosis,' she supplied in answer to Rosamund's querying look. 'Came in during the night. She got worse and worse, and we're waiting now for the ambulance to transfer her to the mental side.'

'Poor girl. Where's the baby?' asked Rosamund.

'With grandparents. She rejected it. Said it wasn't hers – that she'd never had one.' A knock came on the office door. 'Ah, this'll be her husband.'

A young man appeared, pale with anxiety. Staff went out to speak to him. Saddened, Rosamund sat to read the report. Soon there was the rumble of trolley wheels in the corridor as the woman was wheeled away, but the smell of largactil lingered in the corridor for a long time.

The rest of her duty passed as usual, except for the presentation which the patients made to her before she left. Touched by the signed card and cut glass vase they had clubbed together to buy her, she left the ward finally in high spirits, looking forward to her wedding next day and whatever the future would bring.

29

As the aeroplane crossed the south coast of England, Rosamund peered down through the cabin window to see nothing but occasional dots of ships tracing haphazard white trails on the English Channel. She glanced at Laurence beside her to ask him to look too, but he was leaning back against the headrest with his eyes closed.

Why aren't I feeling tired too? she thought. I suppose it's the excitement of flying for the first time that's keeping me awake. What a day! She leaned against his shoulder, and he opened his eyes and smiled at her.

'Happy, Mrs Grainger?'

'Mmm. Just remembering the day, and how quickly it passed.' She put her hand through his arm.

'All over in a flash. Do you feel married?'

'I'm still getting used to it. You?'

'It's a bit strange. I feel I'm the same, yet not the same.' Was that a note of regret in his voice, she wondered? 'There's a different life ahead.'

'I know what you mean. Lots of adjustments to make.'

Laurence laid his hand over hers where it lay on his arm, and traced the rings on her finger. They each subsided into their own thoughts, and the plane droned on, crossed the French coastline and flew south toward the island of Majorca.

Rosamund remembered how she had walked into church on Philip's arm feeling strange and lonely in her gown of ivory satin, the weight of the train pulling her back at every step. Laurence stood at the chancel steps, straight backed with arms stiffly by his sides, and she realised he was nervous too. Reality struck her. In a few minutes Rosamund Hambly would be gone for ever, and Mrs Laurence Grainger would walk out of the church in her place. She'd trembled behind her veil, and clutched her bouquet of roses and sweet peas with a suddenly clammy hand. The church was full of music and the murmur of people waiting in best clothes for her arrival. Pa should have been here to give her away. How she missed him. And not just Pa. Through a blur of tears, she saw a misty copper head outlined momentarily beside Laurence's black and silver. Then her vision cleared, and it was only dust motes dancing a rainbow in shafts of sunlight as it streamed through the purple and crimson, blue and gold of the window. The scent of flowers, beeswax and faint traces of incense flowed towards her and enveloped her like a blessing.

Philip had squeezed her hand. 'Are you okay?'

She'd smiled her reassurance, lifted her chin and stepped out towards…

'You and your sister are not in the least alike, are you?' Laurence interrupted her reverie.

She started. 'No. Edith's like Pa, a dark haired Celt, and I'm supposed to be the image of my mother. I'm glad they came to the wedding. It's seven years since I saw her last at Pa's funeral. Edith looks older.' In fact her skin had aged in the African sun, dried into crinkles and folds like an amiable monkey. Rosamund chuckled. 'However long it is between seeing each other, we always get on. It would have been nice to have spent more time with her. I hadn't seen the twins before. Imagine! We have ten-year-old nephews. When they were little they used to write to me, and send me funny drawings. Leslie says they're thinking of coming back to live in Cornwall again in another few years.'

'We'll see more of them then, I expect. I might even persuade you to take me to Cornwall,' he teased. 'I can't think why you won't go back there.'

Rosamund glared at him.

'All right, I won't go on about it.' He steered the conversation into safer waters. 'What a surprise to see Mother and your Addy get on so well.'

'They looked like lifelong buddies, didn't they.' Rosamund pictured the two old ladies, one elegant and upright in lavender silk, the other plump and shiny in a tight brown dress splashed with orange flowers, heads together, glasses in hands, laughing fit to burst. 'The beginning of a beautiful friendship? Wasn't Sally sweet? She adored being a bridesmaid, and she's so good with little Joe.'

'He seems to be rather a handful – trying to climb onto the table, running off whenever he was put down: and squealing.'

'He's only fifteen months old – he'll grow out of it. Amy does find him hard work though.' She thought of Amy's careworn face and thin body. 'Thank goodness Cyril stayed away. No doubt that's Amy's doing. She told me she's pregnant again.'

Laurence pressed his lips together, and didn't reply.

'Anything more to drink, sir?' The air hostess was at their elbow again.

***

It was dark when the plane touched down with a bump on the tarmac at Palma airport. The roar of the engines as they went into reverse thrust startled Rosamund, and she clutched Laurence in alarm. Soon she stood at the top of the landing steps looking out over the lighted airport, Laurence's hand on her shoulder. The smell of hot dusty earth and aircraft fuel, spiced with strange foreign scents, was warm and heady with promise. Rosamund filled her lungs and a sense of adventure flowered. Laurence, no stranger to travel, steadied her as she set off down the steps, almost tripping in her eagerness to discover this new country.

It was the small hours of the morning when the coach which had rattled and banged its way across the island, mysterious in the darkness, decanted its weary passengers in front of their hotel.

But Rosamund was far from weary. Everything enchanted her, even at this hour. Impressed with the spacious marbled foyer and staircase, she gasped with delight when she saw their room, and immediately went out onto the balcony to look down into the pink blossoms of an oleander tree, and beyond to the blue of the lighted hotel pool and the moonlit sea. Strains of music floated up from below.

'Laurence, come and look. It's magical.'

'I'm sure it is, but I just want to get out of these sweaty clothes and find something to drink. I noticed the bar's still open.'

He set down a suitcase on either side of him, and stood with exhausted face and dark shadows beneath his eyes.

'I'm sorry.' She came back into the room and put her arms round him. 'I'm parched too. We'll go right down.'

She kissed him gently, and he leaned into her and nuzzled her neck.

'You're such a comfort, Mrs Grainger. Don't worry, I'll soon revive.'

***

'Let's go out by the pool.' Thirst slaked, Rosamund put down her glass and got to her feet.

'There's no rush.' Laurence took another sip of brandy.

'But it's lovely out there, so romantic. Come o-on.'

'Impatient?' he raised an eyebrow.

She blushed. 'Well, it *is* out honeymoon.'

The warmth of the night embraced them as they threaded their way, serenaded by whirring cicadas, among empty sunbeds on the terrace, to wander round the rocky promontory enclosing the pool, arms around each other's waists.

'Just look at those stars, I've never seen so many, so bright.'

'I love the way you get excited about every new thing.'

'But this is wonderful. How could anyone ever take it for granted?'

He held her closer, and they stood listening to the murmur of the sea. Rosamund felt shy and a little confused. What were they supposed to do now? It seemed the hardest thing in the world to make the move to go up to their room, but it was what she wanted to do. Perhaps Laurence felt shy too. She turned and buried her face in his shoulder.

Almost in a whisper she said, 'I'm going to our room now, Laurence.'

He turned her to face him and took her in his arms.

Surfacing from their first long kiss, he said, 'Would you like some time to yourself before I come up?'

'Yes, I would. But don't be long will you?' Her voice was shaky.

'I'll smoke another cigar then I'll be with you.' He took the room key from his pocket and gave it to her.

***

Rosamund closed the door behind her. Bedside lamps were already lit, and she stepped over remnants of confetti scattered on the floor.

The bed lay vast and virginal, the sheet turned invitingly back. Pale blue pyjamas lay on one pillow, and her own lacy nylon nightdress was prettily arranged on the other.

She smiled to herself. 'Good. That takes care of who sleeps where.'

The marble floor was warm to her bare feet as she stepped out of her clothes, her nightdress soft as thistledown as she tossed it in the air to settle over her in a sensuous cloud. Cellophane crackled as she unwrapped the bottle of Chanel No 5 which Laurence had bought for her at the airport, and she breathed in luxuriously as she misted her body with perfume.

At the mirror her eyes gazed back at her, huge and dark blue as the night sky. She paused, hairbrush in mid air, and leaned forward to look closer.

'Is this really me?' she asked.

There was no reply, but the eyes stared back with – could it be – reproach? The diamond on her left hand caught the lamplight, and she flickered her fingers at her reflection. Then she spun away from the mirror, round the foot of the bed and back, and whirled through gauzy curtains onto the balcony, where she fetched up with a thud against the rail.

She leaned over. There was no one on the terrace, and no more music from the bar below. Only the cicadas whirred on, loud in the darkness. A blue glow from the pool lights illuminated Laurence's silhouette as he stood looking over the sea towards the waning moon. His cigar tip flared briefly as he raised it to his lips, and even from here she could see the elegant curve of his fingers. A warm breeze gusted. Her nightdress blew against her, making her shiver. As though she had called, Laurence turned and saw her. There was a red arc as he spun his cigar into the sea, and began to make his way purposefully towards her.

***

Faint guitar music filtered from below as Rosamund woke, hot and sticky in the rumpled bed. The room was still shady, the morning sky apricot and azure through the open balcony doors. She put out a hand, and the bed was empty beside her.

'Laurence?'

No reply.

She threw off the sheet, and was halfway onto the balcony before realising she was naked. Disregarding her nightdress which lay in a heap beside the bed, she pulled on a robe and peered over the balcony. Waiters were wiping the tables on the terrace, a swarthy young man lazily swept last night's cigarette ends under the bushes at the side, and a few sunbeds already had towels spread on them. There was a splash from the pool, a dark head streaked with silver surfaced and its owner struck out in a strong crawl, leaving a glittering wake.

Minutes later Rosamund, hair already wet from a quick shower, dived in and bobbed up in front of him as he turned.

'Race you!' She was already several yards away when Laurence gathered his wits and came after her. They arrived together at the far side of the pool, gasping. They hung by their arms, backs to the concrete side. Rosamund looked down at their legs, pallid and wavering in the water. Her own were slender and smooth beside his, dark haired and well muscled.

'Are you all right?' Laurence searched her face.

'Perfectly, thanks.'

'I'm sorry about last night…'

'Don't worry, it'll happen I'm sure.'

'I'm so embarrassed. I didn't want to disappoint you.'

'Forget it. Truly, it's all right.' She kissed his wet nose. The sun was already hot on her back and she had no sun oil on. 'There and back again? Then let's find breakfast. I'm starving.'

***

Breakfast finished, they sunbathed on the terrace, then swam again. The sun was hot, the light bright, and they moved into the shade of an oleander. After the wedding and long journey the day before they were both content to do little but relax. There was plenty to see: the terrace was full of sunbathers and striped towels; yells and laughter came from the crowded pool where blue, yellow and red plastic water toys bobbed in competition with glistening bodies; waiters balanced trays of drinks on one hand as they threaded between sunworshippers of varying shades from deepest copper to palest white like themselves.

A gentle snore came from beside Rosamund, and she looked across to see Laurence's abdomen rise and fall, mouth slightly open and beads of sweat on his forehead. A wave of affection swept her. What a pity last night had been a disappointment. They had grown close during the months of their engagement, but with little real intimacy. She would have gone to bed with him long ago, but Laurence wanted to wait until they were married.

'Puritan,' she'd chided, teasing.

'No. It's not that at all. You see, I've never slept with a woman before, so when I do I want it to be quite perfect.'

'Hmmm' she'd said, thinking can he really be that naïve? 'A real virgin bachelor!'

'Well. I...'

'We'll soon change that, won't we?' she went on. 'I've only a few months' experience myself. It'll be fun to teach each other.'

And she had looked forward to it. In truth, last night had been wonderful until the ultimate moment when it had all somehow gone wrong. Never mind, she thought. There's no rush.

She threw the sun oil bottle top at him, and it landed on his chest.

'What...?'

She laughed down at him.

'People are starting to go in to lunch. If we want another dip before eating, there's more room in the pool now. What do you want to do?'

He sat up. 'Let's swim again. I don't want to sleep the day away, then not sleep tonight.'

'Why not?' she flirted.

She couldn't see his eyes behind his sunglasses, and before she knew it he was up and on his way to dive into the pool.

Rosamund took a siesta in their room after lunch, while Laurence took a book down to one of the leather couches in the cool of the lobby.

She lay on the bed. It was still hot, even though a breeze stirred the gauze curtains. The bed was soft, distant sounds soothing, and she drifted off.

Two hours later, when Laurence returned he found her sitting on the now shady balcony with a book, refreshed and cool in shorts and a sun top.

'I've been looking at a map,' he told her. 'If we follow the road along from here there's a fishing harbour. It's not far. Do you feel like a walk?'

She jumped to her feet. 'Ready, willing and able, senor,' she smiled, then could have bitten her tongue out. Oh, no, she thought as his eyes clouded. How could I have been so insensitive!

He said nothing, and they set off, linked hands swinging, to explore the tiny harbour where painted boats piled high with nets lined the quay. A string of straw hats dangled in the doorway of a shop, and Laurence counted out pesetas to buy one for each of them. They found a bar where they ate hollowed out melons, filled with slices of peach, melon and strawberries drenched in liqueur and piled high with ice cream. Rosamund scraped out the last drops of liqueur.

'I could get addicted to these,' she declared. 'I'm going to have one every day we're here.'

When it came to making love again, once more it ended in failure. And again, and again. On the third day during siesta, Laurence rolled away yet again defeated, and lay with an arm across his face in silence. Rosamund lay on her back and stared up at the cracks in the ceiling, trying to hold back tears of frustration.

'It's no use.' He sounded close to tears himself. 'There'll never be a child if I go on like this.'

Rosamund couldn't believe her ears. She reared up on one elbow to face him.

'Is that all it means to you?' she flared. 'What about me? What about us?'

'I care about you of course. About us. I never expected to be like this. I'm no use to you,' he moaned. 'I'm too old. A failure.'

'Laurence, we've been through all this. There's plenty of time.' She had been patient and loving so far, but now she was impatient with him. He was so childish at times – the dignified consultant was just a little boy when he couldn't do what he wanted. I'm no better, she reminded herself ruefully. I shouldn't be resentful.

She touched his shoulder.

'I'm going out. I want to be on my own for a while.'

Laurence turned over and buried his face in the pillow.

She dressed quickly, and grabbed her straw hat and sunglasses.

'I don't know how long I'll be.'

There was no reply, and she left, closing the door with exaggerated care.

Taking the opposite direction from the harbour, she set off along the road that curved round a wide sandy bay, ending in a promontory crowned with a small tower. In spite of the heat she walked fast, ignoring the empty dunes beyond the road, the sparse traffic and the tourists on the beach. Her stomach seethed with pent-up emotion, and thoughts whirled like bits of torn paper scattered to the wind. Her feet slapped angrily against the pavement, but gradually she found she could think straight again. It's no use feeling angry with Laurence, it's not his fault, she thought. How he's feeling I can't tell – only another man could, but it's plain that he's suffering. What can I do? He won't let me touch him and I don't know how to help him. Perhaps it's me – something about me that puts him off. Is it because I've already been with someone else before marriage? She felt soiled and humiliated, as if she wanted more than she ought to want. More than he could give.

The road ran out, and she found herself at the foot of a sandy path which rose through rough scrub. You're both being ridiculous, she realised with a jolt. Lots of people have difficulties on their honeymoon. It's not the end of the world.

Her pace slowed as the path became steeper, winding seaward to end in a flat area in front of the half ruined tower she'd seen in the distance. A couple with a boy and a girl were entering the tower, and the excited cries of the children rang across the dusty air. There were several other people in the open space, and a line of tall rawboned horses were tethered to a rail in front of a low ramshackle bar.

Rosamund explored the tower first. She climbed the winding stairs inside thick walls, wrinkled her nose at smells of dankness and old urine, hoping for a breeze at the top. When she arrived the sun beat down and there was no wind. She leant on the hot stones of the ramparts. The view was worth the climb, all blue sea and sky and golden sands, straw-coloured dunes.

At the bar she took a weathered table outside in the shade of a sun umbrella, and was served a tumbler of rough local red wine by a fat Spaniard, whose black eyes disappeared into the creases of his face when he laughed, revealing a battery of gold teeth. The wine rolled down her throat slaking her thirst, the glass cool and solid in her hot hand. The scent of horses and leather filled her nostrils, and the jingle of harness mingled with conversation from other tables, English, Spanish and German. She leaned back in her chair and let peace flow over her.

Back at the hotel she found Laurence on the terrace, cigar in hand and glass at his elbow, looking his usual urbane self. She flopped down on the chair at the other side of the table and fanned herself with her hat.

'You look hot, Rosamund. Would you like a drink?'

'Would I! A large orange juice with lots of ice, please.' It had been a long walk in more senses than one, and she wasted no time.

'Laurence.' She leaned towards him across the table. 'I don't want us to go on struggling to make love. It's making us both miserable, and it really doesn't matter much at this stage. Unless we let it.'

He looked out to sea, expression unchanged except for a small tightening at the corner of his mouth.

Rosamund paused, her heart fluttering, then plunged on. 'I'd like us to enjoy being here together, in this wonderful place. Let's just have a holiday, without any sexual obligation. Oh, I'm not saying don't let's kiss and cuddle – I'd like that anyway. And if it goes further then we'll let it. If not, that's all right too. We've got years and years for the rest to happen. What do you think?' She sat back and waited.

Laurence picked up his glass and took a swallow of beer.

'I think that's a very good idea,' he said to the horizon, then turned to her with a smile. 'Could this holiday include the hire of a car, and exploration of the island?'

Rosamund was taken aback for a moment, then she chuckled. 'I think that's a very good idea' she echoed. 'When?'

'I've booked a car for tomorrow.'

She was amazed how much enjoyment they packed into the remainder of their holiday. There was so much to do and see and they did it all: from the spectacular rocky north coast to the bustling city of Palma with its beautiful cathedral. A boat trip took them to silvery sea caves full of limpid blue water and reflected light; there was a barbecue under pine trees at the sea's edge; a flamenco evening, and red wine poured in a thin stream from a long thin-spouted glass straight into their mouths. Once they sampled liqueur tastings in a dim bodega, and afterwards staggered back to their room to sleep it off, and missed supper. There was a moonlit dance on the hotel terrace, and shady roadside bars draped with vines.

Not once did they try again to make love. Privately Rosamund was relieved. She felt sure it would happen spontaneously when they settled to normal life together. What Laurence thought she didn't know – the subject was not mentioned again.

30

Rosamund placed the last china cup in its place and closed the kitchen cupboard. 'What time does the concert start, Laurence?' she called as she folded the damp tea towel and hung it over the oven door to dry.

'Seven thirty, but we'll want to be in time for a drink before. Do you want to have your bath first, and I'll tidy up in here?' Laurence answered from the drawing room.

She poked her head round the door. 'It looks all right to me.' But he was already drawing the curtains, plumping up cushions, straightening magazines. 'Oh, all right then.' All he needs is a frilly apron and a feather duster, she thought with irritation.

A few minutes later as she relaxed in the steamy warmth, her irritation subsided and other feelings arose as her skin accepted the caress of scented water.

'Will you be long, Rosamund?'

With a great swoosh she and her sudden anger lifted out of the bath and a gout of water slopped over the side onto the floor.

When will I ever be a proper wife? she yelled silently, but it came out in a meek 'No, I'll only be a few minutes.'

She towelled herself back to equilibrium, and emerged pink and glowing in a cloud of perfume.

'That feels good,' she said and threw her dressing gown across the bed. Tight lipped, Laurence picked it up and hung it behind the door. He sniffed.

Rosamund laughed. 'It's a bit strong isn't it? It came out of the bottle rather quickly. Like it?'

'Hmm. Not sure.' And he strode off, straight backed in the direction of the bathroom.

A few moments later there was an exclamation of outrage. Rosamund dashed to see what was the matter.

'You really are the limit, Rosamund. I put up with tops off the toothpaste, and shampoo and a wet bathmat, but this time you've excelled yourself.'

He picked up the bath towel and began to mop the puddled floor.

'There's more talcum powder on the floor here than you could possibly have on yourself.'

Rosamund stood in the doorway with her arms folded as he righted a bottle of lotion that was spreading a pink tide down the sink side.

'Don't be such an old woman, Laurence.'

He hunched his shoulders and continued to scurry about clearing up.

'Here, give me that.' She took the soaked towel from him and flung it in the linen bin. 'I'm sorry it's a mess, but I wouldn't have left it like that if you hadn't rushed me.'

She rammed her discarded petticoat, pants and stockings into the bin with the towels, then grabbed a bag of cotton wool and a jar of cold cream in one hand. As she wrenched open the door of the bathroom cabinet, a bottle of Dettol fell into the sink and smashed.

'Now look what you've made me do,' she yelled as the pungent smell of disinfectant added itself to the explosive atmosphere.

'My God. What have I married! This flat was always clean and tidy. I knew where everything was. I could bring anyone home any time, and be proud of the place.'

'But *was* it a home? Clean and tidy, yes. But *clinical!*' Rosamund shot at him. 'I can't sit down for fear of creasing the cushions, can never leave a book out until I want it again. *You* never even rumple the bedclothes!'

She stopped. They gazed at each other speechless, the real root of their anger stark between them.

Laurence turned on the bath taps, and Rosamund left the room in silence.

***

The atmosphere between them remained cool for several days. Rosamund thought about what had happened. She knew herself to be frustrated.

After so many years of keeping her emotional and sexual feelings under lock and key, she had opened the door only to find disappointment and humiliation. The trouble was those feelings didn't want to be locked away again. She longed to confide in Helen, but loyalty to Laurence prevented her. She knew he would be mortified if their personal difficulties were shared with anyone else. It must be awful for him too. She could see his increased pernicketiness was due to frustration. But where did that leave her? He had been clear that he wanted marriage in order to father a son, and she wanted children too. Oh, how she wanted children. Here he was, giving her not the remotest possibility of conceiving. There must be some way they could be helped. She would have to talk to him.

***

Rosamund came in from weekend duty the following Saturday evening. She dropped her coat on the hall chair, checked, then hung it instead on the hook which Laurence had allocated to her in the hall cupboard. He was in the kitchen.

'Mm, that smells good. Like me to set the table?'

'I thought I heard you come in. Please. We're having fish, so we'll need the fish knives and forks, and the white wine glasses.'

She pulled a face behind his back, loaded a tray and took it through to the drawing room, where they now had their meals at a small Chippendale table. Rosamund stopped in the doorway. A heap of dented cushions lodged at one end of the sofa, an open book on the floor partly obscured a newspaper, and a pile of records lay with assorted sleeves near the music centre. She began to smile, then giggle.

After setting the table she poured two glasses of sherry and with a straight face carried them into the kitchen.

'A drink for the cook. Here.' She put the glass in his hand. 'Anything else I can do?'

'Thanks, no. It's all taken care of. It'll be ready in fifteen minutes.'

Rosamund leaned against the sink and said casually. 'It looks as though you've been having a cosy day.'

Laurence continued to stir the sauce.

'Yes. Most relaxing. I enjoyed leaving things lying around. Quite liberating.'

'Why did you? Leave things around?'

'I've appreciated the toothpaste top in place, the towels hung up and the absence of talcum powder on the bathroom floor, among other things.'

'So-o-o ?'

'So. I decided to meet you halfway. It'll take a little getting used to, and I will try not to be such an 'old woman'.' He slanted a grin.

'I'm trying too. It's not easy is it?' She sipped her sherry.

He stopped chopping parsley, smiled and nodded in agreement. Encouraged, she went on.

'That's not all that's between us though, is it?'

With quick jabbing movements he scraped the parsley together with the edge of the knife.

'I don't think I can do anything about that. Don't push me, Rosamund.'

'I'm not pushing you, but I'm flesh and blood too, remember. Don't you think we should get some help?'

'No, I couldn't do that. We'll just have to let things take their course. Sorry.'

She had to accept it. At least the subject had been broached.

Occasionally, but without success they continued to attempt consummation, Laurence with grim determination, Rosamund with resigned acceptance. All to no avail.

Sometimes she was querulous. 'Why bother?' she flung at him once. 'You know we never get anywhere. It just makes it worse to try.'

'You want children, don't you? You promised me.'

'*I* promised *you*. Of all the…!'

***

Alicia rang to say she had a slight chill, and could they come down, so Rosamund and Laurence drove down to Clavercote at the weekend to visit.

With no sign of ill health she sat on her drawing room sofa, a fire crackling up the chimney although it was a fine autumn day and the sun shining.

Rosamund stood on the hearthrug and picked up a photograph of Laurence as a child, which had pride of place on the mantelpiece. It was a studio portrait showing him standing stiffly to attention beside a high spindly table topped with a potted plant. There was something lonely about the formal little figure, and the smile he was directing at the camera was both charming and apprehensive. Thoughtfully she replaced the silver frame.

'My precious boy!' exclaimed Alicia. 'That was taken at the end of Laurence's first term at boarding school. He was a sensitive little boy and took a long while to settle away from home. I should liked to have kept him with me a little longer, but my husband – Laurence's step father, you understand – said it was a man's world, and children had to grow up sometime.' She sighed, then looked straight at Rosamund.

'Are you happy with Laurence, dear?' She sounded slightly more anxious than the question warranted.

Unprepared, Rosamund paused before answering. 'Yes, Alicia. Laurence and I are getting on quite well, thank you. We're both having to make adjustments, of course.'

'There's no sign of a family yet?'

Embarrassed, Rosamund was silent, but as she gathered herself to reply Laurence came into the room carrying a knobbly brown paper bag.

'Mother, really! You'll get your grandson all in good time, it's early days yet. Now where do you want me to plant these new daffodil bulbs?'

'You've been married four months now, and neither of you are getting any younger, are you? And the daffodils over by the sundial, darling. Then I'll be able to see them from in here.'

Laurence departed to the garden with a decidedly petulant set of the shoulders.

'There, I've upset him. It will take him a while to come round, I'm afraid,' Alicia said in a matter of fact tone. 'I want to show you some snaps of Laurence when he was a little boy. Would you mind fetching the album, Rosamund? It's at the bottom of the bookcase on the right.'

The two women were soon immersed in sepia and black and white snatches of the past. In these images Rosamund discovered a Laurence that she hadn't seen before. The stiff pages of the album turned to reveal a dark-haired baby with wide bright eyes propped against a cushion and wearing a long lace christening gown. Even at this age she could recognise the Laurence she knew, and with a twinge of excitement wondered if a child of theirs might look like this. Then she remembered, and turned the page hurriedly to find a square faced man looking grimly out at her above a spreading waistcoat girded with a watch chain, and a serious eyed toddler Laurence perched uneasily on his left knee.

'My husband. He was a strict stepfather,' explained Alicia. She stroked the next page with tenderness as though it was a baby's cheek. 'Ah. Here are some of Laurence and myself together – some of the happiest times of my life.'

Easily recognisable, the pretty young mother and already handsome boy made a sandcastle, paddled in the edge of the sea, walked on a pier.

'I like this one.' Rosamund felt a curious kinship when she saw the boy astride a pony, the mother holding the reins and laughing up at him. There had been a snap of herself on a pony about the same age in a farmyard, but it hadn't been her mother laughing up at her. It had been a teenage boy with copper hair and freckles.

'It was his first pony, Tandy. Here he is with his first bicycle. He's older on this one of course.'

Wearing knickerbockers and a floppy cap, the pride of ownership was apparent.

'He still looks like that sometimes when he looks at the Jaguar.' Rosamund was amused. 'Oh look, he was in the scouts. Here he is camping.'

'I was so worried about him sleeping on the damp ground,' Alicia reminisced, 'but he never came to any harm.'

So it went on. School groups, rugby teams. Laurence in groups with other young men, rowing, sailing, sprawled on a river bank sporting a curly pipe; with a succession of cars; and a full page photograph of him in cap and gown.

'Who could have guessed that I would have a son with such a distinguished career,' his mother said with satisfaction.

Laurence returned, ill humour gone. He lowered himself onto the sofa beside Alicia and kissed her cheek.

'Sorry I was grumpy, mother.'

'That's all right dear. We all have our little problems.' She patted his hand.

Rosamund glanced up from the album and caught her looking at her with an odd expression. She looked down quickly at a photograph of Alicia with a laughing young man on either side of her, one of them Laurence, hands deep in the pockets of plus fours. She was not sure what she had seen in Alicia's eyes. It's nothing, she told herself, and smiled at Laurence.

'Come and see this.'

'Ah, a family history lesson. I hope you haven't poisoned Rosamund's mind with tales of my lurid past, mother.'

He slid to the floor beside Rosamund. She leaned into him, and they laughed and exchanged childhood stories about each other until it was time to draw the curtains and toast muffins.

***

Life was less fraught after that weekend. Living together became a matter of fitting in with each other's ways and practising tolerance – most of the time.

They began to entertain. Laurence was an accomplished cook, Rosamund discovered. Her own cooking skills, although competent, were of the farmhouse, Aunt Maud variety, and she was happy to play the hostess, bringing flair and grace to their dinner parties.

On one such occasion on a rainy weekend in late January, the doorbell rang while Laurence was still busy in the kitchen.

'Can you go? I'm in the middle of the starter,' he called.

'I'm on my way.' The bell rang again, several times.

'Hello Sandra. I knew it would be you,' Rosamund laughed as she opened the door. Her eyes travelled to the tall rangy figure behind her friend. 'Come in – both of you.'

'I know we're a bit early, but we had the chance of a lift. Roz, this is Danny Heaney, new houseman on surgical. He's fresh from the bogs of auld Oireland. Only arrived yesterday.'

'Hello Danny Heaney. So you're Sandra's mystery guest.'

The newcomer took her hand, and she looked up into wicked blue eyes under straight black brows and unruly black locks thrown into relief by the dim overhead hall light, and his smile flashed through cast shadow as he spoke.

'Hello Mrs Grainger. It was kind of you to invite me to your home. I don't know a soul yet in this heathen place, except for Sandra here. She's taken pity on me and brought me with her to share your hospitality.'

'Not at all. Come right in both of you, and let me take your wet things.'

Sandra shook the raindrops from her plastic hood.

'Roz, have you heard? Helen's had her baby today. A little girl.'

'Yes, Phil rang this afternoon. He was gabbling so much with excitement I could scarcely tell what he said.'

'Seven pounds six ounces. They're both fine. Helen's already sitting up and looking wonderful by all accounts.'

She continued to chat as they went through to the drawing room where Laurence, still wearing a blue and white striped apron, not at all consultant-like, was pouring drinks.

'Sandra my dear, hello. And…?'

'Danny Heaney – Laurence Grainger. You hadn't met yet, had you? He's the new houseman on surgical. Don't you think he's gorgeous?'

'I- er… Hmm. How do you do, Mr Heaney.' Laurence extended his hand.

'I'm pleased to meet you, sorr. And the name's Danny.' His eyes twinkled with amusement as he regarded Laurence's apron.

'Sandra!' Rosamund hissed in admonishment.

'What's the matter? He *is* gorgeous, aren't you Danny?' She linked her arm in his. 'Bring your drink over here, and you can fascinate me with your Oirish Charm.'

'She's incorrigible,' Rosamund told him laughing, as he was led away to fold himself onto the low sofa like a friendly grasshopper. 'There goes the doorbell again. This'll be Angie and Henry.'

And she dashed out to let in her senior colleague on the children's ward, and her husband.

***

'No more, thank you, Rosamund. That was grand.' Angie laid her napkin on the table and eased the already ample waistband on her skirt. 'Aren't you lucky having a husband who's such a good cook. Henry wouldn't even know what to do with a baked bean if it didn't tell him on the tin.'

'Not true, not true,' protested Henry, who wore black-rimmed spectacles and a lugubrious expression. 'I can boil a kettle without any trouble.'

There was general laughter.

'How about you, young man? You look as if you could do with fattening up. Can you cook?'

Danny put his head on one side and turned the full force of his blue eyes on Angie.

'Sure and I can t'row an egg or two together, if I must, but I'd be cookin' my own goose if I tried anything fancier.'

'You could learn a thing or two from Laurence, then. Seriously, Laurence, where did you learn to cook like that?'

'It started when I was a student in digs, then when I could afford it I became more adventurous and it became a hobby of sorts. I've always been interested in food, especially foreign food.'

'Hence the French menu tonight. He's a devotee of Elizabeth David's recipes,' said Rosamund. 'When we came back from Majorca, he tried his hand at Spanish dishes.'

'And?' Angie was fascinated. 'How did you get on?'

'I'd bought a recipe book, so it wasn't too bad.'

'Don't be modest, Laurence. It was very good,' Rosamund told them. 'But he hasn't *quite* mastered paella yet.' She exchanged knowing glances with him, grinning.

Angie turned to Henry. 'We like going out to eat, don't we, love? One of them Berni Inns, usually. But I've not had anything as tasty as Laurence's Berf Boobig Nonn, and that Lemon Mousse was a dream. You'll never want for a job while you can cook like that.'

'Have some more, Angie,' urged Rosamund.

'Oh, I couldn't eat another morsel. I shan't be able to bend over the kiddies' cots if I go on at this rate.'

Henry rolled his napkin and inserted it back into the napkin ring.

'Well, you won't have to much longer, Angie.' He turned to the others. 'In another six months I'll get my wife back, and mebbe she'll have time to mother me instead of all those kids.'

'Get away with you, Henry Ollerenshaw.' She nudged him affectionately. 'Well there's nobody more capable than Rosamund of taking over from me. We've worked well together, haven't we lass? And I've got her well trained.' Angie's eyes shone behind her round spectacles. 'She's got a heart of gold, has that lass. If anything she cares for those little ones too much.'

'Some of the little mites do tug at your heartstrings,' Rosamund murmured.

'I know. You see some terrible things at times.' Angie spoke from twenty years' experience of nursing children. 'The little devils can get under your skin. You just have to keep a bit of yourself uninvolved, then when the time comes you can let them go.'

There was a short silence, then Sandra said 'Have you seen Amy recently, Roz? Her baby's due this week.'

'We saw her yesterday. We took Sally and Joe out, to give Amy a break. She looks dreadful. I don't know how she'll cope with another one. Joe can be a little fiend, but Sally's an angel. Tries to help her mum.'

Laurence, acid in his voice, spoke from the other end of the table. 'The latest thing is – that Cyril has bought a motor bike.'

'Oh, my Lord,' Sandra exclaimed. 'That'll really help with transport for the family, not to speak of finances. What does Amy say?'

'What can she say?' Laurence shook his head. 'She has no say in his doings, and he doesn't consider her at all.'

'Coffee everybody?' Rosamund rose from the table. 'I'll bring it into the drawing room.' She sensed a diatribe from Laurence brewing. He couldn't abide Cyril, and neither could she. They saw as little of him as possible, and that only for the sake of Amy and the children.

She carried the tray of coffee into the room and set it on a table.

'…so I'm not fresh from an Irish bog at a-all. I've been working in London for a while before I took this job.'

Danny relaxed back in a long armchair, flicking glances from one face to another as they hung on his words. Sandra sat on the hearthrug, hugging her knees. Henry, busy with his pipe, watched from a chair by the window, while Angie gazed into the Irishman's face with happy absorption. Laurence, busy with glasses and brandy, had his back to the scene, but Rosamund could tell by the slight tension in his shoulders that he was listening.

Danny broke off and leapt to his feet.

'Hey, Mrs Grainger. Let me help.'

He dispensed cups of coffee, all elbows and angles, face serious, intent on not spilling.

He's charmed them all, Rosamund thought, including me. Once launched, he's taken no drawing out. Henry's no fool, and now Danny's discovered he's a fisherman they're thick as thieves. Angie's obviously smitten, and you can see she'd like to take him home and mother him.

Laurence came and sat close to Rosamund. As they watched and listened, he took her hand and whispered 'It looks like a successful evening.'

She nodded and squeezed his hand.

Eventually the flow of conversation dwindled. Sandra sat up, crook-kneed on the hearthrug, and smoothed her skirt over her legs.

'I have an announcement to make.'

Rosamund held her breath. Whatever it is, it's just like Sandra to make a performance of it. Could she be about to announce her engagement? But I don't think she's got a serious boyfriend, although she's the biggest flirt ever.

'I'm leaving Leadersfield. I'm going to Leeds to train as a midwife.'

Rosamund was first to move and knelt to hug her. 'Good for you! What's brought this on, Sandra?'

'Stagnation. I'm happy enough, but you've got to progress haven't you?'

'Are you sure that's what you want?' Angie asked.

'I'm sure. I've been thinking about it for ages.'

There was a hubbub of surprise and congratulation, and soon the evening drew to a close. Angie and Henry left first, and Sandra insisted on helping to clear up, so Danny had to stay too.

When she finally saw them off, Rosamund told Sandra, 'I'm pleased you've discovered what you want. Don't lose touch, will you?'

'Course not. I'll be here to deliver your kids – when you get round to having them, that is.'

Laurence gave her shoulders an affectionate squeeze.

'You'd better hurry your training then, we might beat you to it.'

Rosamund felt hollow inside, but she smiled brightly, and said to Danny, 'It's been lovely meeting you. Do come again, won't you?'

'I will,' he said, and looked directly, first into her eyes then into Laurence's. 'I will.'

***

Looking back, Rosmund wondered whether it was because of Sandra's words about delivering their babies that Laurence became more romantic, or perhaps he suddenly realised time might be running out for them. Whatever the reason, in the weeks that followed he became more attentive. She would find a flower or a few chocolates by her place at supper time. Instead of sitting in his big leather chair, he would sit with her on the blue velvet sofa and whisper sweet nonsense into her hair. He became more ardent, and for a while it seemed possible that they might make love completely, that they might even make a child. But no. After a month or so it all changed again. He became moody, edgy. For the first time since she had known him, he was dissatisfied with his work. There was a restlessness about him that was unsettling, and he was unwilling to say what was the matter. Alicia was going through a patch of ill health, and he spent a good deal of time on the phone talking to her. They went together to see her, and once Laurence went on his own.

Trying to suppress her disappointment, Rosamund sought solace with her friends. She went with Sandra to see Helen and her new baby, Anna. The rosy little face peeped out at her from the folds of her shawl, and Rosamund felt a twist of pain as she felt the weight of the child on her arm.

'She's beautiful, Helen.' She was near to tears as she rocked her. 'She's so lucky to have you two for parents.'

'It'll be your turn soon, Roz. You'll see.'

'I'm not so sure,' she replied in a small voice.

After a difficult labour, Amy had another girl, a pale and puny wisp of a child with a club foot. Amy was so weak she couldn't hold her, and for a while it seemed she might drift away. Alarmed, Rosamund defied hospital rules and took Sally to see her. Sally leaned over her mother and put a fat hand on either side of her cheeks.

'Wake up, Mumma. Joey and me wants you to come home.'

Amy reached out for her and promised, 'We'll be home soon, love. Me and your new sister.'

'We love you, Mumma.' She planted a big wet kiss on Amy's nose.

After that Amy made progress, but the spirit had gone out of her. She went home and her own mother moved in to care for her. Rosamund did what she could. Sally she could take home with her, but Laurence wouldn't have Joe in the apartment.

'He's such a little tearaway, we'd have too many breakages. He'd ruin our things.'

Reluctantly, Rosamund had to agree about Joe, although it saddened her to think this could be how he would react to a child of his own.

Sandra continued to drop in at the apartment, often with Danny in tow. Sometimes he came alone, drank a cup of tea and had a yarn, or he'd stay to supper and Laurence would cook for them all. They never knew when he was going to turn up. Mostly they were both in, sometimes one or the other of them would be there on their own. It didn't seem to matter to Danny, he was always pleasant and helpful, easy to get on with, and after a while it seemed to Rosamund that he had always been around.

One evening when Danny had left early as he was on night calls, Laurence heaved a sigh of relief.

'Thank goodness he's gone. We never seem to get any time alone together these days.'

'That's true.' She smiled at him, relieved that he should feel that way.

'I've been waiting for a chance to talk to you, Rosamund.'

He led her to the sofa and drew her down beside him.

'What would you say to our moving away from Leadersfield?'

31

FRANCIS

Treblissick, 1964

'Da-addy. Can we play in the hayfield?'

Francis shook the earth from the potato plant he had just dug up, and leaned on his fork. Two rows away Alan dug and lifted at a steady pace. Behind them his mother and Betty filled sacks, chattering nineteen to the dozen. Meri, Alan's two and Jimmy's younger brothers hung about, ostensibly helping. He looked through the open gate into the next field where they had carried hay last week, and Dan was trundling the tractor towards them, returning with an empty trailer for another load of sacks of potatoes. At the edge of the field a ladder leaned against the rick still to be thatched. Must get that done as soon as we've finished here, he determined.

Meri danced up and down, black curls bobbing about her impish face as she waited for his answer. A leggy, wiry seven-year-old, she was never still for an instant. Her check shirt was half hanging out and there was a tear in the leg of her shorts, and both knees were crusted with dirt.

'Can we Daddy, can we? Paul wants to fly his aeroplane.'

Four-year-old Paul clutched the bright blue aeroplane he'd had for his birthday, while his sister, Jane, hovered protectively. Jimmy's young twin brothers hadn't waited for permission, and were already galloping across the short grass slapping their behinds as they whooped along. Francis looked across at Alan.

'Okay with you if Jane and Paul go with the others?'

'Sure.' Alan shaded his eyes with his hand against the sun. 'See Jane looks after Paul, won't you Meri?'

'Course. We both will, Uncle Alan.'

'All right, Meri,' Francis told her, 'but keep off the hayrick, remember.' He fixed her with a look. 'And mind the tractor.'

'Yippee. Yes, Daddy.' She skipped away along the rows, two white butterflies dancing round her.

Alan pulled a packet of cigarettes from his shirt pocket and lit up. He shook out the flame of the match with care, flicked away the charred stalk, and stretched his long limbs in the sun.

'That'll keep 'em happy till dinnertime,' he grinned.

Francis wiped the sweat from his forehead with the back of his hand. 'Pity Gwen couldn't be here too, it's such a nice day.'

'She says she'll be glad of the peace and quiet. I hope she'll put her feet up like the doctor told her – she's been a lot tireder carrying this one. She won't get much rest when there're three of them to look after, that's for sure.'

'Hmm.' Francis knocked a clod of earth from a potato.

Children. He envied Alan and Gwen their family and regretted that he'd never fathered a child himself. Meri was a blessing, and he was lucky to have her, he knew. Ruth had refused to consider another baby – gone to Family Planning without telling him – but that was beside the point now. They'd seen or heard nothing of her for four years since the day she ran off, and soon after that Bill and Beryl Nankivell had sold up and moved on to nobody knew where – and no loss to the village either.

The children's voices floated over the fields, and he looked across to see what they were up to. Paul's plane banked in the light breeze and glided to the ground. Jane ran to retrieve it and threw it back in the air towards the little boy. Meri was doing handstands and the twins still charged around. He smiled. They were all right.

He took a deep breath, absorbing the scent of fresh earth and the tang of freshly pulled plants, and looked along the rows with satisfaction. Jimmy was looking after the heifers and calves. Good ones, by the look of them. I'm glad I took him on. He's a hard worker and a quick learner, with a real feel for the land. On the whole, he mused, I've nothing to complain of. Meri's happy and healthy, growing like a weed. Dan and Mother are still billing and cooing like a young couple, not like a pair in their mid-sixties gliding gently towards old age.

Francis smiled to himself, and moved on to another row.

Dare I say it? The farm's prospering at last. Even won third place at the Royal Cornwall Show last year with my best shorthorn. All done by hard graft and good husbandry. With Betty Sandey to take care of Meri and the house, I manage fine.

Betty had been his saviour in many ways, since she'd answered his advertisement for help after Ruth walked out. His own age, and one of the group he'd grown up with, Betty was the girl who'd asked him to go on the big wheel with her at the fair, unknowingly keeping him out of Ruth's clutches for a while the night she… He pushed away the memory. Plain and unmarried with a kind and no-nonsense approach, Betty'd been looking for a job after her widowed mother died. She came to Pennygarra for an interview, and stayed to cook supper and put Meri to bed. She'd worked here ever since, returning each night to her council house in the village. His mother always said that a farm needed a wife, but he was never tempted to court Betty. She was a good pal he could depend on. He sighed. Wherever she was now, he was still married to Ruth, but no one could fill the space in his heart which would always be reserved for the possibility of Rosamund.

The breeze freshened. It blew across the rick; teased the children playing in the hayfield, where it snatched the aeroplane and tossed it high into the air. It gusted down across the rows of potatoes to where Francis felt it urgent on his cheek and lifted his head. Smell of burning. He stiffened and straightened up, looked over into the hayfield just in time to see Paul halfway up the rick climbing the ladder towards his bright blue plane where it had lodged on top. The twins oblivious, wrestled by the hedge. Jane stood transfixed, her hands fisted against her mouth, but Meri, elbows pumping and hair flying, was running towards the figure of the child, tiny against the bulk of the rick.

'Paul, Paul! Come down. We mun't go up there. Come down Paul!' she yelled.

Francis dropped his fork and raced towards them as Meri started to climb the rick behind Paul.

'No, Meri! No!'

His voice was frantic as he pounded across the field, heart thudding faster than his feet, his mouth dry with fear.

The smell of burning was stronger. Paul was nearly at the top now, and a skein of pale blue smoke above him wavered across the deeper blue of the sky.

Francis reached the rick and in a frenzy grasped the rungs, his boots scrabbling for purchase. The fragrance of hay mingled with the pungency of smoke.

'Meri, go back.'

He caught up with her and pushed her hard sideways as he stretched high to grab at Paul's ankles.

Too late.

The top of the rick collapsed inwards as a wall of flame erupted into the sky. Francis felt the searing heat on his hands and face as Paul flung up his arms and screamed, saw him spread-eagled against the white-hot brilliance. His foot slipped from Francis's grasp, leaving an empty sandal in his hand, and Paul toppled headlong into the burning heart of the fire, spread fingers still reaching for his bright blue aeroplane.

The fire surged and roared. Francis jumped backwards as the greedy flames snaked over the rim of the burning rick, and collided with a jumble of flailing limbs in mid air – to land gasping, face down in a tangle of bodies.

Spikes of hay dug into his raw hands and cheek, and against the roar and crackle of the fire he heard shouts, howling and shrill screams. He opened his eyes to look sideways through a haze of sooty smoke and wisps of burning hay to see Alan with contorted face kneeling with Jane in his arms, her mouth wide with terrified screams. The howling was Alan's. The acrid smell of burning filled his nostrils, and he became conscious of the weight of other bodies on his. He extricated himself with a heave and rolled over. There was a hand near his face. Meri, thank God! He reached out painfully to touch her small fingers. She opened her eyes, a few inches from his own.

'Daddy.'

A strange arm, wiry and muscular with black curly hairs and a rolled up tattered red sleeve, lay across Meri. She moved, the arm withdrew and its owner sat up.

Francis looked up across his daughter's sprawled body into the thin brown face of a man with snapping black eyes and wild black curls. Unwilling to believe what he saw, his eyes returned to Meri's face. Thin, brown, pale with shock, bright black eyes and wild black curls.

Looked back again in certain recognition.

'Eli!' His mind grappled with the knowledge. 'You?'

Meri lifted onto her elbows. 'It's my Man in the Woods. He saved me.'

Francis tried to get up but there was a buzzing in his ears, and a misty grey world flickered and swung until, as his vision faded he saw the two faces side by side. Then nothing.

***

He came to as they loaded him into the ambulance, and looked over his blanketed feet to see Eli's figure outlined against the sun. He tried to shout, but the words came out in a croak.

'You stay until I get back. Do you hear?'

'Ain't goin' nowhere, mister.'

The ambulance man blocked his view, and Francis sank back on the pillow as the doors closed.

***

He returned to the farm with bandaged hands and a skin graft on his right forearm. His face, still scorched red as a beetroot and smothered with white ointment, had escaped the worst, but his eyebrows and the front of his hair were badly singed. The pain of the burns was nothing compared with the pain in his heart.

There had been plenty of time while he lay in hospital for waves of horror and guilt to swamp him for his part in Paul's death. He blamed himself. It was not uncommon for hayricks to combust spontaneously, and in the annals of farming many lives had been lost that way. It was why he'd warned Meri to keep off the rick. But the others hadn't heard. The children should never have played in that field without supervision, and it was his responsibility. The rick had been properly built he knew, and Meri had done her best to save Paul. His blood ran cold when he thought of what could have happened to her too. Thank God Eli had been near and seen what was happening. But Eli was something he didn't want to think about just yet. With difficulty he pushed the vision of the two faces away. If only he had smelled burning sooner. He had been so close. Another few seconds and he could have pulled Paul back from the brink. Over and over the nightmare replayed itself. Paul climbing. Meri climbing. His own mad scramble up the ladder. The feel of Paul's foot slipping out of his sandal, and his scream as he fell into the inferno.

Dan brought him home from hospital, and on the journey back from Truro after several futile attempts at conversation, he left Francis to his thoughts.

He was sunk in sorrow. To have brought such tragedy to Alan and Gwen – and with another baby due. He couldn't imagine how they must feel. And how had it affected Jane, whose anguished screams still echoed in his ears. How was he to face them? But face them he must, and soon.

'Here we are, boy.' Dan turned into the farmyard, and pulled up in front of the scullery door. He came round the car to open the door for Francis and helped him out.

'You'm all right now? Maud'll be somewheres about.'

Francis stood shakily and nodded, thankful to breathe in the familiar farmyard smells under a damp grey sky as heavy as his heart. Maud hurried out of the doorway, and seeing his bleak look put her arms round him without a word and led him into the house. He lowered himself into the Windsor chair. Maud got busy with the kettle.

'Where's Meri?'

Maud poured tea into two mugs before she answered.

'She's... Francis, she's... you must...'

Slow footsteps dragged into the room and Meri appeared. She took one look at him and turned away, her face blank.

'It's all right, sweetheart. I'll soon look like me again.' With the bandages and ointment, and his scorched face stubbled with the beard he was being forced to grow until he could shave again, he'd worried she might be frightened by his appearance.

She kept her back to him.

'Meri, look at me.' His voice was gentle, trying to understand. She stood with her head bowed, the pale backs of her knees vulnerable.

Francis waited, sure she would respond soon. Tilly got up from the hearth, padded over to rub herself round the little girl's legs as though to offer comfort. Meri bent to scoop the cat into her arms, then crept out of the room.

Francis stared, appalled. Maud put a mug between his bandaged hands then sat down opposite with a sad sigh.

'She'll have gone over to the hayloft. She's spent most of her time up there since the accident. She comes in to pick at her food when she's called, and goes to bed when she's told, lying there for hours with her eyes wide open. She hasn't spoken a word since that day.' There were tears in Maud's eyes and she plucked at the edge of her apron. 'I hoped when you came home she'd come round, but now – I don't know.'

'Has the doctor seen her?'

'Yes. He says she's physically all right, but her mind's protecting her from the shock of what happened. It's just a matter of time before something triggers it and she'll come round.'

'Oh, Meri.' He groaned, and closed his lashless eyes. And Eli. His mother must have made the connection. 'Eli?' he asked without opening his eyes.

Maud, gentle, 'Dan found work for him until you're ready to talk to him, and he's sleeping out in Bull field. He's kept away from Meri.'

'Thank God.'

***

'What's Eli doing today, Dan?'

'He'm on the moor. Spotted some lamed sheep, so I asked him to sort 'em out.'

'Right. I'll go find him.' He called Floss. She hobbled towards him, stiff now with old age. 'Come on, girl, we'll go and help Meg and Eli with the sheep – two old crocks together, aren't we?'

Her plumed tail wagged and she started eagerly out of the yard.

Out on the moor, with the scent of peat and grass blowing over stunted trees and brakes of gorse, he could see the slight figure of Eli and Meg in the distance. Meg, ostensibly Meri's dog, had taken over most of the work Floss could no longer do, since the loss of her hind leg and old age had overtaken her. A group of sheep were penned together near a heap of granite rocks, and the Gypsy bent over one of them while Meg kept watch on the rest.

Francis had no idea what he and Eli would say to each other. He pulled down the soft cotton sunhat Betty had lent him to protect his still tender scalp, and shield his eyes, although the day was soft and grey. His hands were free of bandages now, but he couldn't yet use them for much. The skin graft on his forearm was still covered, and would be for some time. He knew he still looked a freak, and Meri had still not spoken to him. After today he wondered if she ever would again. Don't be silly, he told himself. She thinks the world of you, always has done, and nothing that passes between Eli and you will alter that. But things'll be different, bound to be.

As he approached, he saw Eli with a sheep on its rear, leaning back against his legs. With a knife in one hand, a hoof in the other he looked straight at Francis.

'Mister?'

'Eli.'

'There's a few with hoofs needs paring. Go lame, else.'

'Finish that one then we'll talk.'

'Aye. Tis time.' He turned and carried on paring the hoof held between his legs, while the sheep bleated in protest, and turned its head trying to see what he was up to.

Francis sat nearby on a rock and watched him work. His hands moved with deftness, and in a few minutes he released the sheep and watched it run off to join the others. He walked over and seated himself on a rock nearby, a quick glance at Francis from under dark brows the only indication that he might be nervous.

He plunged in. 'How did you get to know Ruth?'

'When I were down west that springtime. Family camps there, same as every year, and I joins 'em. She hanged round the camp, like.'

Francis was silent, his eyes on the other man's face.

'Girls do, y'know. S'romantic, caravans and th'open fire and such. They thinks we're different from their own men. But we're not, an' when a wench throws hersel' at you there's nothin' to lose when y'can move on quick if there's a need.'

He took out a packet of cigarette papers and a screw of tobacco, and busied his hands rolling a tight little cigarette, and he didn't need to look at Francis.

'Didn't know she were so young,' he muttered, then lifted his chin. 'Not innocent, she wasn't. An' I takes what I'm offered, if you takes my meaning. Bein' single and footloose.'

He drew on the smoke, and they both watched the tip as it glowed bright.

'Lasted 'bout three week, no more. Then Eli moves on. Never sets eyes on her again till I sees her here at your place, your lady wife as may be. She at her full time, and Eli knows what he knows.'

Francis pictured Ruth heavily pregnant, when he and Eli had seen her feeding the pigs as the storm gathered.

'Meri was born that night, in the snow storm,' Francis told him. 'I had to deliver her.'

Eli nodded. 'Knew it had to be mine. Kept away after that. Didn't want to mess you 'bout, see.'

'I wondered why you didn't come for years. But you saw Meri, didn't you?'

'Watched that little un grow. Kept out of sight, I did.'

'She saw you though. She calls you her 'Man in the Woods '. It was you who helped her when Floss's paw was trapped, wasn't it?'

'Couldn't stand to see her in trouble. I never set the trap though.'

'It's lucky you were here when the rick caught fire.' Francis's voice was quiet, steady, and he looked straight at Eli. 'Thank you for saving her.'

Subtly the mood changed.

'Had to. She's my flesh and blood.'

'Meri's mine by law. She has my name, and I'm her father by rights and by love and by care.'

Their eyes locked. They'd got to the kernel of it at last.

32

'Ain't challenging that. Want to be part of her life. Like her to get to know me some day, so she knows who I am.'

Francis rubbed his neck. 'It's along the lines of what I thought too. When the time comes I'll be the one to do the telling, but not yet, specially as she is now. She's still not talking.'

'Ay, there's a deal of healing needed. You too.'

'Don't think I don't know. But we aren't here to talk about me.'

Eli nodded, acquiescing.

'I'll come to the farm like before now and again – when there'll likely be work?'

'Do that. I missed you, you know, and not just for the work.'

There was a silence, punctuated by bleats of sheep and the distant sound of a lorry rattling down the road to the quarry. Meg, stretched out with her head on her paws, snapped at an inquisitive fly. Floss opened one eye, decided it was of no interest and closed it again.

Eli said suddenly. 'Meri has kin. Romany kin, as wants to claim her as such.'

Francis hadn't thought of that, and took a while to marshal his thoughts. Initially he felt threatened. He supposed that it stemmed from old stories about children being stolen by the Gypsies. If Eli wanted to introduce her to his family, he couldn't stop him. Besides, she had hardly any relations – just himself and Maud and Dan. He didn't know of any more, even distant ones; and Merry's other grandparents, Bill and Beryl Nankivell, had removed themselves from her life as effectively as her mother had done. No uncles, aunts or cousins – there'd be those in plenty on Eli's side.

'Let's wait until she knows her full parentage. When she's used to the idea, let her decide for herself if she wants to meet your people. I think she will want to, but we'll let things take their course. Will you tell them?'

'Ay. Ma'll find waiting hard, but she'll respect what you decide. The rest'll do what she says.'

Francis was relieved that he hadn't wanted to make things difficult. Meri hadn't been worried by his secret presence since she was a toddler, and already trusted him. It would just be a matter of her getting used to Eli being around. He wanted what was best for his precious child, even if there was pain in it for himself, but he didn't want to lose her. Ever. Although he'd wondered who her natural father was, life was simpler before he did know.

There seemed little to add to what had been decided, but the two sat for a while longer. Francis told Eli how Ruth had forced him into marriage, about their life together and Meri's early life. Then talk turned to farming matters, sheep and cattle and crops and the state of the weather. At last Francis left Eli to finish paring hooves, and strode away, leaving the dogs behind, to walk alone on the moor.

***

At the end of the afternoon Meri came tearing into the yard from school, miles ahead of Betty who was still panting up the lane.

'Da – addy!' she yelled, just as if there had been no days of dumbness, no turning away when he came in sight.

Francis rushed from the dairy and caught her in his arms as she charged full tilt at him. She burrowed her head into his stomach and gripped him round the waist as if she couldn't get close enough. He stood and rocked her, his heart full, until she raised her head to look up into his face.

'Sweetheart. What is it?'

He knelt and encircled her in his arms.

Her face was alight with excitement.

'Jane says you're a real live hero, Daddy. Auntie Gwen and Uncle Alan say you nearly died when you tried to save Paul from the fire.'

'Is that so? And what do you think, Meri?'

She became still, and her lips began to tremble. He felt her slightness and fragility under his hands as she fought the tears that filled, then overflowed her eyes and ran in a deluge down her cheeks. He had to bend his head to hear her whisper.

'I thought – you ki-illed P-Paul. You p-ushed him into the f-fire.'

'Oh, Meri. How could you think that?'

'You c-climbed the rick all cross an' shouting, and you pushed me till I fell, an' I was only trying to make Paul come b-back, and he wouldn't. Then you p-pushed Paul as well and he fell. Only he fell in the f-fire and my man in the woods saved me'.

By this time Francis's eyes were full, too. She began to sob, great heaves that racked her.

'I hated you, Daddy. I really hated you for making Paul die,' she told him when she could speak again.

'Sweetheart, sweetheart.' Francis spoke in anguish against her curls.

'I didn't know why, and I couldn't bear it.'

He fished in his pocket for a grubby handkerchief and wiped away her tears.

'So what made you change your mind?'

'Jane did, when she said you're a real live hero. She said you only pushed me and Paul to get us away from the fire, and it wasn't your fault you couldn't hold Paul. Uncle Alan said so.'

She began to cry again, this time flowing, healing tears. Careless of his still tender arm, he lifted her and carried her into the kitchen. Sitting in the embrace of the big chair, he held her close until the crying stopped, grateful that she had learned the truth. Her silence was not what he had believed, but infinitely more painful for her, and he was full of compassion for her suffering.

'Why did Paul have to die? He was only little, littler than Jane and me.'

'I don't know. It just happened. I wish we'd been able to save him. It was a brave thing that you did too, Meri. We can only remember all the lovely things about him, and the happy times we had with him. And be specially kind to Jane and Auntie Gwen and Uncle Alan.'

'Don't forget baby Andrew. I saw him when Auntie Gwen came to meet Jane from school. He's lovely, all creased up and pink like a baby pig and I'm going to help Jane look after him.'

'That's my girl.' Francis kissed her. 'Your face is all streaky. Go and wash it and change out of your school things.'

She examined Francis's face intently. 'Your face's getting better. Was it very sore?'

'It was, and my hands and arm. But I'll mend.'

She stroked his beard, and put her head on one side. 'When are you going to shave this off?'

'Don't you like it?'

'I don't think so. But I might if you really wanted to keep it. It's very red,' she observed solemnly. 'Nearly the same colour as your face, but a bit gingerer.'

Francis started to laugh, feeling it rumble up from the depths of his gut. Meri felt it too, and put her hand on his chest. She began to chuckle then to laugh, and soon they were both rolling around in the old chair, helpless.

Betty came into the kitchen, trying to hide her grin.

'Can I get tea ready now?' she asked.

***

Eli disappeared as mysteriously as he had come.

'Where's my Man-in-the-Wood?' Meri demanded after a while.

'He'll be back when he's ready. And his name's Eli.' Francis told her. 'He's a Gypsy, and they like to travel, so we'll only see him now and again.'

Francis was relieved when she asked no more. She was all his for a while longer.

Harvest was gathered and the swallows departed; St Hyldroc's Fair came and went and soon the grey Fergy was trundling the new plough up and down the fields, turning faded stubble into cords of purple-brown earth, while following gulls screamed grey and white skeins across the sky. Bare trees lined the hedges, and the first frost rimed the drifts of dead dark leaves in the lanes, and folks blew on their chapped hands and stamped feeling into their frozen toes. Then it rained, and rained and rained. Bank after bank of laden purple clouds swept in from the south-west, to dump their loads onto the sodden fields. Francis and Jimmy worked in a sea of mud; sticky, clogging mud that stuck like glue, and Francis kept Dan on indoor work out of the constant damp. The cattle stood steaming, ankle deep in the stuff, seeming not to care. Tractors and farm implements came off the fields coated with it, slinging gouts of muck mixed with reeking manure onto the roads and yard. It seemed to sink into the very pores of Francis's skin, and the air was thick with its earthy smell.

Then drier days and December arrived, and ungainly angels and lopsided stars appeared in the tall windows of the schoolhouse, and the ragged strains of 'Once in Royal David's City' and 'Hark the Herald' in high sweet voices issued from its worn green doors.

'I'm going to be a Shepherd in the Nativity Play, Daddy. Miss Dunn wanted me to be the Angel Gabriel, but I didn't want to be an angel. Do you think Paul's an angel now, up in heaven?' Without waiting for an answer, Meri burbled, 'An' I have to have a dressing gown or something, and it has to be striped, and a tea towel will do for my headdress. Oh, and can I borrow a crook?'

She stopped to draw breath. Francis tried to keep his face straight.

'Yes, you can borrow a crook, but you'll have to talk to Betty about the rest – or Grannie. I think Dan has a striped dressing gown. When's the play?'

'The day before we break up, and we're having a party on the last day, and Father Christmas is coming, and Daddy, can I have…'

'Slow down, Meri. There's plenty of time.' With a pang he realised he was wishing Rosamund could see her, hopping up and down with shining eyes. Her whole face lit up when she was happy. No sign now of her distress after the accident, although she did have quiet moments when she was still sad at the loss of Paul. How resilient children are, he thought, but it all makes its mark somehow, and I just hope I'm handling things right.

***

It was dull and cloudy on the second of January. The morning yard work was done and the cows, steaming on the cool morning air, were turned into the field to munch at the rack of silage. Francis, hungry from his six o'clock start, attacked the plateful of bacon and eggs, sausage and fried bread that Betty put in front of him.

'Meri up yet?' He poured a dollop of tomato sauce over the eggs.

'Yes. In her room painting a picture with those new paints she had for Christmas. Had breakfast early – said she couldn't wait to get back to it.'

He grinned indulgently, and turned his mind to the day's work.

The autumn sowing of barley was greening well, and he'd get a good start today ploughing Home and Bull fields ready for the spring corn. He enjoyed ploughing, took pride in driving a straight furrow, watching the blades of the plough fold the earth into clean shining ridges, gulls screaming in the wake of the tractor. He spooned three sugars into a mug of tea and picked up the Western Morning News.

The headlines leapt out at him.

'Oh my God!' White as a sheet he stared at the photograph. The picture was blurry, but there was no doubt.

'What is it?' Betty put the lid back on the bread bin with a snap.

'Just a minute.' In stunned silence he read the report.

'It's Ruth. She's been murdered.'

'Murdered? Ruth?'

'There's no doubt. See this photograph.'

'I don't remember her looking like that.'

'Her hair's dyed, but it's the same face, long and narrow. And I'd know those eyes anywhere.'

'What happened?'

'Found strangled in an alley near Ruby Mary's in Union Street in Plymouth – in the early hours of New Year's Day.'

'Oh, the poor girl.' Betty leaned over his shoulder to read the report. 'It says here she was called Gloria – blah, blah – identified by her flatmate – nothing else known about her.'

'It's Ruth all right – snapped by her flatmate last summer on the Hoe, it says.' There was sadness in his voice as he looked at the once familiar figure in tawdry clothes and the parody of a smile, and traced the outline of her face with unsteady fingers. 'She looks ancient, and she'd only be twenty four.'

'Yes, well. With that kind of life…' Her voice tailed off in embarrassment.

Francis didn't notice.

'She never stood a chance, poor maid.'

He picked up the newspaper and went to the telephone.

***

It was early evening before he was back from Plymouth, with an expression bleak and blank as a concrete wall. Without a word he got out of the Land Rover, and strode away up to the winter wastes of the moonlit moor.

33

ROSAMUND

Leadersfield, 1963.

'Move away from Leadersfield?' Rosamund couldn't believe what Laurence had just said. 'Right away? From the hospital, this flat?'

'Yes.'

'Why? We're happy here, aren't we?'

'There are several reasons.' His voice was quiet, equable. 'You know Mother's health hasn't been good recently – and she's not getting any younger. If we lived nearer, when things do go wrong we'd be on hand when needed.'

'And?'

'I'd like to start doing some private work. I can't bring patients here to the flat, so it would mean moving somewhere with space for a consulting room.'

'I see. Go on,' she answered calmly. She didn't feel calm, she felt as if she had been tipped out of a boat into a raging sea.

Laurence shifted his position and avoided her eye.

'Well. As a matter of fact there's a medical consultancy going at Warwick Hospital. I thought I might try for that.'

'And Warwick just happens to be a few miles from Clavercote.' A thought struck her. 'Does Alicia know of your plans?'

'Er, actually it was she who mentioned it to me. She knows someone…'

Rosamund stood up abruptly and kicked the log basket. The poker fell, clattered across the hearth and landed on the rug, leaving a black smear across the cream wool.

'Where am I in all these wonderful plans?' Hands on hips, eyes blazing blue ice, she faced him. 'Do I, your wife, have any say? Have you considered how I might feel about being torn from the hospital that has been home and family to me the past eight years? To be at the beck and call of a scheming old woman, who will stop at nothing to keep her son's allegiance; who demands grandchildren, but puts every emotional obstacle she can in the way of her son's proper relationship with his wife? I sometimes think, Laurence, that you married me in order to satisfy your mother's dynastic ambition.'

He covered his eyes with his hand. 'Sit down, Rosamund. I can't talk to you like this.'

'I can't sit down. I'm too angry.' Shaking, she paced across to the window.

'I didn't know you felt like this about Mother.'

'Neither did I until now. But it's true, isn't it?' She flung round to face him again.

Laurence took a long time to answer, then with reluctance said, 'There's some truth in it, perhaps. I chose you and married you for yourself – for the person you are, and I care about you very much. But to be honest, I don't think I would have been looking for a wife if Mother hadn't been intent on my continuing the family line.'

'Ohh.' All fire extinguished, she dropped into the leather chair. 'You can't know how that makes me feel.' She hid her face in her hands.

He remained silent.

When she could speak again, she took a deep breath and said, 'As your wife – apart from how it came about – as your wife, I know Alicia needs more of our time and care, and I don't begrudge her what she really needs. As your wife, I also want what's best to make you happy in your career. But you're asking me to give up an awful lot. I've worked hard from nothing for what I have now, and Addy, Helen, Amy and the children, Sandra – they mean so much to me. How could I leave them behind?'

'I know, Rosamund. That's why I was afraid to talk to you before. I thought you'd say no outright.'

'Am I so selfish? I wish you had talked to me earlier – given me time to think. It makes me feel like rubbish that you didn't.' She rubbed her palm over the polished leather of the chair arm, as if rubbing away the hurt. 'When's the application to be in?'

'Next Tuesday.'

'So soon. That's only a week to decide.' (Then she remembered – I made up my mind to leave in an instant eight years ago.) She looked at Laurence waiting, tense, expectant.

'You really want to move, to have this job, don't you?'

'I might not get it.'

She sat back and closed her eyes. Of her close friends she was the only one left at the hospital. Helen, wrapped up in motherhood, had no intention of returning to nursing. Amy, trapped in a destructive marriage with three children, couldn't, while Sandra had turned her face in another direction. There's really nothing to keep me here, she realised. I could keep in touch with them all. Visit them here, have them stay with us. I'd enjoy having Addy, spoil her a little in return for all she's done for me. I could give Amy and the children holidays. Perhaps when she's older have Sally to stay on her own. It shouldn't be difficult to find another job, either. Who knows, it could be a new beginning for me. If I let it.

Laurence interrupted her thoughts.

'Don't try to give me an answer straight away. Sleep on it at least. But please don't dismiss it out of hand.' He hesitated. 'Mother's not so bad, really.'

Rosamund lay awake most of the night, turning things over and over in her mind.

Whatever his reasons for marrying me, she thought, we're reasonably happy, except for that One Thing. I know we row sometimes, but that's normal. I'm sure I shall handle Alicia now I've realised what she's doing. I like her, and we ought to be able to get on. I wouldn't want to live next door to her, though.

We could look for a house in the country. To live among fields and woods and hills again! It wouldn't be Cornwall, but it'd be wonderful to get away from city streets and grime. Clean fresh air. A good place to bring up children, where they could roam free and grow up close to nature as I did. It might be that Laurence and I could make a child if things were different.

'Yes, Laurence,' she said as she put the toast rack on the breakfast table.

'What did you say?' he spluttered through a gulp of coffee.

'I said, Yes, Laurence. Yes, yes, yes. Let's go south. Let's live in the country – but not too near your mother. Let's start something new.'

'You really don't mind?'

'No. I did at first, but I've thought it through. Let's do it. This flat's *your* home, that I've shared since we married. I want us to have a home that's *ours,* that we've made together.'

'You're sure you're ready to do this? It's too sudden after what you said last night.'

'I've been thinking all night, and I believe it will be right for us, for what you want and what I want. But I haven't agreed because your Mother wants you near her. I will not play second fiddle to her. I'm your wife, and I expect to come first with you. On that understanding I'll do all I can to support you, and… When shall we start looking at houses?'

'Steady, steady. I haven't applied yet.'

'Write today. You'll get it, I know you will.'

He did.

***

Warwickshire mud is just as sticky as Cornish mud, Rosamund decided as she picked her way round the edge of a ploughed field, the feet of her wellies clogged and heavy. Sam, Laurence's black Labrador, was muddy all the way up his legs. She turned her face to the cold wind and louring early November sky as she absorbed the dark smell of the earth and dank dead leaves that lay at the foot of the skeletal hedge to her right.

At the edge of the wood, the grass was yellowed and spiky with dead stems of dock and cow parsley. She scraped the worst off her boots, and turned to look back the way she had come. This was the view of the house she liked best. Ribbed fields bordered by hawthorn hedges sloped up to the Edwardian house of mellow brick framed by evergreen bushes and elm trees, which stood on the skyline, alone on a low bluff. From this side the house appeared to sprawl a little, to relax the formal front it presented to the world at the other side. The wide french windows of the drawing room reflected the sky, and above, the generous bay of their bedroom sheltered under deep eaves, overlooking the terraced garden and valley beyond. When they found the house she'd teased Laurence for preferring the more 'swanky' front entrance, with its formal porch and symmetrical high windows, where he had his consulting room.

Sam dashed enthusiastically into the midst of a flock of rooks, which had been picking for grubs among the furrows. They scattered across the sky, cawing in derision as he halted, one paw raised, and gazed ineffectually after them.

Rosamund laughed and entered the wood.

Unable to find what they wanted, she and Laurence had considered this house on the fringe of Clavercote as a last resort, Rosamund fearing it would be too near her mother-in-law in the centre of the village by the church. But as soon as Laurence turned into the driveway and she'd seen the name of the house carved on the stone gateposts she'd exclaimed, 'Arthur House! Pa's name.'

'It's got to be the right one then,' Laurence grinned as he pulled up at the door.

It wasn't until August when the fields were harvest gold, and the mealy scent of cut corn blew dusty on the hot wind that they'd moved in. Now it was hard to believe it was nearly fifteen months since they'd sat on the terrace that first evening in the glow of sunset, with the chaos of removal in the house behind them, and eaten corned beef sandwiches washed down with a bottle of hock.

In the wood, Rosamund's feet made no sound on the loamy path where tree roots snaked at random to trap the unwary, and a robin piped bitter sweet in the depth of a holly bush.

It had been a good move, she reflected. Laurence was happy at Warwick Hospital, and the trickle of private patients had grown to a steady stream. She didn't know whether Laurence had spoken to his mother, and she wouldn't ask, but Alicia no longer made remarks direct or indirect about grandchildren, and generally kept her nose out of their business unless included – which she often was. She herself had been happy homemaking for the first few months, and had discovered that she didn't want to go back to hospital work.

'Why not try District Nursing?' Alicia suggested one afternoon soon after they had moved in. She wielded a yellow duster over the book she held, then added it to the pile beside her.

Rosamund picked up several books together. 'Why not?' she considered with her head on one side trying to read the titles. She stowed the books on the bookshelf and pushed them together with a satisfying snap. 'Yes. I do fancy being a District Nurse. But I'll have to learn how to drive first.'

She hadn't minded Alicia making the suggestion. It no longer seemed like interference. There had undeniably been a problem between them, but Rosamund now acknowledged that part of it had been of her own making. Oddly enough living nearer had brought them closer, and Rosamund relished having family.

Sam had forged ahead of Rosamund to splash through a small stream, and looked across at her from the opposite bank to see if she was following.

'I'll stay dry, Sam,' she called, resting her back against a beech tree, its bark silky cool under her hands. Smelling sweet and fresh, the stream tumbled over a low waterfall to a pool below. Filigree branches of next spring's beech buds dipped into translucent water, gathering last summer's leaves at their tips. Sam explored the shoreline, nose down.

She returned to her thoughts. Saw herself learn to drive, and after the first Christmas take a course in District Nursing; be issued with navy blue uniform with a felt hat, a battered Gladstone bag packed with nursing necessities: and a dark blue Morris Minor – which to her delight she was allowed to use for private purposes, provided she bought her own petrol. Her rounds in neighbouring villages enabled her to explore the byways of the countryside, and she realised how alien to her true self town life had been.

True to her intention, from time to time she returned by train to Leadersfield to see her friends, who in turn came to visit. Even Amy struggled on the train with three children when Cyril had got on his motorbike one day and ridden out of their lives. 'Good riddance too,' Sandra'd said, although Amy herself wept bitterly. Helen and Phil, with little Anna, arrived with the car piled high with baby equipment, and it was on the terrace of Arthur House that Anna took her first steps. Laurence's Mother and Addy progressed the friendship thay had begun at the wedding, and Addy spent almost as much time with Alicia at Berry cottage as she did at Arthur House.

Rosamund hadn't realised how much there was to see and do in the area. They were within easy reach of Stratford with its Shakespearean connections, and hordes of tourists. All the world seemed to visit Stratford-upon-Avon – she'd even met an ex-patient on a day trip from Leadersfield queuing at the riverside for a boat trip! She loved Warwick with it's magnificent castle, and there was Kenilworth and Leamington Spa. Laurence relived his youth as they explored all of these, and places tourists didn't find – tiny hamlets, woodland, canals and streams. She had grown to love the 'leafy lanes' of Warwickshire and the rosy brick of its old farms and cottages. The furniture they had brought with them from Leadersfield was not enough to fill their home, and wherever their expeditions took them they rummaged in junk shops and searched more upmarket antique shops in town to grace the high-corniced rooms of Arthur House.

Yes. Life was good on the whole. Not perfect, nothing ever was. They still bickered from time to time, but nothing serious. But there was still no possibility of a child, and sometimes frustration tied her in knots. She sighed and shuffled her toe in an arc in the bare soil at the foot of the tree. She hadn't given up hope, but in her heart she felt cheated.

An invasion of homecoming rooks clattered, raucous into the darkening wood. Between the thinning trunks a narrow band of yellow light stretched low in the sky. Time to go home. Laurence would be back about six, and she had a pheasant casserole simmering in the Aga. She pushed herself away from the beech tree and whistled for Sam.

***

Laurence came in from the bathroom, smelling of soap and toothpaste, his hair almost completely silver now, neatly combed. Rosamund wanted to ruffle its precise waves, but because he had been irritable lately, edgy and distracted, didn't dare. She slipped on her shorty nightdress and scrambled into bed. He wound his wristwatch, laid it on the night table six inches from the edge and climbed in beside her.

She reached for her book.

'You're going to read?' His voice was querulous.

'Just a few minutes, if you don't mind.'

'Don't be long, will you? I need to sleep.' He turned away and pulled the sheet over his shoulders.

'Okay, I won't bother.' She put her book down and switched off the lamp. 'Goodnight.' She leaned over to kiss the back of his head, which was all that was available, and snuggled down.

Perhaps it was because of her long walk, but Rosamund fell swiftly into a deep sleep, and only half roused when she felt Laurence turn over towards her and lay his arm across her waist. He mumbled in his sleep, and she wriggled back, spoonlike, into the curve of his body. As she drifted back to sleep she thought she was dreaming when he mumbled again and clutched her to him, and she felt him slip inside her from behind. This couldn't be happening. She moved slightly, and knew that it was. He began to move his hips, then to thrust, and thrust again. Almost immediately he cried out. She felt him convulse.

Fully awake now, she waited for something else to happen, but nothing did. They lay immobile, folded together under the weight of the blankets until she felt his breath on her neck and he whispered, 'Do you realise what just happened?'

She opened her eyes. Moonlight stretched a silver finger through the slit between the curtains, and a shiver of certainty rippled through her.

Scarcely daring to breathe she answered, 'Yes.'

'Oh, my God, Rosamund.' He buried his face in her hair and sobbed.

In tears herself, she turned over and took him in her arms.

Daylight found them still dazed. At first they treated each other with utmost care, as if something fragile and precious would break if they were to speak loudly or move suddenly.

But gradually real life returned.

Each morning after breakfast, Laurence gave Rosamund his customary kiss on the cheek and drove off to the hospital, conducted clinics, ward rounds, held consultations for his private patients in the front room of Arthur House.

Rosamund washed the dishes, fed the dog, and drove round the Warwickshire lanes in her Morris Minor, stopping to carry her shabby black bag into cottages and houses, to change a dressing here, give an injection there, care for someone dying, take out stitches, all with a sure and gentle touch. She shopped at the village store and visited Alicia, brought her back to Arthur House to spend time with herself and Laurence. She felt different, special, but not in any superior way, but flowing and generous, so that each contact she made and each task she performed was imbued with more than its actual meaning.

And by the time the New Year arrived she knew for certain that unbelievably, wondrously – she was pregnant.

34

'You can't be!' Laurence gaped at Rosamund in disbelief and dropped the open pages of The Times onto his toast and marmalade, then with cautious hope asked, 'Can you?'

'Yes, I can. Unlikely as it seems, I'm pregnant – going to have a baby.' Rosamund heard the sound of her voice as though it belonged to someone else.

'But, I – we only – just that once…'

'I know,' she said. 'Bull's eye, Laurence.'

It was the morning of New Year's Day, and Rosamund had been wondering how to tell him. Half of her wanted to keep her secret for ever, it felt so fragile. Her miracle. It was a golden bubble in her consciousness, too precious to share. For in telling, the bubble might burst and scatter her hopes to the four winds. Laurence and his mother would take over this baby, she just knew they would, and it would have to be a boy, of course.

She'd looked at her silver-haired husband across the breakfast table where he sat in his paisley silk dressing gown sipping coffee, his eyes scanning The Times over half spectacles. She was being irrational she knew, but pregnant women were allowed to be irrational, weren't they? It's his right to know, she'd conceded to herself, and he'll be so proud that he's succeeded in fathering a child after all the difficulties, arbitrary as its conception was. She'd pushed away the remains of dry toast on her plate and the cup of hot water which Laurence hadn't noticed in nearly a month, and looked out over the wintry garden to the bare fields beyond. Then she'd tightened the girdle of her blue housecoat, and just blurted it out.

Now he sat very still, and as she watched him with her hands over her abdomen, her heart fluttered like a trapped butterfly.

Sam's tail rose, and fell with an enquiring thud on the polished floorboards, and Laurence without moving his eyes from her face, reached down to caress the black velvety head which nudged his thigh. His eyes were full of tears.

'I'd given up hope.' His voice thick, face working. 'Ohh!' He rubbed his eyes with thumb and forefinger. 'I don't know what to say.'

'Then don't say anything.'

They sat for a while in silence, then he asked, 'When?'

'Late August.'

'It was that night then.'

'Laurence, it was the *only time*.'

'Yes, I'm sorry. I couldn't quite believe it's mine.'

Rosamund was stunned, wounded.

'I wouldn't have blamed you,' he went on.

'Why on earth not?'

'I felt like a useless old man.'

'Not so useless after all, it seems.' This wasn't the conversation they should have been having. 'Aren't you pleased?'

'Of course I'm pleased. More than pleased.' He rose and came round the table, lifted her bodily from her seat and whirled her round and round. 'I'm bloody ecstatic. A child at last! You clever little creature.' And for the first time since she couldn't remember when, he covered her face with kisses.

'We must tell Mother as soon as possible. She'll be absolutely delighted,' he said, still holding her round the waist. 'I'll ring her up immediately.'

'Can't it wait until this afternoon when we go down to Berry House?' Rosamund pleaded. 'Let it be just between the two of us until then?'

'I should have thought you'd want to shout it from the rooftops.' He looked curiously into her eyes.

She pulled away, and sat down again, arms crossed over her stomach.

'Well, I don't. Besides, there's Addy.'

'What about her?'

'We'll tell them both together. It'll give them something to twitter about.'

'Rosamund, my Mother doesn't twitter. Where is Addy? She's usually about by now.'

'I took her breakfast in bed, and told her to take her time.'

'Very well, but I think it's odd. Couldn't you have waited until she'd gone home next week?'

'What do you want? First you're all for racing off to your mother with the news, next minute you want to delay her hearing it.' She stopped. 'I'm sorry, Laurence, I'm being silly. There's a tiny baby in here that we've both longed for, and who's going to be welcomed with love. Of course I want Alicia to know, but not until this afternoon. Please?'

He capitulated. 'Anything to make you happy. I'll take a bottle of champagne, and we'll celebrate the New Year *and* the baby in style.'

***

'You've made an old woman very happy.' Alicia embraced them both. 'You've no idea what this means to me. I've so looked forward to becoming a grandmother before I die. Although you took your time about it, I must say.'

Laurence ducked his head slightly, and said, 'Nonsense, Mother, you'll have years and years to enjoy your grandson.'

Addy joyfully hugged Rosamund. 'Ay, lass, I'm right pleased for you – and you Laurence, o' course.' She turned to kiss his cheek.

'Yes, don't forget Daddy,' Rosamund teased. Then, as the colour rose to his cheeks, 'Laurence! I didn't know you could blush!'

'Yes, well. Who's for a glass of champagne?'

He popped the cork with a 'thwack ', and caught the first fizzings expertly in shallow crystal glasses.

Alicia seated herself with arthritic care into her wing chair. Addy lowered her bulk onto the couch and plumped a cushion to make room for Rosamund.

'Here's to nineteen-sixty-five, and to our little baby.' Laurence stood tall, an expression of pride and happiness on his face as he lifted his glass.

Rosamund felt a warm glow as she sipped, tasting the prickles of champagne on her tongue. This had been the right way to make the announcement, and Laurence had had a little time to get used to the fact of his impending fatherhood. She giggled.

'What is it?' Addy nudged her.

'I was just trying to picture Laurence changing a nappy.'

'Not up my street, my dear,' he said with uncompromising firmness.

That's telling me, she thought. Well, I'm not really surprised.

They drank and talked, and Laurence opened another bottle of champagne. The room lapped them in comfort. Lamps glowed against the gloom of the late afternoon, and flames from the log fire shed warmth on the small but exquisitely decorated Christmas tree, and cards perched on every available polished surface. Bowls of early forced hyacinths added their perfume to aromas of roasting pork and stuffing that wafted from the kitchen.

'I mus' baishte the joint.' Alicia struggled out of her chair.

'I'll do it.' Rosamund jumped to her feet, only to feel the room swim round her. 'Ooh dear. I think I'm a bit tipsy.'

'You will not-t do it. *I* do the cooking in my own ki-kitchen.' Alicia with her patrician nose in the air stalked unsteadily towards the door. 'S-sit down, Roshamun ', you've got my gran'son to think about. You can help later with th' shervin'.'

'Laurence?' Rosamund subsided with a slight thump into her seat. 'D'you think she should?'

Laurence leaned back in his chair and waved his glass. 'Leave her to do what she wantss. She's an imm- immovable o'ject.'

Addy, perspiration standing in beads on her forehead, shuffled about as though dying to help, but good manners as a guest kept her where she sat. Rosamund put her glass down and leaned her head against the settee back. No more for me, she thought, Tiddler mightn't like it.

Moments later there was a crash and a thump from the kitchen, a long wail tore through the sitting room.

'Mother!'

Laurence was out of the room like a shot, Rosamund close behind.

Alicia lay on the floor with the roasting tin beside her, the joint half out of the tin, potatoes and gouts of melted fat scattered around. Splashes of fat stained the front of her dress and lisle stockings, too. She lay with her left leg under her, the oven cloth still in her hand.

'Sshilly me,' she said, and passed out.

Laurence, instantly sober, examined her quickly. Rosamund fetched a rug and a cushion for her head, all feelings of insobriety gone.

Lumbering into the kitchen behind them, Addy took one look and said, 'Strong coffee. Where's it kept?'

On her knees beside Alicia, Rosamund told her, and looked anxiously at Laurence. He looked back, pale-faced.

'Ring for an ambulance, Rosamund. She's broken her leg – if that's not all.'

It wasn't quite all, and it was bad enough at her age. She'd fractured the neck of her femur, which had to be pinned; twisted her right wrist in trying to save the tin from falling; and there were several small burns on the front of both legs. Enough to keep her in hospital for several weeks.

Addy returned to Leadersfield, and bombarded Rosamund with enquiries. She couldn't keep away, and soon arrived again to stay, laden with home baked goodies and an enormous potted azalea to take to her friend in hospital.

Returning from a visit she announced, 'Alicia's asked me to come and look after her when she comes out of hospital.'

Rosamund and Laurence looked at each other.

'What a relief,' he told her. 'We thought we'd have a battle to get her to have help.'

'She might be stubborn, but she's not stupid. It'll be comp'ny for us both. 'Sides, it'll get our Wendy used to not having me at her beck and call. Did I tell you they've applied to go to Australia on one of them assisted passages?'

'You'll really miss her, and your grandchildren, won't you?' Rosamund knew how she'd revelled in her family.'

'Well, they're growing up now, don't always want me fussing ovver them. It'll be a grand life for 'em ovver there, and I can go an' see 'em when I want. Looking after Alicia'll take my mind off it – and there'll be your little mite to enjoy soon.'

'That's something we wanted to talk to you about, Addy.' Laurence broached tentatively. 'We wondered if you'd like to look after Rosamund and the baby when it arrives – just for a few weeks, you know?'

Addy's smile grew until it stretched right across her face, and her cheeks glowed.

'There's nowt I'd like better, and I'll stay as long as you like.'

'Thank you. That's settled then. But we shall have to get Mother well first.'

Rosamund beamed, but she couldn't hold back a small sob. She suddenly felt far from family of her own. It seemed wrong to be having a baby without her own mother, but with Addy it would all be all right. Before she knew it tears flowed, and she was folded into Addy's capacious bosom.

'There, don't tek on, love. It's your hormones as is mekking you weep. Now dry your eyes, and let's think about getting Berry Cottage ready for your mother-in-law to come home.

***

'What's the hurry, Laurence, you've got heaps of time?'

He grabbed a piece of toast, buttered it at speed, and crammed it into his mouth without sitting down.

'Got some casenotes I want to go through before clinic starts,' he mumbled with his mouth full. 'Pour me some coffee would you, please – not too hot.'

She did as he asked, moving her eight-month bulk ponderously to the fridge for more milk, then returned to the table.

'Will you need lunch, because I planned to go into Stratford today, and it'd be a rush to get back.' She picked up an airmail letter from Edith and put it on one side to take with her to read.

'No, I'll grab something in the canteen.' Laurence ignored the pile of letters beside his plate and slapped his cup down half drunk.

Rosamund watched the coffee slosh onto the clean yellow cloth.

'You *are* in a hurry. They must be fascinating casenotes. Are they about a very beautiful blonde?' she teased.

He threw a look of disparagement in her direction, and smoothed his hair with both hands as he passed the mirror.

'By the way, we're having a guest for supper. Sorry it's short notice.'

'That's okay,' she answered, mentally rearranging the menu. 'Is it anyone I know?'

'Danny Heany.'

'Danny Heaney? I didn't know he was down here.'

'He joined us a few weeks ago, men's surgical. Didn't I tell you?'

'No.' She pictured the lanky Irish surgical houseman at Leadersfield, with his wicked blue eyes and a neat line in blarney. 'It'll be nice to see him again, but I hope he's not intending to make himself quite so much at home here as he did at the flat. It began to feel as if three people were living there, and we'd only been married a few months.'

'Things have moved on since then.' He grabbed his briefcase, and kissed her briefly on the cheek. 'I'll see he doesn't. Enjoy Stratford.'

'I will,' she said to empty air.'

***

She squeezed behind the wheel of the bright red Mini Laurence had bought her for her birthday, and backed out of the garage, humming gaily. She wound the window down to enjoy the feel of warm air on her face and bare arms. Glad that Laurence wouldn't be back until suppertime, she would give herself a day out in Stratford. He'd been over-solicitous of her pregnancy at first, as she'd known he would. In the end Alicia wasn't a problem. In any case, her interest was in the baby rather than in Rosamund, and she'd more to occupy her now that Addy had gone to live with her as her permanent companion. Rosamund smiled as she thought of how Addy had embraced village life with enthusiasm. She'd dragged Alicia, lame as she now was, and who'd lived in the village for thirty years and had always considered herself above such things, into bring and buy sales and beetle drives and concert parties, and had even joined the Women's Institute – though she did draw the line at jumble sales.

Rosamund drove at first towards Warwick, then turned right at the station to wind her way through country lanes. Roadside verges were high with grasses and wild flowers, and the hedges dotted with pink and white wild roses. The scent of haymaking filled the air and reminded her as it always did of Cornwall and Francis.

Laurence's attentions had lasted through her early pregnancy, and together they'd bought baby things and planned the nursery. But it was Rosamund who'd papered the walls with pale green paper decorated with baby rabbits, and hung green and white curtains at the window. He'd become edgy of late, and short-tempered. She saw him at breakfast times, but he was increasingly late home in the evenings. Weekends he spent on the golfcourse – anywhere, it seemed except with her. She put it down to her increasing bulk and slowness, and general unattractiveness. I suppose it's to be expected, she sighed. Lots of men go off their wives during pregnancy. It'll be different when the baby comes.

She pulled in to let a tractor pass and returned his cheerful wave. It was too nice a day to worry about Laurence. If he wouldn't take her anywhere, she would take herself. He had at least provided her with the means to do so.

She turned onto the Warwick Road. Soon traffic began to build up as she approached the outskirts of Stratford. Then she swept round the bend of the Birmingham Road, and turned left into Riverside, where she was lucky to find a parking space.

She sat for a moment to enjoy the gentle kicking inside her. You know we've arrived, don't you Tiddler? I'll show you the river and the swans, and I might even buy you something. Eased from behind the wheel, she stood to stretch and gather herself. It was hot. Children ran laughing across the grass in the gardens, summer-clad figures strolled among flower beds and along the river bank and round the statue of Falstaff, where he sat with a tide of antirrhinums at his feet watching the traffic flow by over Clopton Bridge. There was a red and green painted barge in the lock, and a crowd of holidaymakers clustered round to watch the boatman tie up. The Theatre first, she decided, it was after ten thirty and the Box Office would be open now. She slung her bag over her shoulder and started towards the brickbuilt theatre facing the gardens.

Rosamund emerged from the foyer feeling pleased. She had two thirty shilling seats in the centre of the dress circle in her purse for The Merchant of Venice on November twenty-seventh. It was to be a surprise for Laurence's birthday, and with Eric Porter playing Shylock she knew how delighted he would be. Now, where next? I need some more Bisodol tablets for my dyspepsia. Being pregnant isn't all sweetness and light. Boots was in Bridge Street, round the corner, and with the blue and yellow packet in her bag, she dawdled up the street, looking in shop windows. She stopped to admire elegant clothes in one shop. Just what I like, but no good at present – maybe after the baby. There was an antique shop on the opposite corner of High Street. There might be something Laurence'd like for his birthday. It's not for ages, but that doesn't matter. I'll be too busy to shop soon, anyway. She drifted up to the window and searched through the display.

A Georgian barometer was the first possibility, then a Bow figurine of The Doctor, which she thought might amuse him. A pair of Chinese ginger jars entwined with green dragons, perhaps, or a set of amber wine glasses? Ah! Set on a low table, she spotted a pair of ivory anatomical figures, male and female, in a velvet-lined case. Each figure, perfect in detail, lay on a miniature couch, and had a hinged cover to display tiny internal organs. This was perfect. And the cost? Hmm. Yes. But she had to have them.

She made for the doorway, and paused inside to let her eyes adjust. Bright against the comparative gloom, the broad shoulders of a man in a soft yellow shirt bent to examine the underneath of a Pembroke table. As if he knew she was there, slowly he lifted his copper head to look straight at her with eyes of deepest green.

Francis.

Rosamund stood paralysed with shock, her hand on the door jamb. Recognition bloomed in his face, and she panicked.

No! No! It mustn't be!

She turned, fled blindly out of the shop and across the road, oblivious to the stares of passers-by and the honking of alarmed motorists, as she wove between chrome bumpers amid the squeal of brakes. She hugged her bump as she ran. Her bag fell off her shoulder onto her arm, and banged against her legs. Safe by a miracle on the opposite pavement, she swerved round the corner of a jewellery shop into Sheep Street. She knew he would come after her. Gasps came ragged in her constricted throat and her sight began to blur. I can't go on much longer! Francis mustn't catch me! Mustn't catch me!

She saw an open door and stumbled into dimness, the murmur of voices and clink of teacups, and a smell of coffee and ice cream. There was an empty table in the far corner, near a flight of stairs. She made for it and sank onto the seat without looking round. Elbows on the table, she leaned over and thrust her fingers through her hair so that it fell forward to hide her face. She tried to still the banging of her heart against her ribs. Banging with shock, panic, the effort of running, and most of all with pain. All she'd wanted to do when she saw him, was to throw herself into his arms and beg forgiveness, to feel his arms round her and his mouth on hers. Why? Why now? After all these years?

The table moved slightly, and someone slid into the seat opposite.

He'd found her.

35

Francis's heart pounded like an over heated tractor. He'd known in an instant that it was Rosamund, and now, unbelievably, he was looking at her bowed head across the salt and pepper pots and today's menu in the middle of a red tablecloth.

Her fair hair was longer, darker than it used to be, but streaked blond by summer sun. Elbows on the table, her face covered by her hands, he could see the glint of a wedding ring between the locks of hair which swung forward. It had been obvious at his first astonished glance that she was heavily pregnant, and she'd amazed him with the speed of her flight.

Give her time, he thought, content yet just to look, to believe that it truly was her. There'll be all the time in the world after these long years.

He spread his hands on his thighs to stop them trembling, but Rosamund shook all over. Longing to take her hands away from her face, to hold them still as he looked into her eyes, he knew he must wait patiently, as he would for a frightened animal to still.

'Are you ready to order, sir?'

A waitress in check gingham and a white apron stood with notepad and pen poised.

'Tea for two, please,' and with a look at Rosamund's still quaking shoulders added, 'and a plate of biscuits.'

Rosamund didn't move, but he heard a surreptitious sniff. Will her voice still be the same, he wondered. Sounds of the busy tearoom swirled round them: chatter, a sudden burst of laughter; the clatter of crockery; a spluttering coffee machine somewhere in the depths of the room at the back; and the surge of passing traffic.

'Here we are, sir.' The waitress was back with a loaded tray. She glanced from Rosamund's still bowed head to Francis, winked, but said nothing.

When she'd gone he picked up the teapot, poured two cups, added milk.

'Here.' He placed the cup and saucer near her elbow.

She laid her hands in her lap and raised her head. Blue, blue unforgotten eyes gazed straight into his soul. Without breaking their gaze he pushed the sugar bowl towards her.

'You know I don't take sugar.'

Musical before, her voice was slightly deeper now in maturity. Suddenly elated, he siezed the sugar bowl and heaped his usual three spoonfuls into his own tea.

'I do – as if you didn't know.' He raised an eyebrow and stirred. They both watched the miniature whirlpool.

'You ought to be fat as butter.' She picked up her cup and sipped.

He saw that her hands were steadier. How calming mundane activities are, he thought as he began to relax, feeling the bunched muscles of his shoulders soften. She was studying his face, and he gazed steadily back.

She saw a beloved face that the years had enhanced: the jawline wider, the features more rugged. The curve of his mouth was as she remembered. There were deeper crinkles round his eyes, with shadows that shouldn't have been there in the green depths. His hair, deepened to a dark mahogany, had receded, revealing a crop of freckles across a weathered forehead, and she remembered why she'd had to flee. He resembled his father, and this was her half brother.

Francis saw her eyes cloud, and held his breath.

She searched for a likeness to herself and found none. That meant nothing. The letter her mother had written to his father was unequivocal. *'The child is the image of you, and I have called her Rosamund'*. Babies soon change their early likenesses, and she knew that as a girl she had resembled her mother. Instinctively she cradled her own unborn child.

He could see she was withdrawing, and asked quietly, 'When is your baby due?'

She came back with a start.

'Tiddler?' she patted herself. 'In about a month – the end of August.'

'You look well.'

'I am.' Then after a pause, 'It's my first – Laurence is determined to have a boy.'

'Your husband?'

She nodded. 'A medical consultant.'

Are you happy?' He hardly dare ask.

She considered, her head on one side. 'Yes, I suppose we are. You married?'

'I was – my wife died last year.' He sobered, then his face brightened. 'I have a daughter of eight, Meri. She's a delight, a real livewire. We're great buddies.'

Rosamund's chest constricted. Laurence and Alicia were so set on a boy and no one had asked her what she would like.

'I'd like a daughter, but I don't really mind.

They drank in silence, then Rosamund asked, 'How come you're here in Stratford?'

He smiled and leaned over the table. 'You remember Alan Phipps? He married Gwen Trethewy and inherited his dad's auctioneer business when he retired.'

She nodded, and he continued. 'He and I came up country for the Royal Show at Stoneleigh Abbey.'

'I know, I've read about it. It reminded me of the Royal Cornwall, how we always had grand days out there.'

'I got a Second place in Best Heifer there this year with a shorthorn called Angel – Meri named her, not me.'

'That's really good.'

'Yes. But I was telling you – Alan and I are staying with a cousin of his who lives at Kenilworth. Mother and Dan are looking after the farm while we have a few days off. We've seen the show, and now there's chance to have a look at some of the places round here. Alan's gone to Birmingham with the family today, and I've always wanted to see Stratford. So – here I am. And you?'

'I don't live far away. We moved from Leadersfield two years ago to a village near Warwick when Laurence got a consultancy at the hospital there, and he does some private work at home.'

'Lucky you. It's a lovely part of the country.'

'Towns are all very well, but it's good to be in the country again.'

Rosamund felt easier, more confident. I'm safely married, about to have a baby, she told herself. Francis is an old friend, a relative, and there's no reason why I shouldn't enjoy his company for a while.

'Here, have a bourbon,' she offered the neglected plate of biscuits. 'Before I eat them all.'

Laughing, Francis bit into the chocolatey crispness. It was ironic that now he was free, she belonged to another man, but he'd no intention of trying to take her away from him, lucky devil. Why shouldn't they enjoy meeting as old friends, with no strings attached. He was just full of joy that he'd found her again.

It was as if a dam had burst. In a torrent of words they told each other about their lives in the lost years; of high times and low times, of friendships and relationships, interspersed with reminiscences of their shared years in Treblissick. Francis ordered another pot of tea, other customers came and went. People squeezed by their table to the stairs, and every now and again Francis got a whiff of the perfume Rosamund wore – something light and flowery that went straight to his senses.

Have you thought about marrying again?' Rosamund, without thinking, and full of pity for his motherless child, asked him when he told her about Ruth's desertion and death.

He gave her a level look. 'No. There's no one available I'd want to marry.'

She picked up the teapot. I've gone and wrecked it, she thought. Dangerous ground.

'Another cup?'

Francis didn't answer, just kept looking at her. The question which had lain between them ever since he'd slid into the seat opposite was in his eyes.

She put the pot down. 'It's empty, anyway,' she said with a nervous laugh.

'Rosamund, why did you run away?'

She stared back. Should she tell him? Maybe it was time. She'd hurt him immeasurably already, and there'd be more pain, but at least things would be in the open between them. Perhaps if he could accept her as a sister she could go back to Cornwall, take her baby and Laurence and be part of the family again. Even as she thought it she knew it was impossible. She thought then of Aunt Maud. No, she wouldn't wreck her happiness. As long as Aunt Maud was alive she must keep silent, whatever it cost.

Francis saw her hesitation. Would knowing now make things any easier? he asked himself. Yes it would. However bad the reason – and it must have been something terrible, for he knew how much she'd loved him – it would be better than all these years of not knowing. He recognised the moment she made up her mind, and knew before she spoke what her answer would be.

'I can't tell you, Francis. Don't you know that if I could, I would have done so ten years ago?'

'Ten years eight months,' he said with bleak eyes.

He rubbed his neck, revealing the dented scar she knew so well. How many times have I seen him do that? she thought.

'Tell me this much, then – was it anything I said or did?'

'No, Francis. It could never have been anything you said or did.' Her eyes were soft with regret.

She picked up her bag and pushed with her hands on the table to stand, and eased out of her seat. 'I have to go now.' She stood for a moment looking down at him, with shadowed eyes, one hand holding back her heavy hair.

He watched her mount the stairs, dragging herself up by the handrail.

The waitress approached with the bill.

**

Once upstairs, Rosamund took as long as she reasonably could in the Ladies. Sweating and uncomfortable, she ran her wrists under the cold tap for a long time, then splashed her face, and a refreshing trickle ran down her neck into the damp hollow between her breasts. In the mirror a pale faced woman with haunted eyes and dishevelled hair, stared back at her.

What a sight! she thought. It was silly in the circumstances, but she felt chagrined to think that after ten years' absence Francis had to see her in this state. It was bad enough being the size of a house with Tiddler. She sighed. It was too late now, and what did it really matter anyway? Who'd have believed that they could have met at all, let alone here? She'd often wondered how she'd react if she ever did see him, but nothing could have prepared her for this. And Francis? It had been quite possible that he'd turned against her, stopped caring after she'd treated him so badly. But it wasn't like that, she could see. Very much it wasn't like that.

She dipped into her bag for her comb. It was snagged on the string bag she kept there. She tugged it free and broke three teeth. Damn. She dragged the comb through her hair until it fell in waves either side of her face to curve in towards her chin. Out came her lipstick, and she smoothed the rosy colour onto her lips, then pressed them together to even it out. She looked critically at herself. There was nothing she could do about the shadows under her eyes, but she pinched her cheeks to encourage the colour back. That would have to do. It was enough to give her courage to go back down the stairs and say goodbye to Francis. Goodbye to this wonderful, agonising interlude, which would have to last her for the rest of her life. She must drive back to Clavercote, call into Berry Cottage to see Alicia and Addy. Then she'd pick up some boiled ham for supper and a bag of dog food from the village Post Office, and there'd still be time for a rest before Laurence was home. It was going to break her heart.

Tiddler kicked, or waved an elbow or a knee – whatever. With tenderness she pressed the bulge beneath the thin fabric of her dress. 'At least you've met your Uncle Francis,' she told him.

When she came back down the stairs she wondered if he would have gone – it might be easier on both of them that way. She couldn't see him in the teashop, but when she stepped out into the heat of the late morning he was across the road, leaning against the narrow brick wall between a baby linen shop and the window of a souvenir shop crammed with busts of Shakespeare. One foot rested against the wall behind, his light jacket slung over one shoulder and a paper package under his arm.

He saw her and pushed himself upright. As she crossed the road, even the waddle and swayback of advanced pregnancy couldn't hide the slightness and elegance of her body. *She's tougher than she looks, my Rosamund.* No, he reminded himself firmly. *She's not your Rosamund.* Her approaching face was determined. He knew that look.

She stood in front of him, chin up. Unheeding pedestrians steered round them, and as she opened her mouth to speak, he said in an easy tone, 'As it seems obvious that we're unlikely to meet again, will you let me take you out to lunch? Spend a couple of hours together, no strings attached?'

It was almost funny, the way her mouth stayed open, and it would have been if the rest of his life didn't depend on her answer.

He pressed on. 'It seems a pity not to share Stratford with someone who knows the place.'

Rosamund clapped her hand to her mouth, the wind taken out of her sails. Then she laughed, and capitulated. After all what else would she do, just go home as if nothing had happened? A few hours would make no difference now.

***

She waited in the foyer at the Memorial Theatre where earlier she had bought tickets to celebrate Laurence's coming birthday. While Francis booked them a table in the restaurant for an hour's time, she inspected the black and white photographs of past Shakespearean productions. Outside again they sauntered round the gardens then made their way past the theatre and Holy Trinity church where the bard was buried.

'Don't you want to go in?' queried Rosamund, ready to swing into guide mode.

Francis shook his head. 'I just want to be with you.'

It looked cooler along the riverbank, where there were trees and the green smell of the river. They wound their way along the path, pausing to laugh at the ducks with their fluffy yellow retinue, until Rosamund stopped.

'Whew, it's hot!' She rubbed her back. 'I haven't seen an empty seat yet.'

Francis looked about. 'There's a tree over there with a spot of shade. D'you think you'd be comfortable on the grass?'

'Anything,' she said.

He spread his jacket between the tree roots and, with a sigh of relief she sat with her back against the tree trunk, legs outstretched. Francis sat beside her feet, facing her with his knees crooked.

'Here,' he said and tossed the package he had been carrying onto her lap.

'What is it?'

'A present for Tiddler from Uncle Francis. With love.'

Her eyes widened. Did he know? Of course he didn't. 'Francis, I…'

'Don't say a word, just open it.'

The paper bag was printed with the words 'Tiny Tots of Stratford-upon-Avon'. She opened it with care and drew out two tissue wrapped parcels.

'The funny shaped one first,' he directed.

It was a soft pink pig, with grey spots, a squashed snout, and a comical expression. She giggled, as he'd hoped she would.

'It's just like the piglets you used to have.'
'Still do. D'you think Tiddler'll like it?'
She rubbed her nose on the pig's snout. 'It's perfect.'
The other parcel fell open, and she unfolded a shawl of pure white which billowed over her hands, soft as thistledown.

'I don't know what to say. When could you have done this?' She held a fold of the shawl to her cheek.

'I'd just time to nip over the road to that baby shop before you came out of the tearoom. I was afraid you'd think I'd gone.'

'I did,' she said. 'Thank you, Francis.'

Her expression was thanks enough.

***

Rosamund ate little in the restaurant above the river with its view of the busy waterway and watermeadows beyond, content to sip lemonade while Francis ate with gusto.

'Would you like a row on the river?' he asked afterwards as they left the theatre.

'Yes, I would,' she said, wondering how she'd get in and out of a boat.

She managed without help, and soon reclined in the stern of a varnished rowing boat, a rope for steering in either hand. Francis rowed well, his big farmer's hands sure on the oars. Rosamund watched the play of his muscles, and wondered about the burn scars among the curled copper hairs of his forearms. He pulled strongly, turning now and then to check their progress. She relaxed against the warm wood, and stretched her feet towards where Francis's were braced against the footboard. The boat passed into the shade under Clopton Bridge, then they were gliding past houses with green and flowery gardens that ran to the water's edge, until a sign directed them to turn back. Swans kept pace with them for a while, but soon lost interest when they had no food to offer.

Leaning into the rhythm as the oars dipped and rose, dipped and rose, each time sparkling with diamond drops, Francis kept his eyes on Rosamund with the silver wake of the boat fanning behind her, as she dreamed through the sliding landscape. He gazed with hunger, knowing this would be for the last time. She was even more beautiful than she had been as a girl. With maturity her face had filled out, bringing her long nose into balance with her delicate bone structure. The pure line of her chin moved him unbearably and she held her head with heart-stopping grace. Pregnancy gave her a mysterious opulence that stirred him to the core. Beneath the heavy breasts of impending motherhood, the swell of her belly and inverted navel pushed against the daisies scattered over the blue of her dress. His breathing became ragged, hands sweaty on the oars, and he pulled harder and faster.

Rosamund leaned against the sloping back of the seat in a half trance, mesmerised by the creaking of the oars in the rowlocks and their rhythmic sweep as they sliced through translucent turquoise. Sunlight beat a dancing shield on the water. Francis's face, red with exertion and slick with sweat, filled her horizon. She met the blaze of his eyes and felt herself softening and opening. The riverbanks streamed by in a haze as Francis rowed on and on, riding the current, and Rosamund felt she was drowning.

Suddenly the pressure was unbearable. She drew her swollen feet under her and struggled to sit upright.

'Take us back, Fancis,' she said. 'It's time.'

As if a switch had been thrown he stopped rowing, and bent gasping over the oars.

'I know.'

He dug one oar into the water, and swung the little boat round to labour back against the current.

A huge blue-black cloud inched over the sun, but the heat, if anything intensified, and fingers of lightning flickered across the horizon. A pleasure launch chugged past and a laughing crowd waved and called to them. The river scent was strong.

***

They walked in silence, side by side yet separate, across the crowded gardens to where Rosamund had left her car. She steeled herself for this parting, filled with mourning and guilt. Francis, already feeling the agony of impending loss, was flooded with shame. Thunder growled in the distance.

They reached the kerb beside the red mini.

'Nice car,' he managed.

'It's still new. Laurence gave it me for my birthday.'

She fumbled in the bottom of her bag for the car keys. They were tangled in the string bag, and she tugged at them in agitation, tears blurring her vision. They came free, and she groped for the keyhole.

'Here.' Francis took the keys from her, and for the only time that day their fingers touched.

With an unsteady hand, he unlocked the car door. A wave of pent-up heat gushed out, and he leaned in to put the keys in the ignition, then wound down the window.

Rosamund got in, and stowed her bag and the Tiny Tots package on the seat beside her. He stood beside the closed door, imprinting the image of her profile on his brain. She couldn't look at him. The steering wheel burned under her hands, and she depressed the clutch, anxious now to get away, only to struggle with first gear that she'd forgotten was stiff. It was free at last, and without a word or a look at Francis she bit her lip, signalled left, and pulled away into the traffic.

***

Rosamund drove between the stone gateposts and round the shrubbery of Arthur House without having remembered to buy anything for supper. All she wanted to do was hide and howl, but Laurence's car was outside the door, a blue Cortina parked beside it.

She let herself into the hall. All was quiet, so she dumped her bag and the Tiny Tots package on a chair by the telephone table at the foot of the stairs and went to the drawing room door.

The first thing she noticed was that the curtains were drawn, although it was full daylight. The second thing she saw in the dim light was two pairs of bare feet sticking out from the end of the sofa.

'Laurence?'

There were two appalled gasps from the sofa, and slowly Laurence's tousled head and naked shoulders appeared. Another figure, also naked, unfolded itself to stand behind him.

She recognised him instantly. 'Danny Heaney!'

The Irishman yelped, and hopped on one leg to struggle into his trousers.

'Rosamund!' Laurence's anguished tones were shrill. 'I – I can explain…'

'Don't bother. I've seen enough.'

She turned on her heel and stumbled across the hall. The stairs were steep, but she started up them as fast as her bulk would allow. Sobbing with anger, she missed a step, scrabbled wildly at the banister, and fell with sickening thuds to the foot of the stairs. The telephone table went flying as her head connected with it. Finally she lay still.

***

36

Francis stood at the pavement edge with his hands clenched deep inside his pockets, and watched the red mini travel to the end of the road, turn right and become lost in the outward bound traffic. Crushed with regret and despair, and sorrow deeper than he could remember, he was oblivious to his surroundings until a car pulled in beside him to take up the space left by Rosamund's mini. Already their time together was a memory. He moved away to let the occupants of the car get out, and his foot struck something lying on the pavement.

It was a brown leather purse with the blue and red of an airmail letter caught at an angle under the edge of the flap. He picked it up. They must have fallen out of her bag when she tussled with her keys. The leather was warm in the curve of his hand, and he held it to his cheek as he examined the letter. Unopened, it was from South Africa and addressed to Mrs L Grainger. His mother had letters in this handwriting occasionally from Rosamund's sister, Edith. Never a word had she ever written about Rosamund, and he could only suppose that she'd promised not to.

What was he to do with the purse? He could post it, or… His spirits rose, just a little. What had she said? *'I don't live far away – a village near Warwick?'* He had a map in the car. It wouldn't take long – it was on the way back to Kenilworth. No, he shouldn't go near. She'd made it perfectly clear she wouldn't see him again. And what of her husband? I wouldn't upset things, he told himself, just hand in the purse and letter.

As Francis retraced his steps through the town, which no longer held any attraction for him, he argued with himself. Should he take the purse or post it? In spite of the heat, he hurried back to where he'd left his car in Market Place. The Austin Cambridge was baking inside, so he reached in for the AA roadmap on the back seat, and leaned against the car to search for Clavercote. There it was on the page he'd opened to come to Stratford. Without having made a conscious decision, he got into the car and turned on the ignition, the map beside him on the seat.

Traffic was heavy, and he concentrated on reading the roadsigns to find the right lane out of town. The sky darkened, and he switched on his lights. The storm would not be long in coming.

***

Finding his way through winding lanes and farmland, he turned left opposite the station onto the main road from Warwick to Clavercote, filled with apprehension and a guilty expectation. As he took a left hand bend, a blue Cortina driven like a bat out of hell careered towards him on the wrong side of the road. At the last minute he managed a wild swerve, and with a squeal of brakes brought the car to a halt on the verge. Shaken, he leaned on the steering wheel to get his breath. There were black marks on the road where the Cortina had skidded, but no sign of it now – no one to vent his rage on. Calm down, he told himself. You can't turn up on Rosamund's doorstep in a temper.

The louring sky had a yellow tinge. Thunder rumbled nearer, and the smell of ripening wheat intensified in the sultry air as he continued along the country road between hawthorn hedges and rolling fields. A white village sign loomed in the distance, and a large Edwardian house lay to his right, on its own and set back from the road. Two stone gateposts marked the entrance to a drive that curved round a shrubbery, and he slowed to read the engraved name. Arthur House. He was there. He'd signalled right to turn into the drive when an ambulance burst out of the opening, its bell clanging. It sped away in the direction of Warwick, and he drove between the gateposts with a dry mouth.

There was a dark green Jaguar parked in front of the open door, and Francis pulled in behind Rosamund's car. A slim man in his mid fifties, of medium height, and with rumpled silver hair and acquiline features stood on the gravel, his expression bewildered, distraught.

As Francis got out of the car and went towards him, Rosamund's purse in his hand, he felt the first heavy drops of rain on his shoulders.

'Doctor Grainger?' He hadn't thought of him being so much older.

The man turned a puzzled face towards him and ran his hands through his hair in a distracted manner.

'I am. Who are you?'

'Francis Durrant, an old friend of Rosamund's. We met earlier by chance in Stratford, and she dropped her purse.' He held it out.

There was a brilliant flash of lightning followed immediately by an immense crash of thunder which rolled on and on. The heavens opened and rain sheeted down as if a dam had been opened.

'Come inside.' Laurence shouted over the hissing rain, and ran for the open door.

Francis hesitated.

'Come on, man, don't be stupid.'

They were both soaked by the time they gained shelter. A dog barked once in the recesses of the house. Laurence flicked a switch, and Francis found himself in an elegant hall with a parquet floor, where he could see through an open door into a room where lamplight fell on the back of a blue velvet sofa. A table and carved chair were on their sides at the foot of the stairs, the cable from a black telephone tangled round their legs. Lying in a dark puddle on the floor were a broken vase and a scatter of roses, and the scent of crushed petals filled the air with inappropriate perfume. Near them, half covered by the folds of a displaced Persian rug, was Rosamund's bag and the Tiny Tots parcel. What in God's name had happened here – this mess, the ambulance? And where was Rosamund?

'Who did you say you were?' Laurence asked.

Francis wiped the rain from his eyes and told him again, gave him the wet purse and letter. He took them with his fingertips, and laid them aside without looking at them.

'Thank you.' He gestured at the disorder. 'Excuse the – er... My wife fell down the stairs a few minutes ago, and she's pregnant. But of course you know that, you saw her.'

'I don't want to intrude.' Francis made towards the door. 'I hope they'll be all right, her and the baby.'

Laurence slicked back his rapidly drying hair and gathered himself. 'You say you're an old friend of Rosamund's?' He looked keenly at Francis. 'You wouldn't be the ex-fiancé, would you?'

There was a calculating look in his eye.

Francis, puzzled by the look, said, 'Yes. That was more than ten years ago.'

'Why don't you go and see her. In a day or two when she's over her fall?'

I can't believe he just said that, thought Francis. He's pushing us together. Why?

'No, I'm going home to Cornwall soon. Let's leave things as they are.' He wasn't going to get himself entangled, much as he longed to do as Laurence suggested. 'But I would like to know how she is, and when the baby's born.'

'I'll get Rosamund to add your name to the list of birth announcement cards.' The voice was courteous, but Francis detected a hint of malice. 'She'll know where to send it?'

'She'll know. It's where we grew up together.'

'I see.'

Francis doubted he did see. 'I mustn't hold you up – I expect you'll be wanting to follow the ambulance.'

'Oh.' He looked confused, and shot an uncertain look at the open drawing room door. 'Yes – I suppose I should…'

'Goodbye then.' Good manners dictated that Francis should offer his hand.

Laurence ignored it, and held the door open. 'Good afternoon, and thank you.'

Following the red tail-lights of teatime traffic in the relentless rain amid mists of spray and hiss of wheels on tarmac, it suddenly hit Francis what was puzzling about Laurence Grainger.

He clapped his hand to his head. My God, he thought, the man's queer! He groaned aloud. How has Rosamund got into all this? He drove on, deeply disturbed. There's nothing I can do, and I'll only make things worse if I try, he agonised. Still, she does know where I am if she needs me.

It was the only comfort he could find.

***

Rosamund opened her eyes to find herself in a hospital side ward, and instead of the taut mound of her pregnancy her hands rested on loose wobbly flesh.

'Tiddler! What's happened?' In a panic she struggled to sit up.

'It's all right, he's here, right beside you.'

Sister reached into a canvas cot and placed the white bundle into Rosamund's outstretched arms.

She received the warm weight of his body and gazed at the tiny crumpled face. His eyes were tightly closed, and she cupped her hand round the velvet head.

'Hello, my beautiful boy,' She brushed her lips in a featherlight kiss on his cheek, as she breathed in the newborn scent of him.

The baby pursed his lips and turned a peachy face to her. He knew her voice, she was sure. She kissed the tip of his little round nose, and looked up at Sister.

'Is he all right?'

'He's perfect. Doctor Smith examined him, and we kept him in Special Care for a few hours for observation. He's a sturdy five pounds six ounces, so he should be okay. We thought you'd want him to be here when you woke up.'

'I don't remember being in labour!'

Sister laughed. 'You were concussed when you were admitted, and your blood pressure was sky high, so we had to give you strong sedation and induce the birth.'

'No problems?'

'Quick and easy. He was born at three minutes to midnight last night.' She looked at the watch pinned to the bib of her apron. 'That's almost fourteen hours ago. Baby's fine, and your blood pressure's normal now. You'll be sore for a few days. Apart from the concussion, you cut your head in the fall, and there are a few bruises. You've a lovely black eye and a grazed cheek, but nothing serious. You – and baby – were lucky.'

Rosamund sighed with relief, and resumed her inspection of her son. Totally absorbed, she unwrapped the blanket and drank in each feature of his rosy body. Savoured each crease of skin; stroked each limb, the roundness of his tummy; and approved the stump of his umbilicus, the severed connection with her own body. She uncurled the shells of his hands, and kissed the tip of each tiny finger.

'There's no doubting you're a fine young man,' she told him as she examined his nether regions.

Sister tiptoed away with a smile.

Rosamund turned him over. His spine was straight, his buttocks soft and dimpled. Everything as it should be. She rewrapped him, and it was perfectly natural to put him to her breast, and watch the steady pulsation of the soft spot on the top of his head as she held him to her. He opened his eyelids a crack, and she glimpsed a spark of blue before he screwed them up again. Then his head fell back and he was sound asleep. Totally relaxed in her arms, the vulnerability of his neck moved her to tears. Whatever lies in store for you, my wonderful little man, I'll always love and protect you the best I can.

Her head was sore, and her probing fingers discovered stitches under the hair on her forehead. She ached all over, especially her head, so she lay back on the pillows, the baby curled against her chest. It wasn't long before she too slept.

She woke again as the door opened, and Laurence's head appeared round the door.

'She's awake,' he told someone behind him in the corridor. 'Come on in.'

Alicia limped through, leaning heavily on her stick. She approached the bed and gazed down with a curious look of anguish at her long awaited grandson, and without taking her eyes off the sleeping baby she said to Rosamund, 'A little boy! Who does he resemble, I wonder?'

Laurence was at the window with his back to them, legs astride, hands in his pockets.

'Have you seen him yet, Laurence – before I woke up?' She steadied the baby's head as she hitched herself higher in the bed.

'No. They told me you were both all right.'

'Aren't you going to look now?'

'Mother first.'

Puzzled and hurt she said, 'Then put a chair for her, so she can hold him.'

'In a moment, dear.' Alicia said.

Rosamund turned to Laurence. She pulled at her hospital gown. 'Did you remember to bring my case? I've no clothes or toilet things.'

'Sorry, I didn't think.'

'Please look at your son, Laurence,' she pleaded.

He didn't move. She looked desperately from him to his mother.

'What's going on?' she asked.

In icy tones Alicia said, 'I hear that your ex-fiancé has appeared.'

'Yes, if you can call it that. We met by chance in Stratford on – was it yesterday?'

Laurence nodded.

'I didn't get a chance to tell you when I got home because – because...' Her voice faltered. 'How did you know?'

'I was never sure this baby could be mine.' Laurence said very quietly.

Then Rosamund knew that Laurence wasn't going to admit to what she'd seen when she got home yesterday afternoon. What's more, he intended to, had already, blackened her own name instead.

Laurence went on. 'Francis Durrant turned up at our home, I repeat, our home, after the ambulance had left with you, purporting to have found a purse that you had dropped, together with an unopened letter from your sister. So he had the address conveniently to hand.' He tossed the letter with its smudged writing and stains of rain onto the bed.

Rosamund closed her eyes and allowed the fog of pain that swirled round her to envelop her in its folds.

***

There were no further visits from Laurence, and Alicia couldn't have come without being brought even if she'd wanted to. Rosamund had never felt so far from family, and was more than glad when a beaming Addy appeared the following day, lugging Rosamund's suitcase.

'Eeh, love.' She enveloped Rosamund in an enormous hug. 'I'm right proud of you. Let's have a look at the little darling.'

For the first time Rosamund was able to share the joy of her new child with someone dear to her. With the baby on her capacious lap Addy looked appraisingly at her. 'Well, you've spoilt your beauty, I must say. It does look sore.'

'It's not so bad now. I'm so pleased to have my case, Addy, thank you. I'll feel more human once I'm in my own things, and baby can wear his own clothes, too.'

'You haven't given him a name then?'

'I wanted to talk to Laurence about that, but he hasn't been to see us alone yet.'

'I see.' She was wise enough to say no more, although she clearly knew there was something amiss. 'Look, he's opened his eyes. Havin' a good look at Addy are you, little man. Coochi – coochi.' The baby screwed up his face and started to whimper. 'There, you want your mummy, I know.'

She passed him back to Rosamund, and rummaged in her bag. 'I've made you a bit of parkin to keep your strength up, love.'

'Oh, Addy. You are a treasure.' She took the paper bag and dipped into the sticky cake. 'Will you be able to come again?' she asked as she licked her fingers.

'Tomorrow if you'll have me. It's Alicia's bridge afternoon, so she won't miss me.'

'D'you think you could call into Arthur House and bring me a couple of things?'

'Course I can. What do you want?'

'My camera. It's in the second drawer in my dressing table. And my shoulder bag and a package from Tiny Tots in Stratford. I don't know where they'll be. I'd only just got home and popped them on the hall chair. Then I had the fall.' She hid her face with her hands.

'Don't take on, Rosamund. I'll find them. Now dry your eyes, you'll curdle your milk if you go on like that.'

Rosamund managed a laugh and a hiccup. 'Addy, what would I do without you!'

***

On a dull warm day Laurence fetched them home in the Jag, the baby snug in his white shawl in Rosamund's arms. Addy, who was to help in the mornings, was there when they arrived, and clucked round them all like a mother hen. Then, with a chicken salad on the table, she put on her cardigan and said, 'Well, I'll leave you to it,' and bustled off to Berry Cottage to report to Alicia.

After an uneasy lunch, Laurence had private patients in the consulting room at the front of the house, and Rosamund carried the baby upstairs to their bedroom to feed him and rest. Only to find that it was now *her* bedroom. Laurence had moved all his things out. In the present circumstances it was a relief.

With the baby laid to sleep in the carrycot beside her she stretched out on the white cover and snuggled her head into the pillow. Only home for a few hours and I'm tired out. It wasn't the happy homecoming I wanted either. As she relaxed, a vivid picture of a naked Laurence with Danny filled her vision yet again, and hot tears spurted. She rolled over and curled in a ball. Why, oh why? With the agony of parting from Francis still raw, she'd gone home determined to relegate thoughts of him to the recesses of her mind where they'd lain almost dormant for so long – only to be confronted by Laurence's betrayal. How naïve I've been not to have realised what he is, and I thought I knew him so well. Then there's his hurtful attitude over his child. A new baby needs peace and calm to be contented, and I'm in such a state…

As if he knew she was thinking of him, there were snuffles and wriggles from the carricot, and soon a cry that she already recognised as hunger stung her breasts into response.

***

After supper she drooped over the washing up, longing for bed and sleep.

'Laurence, will you give me a hand to dry the dishes please?' she called.

'We shall have to decide on a name for this child,' he said as he came into the kitchen, obviously reluctant, and picked up a teatowel.

'I did that yesterday, at the hospital. I registered his birth when the Registrar came round.'

'What? Without me?'

'You didn't come to see us again, so I couldn't discuss it with you.'

'I shan't forgive you for that.' He picked up a handful of knives as if they were daggers. 'What name did you give him?'

She put down the dishmop and turned to face him. 'Michael Laurence Grainger.'

'Why?'

'Because I like the name – and Michael's the patron saint of Cornwall.'

'I don't mean the name. Call him what you like so long as he has my name too. Why register him there?'

'Insurance. You were querying his paternity, and I wanted to make sure he was legally yours – as he is.' She turned back to the sink and scrubbed with a Brillo pad at a reluctant patch of burned fat on the grill pan. 'Did you really think he wasn't yours, Laurence, or was it a smoke screen to hide your grubby affair?'

He slammed a plate down on the work surface. 'That was below the belt.'

'It was not. What am I supposed to think? I find you naked with your boyfriend, and *I'm* the one in trouble?' She was shaking with rage and hurt. 'How do you think I felt when you made your accusation? In front of your mother too. I saw her face when she first looked at Michael. You ruined what should have been a very a special moment for her – for us all.'

She flung the wet dishmop at him, and fled upstairs to the refuge of her room, where she collapsed on the bed and sobbed.

***

Rosamund lifted her head from the soaked pillow. Michael was crying downstairs. She looked at her watch. Another feed, she sighed, it's only two hours since the last one. She swung her feet over the edge of the bed. There was a knock at the door and Laurence came in with a yelling baby over his shoulder.

'I think he's hungry,' he said. It was the first time he'd touched him.

Later, with a satisfied baby once more in his carrycot, Rosamund sat on the bed and looked at her husband, who stood in the bay window gazing out into the sunset sky, hands in pockets.

'Well?' she challenged.

'I don't know what to say.'

'Start by telling me why you tried to set me up.'

'I didn't – I…' He dropped his shoulders. 'I suppose I panicked. I was afraid you might tell people, divorce me even, and I couldn't afford for it to get out. When that fellow turned up I thought…'

'Francis,' she supplied. 'What did you think, Laurence?'

'That I could scare you into keeping your mouth shut. It was stupid, I know, but I was upset about Danny, and out of my mind with worry for you and the baby. Then when I'd let Mother believe it might not be mine, I couldn't get out of it.'

'You idiot, you stupid, cowardly idiot. How could you be so cruel?'

'I know,' he said, distressed. 'What I am, what Danny and I do – it's illegal, and any hint of scandal would ruin my reputation, my career, and might even lead to prison.' He flung himself onto a chair and buried his face on his hands. 'What will you do?'

'I don't know. I won't expose you publicly, but not to save your face. What's important is that Michael has a father.' Rosamund felt utterly weary. 'I think – we'll have to try to go on – together – somehow.'

'Rosamund … .' He came towards her with outstretched hands.

'Don't touch me,' she warned. 'You must tell your mother you were wrong. And if you bring *that man,* or any like him here, I shall walk out and you'll never see your son again. Now go away, and leave me in peace.'

37

ROSAMUND

Even with Addy's help, Rosamund became more and more tired, submerged under heaps of nappies and washing and stacks of ironing, the cooking and washing up. They were tasks she and Laurence had shared before. She supposed the mess of soiled nappies and the smell of baby sick offended his sensibilities. Although she insisted that he walk Sam, the only other thing that he helped with was washing up the supper things – but only when asked.

Michael was insatiably hungry, and she had little rest night or day. She'd been determined to breastfeed, but when the health visitor, concerned for her, and for the baby's weight, suggested she try him on the bottle, she gave in and added mixing feeds and sterilising bottles to her tasks. Michael was immediately more contented, but Rosamund, struggling also with a sore heart, had sunk into an abyss deeper and darker than she could have imagined. Even the milky smell of him when she buried her nose in the baby's neck, or the smiles he bestowed on her, which were definitely not wind, gave no comfort. Laurence did nothing to help, except talk to their GP, Mark Venning, who prescribed an antidepressant. Unable to function at all in a zombie-like fog, she refused all medication.

Sandra arrived, on holiday from midwifery practice in the Leeds suburbs, bringing Sally on her own to visit her godmother and the new baby. She took one look at Rosamund's hollow eyes and lank hair, and tackled her at the first opportunity.

They sat on the terrace with a coffee. Sally, wheeling Michael's pram at the far end of the garden, chatted to Herbert, the gardener they shared with Alicia, who was turning over the compost heap with a garden fork. Laurence was out, and they could hear Addy vacuuming inside the house. Across the fields a combine harvester buzzed to and fro.

'You look worse than a wet week, Rosamund.' Sandra lit a cigarette and leaned back in her chair. 'What's up?'

'I'm just tired. Everything's an effort, even Michael.'

'Rubbish. There's something else, isn't there?'

For the first time Rosamund let her fear show. She put her mug on the table.

'It sounds daft, but I think I'm going mad.'

'Unlikely. What makes you think that?'

'I'm in a daze all the time, can't think straight, and I find myself doing the silliest things. I put the clean nappies in the oven last week and emptied a packet of raisins into the dog bowl. I can't face going anywhere, and I sometimes find myself just sitting and rocking.'

'That doesn't sound too dreadful to me.'

'Well, it's frightening. D'you remember that woman on Women's Medical, the one with post natal depression? She'd had to leave her baby when she was admitted to hospital. She rocked all the time with a dreadful, lost look. I remember it because it was the day before I got married. The poor demented woman thought we were going to kill her. She kicked and screamed and swore, and I had to lean on her legs to hold her down so that Staff Daley could get an injection of largactil into her. Her face was only inches from mine, and I'll never forget the fear in her eyes. They carted her off to the mental side with full-blown puerperal psychosis. I still get that awful sickly sweet smell of largactil in my nostrils.' She said nothing about Laurence, or about the other pain in her heart. The one she was used to. The one that was ten times worse now.

Rosamund ran her hands through her hair and hunched her shoulders. 'And there's something else. Remember how, when we were in Training School, we had to use the mental ward toilets? I saw a young woman all alone in that huge ward one day, rocking backwards and forwards. Just rocking. I'm so afraid it's going to happen to me.'

'You poor kid. How long have you been feeling like this?'

'Soon after I came home, but it's getting worse. I'm terrified they'll take Michael away from me and put me in a mental ward.'

'Have you told Laurence?'

'No, I can't.'

'Well, I don't think you're going barmy. You wouldn't know about it if you were, I think you're very tired and very scared. And whatever else is going on in your head, I'm damn sure you're not psychotic.' Sandra put her arms round Rosamund. 'You need to talk to your doctor though, without Laurence, just to confirm it. Will you do that, Roz?'

Dr Venning did confirm Sandra's assessment, and she was able take her first tentative steps out of the abyss.

She took Michael on outings with Sandra and Sally. Avoiding going to Stratford, she sent the tickets for 'The Merchant of Venice' back to the box office for resale. When Sandra had returned north she plucked up courage to tell Laurence how she felt. After that he treated her with a cautious kindness that made her want to scream, and started to take Michael out in the pram for walks, even wheeling him down to the village to visit his mother, so that she could have time to herself. Gradually she began to feel almost normal. Motherhood had changed her, but her anguished denial of Francis after meeting him in Stratford, and Laurence's double betrayal had left their mark. She would never be quite the same again.

***

FRANCIS

Late August in Cornwall, and holidaymakers crowded the roads, filling guest houses and beaches in their frantic search for the sun, while on Pennygarra Farm harvesting was in full swing. Back in his usual routine, Francis felt as if his meeting with Rosamund had been a dream, except that the renewed pain of her loss flared like a sore that wouldn't heal.

He had been up most of the night with a cow in labour. It had been a difficult birth, but he'd cleaned up, then left her with her calf happily sucking away. He always felt good after a successful birth. Most of them managed fine on their own, but this calf had needed quite a bit of turning and tugging. Jimmy had done the milking and the other farmyard chores, and been into the barn with Dan to inspect the calf before going off with him to Top Field, where they were carrying corn. His stomach satisfied by a large breakfast, Francis went to his desk in the parlour before he joined the others. There was a set of forms that should have gone back to the Ministry of Agriculture last week. He sighed, and pulled the papers towards him. Farming seemed to be more and more about form filling, and it was difficult to keep up with.

As he worked, he could hear Meri moving about in the kitchen across the passage. Betty didn't come on a Saturday, and it was Meri's job to take care of breakfast as well as feed the hens. Even so, he knew she'd been up earlier, ranging the fields, or up on the edge of the moor or along the river bank. She came in after a while, with a glass of milk in one hand, the morning's post in the other and a ginger biscuit between her big adult front teeth. Tall for eight, she was wiry, straight as a hazel wand and brown as a nut. Her gypsy origins, which she'd known about for a year now, were becoming more obvious in the sharp structure of her face, her eyes large and bright as blackberries.

She sat on the floor, bony knees already grubby, sticking out of the legs of her torn shorts. Leaning back against the Chinese cabinet, with its inlaid birds and dragons and fish, which Francis had fetched out of storage after Ruth died, she set the glass of milk beside her on the slate floor, and sorted through the post.

'Huh, nothing for me,' she snorted, and tossed them all onto Francis's desk.

'Steady, my handsome, don't upset my papers. Were you expecting something?'

'Jane said she'd send me a postcard from Weymouth, and they've been away a week already.'

He laughed. 'I expect she'll remember eventually.' There were several bills, a circular about fencing... 'Good, the milk cheque's come.'

He opened that first. He knew it would be a sizeable amount – the yield was up last month. A pale blue square envelope was next. He scrutinised the flowing writing, and his heart lurched.

Merri, tracing a mother-of-pearl dragon with a brown finger said, 'Who's had a baby?'

Francis opened the envelope, and a colour photograph fell onto the blotter.

'Rosamund,' he said absently, distracted by the core of hope burgeoning at the base of his stomach. There was a card with a stork flying over improbably green and gold fields, carrying a plump baby in its beak.

Dr Laurence and Mrs Rosamund Grainger are pleased to announce the safe arrival of their son, Michael Laurence, on July twenty eighth 1965,

he read.

Five pounds six ounces. Both well.

***

That's the day we met – her fall!

'Let's have a look.' Meri jumped up and came to lean on his shoulder.

He lifted the photograph. A tiny baby, loosely wrapped in a white shawl lay asleep on a woman's lap, cradled by the spread fingers of her right hand. A pink and grey spotted toy pig was tucked among the folds of the shawl. The photograph cut off the woman's head and shoulders, but he knew. Thank God they're all right.

'Is that Rosamund's baby?' Meri asked. 'He looks very new.'

Francis turned over the card to read in the same flowing hand, *Michael Laurence, 3 days*. He put his arm round Meri's waist and held her to him.

'It's Rosamund's baby,' he said.

'Who is she?'

'Your Gran used to look after her when she was a baby and I was a little boy. When we grew up we loved each other very much.'

Meri's eyes shone. 'Why didn't you get married then?' she demanded.

'She went away.'

'Why?'

'I never knew. Then I met the girl who became your mother, and you were born. Rosamund met and married Michael's father.'

'Will she come back?'

'I doubt it.'

'But she could come back if she wanted, couldn't she Daddy?' She stood on one leg and twisted a black curl round her finger.

'I don't know. Look, Meri, I've work to do. Why don't you go up to the field if you've finished your chores? Eli might be there by now.'

'Goodee – ee.' She danced towards the door, black curls bobbing.

'I'll come when I've finished here.'

'Okay.'

'And take that glass with you, please.'

She skipped back and picked up the empty glass.

'I do love you, Daddy.' She kissed his right ear, and was gone.

Francis looked for a long time at the photograph.

'Hello, Tiddler,' he said softly. 'Michael.'

He touched the baby's head and Rosamund's hand with reverence, then tucked it into the corner of his grandfather's portrait on the wall above his desk.

It wasn't until several days later that he realised that Meri had asked who had had a baby – before he had opened Rosamund's card.

***

ROSAMUND

Michael peeped round the hood of the pram to watch the black plume of Sam's tail and the daffodils blowing in the March breeze. Daffodils always reminded Rosamund of Francis's birthday, now Meri's too. His daughter who was not a daughter, who would be nine today.

There were daffodils in the churchyard opposite Berry Cottage, and on either side of the path to the porch where the last of the winter jasmine bloomed. Addy had seen them coming and was at the door to greet them.

'She's not so well today, Rosamund, but she didn't want you to be troubled.'

'I won't let her know you told me. What's the matter?'

'I don't rightly know, 'though she's mentioned a bit of a pain in her chest. And she didn't eat her breakfast.'

Rosamund parked the pram and lifted Michael out.

'Let's go see Grandma, shall we? I know you'll cheer her up.'

Alicia was in her usual chair in the sunfilled room.

'How's my little man today?' She reached up to kiss his cold cheek.

'G,' he gurgled. 'G, g.' He displayed his first tooth in a gummy grin.

Rosamund kissed her too, and sat on the sofa to remove Michael's mittens and knitted helmet. She unbuttoned his coat while she observed the old lady.

'How are you, Alicia? You look a bit peaky.' She sat Michael on the floor with a rag book and his pink pig.

'I'm all right. Just a bit tired.'

More than a bit tired, thought Rosamund, alarm bells ringing. There's a blue tinge round her mouth I don't like the look of. She knelt in front of her and took her wrist.

'Ever the nurse,' Alicia smiled down at her.

'Your pulse is a bit bumpy.'

'I've had this pain all night. Addy gave me some Anadins, but they haven't helped much.' She rubbed her fist over her breastbone.

Rosamund sat back on her heels. 'Let's see what Dr Venning thinks, shall we? Just to be on the safe side.'

'Well, if you think so…'

'I do.' She stood. 'Addy, will you keep an eye on Michael, and I'll go and ring?'

While they waited for the doctor ,Addy made coffee for them and brought a plate of her Easter biscuits. Alicia sat with her head against the wing of her chair with her eyes closed, her untouched coffee cooling beside her. Michael buried his nose in a mug of Ribena, then sucked noisily on a biscuit, half of which ended in a soggy mess on his bib.

Rosamund took the baby into the kitchen while Dr Venning examined Alicia, and went back into the room when he called her.

'Mrs Grainger's had a heart attack,' he told her, and turned to his patient, eyes kind behind rimless glasses. 'You've agreed to go into hospital for a day or two, haven't you, Mrs Grainger?'

She nodded without opening her eyes.

'I'll ring for an ambulance.'

When he'd gone Rosamund rang Laurence, who was at first none too pleased to be dragged from a ward round.

'I'll be right there,' he said when she told him.

She returned to the drawing room to find Addy on all fours playing peek-a-boo with Michael. Alicia had slumped in her chair, her face suffused with purple, and Rosamund knew that Laurence was too late.

***

They buried her among the daffodils in the churchyard across the road. Laurence, as Rosamund had known he would be, was inconsolable. She held him in her arms while he sobbed like a child. Something had gone out of him with the death of his mother, and for the first time she saw him as an old man.

Addy, too was terribly distressed. 'I know we was chalk and cheese, and had sharp words now and then, Rosamund. But we was right fond of one another, and I do miss her.'

Rosamund too, mourned her mother-in-law. She'd often been difficult, but in the end they'd understood one another, she believed. When the estate was wound up, she was astonished and touched to find that Alicia had left Berry Cottage to her. 'Don't worry,' she told a fearful Addy. 'The cottage is your home as long as you want it to be.' There was a trust fund for Michael and a bequest to Addy. Everything else she left to Laurence, her only son.

Michael, with his sunny baby ways was a consolation, but even he could not breach Laurence's grief. From turning at first to Rosamund for comfort, he became more and more morose, and spent most of his time away from the house. She didn't try to guess where.

***

In May, Laurence told Rosamund he was going on holiday.

'Where are you going?' she asked. She knew better than to ask who with.

'Spain.' The answer was terse.

When he returned, he was bronzed, relaxed, and handsome as she had known him years ago. He spent scarcely any time at home, his manner distracted, excited – and Rosamund knew he was hiding something. It wasn't long before she found out what. He swept onto the drive in the Jag one day, and came into the house with a jaunty step and a blue folder under his arm.

He sat at the morning room table, the folder placed in front of him.

'Come and sit down, Rosamund. I've something important to tell you.'

She slid into a chair with a feeling of dread.

'Danny and I...' he began.

Rosamund mentally raised her eyes.

'...have bought a restaurant in Torromelinos. We're flying out to Spain at the end of June. For good.'

She gaped.

'You'll miss Michael's first birthday...' was all she could manage when she'd got her breath.

'Yes, well. I'll send him something.' He straightened the folder. 'We have to move quickly to get what we can out of the season.'

She said nothing.

'I've used Mother's money to buy the business, with some left over to cover us.'

'She must have left you a lot,' Rosamund murmured.

'She did. Danny's sold his flat to put his share in. You're well provided for.' He tapped the folder. 'It's all in here.'

He opened the folder, and Rosamund, mesmerised, stared at the pile of legal-looking papers it held.

'Arthur House, and everything in it belongs to you now. Here's the transfer document and the deeds.' He riffled the papers. 'There's enough money in Barclay's to keep you going for a while, if you don't go mad.'

'Michael's share?'

He looked at her. 'I think you'll have enough to take care of him. Everything of mine's gone to Spain now.'

'Everything? Is that wise, Laurence, suppose it doesn't work out?'

'That's no longer your business, Rosamund.' His stare was cold. 'Another thing. You can divorce me if you wish. It doesn't matter any more.'

Her heart leapt momentarily, then sank back to the dimness of its accustomed place. I won't divorce him, she thought. I have to have something that'll stop me flying to Francis.

***

The green Jaguar purred out of the drive for the last time, and she didn't watch it go. Michael was having his nap in the nursery. Sam roamed the garden somewhere.

Let him go, she thought. We might have been able to be happy, but we didn't really stand a chance once Danny came on the scene. She drifted from room to room, arms folded tight across her chest. Was this all that was left of their life together? The blue velvet sofa in the drawing room, his Georgian bureau, shelves of medical tomes; the round table they had chosen together for the morning room? Standing in Laurence's bedroom Rosamund felt nothing of him – no imprint of his personality. He might never have been there. She felt very small and insubstantial. Abandoned. Which is what I am, she thought. She turned round and round in the hall, and looked up the wide stairs. What am I going to do with all this space? she asked herself.

Addy was sympathetic.

'What'll you do, Rosamund? You'll rattle about a bit in yon big house. Five bedrooms, and just the two of you.'

'I know. What do you say if we come to live at Berry Cottage?'

'Would you still want me here an' all?'

'Of course I would. I told you this is your home as long as you want it.'

'That's settled then.'

Arthur House sold quickly to a couple who planned to run it as a guest house, but before she moved out there was something Rosamund had to do. Just for once she would fill the house with life and laughter. In July Michael would have his first birthday party there.

The telephone became red-hot, and before long it was all arranged. Sandra would bring Amy and her three children – seven year old Sally, and Joe now five, and little lame Karen, a brave three-year-old. Helen promised to drive herself down with her two – Anna, four, and Richard, who had been a year old just a month before. Plus Rosamund and Michael, the four friends from Leadersfield and their offspring would be reunited for a whole glorious week – with no men. Definitely no men. It was to be the best first birthday party ever.

38

The two cars arrived in convoy, and their occupants tumbled out into Rosamund's waiting arms. After kisses and hugs, and oohs and ahs over the children and each other, the children scattered to the garden, while their mothers unpacked the mountain of luggage they'd brought.

Later, while Addy put the finishing touches to lunch, the four friends sat with coffees on the balustraded terrace, with its urns full of tumbling geraniums and sky blue lobelias, flanking stone steps down to the lawn and flowerbeds beyond.

'Careful, Joe!' yelled Amy, as her five year old cannoned into Karen, his lame sister, as he tore at speed round the lawn. She picked herself up and limped after him.

'I have to watch our Joe, he's such a little devil,' warned Amy. Her freckled face and sandy hair looked just the same, thought Rosamund, but she's thinner than ever. 'Our Karen puts up wi' a lot from him, but she adores him.'

'There're plenty of us to keep an eye on him,' Rosamund assured her.

'You look much better than last time I saw you.' Sandra said. 'I thought with Laurence going you might have hit the doldrums again.'

'No, I'm fine. It's a relief, to be honest.'

'I think you're well rid of him,' said Helen, who had become plump and cosy.

'Forget Laurence, I want to hear about you all.'

News came thick and fast, filling the gaps left in letters and phone calls. Rosamund had put the playpen on the terrace near to where they sat, and Michael and Richard solemnly regarded each other before reaching for the toys scattered on the rug. Excited whoops from Joe, echoed by Karen made the mothers all look up.

Rosamund shaded her eyes and looked across the lawn. 'He's discovered Herbert's sandpit – he's the gardener,' she explained. 'When I asked him to make a sandpit, he stood to attention – I almost expected him to salute – and said, "A bunker for the nippers to play in? Just the ticket. There won't be a better one in the county, trust me."'

They all laughed. 'He's made a super job of it,' she went on, 'And Michael and I had fun choosing buckets and spades and coloured moulds for sandpies.'

Anna, with big blue eyes and a pony tail, climbed up one step at a time from the lawn to cuddle up to her mother.

'Anna's starting school soon, aren't you, love?' Helen pushed the hair out of her shy daughter's eyes.

'Yeth,' she whispered, and hid her face on Helen's shoulder.

'When does Karen start?' Rosamund asked Amy.

'Not till after Christmas. All of 'em at school – Ah can't wait.'

There was a wail from the playpen, where Richard was trying to pull Michael's pink pig out of his grasp.

Rosamund laughed. 'That's his favourite toy.' She offered different toys to each little boy, but both still wanted the pig.

'Can I wheel Michael in the pram, like I did last time, Auntie Roz?' Sally ran up to them from where she had been drifting round the garden, peeping under flowers and bushes, looking for fairies.

'Good idea. Yes, I'll get it for you.'

Helen took Richard onto her lap, and peace was restored. He nuzzled and pulled at her blouse, until she undid her buttons.

'You don't still breast feed him, do you? He's more than a year old!' Rosamund was aghast, and a little envious.

'Only now and again – when he's unsure, like now, or sometimes to get him off to sleep. He likes it, and I like it.' She smiled, contentment written all over her.

'I hope he doesn't bite too often.' Sandra, her amazing blond hair backcombed into a beehive, leaned back in her chair and blew cigarette smoke into the sunshine. She crossed her long legs, barely decent beneath the shortest miniskirt Rosamund had seen.

'This is the life,' she purred. 'Just look at all those kiddies, each one wonderful. I can enjoy them without any of the bugbears of motherhood. Bliss.'

'Don't you ever yearn?' asked Helen, wiping a string of Richard's dribble off her blouse.

'Nope. I have my little house to myself, and all the babies I want in midwifery. It's perfect.' She suddenly scrambled to her feet and skittered down the steps to the sandpit in her strappy sandals. 'Oh, no you don't, young man.' She grabbed Joe round the waist just before the spade he wielded connected with Karen's head. She laid him, kicking and yelling, on the grass. His freckled face was bright red, carroty hair standing on end as she tickled him mercilessly until he gasped, 'I'll be good, Auntie Sandra,' and she let him go.

'Look at this, Auntie Sandra,' Karen called from the sandpit. She was the one most like Amy, Rosamund thought. Same sandy hair and sharp chin. Already with two operations on her clubfoot under her belt she never complained, her face set with determination to do everything other children did.

'Coming, love.' Next thing, Sandra had kicked off her high heels and was on her knees in the sand, digging beside her.

'She's priceless,' laughed Amy. 'Our Joe allus behaves for her. Well – nearly allus.'

That evening, when the children were all in bed, exhausted by the excitement and fresh air, Rosamund outlined her plans.

'I thought we might share the chores – meals and things?' Nods all round. 'And if you all agree, on a rota basis, one of us should keep an eye on the children – unless they want their own mum, of course. Addy says she'll help, and she'd love to come on outings with us. That way we'll have lots of time ourselves to play. We have a whole glorious week together.'

'Sounds wonderful, Roz,' beamed Helen, cheeks blooming even brighter to match the wine in her glass.

'Michael's birthday's on Thursday, so I thought we'd have the party here, hopefully in the garden.'

'I'm all for that. Keeps the mess under control a bit,' Amy grinned.

'There's lots else we can do, so let's not plan too much ahead. We can do what we feel like, weather permitting. We'll have evenings for long natters, and Addy says she'll babysit if we want to have a girls' night out.'

'That's a definite, then. Gives me a chance to check out some local talent.'

'Sandra, that is not the object of the exercise!'

'It's always the object of the exercise. We might even find something for Amy and you, Roz. Pity you're so firmly attached, Helen. Still, you can always admire the scenery.' She held out her glass for a top up.

They were all in fits of laughter. Rosamund didn't think she'd laughed so much for years. *How I've missed this lot. I hadn't remembered how much fun we used to have.*

They went to Warwick on the train from Clavercote station, which had not yet been closed. Although, as Rosamund said, 'Dr Beeching has his axe poised.' At the castle, Joe charged round the ramparts, and gazed round-eyed with wonder at the shiny armour on display. They picnicked on the lawn near the famous Warwick Vase in the orangery, and watched the peacocks display their magical tails. Their piercing screams made the babies quiver with alarm, and even Sally put her hands over her ears.

Next morning Helen looked up as she wiped the table after breakfast. 'What about going to Stratford, Roz?' She scrubbed at a lump of dried-on rusk 'I don't think any of us have been there.'

Rosamund kept her head down in the steam over the twintub. She jabbed with wooden tongs at the sudsy nappies.

'I'd like to go,' Amy called from the drawing room window where she was keeping an eye on the children in the garden.

Sandra came downstairs from making the beds. 'I'm game, whatever it is.'

Rosamund didn't know if she could cope with Stratford. It was almost exactly a year since she'd met Francis there the day Michael was born.

It was difficult, but she managed. She'd found you could manage almost anything if you had to. They picnicked on the grass in front of the theatre, and Michael, trying to do what all the other children could do, took his first three wobbly steps, then plumped down in surprise, a comical expression on his face. Rosamund gathered him to her and buried her face in his curls so the others wouldn't see her tears.

'We must go on a boat,' Sandra decreed, so they joined the queue at the landing stage with their pushchairs and bulging bags. There was a cold east wind blowing over the water, and they huddled in their seats, trying to shield the children. It was almost more than Rosamund could bear to see couples in rowing boats, and her cheeks burned as she revisited the feelings she'd experienced with Francis.

'Who's for fish and chips?' Amy brandished a five pound note when they got back to dry land.

'Me-e- e- !' came the hungry chorus.

It was time for Magic Roundabout on the tv when they arrived back home, and after Zebedee had boinged and said 'Time for bed,' it was bathtime.

The four friends subsided into the blue sofa and leather chairs in the drawing room. Sandra, who had brought supplies with her, broke out the wine.

'I'm not used to drinking like this,' protested Rosamund.

'None of us are, so enjoy,' said Sandra, and poured a drop extra into Rosamund's glass. 'It'll do you good.'

They were on the second bottle when Helen asked Amy, 'Do you ever hear from Cyril?'

'Naw, and Ah don't want to.' She curled up tighter in the corner of the sofa. 'You wouldn't believe how bad it got afore he went. For me and our Sally. I think that might be why he did go – 'cause he'd started on her an' all. He didn't seem to be able to help himself when he was in drink. Like everynight.'

They were all quiet, feeling guilty that they'd not realised. But she'd never told.

'I would've left him, but there were nowhere to go. There were nowt nobody could do. We're better off wi 'out him.' Then after a pause. 'But I still love him,' she said sadly.

In the silence that followed, Rosamund got up and went out through the French windows onto the terrace. She clenched her hands round the concrete balustrade, and thought, I wish I'd told Amy what he was like *before* she married him. She shook her head to clear it. I'm upset by the visit to Stratford today, and now these uncomfortable memories! Woozy with wine and regret, she took several deep breaths of soft night air, and made her unsteady way back into the room. She flopped onto the hearthrug. Sandra topped her up, and automatically she drank.

'You've been quiet all day, Roz. Are you all right?'

Suddenly it seemed to Rosamund to be confession time.

'N – n – o, I'm not aw'right.' She was having difficulty with her speech, but she told them about her stolen time with Francis in Stratford last year. Helen already knew her previous story, and she helped Rosamund recount her story about leaving her love in Cornwall long years ago, although she'd never known the reason she'd left.

'What I can't understand, Roz, is why you don't get in touch with this Francis. He's a widower, you say, and you're obviously still bats about him.' Sandra waved her glass, puzzled. 'Laurence's deserted you. Why don't you divorce him?'

Then Rosamund shocked everybody – herself most of all – by wailing, *'Because I'm his bloody sister!'*

***

It was a subdued group of mothers who next morning crept round the house, fragile as blown glass. Amy's freckles stood out in her white face like currants in a suet pudding; Helen moved in slow motion, and Sandra turned the volume on Radio Caroline unusually low. Even so 'These Boots Were Meant for Walking ' pounded painfully through the sludge in Rosamund's brain, made worse by the four eldest children tramping round the wooden floor of the hall stamping their feet. Moreover, it was raining, so they couldn't go out to play.

When they had at last trailed through the chores, she made an enormous pot of coffee, and put a packet of Anadins and a tin of chocolate biscuits on the table. When Addy had had a good laugh at them, they all sat round the table and tried to be cheerful.

In spite of her headache and nausea, Rosamund felt a curious lightness, born perhaps of releasing the burden of her secret after all these years. After the girls had got over their shock at her involuntary announcement last night, they'd been wonderful, and she'd taken her mother's flimsy yellowed letter from the depths of her purse and shown them the spidery writing. A thought struck her. Had Francis, when she'd dropped her purse in Stratford, and before he returned it to her, discovered the letter? She'd never know.

The rain had stopped by dinner time, and a tremulous sun hovered overhead, like a pale yellow balloon bobbing among the scudding clouds. They packed the children's swimming costumes and went back to Warwick on the train, to the park by the river this time. Here Joe jumped and splashed in the paddling pool to his heart's content, while the little girls played at the edge with boats and buckets. Even the babies enjoyed sitting on the round parapet to splash their chubby legs. Sandra supplied them with ice creams, then hands and faces de-stickied in the pool, they steamed back on the train to Arthur House for tea.

Next day was the big day, and preparations for the afternoon's party started early. Yesterday's rain had chased away the chilly east wind, and the day dawned bright and sunny. Rosamund and Sandra drove off to the shops while Amy and Helen started preparations. The children were excited and wanted to help, so Helen organised a session of making cheese straws. It was very hot by midday, and Rosamund suggested that after lunch the children should have a quiet time in their rooms to calm them down, and give the adults time to arrange the party. She hosed water into two inflatable paddling pools on the lawn near the sand pit, while Amy huffed and puffed a rainbow of balloons, which she attached to every surface she could find indoors and out. Helen and Sandra prepared the feast, ready to carry outside at teatime.

When all was ready Sandra took Sally, Anna and Karen off to her own room, from where the little girls emerged later giggling, in clean shorts and tops, wearing lipstick and nail varnish. Mercifully, the babies, tired by the heat, slept for nearly two hours.

It was quite a party. Michael, the guest of honour, pushed the truck of coloured bricks, Rosamund's present, everywhere. He'd little sense of direction, but wouldn't be parted from it. Rosamund bursting with love and pride in her little golden haired son, was saddened that Laurence hadn't been in touch for weeks, and no present had arrived from Spain.

They played Oranges and Lemons, Ring o' Roses, Farmer's In His Den, and every thing else the adults could think of. Then a clown arrived with a red nose and a hat with a wobbly flower. For some reason Sam, who usually liked everybody, crouched and barked at him, and had to be shut in the house, much to Joe's disgust. Bozo, the clown juggled and did conjuring tricks, and finished with a flourish by pulling a white rabbit out of a hat. Afterwards, while Rosamund saw him off, Amy and Helen went indoors to fetch the last plates of sausages and cheese straws, while Sandra supervised the children's visits to the toilet before tea. For a few seconds, no one was near the party spread on the grass. There were tumblers of orange squash and coloured plates set round the edge of a cloth, and dishes piled with goodies, and a Smartie-covered white iced cake with a single blue candle in the centre.

Then disaster struck.

Joe was the first one out of the house, and he went tearing across the garden, arms spread like a veering aeroplane, and curved round towards the laden cloth.

'Ee-ee-ee-yo-o-ng!'

'Careful, Joe!' Helen shouted, as she descended the steps with a full plate in each hand.

It was too late. He ran straight across the middle of the feast. Plates and tumblers of squash went flying, sandwiches and butterfly buns scattered. The Smartie covered birthday cake had a large footprint in the middle, and the single blue candle was broken, squashed into the white icing.

'Joe! I'll murder you!' Amy went to grab him, but he dodged her and ran full tilt into Sandra. She took hold of both his shoulders and turned him round.

'Look what you've just done, my lad.'

Joe stared. 'The party!' his eyes filled with tears. 'It's spoilt.'

'Not quite. But it's not for want of trying. You're going to have to put it right, and it can be done. Now, first. What do you say to Auntie Rosamund?'

After apologising to a dumbstruck Rosamund, almost in tears herself, and to Michael, who thought it was great fun anyway, Sandra helped Joe to rearrange as much as he could onto the plates, dusting off bits of grass. Helen and Amy occupied the other children by running piggyback races with them. Addy took the cake away for repairs, and returned with more Smarties heaped in the crater of Joe's footprint, and a new blue candle.

In spite of everything, the party was a great success. Michael had everyone's help to blow out his candle, which had to be relit three times and blown out again.

'Thank God for Tupperware,' said Rosamund, as they discussed the near catastrophe when the exhausted children were all in bed.

***

On the last evening, after a lazy morning and a visit to a nearby farm and donkey rides for the children, the four girls had the night out which Addy had promised.

'What sort of food does this pub do, Roz?' asked placid Helen all in white, for once unstained with baby dribble, as they walked along the road into the village. The sound of church bells floated towards them on the evening air, heady with the scent of meadowsweet.

'The Golden Horn? Mostly steaks, I think. I've never been there, but it's supposed to be good.' Rosamund had taken trouble with her appearance, as they all had. She wore a slim fitting pale yellow dress that was one she'd bought when she and Laurence had a social life together, and had only worn once. She felt buoyant and confident as she swung along in white low-heeled shoes.

Sandra, dressed to kill in a scarlet mini-dress, took deep sniffs of summer air.

'Great stuff, this country life. Very romantic.'

'You think this pub's going to be full of country yokels dying to meet you?' Amy teased. Her green and white spotted sleeveless dress swirled round her, softening the lines of her bony figure.

'You never know, Amy. You might even meet Prince Charming yourself.'

Still chaffing each other, they arrived at the Golden Horn, and found a table in the bar near an open window. The smell of cooking steaks mingled with the cool smell of beer, and they opened the menu in eager anticipation.

As their meal progressed the pub became busier, a haze of cigarette smoke drifted between the rafters and Rosamund smiled and nodded to people she knew. They had got to the coffee stage when a group of men came in together. Laughing and talking, they stood at the bar.

Sandra sat up. 'Who's that, Roz? Do you know him?'

'Which one?'

'The one with wide shoulders and a neat little bum. And he's wearing sexy rimless glasses.'

Rosamund giggled. 'That's Dr Venning. He's my GP.'

'Is he now?' She stood. 'Anyone fancy a packet of pork scratchings?'

She sauntered over to the bar and stood next to him. He was about to take his first drink out of his pint. The three girls by the window watched in amusement as he replaced his glass on the bar, and turned with a courteous tilt of the head to reply to Sandra's opening salvo. There was too much noise for them to hear what she said.

'Bound to be something outrageous,' declared Helen, not sure whether to be disapproving or not.

They saw Sandra turn to indicate their table, a packet of pork scratchings in her hand, and he waved and smiled as he looked across. Rosamund, diverted by Sandra's antics, realised she'd never looked at Dr Venning in anything other than a professional capacity. To her surprise she had to agree he was rather a dish. He was a good doctor, she knew, and kind, and she could see what attracted Sandra.

He came over to their table, and drew up a vacant stool.

'This is Mark Venning,' introduced Sandra. 'Known already to Roz.'

Hazel eyes twinkled at her through his glasses, then he turned his attention to the others as Sandra introduced them.

'Mark's one of the bell ringers,' she told them. 'They usually come in here after practice on Fridays.'

'I didn't know that,' Rosamund was surprised. 'And I live here!'

'I could take you all up the belfry and show you the bells, if you like.'

'I'd love to do that.' Amy was all for it.

'You wouldn't mind all those steps? I'd get claustrophobia.' Helen shook her head.

'We're going home tomorrow.' Sandra reminded them. 'Sorry, Mark, and thanks. I'd have gone up the belfry with you anytime, but no can do.'

'Pity, maybe next time you're here.' He finished his beer, and stood. 'Would any one like another drink?'

They all shook their heads. 'No thanks, we'll be going soon.'

'Well. Nice meeting you.' Mark smiled round at them and rejoined his friends at the bar.

Of course, he was the main topic of conversation, as they linked arms and ambled back home along the moonlit road.

'I have to give it to you, you did find some talent,' said Helen.

'Nice of you to share him with us,' Amy was sardonic.

'Hmm.' Sandra sounded thoughtful. 'I'm not sure it was me he was interested in.'

'It wasn't,' Helen told her. 'It was Roz.'

'Ohh!' Rosamund was shocked at first, then quietly sheepish, admitted, 'I think you could be right.'

'O – o – oh!' chorused her friends.

39

It was quiet after they had driven away, arms waving out of the windows. Rosamund wandered around, Michael astride her hip, reliving the last week. She looked at the flattened grass of the lawn, the wet patch running from the paddling pools, then climbed the steps to the terrace where chairs were pushed back from the table, the result of a concerted last minute dash to rescue Richard from being dunked by Joe in a paddling pool.

'Wasn't he a little terror?' she smiled at Michael.

"Ish.' He answered in his version of Richard, and leaned out to be put down.

She set him on his feet, and held his hand as they went into the house. There were reminders here too, a sticky patch by the table where someone had dropped an eggy soldier, rumpled cushions on the sofa, and a forlorn Action Man in the bathroom. Michael rubbed his eyes and grizzled, so she put him in his cot with his pink pig, and started to strip beds.

***

There were frequent phone calls from the girls in Leadersfield, each of them determined to keep in touch more, and there were plans to repeat their week together at least once a year.

Before she had time to miss them and their children too much, Rosamund was plunged into the melée of removing to Berry Cottage. She and Michael soon settled in with Addy, although the church bells chiming so close took some getting used to at first. She chose the sunny bedroom which had been Alicia's overlooking the garden at the back of the house, and the bells became part of the background.

Now she was living in the heart of the village, she became more involved with the community. Word got round that she had moved there, fuelled by Addy's ready tongue, no doubt. People stopped at the gate to pass the time of day, and admire Michael, who was far from shy.

'No wonder you like it here, Addy. It's different from being up the road away from everything. It's a bit like being back home in Treblissick.'

Except, she added to herself with a pang, it isn't and it can't be.

'Aye well, you know as how I like to be where there's sommat going on,' Addy chuckled.

Rosamund dutifully wrote to Laurence, gave him news and reported on Michael's progress. It was September before a brightly coloured post card with a view of a white town on the shores of a brilliant blue bay arrived from Spain. It told her cryptically that, 'We've had a good season, are very happy here and look forward to a leisurely and warm winter. Laurence.' Rosamund read the words to Michael, and showed him the picture before pinning it to his bedroom wall. Each night she taught him to say 'Night-night, Daddy,' and blow a kiss to the card.

Addy tightened her mouth and said nothing.

Maggie Dent, her health visitor, came to do Michael's eighteen-month development check, which he passed with flying colours. Afterwards, over a cup of coffee Rosamund told her about the week with her three friends and the children.

'I hadn't realised how isolated I'd become, and it was so liberating to be with them.' Her eyes shone. 'It really made me feel like someone who mattered again, especially after the problems I had in the early months. We had such fun, and the children enjoyed it too.'

'I think a lot of mothers feel that way.' Maggie was thoughtful. 'There's not much for them to do here, though.'

It made Rosamund think, and next time she took Michael to the clinic in the church hall, she said to Maggie. 'I'd like to start something here in Clavercote where mums with little ones could meet. Just to chat, and maybe sometimes have a speaker. I've no experience, but I'd like to have a go at organising something. What do you think?'

'It's what I hoped you'd want to do,' Maggie confessed. 'But it had to come from you. Can I come and see you at home, and we'll work something out?'

When she took Michael into the doctor's room for his physical, she was walking on air. It wasn't until she saw Mark Venning's face light up that she remembered the night at the pub. Oh, lor', she said to herself. Watch it, Rosamund.

The mums and babies group, who named themselves Wednesday Chat – or The WC – was a success. Ten mothers with their babies turned up to the first fortnightly meeting in the church hall, and it rapidly grew until there were fifteen, then more than twenty, coming from miles around. Maggie enlisted the WVS to serve cups of tea and run a nursery room so that a mum, although on hand if her child needed her, could make friends and chat to other mums. Rosamund organised a programme of speakers. One mum's aunt had a flower shop, and gave them a flower arranging demonstration, a man from the Gas Board cooked tasty dishes on a Calor gas burner, and they had quizzes and competitions.

Rosamund was happy and busy, and then one evening when she was coming downstairs after putting Michael to bed, the telephone rang in the hall.

'I'll get it,' she called to Addy in the drawing room, and picked up the receiver. 'Hello?'

'Rosamund? Mark Venning here.'

'Oh.' She paused. 'Hello.'

'I hear you're doing a great job with your Mums' group.'

'Yes, it's going well,' she replied cautiously.

'Maggie's asked me if I'll do a talk on childhood ailments. Suggested I ring you to arrange a date.'

'Did she? Yes, of course. I'll get my diary.'

***

Helen, when she phoned her, was enthusiastic. 'Now's your chance, Roz. Better check if he's married, though.'

'I don't think he is.'

'What are you waiting for, then?'

'You don't understand, Helen. I'm not interested,' she said flatly, 'but I'm worried he might think otherwise – though I've done nothing to suggest I might be.'

'I see.'

'He's nice, but I don't want to get involved, and it could be difficult when our paths have to cross.'

'You can't blame him for trying. Are you sure you couldn't get interested? He might help you forget – you know.'

'Not possible. I can't believe how unhelpful you're being, Helen.'

'Sorry, Roz, I really am. I'm sure you'll work something out.'

***

She did – when he asked her out after the talk he gave to the group and everyone else had gone – by being honest with him.

'I don't want to mislead you, Mark. I like you, but I don't want to be involved with anybody.'

'That's all right. Let's just go for the odd drink, be friends for now. You may change your mind when you get to know me better.'

'I won't go out with you. The village would have us at the altar in no time if I did.' Her smile was rueful. She did miss a man in her life, but she wasn't about to hurt him.

'I'll keep trying,' he warned. Snapped the lock on his black bag, turned his gaze full on her, and walked out of the hall.

***

True to his word, over the next months Mark took to calling in after bell-ringing practice, and she resisted his invitation, given with a reminiscent twinkle, to climb to the belfry with him. She didn't go to the clinic so often, as he always seemed to know when she was there. Even the Mums' group wasn't sacrosanct, as he made himself popular with the mothers by holding impromptu advice sessions there.

By Easter the following year, Rosamund was really fed up with him.

'He haunts me, Addy. He's so terribly unsubtle. Please tell him I'm not in next time he calls, even if he can see me,' she implored.

'Well I never.'

'I know it's rude, but he will not take no.'

They were in the kitchen after breakfast, while Michael played on the rug with his cars, brmming contentedly. She picked up an airmail letter from South Africa.

'Let's see what Edith has to say. I wonder what's the latest in the saga of coming back to Cornwall?' and broke open the flimsy letter.

She read. Then whooped. 'They've made it, Addy. Leslie's been over and got a job with English China Clay. He's found them a house in…' She peered at her sister's writing. '…in Penvenna.'

'Where's that when it's at home?'

'It's a lovely little town – on the south coast of Cornwall, on a small estuary.' She consulted the letter. 'The house overlooks the harbour, too.' She clutched the letter to her and danced round the table.

'Me,' Michael reached up.

She took his hands and danced with him.

'They're coming home. Auntie Edith's coming home, and Uncle Leslie, and your cousin Triss, and your cousin Greg.'

Addy beamed. 'When, love?'

'Next month, and they want me to go and stay as soon as possible.'

'And will you, Rosamund? Go back to Cornwall?'

She stopped in her tracks.

Would she? Could she? To be with her own family? It must be fifteen miles or more from Treblissick to Penvenna. She wasn't likely to run into anyone from there.

Her face lit up in a huge smile.

'I might,' she said. 'I just might.'

***

'Oh, look, there's Triss and Greg.' Rosamund spotted her twin nephews. They had just tacked with a flurry of white sails and were slipping across the harbour in the family Wayfarer dinghy. 'Where's Leslie?' She scanned the colourful fleet of small boats for her brother-in-law.

'He's in the safety boat.' Edith pointed to a motorboat with a flag flying. 'There, under the castle.'

'I see. D 'you think the boys'll win the race?'

Edith, laughed. 'It's anyone's guess, but they'll enjoy themselves anyway. We'll go down later and have a drink with them in the sailing club, if you like.'

'It's a lovely sight,' sighed Rosamund, as she leaned on the sill of the open sash window to look at the slanted sails in the harbour mouth. They were beating out to sea between the green headland of Polgissey opposite, and the tudor ramparts of St Anne's castle above its rocky promontory away to the right.

From the tall Edwardian house in Castle Row, she and Edith soaked up the panoramic scene. The golden sunlight of early evening bathed the June foliage of the woods lining the creek across the harbour. It glinted in the windows of the houses stacked up the steep hillside of Polgissey, and painted reflections beneath multicoloured boats cradled at anchor in the silvery blue harbour. A squabble of herring gulls dived past, screaming abuse at each other, then settled in apparent harmony to bob on the tide.

Rosamund turned to her sister. 'It doesn't seem like six years since we saw each other.'

'No. Difficult to believe I'm in my mid forties,' Edith remarked drily.

'I'm glad I came home to Cornwall.' Rosamund spoke quietly. 'Apart from seeing you all, I mean. Nowhere else is really home.'

They were both silent.

Then Edith asked, 'Why did you leave, Rosamund? Surely after all this time you can say.'

Rosamund stilled, then nodded. She could tell Edith now. Fetching her handbag, she retrieved the yellowed paper from the depths of her purse. She smoothed the flimsy letter, holding the ivory fragment of the bird's broken wing in her hand, and handed it to her sister with unsteady fingers.

'This is why,' she said, and gazed out to sea with blurred eyes while Edith read.

'Where did you get this?' she asked at last.

Rosamund told her about finding it in the Chinese cabinet the day the contents of their old home were sold. How, after Edith had left, she'd read the letter and realised what its contents meant for her and Francis. How she'd fled, too overwhelmed with shame to face Francis. How she loved him too much to stay near him knowing he was her brother. How she'd wanted to protect Aunt Maud from the secret of Uncle Edgar's infidelity.

Edith listened without interruption until Rosamund subsided into sorrowful silence. She tapped the letter with the back of her fingers.

'This isn't true,' she said with great gentleness. 'It is not true, Rosamund. Why, oh why couldn't you have asked some one?'

'But it must be true.' Rosamund's face was white. 'The letter's crystal clear. '*My Darling Edgar … the baby is the image of you, with fair hair, and I have called her Rosamund…* 'You'd gone back to Jo'berg, and there was no one else I could ask.'

'The letter's clear because Catherine, our mother, believed it to be true.'

'Catherine?'

'Oh my God. You didn't even know her name?'

'How could I? No one would ever talk about her. When I asked, there were no answers.' Rosamund's voice rose, and she checked herself with an effort. 'So tell me what did happen. Was Uncle Edgar my father? Is Francis my half brother?'

Edith's eyes were full of tears. 'No. Pa was truly your – and my – father.' She paused. 'I can understand why the letter appears to be true. Mother believed that Edgar and she were lovers, that her baby (you) was his. You see, it was all in her mind, a tragic delusion. Have you heard of puerperal psychosis?'

'Of course I have,' snapped Rosamund. 'It's a post natal mental illness.'

The remembered smell of largactil choked her, and she had a blinding vision of the woman who believed the nurses were trying to kill her, of the agonising blankness of her face. And the despair of her own feelings after Michael's birth, though they'd been fuelled by quite different events.

Edith continued, her eyes far away. 'Every one knew about Mother's passion for Edgar, even I did, at ten years old. She was all over him – till he learned to keep out of her way. It must have been dreadful for him, and for Aunt Maud and Pa too. She used to wail and moan – I heard her in the night, and Pa trying to pacify her. In the end she had to go to hospital. She never came home.' Tears ran down her cheeks.

Rosamund gathered her in her arms, her own cheeks wet, emotions in a tumult.

'So we do have a mother, after all.'

Edith drew back. 'Not anymore. Pa moved her from St Laurence's to a private nursing home – that's what that big debt was about when we sold the house – and after three years, she died.'

'Why? She must still have been young.'

'She committed suicide.'

'O-oh!'

With a sigh Edith kissed Rosamund's cheek. 'So you are not Francis's sister, after all.'

'Fourteen years wasted. How much needless heartache.' Rosamund's voice broke. 'Edith, what have I done?'

'It wasn't your fault, my love.'

'I can't get this straight in my head. I need to go out, to walk, to think. Will you…?'

'I'll listen out for Michael. Take as long as you need.'

***

Rosamund walked fast at first, down to the cove, up through the woods onto the narrow cliff path, where evening strollers and dog walkers veered askance round her set figure. Pounded down steep slopes and panted up equally steep hills, head down, until her chest was thumping with pain. She didn't see the pink and lilac sky, the line of billowing spinaker sails bisecting the shimmering sea; didn't see the sheep-dotted sloping fields; didn't smell the damp green scents of evening, hear the herring gull's mewing cry.

Rosamund had a mother to mourn, and through her own experiences her heart was full of sorrow for the sufferings her mother had borne, and for her terrible act of self destruction. In her tumultuous flight she came at last to a grassy hollow, where she threw herself onto a drift of sea pinks and let the healing tears flow.

Calmer now, she returned along the cliff path towards the town, and looking seaward she saw the yachts making for harbour. As she approached the castle, a narrow path led down to old gun emplacements below the castle proper, girded by curved ramparts. There was an easy climb to a narrow piece of turf at the edge of the cliff, where Rosamund sat overlooking the harbour entrance with her back to the sloping rampart. A gentle breeze blew directly into the harbour mouth, and three yachts glided in, swanlike, sails extended on either side.

What of Francis? she thought. Could he forgive her for stealing fourteen years of their lives? For wasting the plans they'd made for their future together? Was it too late to make amends? Tomorrow, she resolved, I'll go to Treblissick, back to Pennygarra Farm. I'll explain everything and ask him to forgive me.

For the first time she allowed herself to hope, to welcome him back into her consciousness, he from whom she'd never truly been apart. The presence of Francis all about her in her dream, she revelled in thoughts of his loving smile, the passion in his eyes, the firmness of his mouth, his hard body, his beloved voice…

'Rosamund.'

It was so clear in her head it sounded real. Francis's voice, warm and full of love.

'Rosamund.'

She turned, and he was there.

He came along the turf's edge and sat beside her among the seapinks. The fresh smell of the turning tide was on the wind, and she could feel the warmth of him close to her bare arm.

'The boats are coming home,' she said, as the yachts dipped and swayed over the bar, wings still spread before the breeze.

He took her trembling hand, and his own hand trembled

They sat still, and the sky filled with the after-light of sunset.

Then they both spoke at once.

'Did Edith ring…?'

'I came as soon as Edith…'

Tentative smiles. Blue eyes and green eyes plumbing each other's depths. Then.

'Francis, forgive…'

'I love you, Rosamund.'

And she was home in his arms. The strength of him encircled her, his breath sweet on her face in the instant before their lips met.

There was so much to say, and they didn't say any of it for a long, long while. Stars glimmered in deepest darkest blue, near enough to pluck from the sky, when at last Francis said,

'Come home with me, my bird. Now. Tonight.'

Rosamund didn't hesitate.

'With all my heart,' she said. 'I'll come home with you, my dearest love.'

**

Michael's sleeping face was rosy in the light of the bedside lamp. Francis stood beside the cot, his arm round Rosamund. They were in her room at the top of Edith's house, with its gable window overlooking the water.

Profoundly moved, he gazed at the two-year-old as he snuffled and turned onto his back, arms above his head.

'I'll always think of him as Tiddler,' he said softly. 'Will he wake if I touch him?'

She shook her head, and he bent to smooth the damp curls from his forehead, and run a gentle finger over his cheek.

'I'd better pack a few things for overnight. I can get the rest when we come back tomorrow for Michael.' She went to her bed, and removed her nightdress from under the pillow.

'You won't need that.' He took it from her, threw it on the bed and drew her urgently into his arms.

When they resurfaced gasping from the kiss, they looked at each other with hot eyes, and his voice was hoarse when he said, 'You don't need to take anything. Let's just go, or I'll devour you here.'

With shaking hands, she picked up her handbag and with a last glance at her baby, walked to the bedroom door on legs that felt like foam.

They heard the telephone ringing in the hall below, Edith's steps as she came to answer it, the murmur of her voice.

She looked up at them as they descended the last flight of stairs, a paper in her hand.

'That was Addy, Rosamund. You're to ring Spain as soon as possible. Here's the number.' She disappeared somewhere into the back of the house, leaving them alone in the dim hallway.

Rosamund held Francis's hand tightly and picked up the phone. With his free hand he dialled the number Edith had given her, and as they waited for the line to come through Francis said, 'Will you tell him about the divorce?'

'Let's see what's the matter first. Then I will.' She held up her hand. 'Ssh, I'm through now.' She spoke into the mouthpiece. 'Hello? Danny!'

And listened.

Francis felt her stiffen, and her fingernails dug into his hand.

Rosamund felt her heart turn to ice, and the frozen particles in her veins crackle with shock.

At last she said in a small voice, 'I'll see to things this end, then. Goodbye.'

Without speaking, Francis held her close, guiltily hoping that there needn't be a divorce.

She pulled away, her face ashen. The words forced themselves through wooden lips.

'Laurence has had a stroke. He's in hospital, ready for discharge. Danny can't – won't – have him home. Says their relationship's finished now, anyhow.'

'What'll happen to him?' Francis felt a leaden weight invade his chest.

'He'll be on a flight to England in three days time. Long enough for me to arrange an ambulance to take him to Warwick Hospital.'

'Then what?' He had to drag it from her.

'When he's been in rehabilitation I take him home to Clavercote.' She turned anguished eyes up to Francis. 'He's totally paralysed on the right side, and his speech has gone. Even with good progress he'll always be dependent.'

'No – o – o!' Francis bellowed like a wounded bull. There was a cry from above, then silence.

'No-o! Rosamund, you *can't do* this to me again. You *can't!*'

'Laurence is still my husband – whatever else I want.' Her heart was breaking. 'It's my duty.'

'Duty. Don't talk to me about bloody duty. He doesn't love you. You owe him *nothing*, Rosamund. *Nothing.*' He forced the word through his teeth. 'If you love me – stay with me. I'll love you as no one else could ever love you. For the rest of our lives,' he pleaded.

She shook her head, knowing it sounded her death knell. 'He has no one else.'

Francis's anger boiled, slowly at first. Then in a rush his neck swelled, his reddened face contorted in a paroxysm of anguish, eyes flashing fire, hands clenched into great fists.

'If you go to this man now, don't come near me *ever again!*' he howled, and stumbled blindly away from her, out of the door.

She watched helplessly as he crashed down the steps outside and his copper head disappeared from sight. Moments later she heard the start of an engine, the grind of gears, and he roared away.

40

It was mid November, and a bright fire burned in the drawing room that was no longer a drawing room at Berry Cottage. Although the blue sofa and an easy chair which Rosamund had brought from Arthur House were still in evidence, and there were ornaments and photographs on the walnut bureau, it was the single bed, with its 'monkey pole' and view of the garden through the French doors that dominated the room, and the commode masquerading as a Lloyd Loom chair which stood beside it. The smell of lavender polish and fresh chrysanthemums couldn't disguise the smell of antiseptic and illness.

Rosamund drew the blue velvet curtains against the early darkness and turned to look at Laurence where he sat beside the hearth in his mother's chair. His head was tilted against the wing, his right arm in a collar-and-cuff sling, and a multi-coloured rug that Addy had knitted for him over his knees. After nearly six months, she was still appalled at the parody of a face the stroke had left him with: the collapsed folds of flesh once his right cheek, the red crescent of his drooping lower eyelid and the sag of his constantly drooling mouth; the cruel contrast with his still normal left side and the unchanged waves of his beautiful silver hair. For such a proud man, the extent of his disfigurement and the humiliation of his disabilities were pitiful. They were also very difficult to deal with.

There were times when the sheer physical effort was beyond him, and he sank into depression and self-pity. It was at such times that his incoherent speech became even more garbled, to culminate in animal howls of distress that pierced Rosamund to the core, and it seemed he would drown in the tears that drenched his face to mingle with dribble and gather under his chin. Rosamund knew that as well as everything else, he was grieving over Danny and his rejection, and the end of their idyllic life together. And it was only nine months since his mother's death.

Sometimes she felt like screaming at him – telling him of the agonising sacrifice she had made simply out of duty, not to him, but to her marriage. But she didn't. She would never tell him that.

'Cup of tea time.' Addy elbowed the door open, a mug in one hand and a spouted cup in the other.

'Just what we need, thanks Addy.' Rosamund took the steaming tea from her and set the cups down on the table beside Laurence's chair. 'Where's yours?'

'I'm 'avin mine in the kitchen with 'Erbert. 'Ee's just coming in with the coal while ours is mashing. He likes his tea strong, does 'Erbert.'

Before anything more could be said, Herbert appeared carrying a full coal scuttle in a knarled brown hand. Tall and thin, he had a military bearing and a huge nose pitted like a strawberry over a flowing moustache. Sam got up from the hearthrug and wagged his tail.

'Here we are, Rosamund. Supplies for the troops.' He patted Sam, and set the scuttle down next to the fireirons. 'That should see you through the evening. Telly says there'll be a hard frost tonight.'

'Thanks, Herbert. We don't know how we'd have managed without you this last few months, do we Laurence?'

Herbert stood straight and dusted his hands together. 'There's more to a military man than gardening, you know. Now. Anything else, before Addy and me murders that pot o' char?'

Rosamund shook her head. Addy beamed as she ushered him out of the room, and they could hear her as she followed him down the hallway.

'You can tek yer coat off, 'Erbert, an' I've put a clean towel for you to wash your 'ands.'

'It's looking serious,' said Rosamund with a chuckle, as she tucked one of Michael's old nappies under Laurence's chin.

He reached for the cup with his left hand.

'Kyeh' he said, and rolled his eyes before he inserted the spout into his mouth. This was one of his better days.

'D'you want to watch tv?' she asked afterwards.

He blinked No.

'You mean 'No'? Why don't you try to say it?'

He picked up the pad and pencil from the table and wrote awkwardly with his left hand. *Tired. Music.*

'Ah.' She crossed to the music centre, and rummaged among the records. 'How about 'Moonlight Sonata' or some Greig?'

He gave a one-sided shrug, and she put the Beethoven on.

The tranquil music followed her upstairs where she checked that Michael slept soundly. She sighed, as she tucked his hand back under the blanket. Laurence couldn't tolerate the chatter and energy of the lively three-year-old for long, and if it hadn't been for Addy she couldn't have coped with them both. She kissed his forehead and went into Addy's room to switch on her electric blanket, then crossed the landing to her own room and set her own blanket.

Should I go down to Laurence, she wondered. No, he's probably fallen asleep, and he's got his bell if he needs anything. I owe myself a few minutes alone.

The trouble was, that alone her thoughts always turned to Francis and the terrible thing she'd done to him. Only by filling her days with other people and work could she hold her anguish at bay. Her nursing instinct was strong, and mostly she was occupied with caring for Laurence, cajoling, encouraging and sometimes even bullying him, not just for his own sake, but in an endeavour to wrest something worthwhile from the wreckage of her dreams. That was all that was left to her. Dreams. Not of the future, but of the brief time she and Francis had together on that precious June evening when everything was once more possible. Then with one stroke she had destroyed not only her own certainty of happiness, but Francis's too. She shuddered as the agony of his wounding echoed in her mind. She didn't blame him for his anger and rejection, but what else could she have done? When she first saw Laurence on his arrival at the hospital, she knew that she could have done no other. Now he was installed here in his boyhood home, and if he didn't make progress it would be no fault of hers.

It was getting chilly up here. She rubbed her arms. Perhaps he'll be ready to go to bed, she hoped. The 'Moonlight' had finished, and she could hear the nine o'clock news was on Addy's tv in her back sitting room. Definitely bedtime. She was worn out herself.

They had a routine. Laurence managed a walk to the French doors and back with the aid of his tripod walking stick, while she turned down the bed and got his washing things ready. Then, when he'd used the commode she helped him into his pyjamas and rolled him into bed.

Tonight his pyjamas were pale blue. 'You wore this colour on our honeymoon, d'you remember, Laurence?' She always tried to talk about something evocative or interesting while she was doing personal things for him.

He shut his eyes, and turned his head away.

'Not tonight, Josephine? Okay.' She saw his grimace. 'What is it?'

He rubbed his hand across his tummy. 'Aighn.'

'Tummy ache? I'll get you something for it.'

Half an hour later he was settled on his pillows. The note pad and pencil and the little brass bell he'd had as a child were within reach on the bedside table, and a bottle tucked handy under the bedclothes, so he wouldn't need to get out to the commode in the night. The church clock was striking ten thirty when Rosamund put the fireguard in front of the embers of the fire. She kissed Laurence's cheek and turned out the light, leaving only the rosy glow from the electric heater set on low. With Sam safely shut in the kitchen she went upstairs. There was no light showing under Addy's door, so she whispered 'Goodnight', before peeping in at Michael once more. She closed her bedroom door and rested her head against it with a sigh of relief. It would start all over again tomorrow, but for now, peace.

It started again long before morning. She was dreaming of Francis in the dairy at Pennygarra, when the clanking of milk churns turned into the urgent ringing of a bell. At first she thought it was the church bell, but the luminous dial of her clock showed twenty past one. She shot out of bed and grabbed her dressing gown. She was still tying the girdle as she arrived in Laurence's room to find him struggling to get out of bed. His good leg was stretched towards the floor, and he was vainly trying one handed to lift the other one to join it.

'Ghagh, ghah.' His eyes rolled frantically towards the commode.

Rosamund lifted the lid and grabbed the tripod before heaving him onto his good foot. He'd already undone the cord of his pyjama trousers, and she was manoeuvring him towards the seat when there was a mighty explosion and faeces poured from him to drench them both. Laurence lost his balance, and she collapsed with him onto the floor. The stench was awful.

When Addy, who had heard the noise, came running, Laurence was sobbing, and Rosamund couldn't tell whether she was crying with him, or whether it was hysterical laughter.

'Help me up, Addy, and for God's sake be careful where you put your hands.' And when she was on her feet she said to Laurence, 'That must be what your stomach ache was.'

It took her and Addy an hour and a half before she said wearily to her, 'Go to bed, now, I'll finish off here.'

When she'd gone, Rosamund sat on the edge of the bed, carefully keeping her feet clear of the newly scrubbed carpet.

She took Laurence's good hand and stroked it. He looked at her from a gaunt yellow face with a softness she'd never seen before in his sunken eyes.

'Don't worry about it, it's over now,' she told him.

They sat quietly for a while, then she said, 'I think we'd better get Mark to have a look at you in the morning, don't you?'

He nodded.

'I'll stay the rest of the night, shall I?'

'No!' It was the clearest word he'd spoken.

She kissed him on the mouth with a new tenderness, and his eyes followed her to the door.

'Good night, Laurence.' She couldn't be sure, but she thought he smiled.

***

Rosamund roused from deep sleep as Michael lifted the covers and crept into bed beside her.

'I's cold,' he said, and cuddled up to her.

Without opening her eyes, she curled round him and pulled him close. There was a distant howl from the kitchen. She lifted her head to listen, and felt the cold on her face. The church clock donged four. All was quiet after that, so she pulled the eiderdown up and snuggled her nose into her sleeping son's warm curls.

Grey light was showing round the edges of the curtains when Michael climbed out of bed and trotted into the bathroom. When he returned he went to the window and hauled back the curtains. Rosamund looked up. There were frost curls round the edges of the glass. Michael clambered onto the ottoman and peered through the gap in the middle. She retreated into the bedclothes.

'Come back to bed, Michael, it's freezing.'

'Daddy's sleepin' in 'a garden, Mummy.' He pressed his nose against the glass.

'What!' She shot out of bed.

Through a lacework of ice fronds, she looked down in the murky dawn to a shrouded garden. Hoarfrost blurred familiar shapes of plants and trees, and carpeted lawns and paths. Silver-white fur veiled the sundial, and cloaked the pale blue mounded figure that sprawled on the crazy paving near the garden seat.

Rosamund's heart lurched, and she caught her breath.

Knowing that it was already too late for haste, she said to the little boy, 'It's too cold to stand here, my love. Let's go in to Addy and you can snuggle up with her, while I go to Daddy.'

Taking him by the hand she led him to Addy's welcoming arms.

She descended through the cold house to Laurence's room. The bed was empty, the covers thrown back. The French doors were wide, and she shivered as she trod the icy path to kneel beside him. His face was hidden, and frost had dimmed his silver hair. The tripod lay nearby, dropped as he'd fallen. Her hand hovered over his head, but she knew better than to touch him. It seemed wrong to leave him uncovered, and she fetched his scarlet dressing gown to lay over his body. Chilled to the bone herself, still she lingered beside him in the freezing cold garden, saying goodbye. Then common sense asserted itself and she went back into the house.

How he struggled out of bed and got so far without help, I'll never know, she thought sadly, he must have been desperate.

She closed the French doors behind her. I've shut Laurence out! For a moment she was panic stricken.

Among the tumbled bedclothes lay the note pad. Pencilled at a crazy angle across the page she deciphered the crooked letters. *Forgive me. Be happy. L.*

Then the tears came. She dropped to her knees and rested her head on the place he had lain and sobbed.

***

After the autopsy Mark, as her GP, came to see her.

'I wanted you to know before the report came through, Rosamund.'

They were in the now restored drawing room, with its bowls of scented hyacinths, all evidence of illness removed.

'Yes?' She stood composed beside the hearth.

'Laurence had a malignant tumour in the lower bowel, and secondaries in his prostate, spleen and lungs,' he told her gently. 'He couldn't have lived much longer.'

'I guessed as much. That last night when...' She remembered the stench and the evidence of blood and pus in the mess she and Addy'd cleared up. '...when he was so ill. Thank you, Mark.'

'Do you think perhaps he knew? That's what prompted him to...?'

'Perhaps, who knows.' And she thought of the crooked message she'd found, and thought she did know – some of it at least.

***

It was February before the estate was wound up. Laurence had made a new will not long before he had his stroke, and Rosamund was surprised to find that she was the sole beneficiary. Her solicitor was having difficulty recovering the monies from Spain, but she wasn't worried about it. It would come eventually, and she wasn't in need of it. She'd informed Danny by telegram of Laurence's death, but there had been no response. No condolences, no flowers, no presence at the funeral. She was sad and angry on Laurence's behalf. He had given up so much for this man who ended up destroying him, for she believed that the cause of his stroke lay in Spain.

Poor Laurence. Looking back I can see how hard he tried to be normal, to be a good husband. If only he could have talked about it, even in my ignorance I'd have tried to understand. The irony is that homosexuality in private became legal the month after he died.

No one seemed to miss him, except herself and Addy. Even Michael was too little to ask about him more than once or twice. It was if he had never existed. Never helped all those patients with his skill and courtly manners. Never loved his mother or had friends. Never enjoyed music or books. It was as if he had melted with the frost of that November morning.

Mark had been kind, made sure she was sleeping all right, helped her deal with the aftermath, the inquest. He didn't push himself when inevitably he suggested he take her out to dinner.

'Somewhere quiet, just to take you out of yourself for a while.'

Rosamund smiled to take the sting out of her words. 'No, Mark. I don't need taking out of myself, thanks. Please don't ask me again.'

'Perhaps later on?' He saw her face. 'There's no hope for me, is there?'

'No, there isn't. I love someone else, you see.'

He bowed his head.

'Thank you for everything you've done,' she said. 'For being there.'

'You're going away, aren't you?'

She was taken aback. Then her heart lifted.

'Maybe,' she murmured.

But the idea grew.

***

It was more than a year since Laurence's death, and Rosamund and Addy were putting the finishing touches to the Spring Cleaning. For the past week they'd scrubbed and polished everything in sight, washed curtains and beaten rugs and vacuumed carpets; swept away cobwebs from high places and low places; turned out cupboards and shelves, and washed all the china they could lay their hands on. In short, the house had been cleaned from top to bottom. Today it was the turn of the silver and brass, and the group of shining articles on the newspaper-covered kitchen table had become larger than the dull group. The last task of all was nearing its end.

'Have you seen Michael since lunch?' Rosamund asked, reaching for the Silvo can.

'Nay, but he's with 'Erbert. They're planting that new hedging to replace yon as died in the frost.' Addy's polishing cloth moved briskly over Alicia's Georgian silver teapot.

'Oh, good. They get on well, don't they?' Rosamund's manner was distracted.

'You know very well they do. What's up wi ' you, lass? There's sommat on your mind, I can tell.'

'We-ell. As a matter of fact there is.'

Addy's duster didn't pause as she waited for what was to come next.

'I've decided to go back to Cornwall.'

'Well, I'll go to our house! Going to your Francis, are you, love?'

'I wish I were.' Rosamund's face was wistful. 'But that's unlikely, given the way we parted. I don't think he'll forgive me for leaving him again when Laurence had his stroke, and I can't say I blame him.'

They each plied their duster, thinking their own thoughts.

'No,' said Rosamund. 'There's nothing to stop me going back to live, now I know the truth about my mother. I'll find a house near Edith, where I'm not very likely to bump into Francis. A house with room for you too, if you want to come.'

'Nay, lass. I've loved being with you, but I'm right at home now, here in Clavercote. I never thought I'd uproot meself from Leadersfield, but I have. Besides, 'Erbert and me's planning to settle down together.'

'I am pleased for you – not that it's much of a surprise. Even Laurence had spotted how the land lay.' She got up and went to hug her old friend. 'Would you like Berry Cottage? I don't need it, and it looks as if I'm going to have more money than I know what to do with.'

'That's right generous of you, Rosamund, but 'Erbert's little cottage'll do us nicely, thank you. It'll take a might less looking after than this place, and it's handy wi' the shop next door.' Then with a satisfied grin. 'After we're wed we're planning on having a honeymoon in Australia, to visit my grandchildren.'

***

'It's not just for me,' Rosamund told Helen on the phone. 'It's true, I've always felt uprooted since I left to come north. But I want Michael to grow up in Cornwall. He couldn't be born there, but this is the next best thing.'

'What about our annual get togethers? It's such a long way.' wailed Helen.

Rosamund laughed. 'It's a wonderful place for a holiday. If you want to come, you'll manage it somehow. I'll be sure to buy somewhere big enough for us all,' she promised.

41

The red mini turned off the moorland road over the cattle grid towards Treblissick. It had been misty over the moor, but it was clear in the twisting lane as it descended between February hedges.

Rosamund hadn't planned it this way. When she'd arrived at Edith's yesterday, she'd intended a lazy day with her sister, followed by a trawl around estate agents on Monday morning. Then, lying in bed last night in the room where she and Francis had last been happy together, every nerve screamed to go to him.

'I know it's a lot to ask on my first day, Edith, but will you have Michael while I go over to the farm?'

Edith looked hard at her.

'I have to know whether he'll forgive me, one way or the other.' Rosamund told her, 'Then I can get on with my life.'

'Yes, I'll look after Michael, I'll enjoy him. But, take care, Rosamund. You've been through so much, I'm afraid you'll be hurt again.'

'So am I, but it's worth the risk.' She hesitated. 'Does Francis know Laurence is dead?'

Edith shook her head. 'I haven't been in touch with any of them since you went back last June, and I haven't heard from any of them either, not even Aunt Maud.'

Now the mini dipped between trees, and rounded tight bends that it seemed to know. Overwhelmed with nostalgia, Rosamund took the right fork that would take her past the Old Rectory. There might never be another chance to see her old home again.

There was the entrance, its granite walls sweeping back on either side of the gateway. A blue and yellow sign reared above the lefthand wall.

Gelling, Gelling and Phipps, Estate Agents,
she read. The house was for sale.

She pulled in and got out of the car. Lovely wrought iron gates newly painted black had replaced the decrepit ones, which always stood open. Pa could never afford new ones. These gates were closed and padlocked. She stood outside and peered through the bars to look along the curving drive, overgrown and mossy in her day, now gravelled and flanked by well groomed laurels and rhododendrons. As she stood there it seemed she heard children's voices, and the laughter of women, and the germ of an idea bloomed in her mind.

She got back in the car and drove on.

Suddenly she came to the stone churn stand at the entrance to Pennygarra Farm lane, with the two cottages on the opposite corner. Rosamund's heart banged against her ribs, and she slowed the car.

I can't go in yet, she panicked. I should have rung first. No, I was right. Without warning him I'm coming, I shall know how Francis feels the instant he sees me. But he might not be there. I might not see him at all.

She found she had driven past the opening, and was nearly in the village proper, close to the green. It was early Sunday afternoon, and she couldn't see anyone about. They'll all be sleeping off their Sunday lunches, she guessed. She didn't want to be recognised – for someone to tell Francis she'd been near if she didn't get to see him. No one knew the car, so she risked a drive round the triangular green. How she'd missed it. Little appeared to have changed. The ancient manor house on the left looked just the same, even to the rosemary bush leaning over the wall by the gate. The field next to the church, where she and Francis had gone to sheep fairs in the mornings and funfairs in the evenings of feast days, had the same muddy gateway. The church itself, the elms and ash trees on the green, all unchanged. The Post Office was still in the old coach house, and she wondered if Annie Keast still spied all that went on in the village. If anyone spotted her today it would be Annie. The Ring o' Bells had a new sign, and the chimneys of the moorland granite cottages at the top of the green trailed blue plumes of smoke into the damp still air.

She headed back in the direction she'd come, and it was decision time.

I haven't come all this way to back out now, she told herself. She signalled left and turned into the farm lane. Fluffy yellow catkins dangled from the hazels, and snowdrops drifted in the hedge where the lane dipped to the stream, and there was an overgrown dent in the grass bank where, if she remembered rightly, a huge beech tree had stood. She gripped the steering wheel with ringless hands and hunched forward as she breasted the rise to the farmyard gate. This was it. She didn't know what she felt. Hope, trepidation – terror. All of these. Every sense was heightened, and if she didn't set eyes on Francis soon the top of her head would blow.

The farmyard was deserted.

Rosamund parked the car to the side where the pigsty used to be. There was a big dutch barn there now, and the end of a blue lorry with 'F Durrant, Pennygarra Farm' painted in black on the side, sticking out of what had been the stable. Beyond two empty loose boxes lay a modern milking parlour, with the wooden doors of the old hayloft above. She got out of the car and prowled round the clean concrete yard, expecting at any moment that someone would appear – Aunt Maud, Dan, Meri, Francis himself. No one did. She could smell familiar farmyard smells, hay and cows and manure and sheep. It was as if she'd never been away. In the holding pen next to the milking parlour soft eyed cattle peered curiously at her, trampling straw into the muddy ground. Through the big gate into the pasture that led over fields to the ruined chapel she could see more cows grazing, and a few sheep. Hens squarked and clucked in the field beside their ark, and a blackbird's golden whistle inscribed the grey afternoon with melody.

The scullery door was closed. She rapped on the weathered wood. Then, knowing it was unlikely to be locked, lifted the latch.

'Anyone there?' she called to warm silence. A red anorak side by side with a wax jacket and a pair of blue overalls, hung from hooks, muddy wellington boots beneath. Resisting the temptation to step inside and bury her face in the tough fabric of what must surely be Francis's overalls, she closed the door softly and considered what to do next. A tabby cat jumped down from the dairy roof and cast a disdainful stare in her direction before leaping onto the tailgate of the blue lorry.

Her mind made up, Rosamund went back to the mini and fetched her coat. Leaving the car unlocked, she dropped the keys into a pocket, and swung out of the gate and up the lane towards the moor and the Jubilee Stone.

***

Francis stood and stretched, his check shirt coming adrift from his trousers.

'I'll be getting along home now,' he said. 'Thanks for yet another wonderful lunch, Gwen.'

'You know you'm always welcome. That right, Alan?' Gwen lolled in an armchair, slippered feet to the fire. Their youngest child Lisa was playing with her Cindy doll, behind the sofa where Alan was stretched out with his feet up. Outside in the back yard of their house in the village they could hear five-year-old Andy screeching round on his three wheeler bike.

Alan took his cigarette from his lips. 'Course he is, he knows that, don't 'ee. boy.'

Francis laughed, tucked himself back in and picked up his jacket from the back of a chair. 'I feel a nice nap in front of the telly coming on. It must have been the treacle pudding, Gwen.'

Jane burst into the room, closely followed by Meri. 'Da – ad! Tell Andy. He's frightening the ponies.'

'It's only for a little while, Uncle Alan. We'll be going off in a minute.' said Meri.

Alan got up and left the room. Jane went too.

'Where're you going, Meri?' asked Francis.

'Oh, anywhere. Just riding.'

'There's mist on the moor.'

'We'll be all right. Poppy knows her way.'

'I don't want you on the moor, Meri.'

Meri put her arms round Francis's waist. 'You're the best Dad ever,' she weedled.

'Flattery will get you nowhere, sweetheart. You're not to go on the moor.' He ruffled her wild curls. 'Take Meg.' The collie lifted her head at hearing her name. 'If the mist comes down thick and you lose your way she'll bring you home.'

She capitulated. 'Okay, Dad. We'll go up the river instead, and take Meg anyway.'

Francis said goodbye to Gwen and Alan, and followed Meri out to the gate where Jane was unhitching Poppy and Candy.

He watched them trot along the green, before climbing into the

Land Rover. Meri had been a tall scraggy child, with a thin Gypsy face and black dancing eyes. Now she was growing even more leggy. She'd be twelve next month, almost a woman – and he would be thirty-nine! He ran his hands over his much receded and, he had to admit, now balding head. Where had the years gone? He switched on the ignition and let out the clutch. Meri's hair was still untameable, but her skin was a translucent pale cream, like her mother's when he first knew her. That was her only likeness to Ruth, except that at times she could be inordinately stubborn.

He turned into the farmyard, and there was a red mini where he normally parked.

Francis closed his eyes, then looked again. It was still there.

Rosamund.

He let elation course through him, only for it to be replaced by sickening doubt. He remembered how they'd parted. Rosamund's decision to go back to nurse her husband, snatching away their own new chance of happiness. His rage, his brutal rejection of her, at a time when she'd needed his understanding and support. His rage had not lasted long, but he hadn't got in touch. Apart from the fact that her loyalty would now be to her sick husband, he felt he'd put himself beyond the pale of her forgiveness. Better to stay out of her life.

She was here. That must mean something. He leapt from the Land Lover.

'Rosamund?' he called.

There was no reply. Only the squarking of the hens and a surprised look from a cow in the pen.

'Rosamund!'

He went into the house and called again. There was no one there.

Outside in the yard, wisps of mist curled round the buildings. He grabbed his wax jacket, pulled on wellingtons and swung out of the yard. He knew where she'd be.

***

Up here the mist had thickened. Gorse bushes and stunted hawthorns hovered ghostlike to meet him as he bounded up the hillside over the wet grass. In the dim light and silence the Jubilee Stone loomed ahead. She was there. A pale figure leaning against the dark rock, hands thrust deep into the pockets of her coat.

Francis breasted the last rise, to stand before her, panting with more than haste.

Droplets of moisture spangled her hair, and her face was still as she looked at him with unforgotten eyes of summer blue.

There was a long moment of silence. Mist swirled and eddied round them. Sheep cries came faintly across the scent of wet grasses.

Rosamund moved first. She shifted her weight from the rock face, and stood straight. She'd seen the message in his face.

'Francis.'

'Can you forgive me, Rosamund?'

She reached forward and put her fingers over his lips.

'There's nothing to forgive.'

He took her fingers away and kissed their tips.

'Laurence is dead, Francis.'

He raised his eyes to her face.

'Then there's nothing more to keep us apart?'

She shook her head, and suddenly there was no space between them as his arms went round her, and all the heartache of the past dissolved in the miracle of their kisses.

When they next looked at the world the mist had thinned, the light a milky pearl.

He touched her cheek, and kissed her eyelids.

'I intend to make you mine before you can change your mind and fly away again, my bird, my darling.'

Rosamund melted against him. There was no need for words.

***

The mist had gone and a pale sun shone as they arrived, hand in hand at the farm. Francis lifted Rosamund into his arms and carried her into the kitchen, where he set her down, laughing, in the old Windsor chair.

'Your feet are soaked.' He knelt and removed her shoes one by one. Took each cold foot in his warm hands, rubbed them until the warmth returned.

She leaned forward to take his face in her hands.

'I love you Francis Durrant.'

The fragrance of her hair was around them as again they found each other's lips. He unbuttoned her coat and helped her out of it to spread behind her in the chair. She thrilled as he touched her throat. His hands slid round her to hold her close, the soft wool of her pale blue sweater dress smooth under his palms.

'Why did you ever leave me!'

She broke his embrace. 'I never got a chance to show you this, did I?' She rummaged in a pocket of her coat and came up with the flimsy packet that had travelled with her since their parting. 'Here.'

Francis unwrapped the paper, and picked up the fragment of ivory. An enigmatic expression came into his eyes. He took her hands and pulled her out of the chair.

'Come with me,' he said, and led her into the parlour.

The light was dim, and he switched on the desklight beneath his grandfather's portrait and the photograph of newborn Michael.

'Ohh!' gasped Rosamund. 'The Chinese cabinet from the Old Rectory. How did it get here?'

The mellow wood glowed in the lamplight. The mother of pearl and ivory dragons and fishes and birds gleamed.

'It's your wedding present. It's been waiting for you all these years.'

She took the fragment of ivory from him, and went on hands and knees in front of the cabinet.

'Where is it?' Her fingers felt for the roughened space where the broken wing had been. She wedged it back into place joining it to the ivory bird from where it had fallen long ago.

'There,' she said, 'it's back where it belongs.' She sat on her heels and looked up at him. 'That's where I picked it up, when I found the letter – under that drawer.'

Francis reached down and raised her to standing. It took another long kiss before he said, 'Which leads me to something else.'

He opened the topmost tiny cupboard and took out a piece of folded cloth.

'That's one of my handkerchiefs.'

'It is. And this belongs to you too.' He unwrapped the cloth.

There lay a garnet and seed pearl ring.

Rosamund's eyes filled with tears. 'My engagement ring.' She went to pick it up, but he held it away from her, and knelt on one knee.

'Rosamund, will you marry me?'

She was laughing and crying all at the same time.

'Of course I will, my love. Do you really need to ask? But I'm glad you did.'

The ring slid onto her finger, and sparkled in the lamplight. 'It looks as though it's been there for ever,' she said.

They stood there in the parlour, lost in themselves and their love.

Rosamund, facing the door, sensed a slight movement. She tensed, and looked round Francis's shoulder to see in the doorway a thin girl with a mass of dark curls, eyes full of bewilderment and hurt.

Francis, with Rosamund still in his arms, turned.

'Meri…' he began.

The girl fled.

Pamela had planned to write another book about Meri and her life, and had left the story with many open ends. I wanted to keep the book true to Pamela's ideas and so have preserved the ending as she intended and left the end of the story open to your imagination.

Cedric